MAKING HOME

THE HOME SERIES

THE HOME SERIES BOOK3

MELISSA WHITNEY

He may be her unexpected gift in this friends-to-lovers
***Mean Girls*-inspired small town holiday romance.**
Summer Michaels just wants to raise her son, get lost in a
good book, and get through a shift at the café without her
boss playing matchmaker. While she's the single mom her
boss wants to set up, to everyone else, she's still their high
school bully.
Except to sexy brewery owner, Todd Kruger, she's more than
the village's former mean girl. The one-time band geek and
the reformed prom queen have formed an unlikely
friendship.
Though Summer isn't just a friend, and she's no longer the
girl he had a crush on in high school. She's the woman he's
falling for, and he's the man she won't let herself have. After a
year of tiptoeing around their feelings, one dance at a
wintery-themed wedding changes everything.
Summer debates whether she is ready for the next step with
Todd. There's her son to think about. The impact of her reputation on Todd and his thriving business. The residue from
the relationship with her abusive ex. Not to mention the

secret she carries that could threaten the life Todd wants to build with her and her son.

Will Summer unwrap her heart to build that life with Todd, or will she do what she's always done—hide?

AI RESTRICTIONS

To the mamas, especially those who fall for gingers.

AUTHOR'S NOTE/CONTENT WARNING

Dearest Reader,

It's strange to think this is the last book in the Home Series. What started as a single story inspired by the work of Jane Austen about a woman coming home to face her past, while reclaiming her heart, spawned two additional books in this interconnected, stand-alone series. Not only does this series play with my girlhood favorites, Jane Austen, *Little Women*, and *Mean Girls*, but it's set in my hometown of Perry, N.Y.

In so many ways, Perry is the fourth main character of these books that follow three different female archetypes, commonly found in small town romances; the "big city" woman, the village doctor, and the single mom. Perry is the fourth sassy lady joining this trio, and it's been a deep honor to introduce you to the village I love so deeply. I only hope you take time to visit the real places highlighted in this book, or that inspired the fictionalized places.

That being said, this is a work of fiction. Any resemblance to real places or people is merely a coincidence. Real places depicted in this book may have details fictionalized.

As well, please take care of yourself while reading this

book. While this is a heartfelt/funny *Mean Girls*-inspired holiday romance with spicy Hallmark vibes, it does deal with very real issues that may be too much for some readers. While I take care with these topics, please do what you need while reading. These topics include use of vulgar language, on-page consensual sex scenes, bullying (description and on page), ableism, discussion of intimate partner violence (not between the FMC and MMC), sexist language (not between the FMC and MMC), depictions of toxic masculinity (not by the MMC), a physical altercation, discussion of death of a parent, discussion of cancer, and consumption of alcohol.

Your mental health is more important than my book, so please do what you need to take care of yourself.

CHAPTER ONE

"Raise your hand if you've ever been personally victimized by Regina George." ~Mean Girls

"I just seated French Fries and Wedge Salad at table three," Cassie crooned, her amber eyes twinkling with mischief as she walked into the café's kitchen.

Summer arched a knowing eyebrow at the café owner's salacious grin. She knew all too well whose order that was. Working at Cassie's Café for the last eight and a half years meant Summer knew everyone by their regular order, especially those that Cassie dangled like man candy for the taking.

"You know Laney's section is mostly empty, so he should be seated there." Summer tipped her head to Laney, who stood beside her packing up a to-go order.

"Laney is delivering the to-go order to Doc Owens' veterinarian clinic, so she'll be plenty busy. I'll be covering her section and keeping the kitchen staff in line, so you'll just have to deal." Cassie pulled a pencil out of her messy bun, releasing some loose brunette tendrils to frame her face.

"Plus, I wouldn't *dream* of standing in the way of true

love," Laney drawled, closing a to-go box and adding it to a nearly overflowing paper bag embossed with *Cassie's Café.*

Summer shook her head. Just like clockwork, there it was. Almost daily, Summer faced not-so-subtle and repeated attempts by Cassie and her younger sister, Laney, to ship her with some of the town's most eligible bachelors. Cassie would coo about Summer's leading lady potential and urge her to find her costar in life.

The only leading man afforded a space in Summer's heart was Liam, her nine-year-old son. It certainly *wasn't* Mr. French Fries and Wedge Salad, despite Cassie's pointed reminders of his good looks, successful business, and his straight out of a Hallmark movie, cinnamon roll sweetness. Mr. French Fries and Wedge Salad was just a friend, nothing more.

"Wait!" Cassie called, halting Summer's shuffled steps toward the swinging door leading into the dining room. "You can't go out there like that."

Aborting an eyeroll before it sneaked out, Summer considered her outfit. A cow-print apron hung loose over her black sweater and dark blue jeans. Her chestnut hair was pulled up in a high ponytail. It was the standard outfit for a busy afternoon shift waiting tables. Hell, it was her go-to ensemble even when not at work. It was a far cry from the days of tiny red Chanel dresses and Louis Vuitton stilettos that filled the walk-in closet of the Fifth Avenue apartment she'd once called home.

Cassie hurried behind her and untied and then tightened the apron around Summer's waist. "This will show off your curvy figure better. Show him the goods."

"Stop!" Summer scooted away, almost dropping the tray of drinks she carried.

Cassie placed her hands on her hips. "I'm trying to help you get a man. Maybe, I should rethink the dress code for staff."

"We could always invest in some cow printed pasties and G-strings," Laney snarked, plopping her trademark Bills cap over her short blonde pixie cut. "You know, rebrand to Chestie's Café instead of Cassie's."

"Don't encourage her." Summer let out a beleaguered breath as she pushed into the dining room.

Sunbeams glided into the dining area from the large windows at the front of the café. Brightness bathed every corner of the room in warmth despite the early December chill. The café hummed with the soundtrack of laughter from the corner table of retirees sipping on their fifth coffee refill, the door's bell chime announcing incoming customers, and the clank of forks against plates. Each sound zinged like the notes of a favorite song.

Summer dropped off the drinks at table seven. Slipping the tray under her arm, her brown eyes were pulled like a magnet to the small two-person booth tucked into the café's front corner. Sometimes he'd be with Veggie Burger and Side Salad, AKA his business partner, Noah Wilson, but today he was alone.

Sunlight haloed French Fries and Wedge Salad's red hair, burnishing its shiny coppery hue. The green of his eyes was reminiscent of lush grass after a rainstorm. A hint of a smile softened his strong jawline as he focused on his phone. The Henley he wore outlined his muscular build. His right bicep flexed as he scratched the small scar above his right eyebrow. It was so small that she doubted most people would notice. But she had.

Laney sidled up to her. "For someone who's *not* interested, you're drooling," Laney taunted.

Summer wagged a finger under Laney's nose. "Hush or I'll tell your sister about you making googly eyes at the new veterinarian at Clayton's clinic."

"You wouldn't."

Her mouth quirked. "If you think she's bad about trying

to set me up, just imagine if she knew her *sister* was crushing on the village's latest addition to the most eligible bachelorettes."

Horror scrunched Laney's features. "She'd be relentless."

"Especially if I reminded her of my friends and family discount for wedding planning services."

"You chucklefuck." A small laugh escaped her pink lips as she hoisted the overstuffed bag. "On that note, I'm off to deliver this order."

"Enjoy seeing Veggie Melt on Sourdough." She made a kissy face.

Since Dr. Ana Singh joined the Village Vet Clinic last year, Laney was smitten. She volunteered to take all the lunch order deliveries to the clinic, even on her days off. Somehow her meddling older sister hadn't caught on yet, but Summer had. She made it her business to pay attention to the people around her. It made her good at her job.

It also kept her safe. A jolt of anxiety always prickled just beneath her skin until she scanned a space taking stock of who and who wasn't there. Scanning the café, her muscles relaxed, and she moved toward table three. "Todd." Summer sauntered up to his table. "Is Noah joining you today?"

As he lifted his face, the hint of his smile stretched into a large grin. Summer's heartbeat stuttered as its brilliance blasted her.

He is just a friend. Your heart shouldn't thump like Beyoncé in the "Single Ladies" video. She dug her nails, coated in a clear nail polish, into her palms.

"He's having lunch with Nat at the brewery, so I'm staying away…far away."

An amused smile curled her lips.

Summer knew all too well what that meant. To say Nat, her bestie, and her boyfriend Noah's physical connection was strong would be like saying Gorilla glue merely had the adhesive power of a sticky note. A tad embarrassed, but unapologetic, Nat shared that Todd had caught she and Noah making out several times and had overheard them *having lunch* in Noah's office. Summer had refined the art of both tormenting her bestie while cheering on her happiness. Nat had been in love with her brother Clayton's best friend since she was ten. It took eighteen years, but the two finally got together and were madly in love.

"Since I'm alone, care to join me?" Todd motioned to the open seat across from him.

"I'm working." She pulled a small pad of paper from her back pocket.

"Don't you get a lunch break?"

Even if Noah was here, Todd still would have asked. Every day he'd invite her to have lunch with him, and every day, she'd decline.

"The usual?" she said, clicking her pen and ignoring his persistence.

He sat back against the black-leather booth. "Yep. French fries and wedge salad with a side of rejection."

She rolled her eyes. "Don't be so melodramatic, Krueger. I'll bring you the last piece of Cassie's famous pumpkin roll to soothe your wounded ego."

"Guess I'll settle for *that* with whip cream on it." There was a flirty undercurrent in the low timbre of his voice.

Summer gripped the pen just a little tighter. An unexpected heat climbed up her spine to her neck and invaded her cheeks.

"I'll go put your order in." She bit her lip to stamp out the tiny hitch accompanying her response.

Slipping the notepad into the front pocket, she moved toward the kitchen. It was unnecessary to hang the tiny order slip under a hook on the kitchen's order carousel. No doubt Zach, Cassie's husband and head cook, had already started Todd's order. The steady flow of regulars ensured that Zach and his team of two prep cooks had customers' orders hitting the stove, oven, or fryer the moment the bell above the door announced their entrance.

After the chaos of her twenties while living in New York City, there was something comforting about Perry, New York's predictability. The village that had chafed her as a teenager now felt like a comfy pair of well-worn sweatpants, despite being somewhat ill-fitting at times, with tattered holes exposing her to the world.

"Can you play hostess for a bit? I need to run to my office and call the meat vendor," Cassie asked, forehead creased in exasperation. "Someone ordered twenty pounds of ground lamb instead of beef."

Summer smirked at a sheepish Zach, who turned around and headed back into the walk-in fridge at his wife's "someone's in trouble" tone.

Summer fought the laugh bubbling within. "Sure. Let me drop off Todd's food and I'll cover the front."

"Thanks. Should only be fifteen minutes." With a distracted smile, Cassie headed toward the office at the back of the kitchen.

Matchmaking tendencies aside, Cassie was the best boss Summer had ever had. When she returned to Perry, few places were hiring and those that were had too many vivid memories of the teenaged Summer Michaels to give her a shot. Cassie, who was three years older, looked past Summer's mean girl reputation.

Not only did she give Summer a job, but she was more understanding and flexible than any boss had ever been. Even with the support from her parents, there were times Summer needed to take off early or swap shifts because of Liam. Each time, Cassie just smiled and said, "We'll make it work."

Summer's gratitude for Cassie knew no limits. After leaving Perry at eighteen, there'd been a string of past terrible bosses. While everyone else from her graduating class headed to college or into the military, she lived in a sixth-floor walkup studio apartment in Astoria with five roommates. At first, she worked as a server for a caterer but then stumbled into a job as a personal assistant for a wedding planner, whose daily latte expenses were more than Summer's weekly grocery budget... then and now. Soon, working in the event planning industry led to more opportunities and meeting Max.

Summer blew out a long breath at the wisp of a Max-related memory. She tried not to think of him, or *that* time in her life, but like a stealthy cat burglar those memories stole inside her, snatching away the peace she'd found over the last few years.

"Will I see you at the rehearsal dinner?" Todd asked as Summer placed his food on the table.

"Well, since I'm the wedding planner and the Wine Down is hosting the rehearsal dinner, it appears unavoidable," she quipped, curving her lips into a teasing grin.

This was just one of the reasons she turned down Todd's advances. Perry was a small town, which meant a smaller social network. After she'd returned almost ten years ago, the residue of who she'd been during her teens was too thick to be washed away. It wasn't until the last year and a half that she'd nestled into a small friend group outside of her parents, Liam, Cassie, and Laney.

The expanded social circle was due to Elle Davidson's return to the village last summer. As little girls they'd been best friends. As teens, Summer had been the book-loving Elle's tormentor.

Despite the cruelty of her past actions, Elle forgave and started anew with Summer. This led to her being pulled into Elle and her soon-to-be husband Clayton's friend group. She'd even hired Summer to plan her wedding and all its associated events.

Because it wouldn't be Perry without everyone associated with the wedding being connected, the Wine Down, Noah,

Clayton's best man, and Todd's wine bar, would host tonight's rehearsal dinner. There was no six degrees of Kevin Bacon in Perry. It was one-degree of Elle Davidson. After years of nights alone with a book or watching a Disney movie with Liam curled up on the couch, Summer didn't want to risk her small social network for a relationship.

It's not just your friends you're not willing to risk.

"How'd Liam's presentation go?" Todd speared a bite of salad.

Anxiety swirled in her belly. "It's today, so I won't know until I pick him up after school."

The computer teacher at the elementary school had assigned each student a two minute presentation on their favorite animal. For her puppy-obsessed son, deciding on what type of animal was the easy bit. Scaling it down to two minutes was more challenging. Liam voraciously devoured information about all things dog related. He'd find ways to weave canine tidbits into just about every conversation.

"I'm sure he'll kill it. He's memorized his script and nailed it in dress rehearsals this weekend," Todd assured, reaching his hand across and squeezing her wrist.

Every muscle melted with his touch, as if easing into a steamy lavender bubble bath. Her head, however, snapped her out of it. She stepped back, moving away from his touch. "Thank you for your help with his assignment. It was kind of you."

They'd run into Todd at the library on Saturday. Whenever Summer had a Saturday off, she'd take Liam to the library after story time at the local coffee/bookshop. They'd find whatever books he'd seen at the bookshop to take out for the week or settle at one of the tables working on any big school assignments. Sometimes she'd slip into the classics section in the basement or search the stacks on the first floor for a swoony romance.

She found Todd in one of the reading rooms, a to-go cup

of tea beside him, flipping the pages of *Jane Eyre*. The same book she had in her hand to read. It was only natural they read together and then for him to join them with schoolwork time. That was the story she'd told herself, while fighting the flock of birds swooping in her belly as she watched Todd assist Liam with his presentation.

"He's such a smart kid," Todd said, licking a tiny smudge of salad dressing from his lips.

You are a perv! Stop looking at his lips! She averted her gaze. "He gets that from…my mom."

"I think he gets it from you. He gets a lot of things from you."

God, I hope he's not like me or like... Abruptly, she turned. "I should get back to work."

Summer strode to the small reception counter near the front door. No matter how long she worked there, she'd never stop smiling at the quirky atmosphere Cassie had created. The café tangoed between modern and old-fashioned country chic with a curious balance of black and white cow décor and sleek lines. Creamy eggshell walls were bedecked with black framed photos of cows lounging in green pastures. Leather booths lined the perimeter, giving the sensation of hugging the cluster of tables at the center of the café.

Cold air *swooshed* into the café, accompanied by the door's chime and a statuesque woman. Her fiery-red hair was arranged in a sleek low bun. In her tailored, black wool jacket, pants, high-heeled boots, and aviators she appeared to step right off the pages of *Vogue*. The only pop of color besides her hair and ruby-red lips was the emerald infinity scarf draped around her neck.

Summer grinned. "Welcome to Cassie's Café."

The woman wore a tight smile. "I have a to-go order under the name Whatley."

"Let me grab it."

Cassie had taken the order before she'd popped back into

the office. Joseph Whatley, a real-estate developer from Boston, had moved to Perry a few months ago. He'd bought up several properties on Silver Lake and was developing them for vacation rentals and a small waterfront with cafés and shops. There'd been an article in the *Buffalo News* about the enterprising tycoon. Not to mention Carmen Herrera, Summer's friend and the mayor of Perry, had gushed about the potential financial boom to the village.

Summer set the woman's order on the counter. "Here you go."

"Excellent." The chic woman took off her sunglasses. A pair of piercing blue eyes scanned the room, a slight chill seemed to follow her icy gaze.

"Do you work with Whatley and Company?" Summer asked, ringing up the order.

"I'm Mrs. Whatley," she said in a clipped voice.

Summer's forehead wrinkled in realization. The article had talked about Joseph's reason for development in Perry. The reason being his wife, who'd grown up in the village. Who'd graduated a year after Summer.

"Amy… Amy Livingston?"

How different the polished put together Mrs. Whatley looked from the lanky, frizzy-haired, and braces-wearing Amy Livingston with her series of ill-fitting *Lord of the Rings* themed T-shirts.

She glanced up, surprise evident in her expression. "Summer Michaels. I'm surprised you remember me—" She pulled out a credit card "—We weren't exactly…close in high school."

Regret churned in Summer's belly. Saying they'd not been close in high school was an understatement. There'd been no sleepovers or giggling while reapplying lip gloss in the bathroom at a school dance. Instead, there'd been cutting remarks about a praying mantis physique and putting bug spray in

Amy's gym locker, with a note to the cannister that read *For your mosquito bite breasts.*

God, I was the worst. She closed and then reopened her eyes.

This was not a new experience. In some ways, coming home was like her own form of high school mean girl purgatory. She feared that her adult self may forever be doing penance for the things high school Summer had done. As much as it left her feeling like the gunk on the bottom of someone's shoe, she knew it was justified. She'd been horrible.

"You look… Different." Amy's gaze drifted down Summer's figure. The tick of Amy's eyebrow and serpentine curl of her lips telegraphed both judgment and perverse joy in Summer's current appearance.

Summer's once perfectly styled blonde locks had reverted back to her natural color and was often left wavy or tossed up into a ponytail. Instead of Mac products painted across her face, she merely smeared on a thin layer of moisturizer with sunblock. Her once thin, athletic figure was softer and curvier. She no longer looked like the Summer they remembered, but she felt like the Summer she wanted to be. At least, the Summer she was trying to be.

"Amy?" There was surprise in Todd's deep voice as he called from across the café.

Amy turned, her stiff posture melting. "Todd Krueger!"

Slipping from the booth, he strode, arms wide, toward her. His muscular arms wrapped around her for a hug as Todd swung her in a circle…

Was that a giggle? Summer's head tilted to the right.

The woman vibrating with happiness in Todd's arms bore no resemblance to the judgy-eyed, stern-faced version who had stood in front of the counter. Her tight features softened, brightened.

"I thought you were going to remain in Boston until

summer. At least, that's what Carmen said," Todd mused, releasing Amy.

Her curt tone was replaced with an almost sing-song sweetness. "That was the original plan." Soft pink color swept across her cheeks. "But Joseph…missed me."

Summer ran Amy's credit card, listening to the chatter of reuniting old friends. She'd not realized Amy and Todd were friends. Had they been friends in high school? Did they still talk now? Todd was two years younger than Summer. That didn't really matter in a high school as small as Perry. With only four to five hundred students, everyone knew everyone else.

Summer and Todd hadn't exactly run in the same circles. Like Amy and Elle, he was more band and academic clubs. Cheerleading and Homecoming Court were more Summer's speed. It was a total cliché, but so was high school. Perry had its defined cliques. There were the popular kids, unpopular kids, and everyone in-between. And Summer had reigned over all of them like a tyrant teen queen.

Except for Noah, who went from the nicest most popular boy in high school to the kindest most well-liked man in the village, none of them were the same person they'd been in high school. The six-foot-tall Todd with his sculpted chest highlighted in the form-fitting evergreen Henley he wore was no longer the scrawny pre-growth spurt, trumpet-playing teenager he'd been.

"Here's your card back," Summer said, clearing her throat.

Amy pivoted slowly, taking the card from Summer. "Thanks."

"Amy, you remember Summer Michaels?" Todd tilted his head towards Summer.

"I certainly do." Her face twisted back to its stoniness. "I'm surprised to see her. I had heard she went to New York City to be a model or something like that."

Summer shifted foot-to-foot. Nothing was more uncomfortable than being spoken about rather than to.

She doesn't know how good she has it, does she? A low rumble from the past ran a chill down her spine. She pushed the memory away.

"Event planning." Her correction was almost croaked.

Amy's judgy eyebrow ticked up.

"Summer is an amazing event planner. She did the grand opening for the brewery Noah and I own." An almost-boastful glint sparked in Todd's eyes.

"Really?"

"Remember Elle Davidson? Summer's planning her wedding to Clayton Owens."

"Well, that's...sweet." The sour lilt in Amy's voice telegraphed that she did not think it was sweet, not in the least.

Clearly Todd had noticed the shift in Amy's voice. His eyes flicked between both women. There was no question in his gaze. He'd gone to school with them. Everyone knew who Summer had been in high school. Even him, but especially Amy.

Everyone had phantoms from their past that haunted them. Summer did. The only difference was Summer was also the monster who had lurked under the bed of so many from Perry. So many that wouldn't let her forget. Could she blame them? She still hated her monster under the bed, so of course they would also.

"I should get going. Joseph is expecting me. It was nice seeing you, Todd." Amy grabbed the to-go bag, flashing a soft smile at him.

"Joseph and you should stop by the brewery or wine bar one night."

"Sure." She nodded and turned towards the door.

"Amy," Summer started, wringing her hands.

She stopped but did not face Summer.

"I am sorry. I wasn't kind in high school. I have no excuse, but I am really sorry for how I treated you."

Amy pivoted, cool iciness in her stare. "I'm sure you are." She slipped on her sunglasses, turned, and walked away.

As the door shut behind Amy, Todd's lips curved down. "Summer, I'm—"

"Don't," she cut him off. Her jaw hardened. "Don't apologize for her. She has nothing to be sorry for. I'm the one who does."

He stepped closer, placing his palm atop hers. Warmth spread through her like the first comforting sips of hot chocolate.

She yanked her hand away. At that moment she didn't feel like she deserved his hot chocolatey touches, understanding gaze, and soft words. Even if she was no longer the monster who'd terrorized others, the past was hard to overcome. She was still that monster to them. In some ways she feared she'd always be.

"Summer, plea—"

"I'm working." She turned and pushed into the kitchen.

CHAPTER TWO

"Why are you dressed so scary?" ~Mean Girls

I *did this.* Astonished pride bloomed in Summer's chest as she took in the transformed wine bar.

Purple string lights twined along the large mahogany bar and across the exposed wooden beams that crisscrossed the ceiling. Shiny silver tablecloths covered every table. The Wine Down was bedecked in Elle and Clayton's wedding color scheme for their tapas and cocktail rehearsal dinner.

Bouquets of white roses and lavender sat center of each table scenting the room with a soft floral aroma. Summer inhaled deeply, holding the delicate fragrance in her lungs. With the Wine Down's staff's help, she'd transformed the bar's hip aesthetic into a picture-perfect romantic backdrop for the purple-loving Elle Davidson.

"This place looks adorbs!" Nat squealed, emerging from the back door and almost tackling Summer to the ground in a big hug.

For as sprite-like as the human embodiment of Tinkerbelle was, Nat Owens had the strength of the Hulk. There weren't quick squeezes from her bestie. She barreled into you like a hug missile.

"You're so obnoxious," Summer groaned.

"You *love* it and me."

The eye roll was half-hearted. She really did adore Nat. It made no sense why they were friends, and yet it worked. Summer was nine years older. She'd gone to school with Nat's older brother and soon-to-be sister-in-law. She was a mom. Nat couldn't keep a plant alive. Although, she'd been doing pretty good with Tink, the golden retriever puppy Noah gifted her when they moved in together a month ago. Nat was beloved. Summer was…

"You're not wearing that, are you?" Nat pointed to Summer's simple black dress pants and white button up.

"It's my event-planning outfit."

Nat made an exasperated noise and tossed her head back dramatically. "But you're *not* just the wedding planner, you're a guest."

"But—"

"No buts, except for the one we're going to show off—" grabbing her hand, Nat led them toward the back office "Come with me."

"But I—"

Fighting with Nat was futile. When the five-foot two doctor had her sights set on something…. Watch out. She adored this about her best friend, as long as she wasn't its focus.

"She *did* wear the slacks and a button up," Willa said, aghast, as Summer was shoved into the office.

The curvy, caramel-haired, and brown-eyed Willa Andrews was one of Elle's best friends and had flown in from California for the wedding. The fashionista psychologist always made sure everyone's outfits were on point.

Nat shook her head, shutting the door behind them. "I told you."

"What's happening?" Summer blinked, looking at the desk covered with makeup and hair products.

"Cue the sugary pop song, it's makeover time!" Willa shimmied, holding up a red dress and heels.

Summer waved her hands. "No."

"Come on, live a little. When's the last time you put on a cute dress and had a little fun?" Nat propped her hands on her hips.

Summer pursed her lips. "I have lots of fun, just in pants. Plus, this is Elle's night. It's *not* about me."

"Isn't it Clayton's night, too?" Nat tilted her head.

They all laughed.

It was no secret that Clayton had zero interest in any of the parties. All he wanted was to call Elle his wife. The events leading up to tomorrow were all Elle. He just smiled and counted down the days on the calendar on his phone. Summer was surrounded by men who adored the women they loved. Her dad. Clayton. Noah. Her heart filled with joy and twinged with something else.

"It is *my* night," Elle sang out as she strode into the room with Carmen. A deep-violet velvet dress hugged her athletic curves. Her wavy auburn hair cascaded over her bare shoulders. "And I say makeover!"

"Yes, please." Carmen's doe-like eyes sparkled with mirth.

Guess I'm getting a makeover. The grimace taking over her features made her skin too tight.

"Yay," Nat cheered as she moved forward and held a dress out to Summer.

Summer stood in front of four beaming faces. The satin dress's hem inched up past her knees. It had been years since she'd worn a dress. Let alone one that was red and molded around her body like a second skin. Part of her worried that the softer bits may be poking out. Would she have to spend the entire night sucking it in? She didn't dislike her body, it just wasn't what it had been. There were days she loved its softness like when Liam cuddled up with her on the couch, reading a book. At this moment, though, she yearned for her cozy leggings and oversized hoodie.

"You look luscious!" Willa crooned. "I just want to drink you up like a fine glass of wine."

"Agreed." Nat winked.

"Wills, you did a superb job. That color and cut look amazing. Although…" Elle nibbled her lower lip. "…It's missing something. I know!" She turned and pulled four purple velvet boxes out of the cabinet behind the desk and handed each woman a box. "I dropped these off earlier."

"Oh, Elle," Carmen gushed, opening the box.

A simple silver tennis bracelet engraved with tiny starfish just like Elle's bangle bracelet, a gift from Clayton, sat wrapped in silky tissue paper in the box. She'd shared the story with Summer about a young girl tossing starfish in the sea, trying to save them before low tide. An old man came along, telling her that she couldn't save them all. In defiance, she tossed another in the ocean saying, "But I saved that one."

"Each of you are starfish savers. You make such a big difference to so many," Elle said, her hazel eyes glossy with gratitude.

Running her fingers along the smooth edges of the embossed starfishes, a large lump formed in Summer's throat. What difference had she made? Amy's icy gaze today reminded her that not all differences are good. Not all people tossed starfish in the ocean out of the kindness of their hearts.

You don't deserve to wear this.

"So sweet." Carmen sniffled and hugged Elle.

"No crying!" Willa wagged her finger. "There's only so much waterproof mascara can do."

"Agreed!" Elle let out her own watery laugh. "Let's go drink some rosé!"

"Tits up, ladies, we've got men out there to flirt with," Willa purred, batting her long lashes.

Elle cocked an eyebrow. "What man are you flirting with?"

"Well, we know it's not Todd since *he's* spoken for." Nat waggled her eyebrows at Summer.

A furrow notched Summer's forehead. "There's *no* spoken for. She may flirt away."

"Sure." Willa drew the word out into several unconvinced syllables. "I have my sights set on some harmless flirting with Elle's married boss. He's always fun at a party."

The corners of Elle's lips pulled into a mischievous grin. "Malcom? He's not married anymore. He and Judith divorced six months ago."

Willa gaped.

"Ladies." A deep voice boomed from the other side of the door. "As much as I hate interrupting girl time, I only get my fiancée for four more hours before we have to go our separate ways for the night."

"Are you *really* spending tonight apart?" Willa guffawed.

"Elle's uncle is insistent. As far as he's concerned our dear Elle is a virgin and he's probably going to have the *talk* with her tonight," Summer teased.

"Pete may be the only person in the wedding who hasn't walked in on the two of you having sex." Nat elbowed Elle.

"Hello pot, may I introduce you to kettle?" Summer gestured between Elle and Nat.

They both flipped her off.

"Ladies, Clayton has his 'I've been away from Elle for ten minutes' face on." Noah's laugh was muffled through the door.

"Look who's talking?" Mathew, Carmen's husband, drawled. "You were all 'Where's Nat?' for the last ten minutes."

"Impatient men!" Willa chortled.

"Alright, ladies, like Wills said… Tits up!" Elle commanded, popping out her chest.

Stepping out of the office, they were greeted by a trio of smiling men. Clayton's grey eyes twinkled as he took in his soon-to-be wife. Noah's sexy dimple popped with Nat's kissing.

"Hey, handsome." Carmen's husband Mathew's entire face lit like a chandelier when she emerged from the office.

Happiness bloomed in Summer's veins at the sight of three *good* men utterly in love with her friends. For a long time, she'd worried good men no longer existed outside of her dad and the man she hoped to raise Liam to be. Standing before her was the proof that they did exist. She saw their goodness not just in their steadfast love for her three friends, but how each man played a role in Liam's life.

Clayton invited Liam to the vet clinic weekly to guide the budding future veterinarian. Noah took Liam to the park or for playdates with Tink. Mathew ensured that story time at Cow Tales, the village's bookshop supported those with sensory challenges like Liam, who was on the autism spectrum.

"Come on, gorgeous, you'll be my date." Willa linked her arm with Summer's, guiding them down the short hall into the bar area.

"What happened to flirting with Malcom?" Her head tilted.

"That ship has sailed. Your baby-making hips look too good in this red dress to not be my date."

"Maybe I should put on a jacket." She tugged on the hem.

"Summer Michaels." Nat spun, her face pinched. "You are gorgeous in that dress. Don't make me go full best friend on you and list all your physical attributes which only pale in comparison to your *many* non-physical ones...because I'll do it."

Mortification inflamed Summer's cheeks. "Not necessary."

Nat counted on her fingers. "You have chocolatey-brown eyes that someone could lose themselves in. You have the perkiest tits despite having breast fed. Your rump is made for grabbing. Your long legs—"

Noah placed a hand over Nat's mouth. "Baby, you're embarrassing Summer," he chided sweetly.

Summer was eternally grateful for Noah, who soon spirited Nat off to get a drink. Although, while the endless supply of support and cheerleading from Nat was unsolicited, it wasn't totally unwelcomed.

While Nat grew up in Perry, she was younger and only knew the Summer of today. The Regina George-level cruel Summer of the past was merely a story to Nat. A fairytale in which Summer was the Evil Queen destined to be slain in the form of coming home pregnant, jobless, alone, and with five dollars in her wallet. A fairytale where the heroine, who once sat on the bleachers watching everyone else, now stood in the middle of a room full of people who adored her.

Summer had been the villain of Elle's story. She'd been the villain of Amy's story. Hell, she'd been the villain of so many other's stories. Many who stood in this room. What twist of fate brought her here? Part of her screamed that she didn't belong. That she didn't deserve this.

She doesn't deserve what I do for her, does she? She knows that, doesn't she? The cold voice of the past growled inside her.

"Mom!" Liam barreled into Summer, wrapping his little arms around her waist. "Todd brought cookies from the bakery! Can I have one?"

Liam's arms around her washed away any sensation of not belonging. In his brown eyes, she wasn't the villain. She was the soother of his tears, the person who knew the perfect ratio for his PB&J sandwiches. The only one who understood what every eye roll, huffed breath, and wrinkled nose meant. She was mom.

"Why, hello to you too," she teased.

He made an exasperated noise and stepped back. "Hi, mom. Can I have a cookie?"

"I do adore a determined young man." Willa raised her cocktail to Liam in salute.

Summer grinned. "Did you have a proper meal?"

"I made sure he ate all his Brussels sprouts," Todd said, stepping beside Liam and placing a hand on the little boy's shoulder.

Summer's heart skipped. Much like herself, Todd tended to lean into his casual wear. Most of the parties they'd found themselves at together over the last year and a half found him hanging behind the bar sporting a Farmer's Ale or Wine Down T-shirt. She'd noticed how those form-hugging shirts accentuated his muscular frame. But in an emerald-green button up shirt that stretched across his broad chest, he stole her breath. A shiny black tie was loosened at the unbuttoned collar of his shirt, showing a glimpse of his throat. His smile teetered between boyishly sweet and something she'd imagine a rogue from her latest Liana De la Rosa novel would flash.

She arched an eyebrow. "You made sure he ate his vegetables?"

"He did," Liam grumbled, his forehead puckered.

"What a good *friend* you are to our dear Summer." Willa enunciated the word "friend" in a way that somehow seemed dirty.

Summer discreetly nudged Willa's ribs.

Willa merely beamed.

"I ran into your parents with Liam at Cassie's having dinner before they headed over for the rehearsal. They invited me to join them." He shrugged.

While Summer was prepping the Wine Down for tonight, her parents were on Liam duty. He was the only child invited to tonight's shindig due to the important role he'd play at the ceremony as official puppy wrangler. Only Elle and Clayton would have their pudgy pug Fitz and flirty pit bull Lizzie be in the wedding party.

"Cassie's twice in one day? I thought you were a master chef?" she teased.

"You'd find out how good I am if you took me up on one of my dinner invitations." A playful dare glinted in his green eyes.

Willa pinched Summer's side, whispering, "Girl, stop turning down nice sexy men who can cook. They are *so* rare."

She ignored Willa, keeping her tight smile aimed at Todd. Yes, he was sexy. Yes, he was nice. Yes, he could cook. He was so much, and that made him dangerous.

"I was just delivering some pumpkin ale to Zach and ran into your parents. You know I can never turn down an invite from my favorite euchre partner." He ruffled Liam's chestnut hair.

Affection squeezed her heart. Here stood a good man who played a role in Liam's life. Todd had taken Liam under his wing, teaching him card games, talking about books with him, and meeting them at the park with his dog, Sheba.

Yet another reason to not cross the line with Todd.

"So, can I have a cookie?" Liam asked with all the annoyance of…well of Liam wanting a cookie.

"Sure, but only one since Grams and Pop will be taking you home soon. It's almost your bedtime." She bent down and pressed a kiss to his forehead.

"Mom!" He pulled away. "I'm not a baby."

"You're still *my* baby," she insisted, peppering kisses all over his cheeks.

He struggled and laughed until he finally relented and kissed her back. "Fine," he grumbled.

"Come on, handsome." Willa stretched her hand out to

Liam. "You can be my date and escort me to get a cookie. I see something sweet over there I'd like to nibble on."

Summer's gaze moved to the tray of cookies where a tall lean man in an expensive suit stood. "Don't corrupt my son," she warned, only half-kidding.

"I'm just broadening his education." Willa winked, then skipped away with Liam.

"What's that about?" Todd tipped his head toward the man, whose smile stretched into a flirty grin with each step Willa took closer.

"Elle's no-longer-married boss."

He shook his head, a silent laugh playing on his lips.

"I'm assuming you got Liam's favorite," she said, watching Liam bite into an oatmeal raisin cookie.

"I got your favorite too."

She bit back the smile that threatened to spread across her face. In moments like this, she wanted to melt into his sweetness. She wanted to sink into the fact that he knew her favorite cookie and brought them. Into the idea that he'd run into her parents and Liam on a Friday night and instead of just saying "Hi" and leaving, he'd joined them for dinner. While she was undergoing a forced makeover in the back office, he was stepping up to entertain Liam.

"Thank you." She finally allowed that smile to curl her lips.

"You're welcome." Crinkles deepened around the corners of his eyes. "How are you?"

Of course, he'd ask about earlier. So many feelings wrestled inside her. How was she? Happy that he cared enough to ask? Annoyed that he'd ask? Frustrated with her past self for creating situations like what he'd witnessed earlier today? Her past actions were like stones tossed into a lake, still rippling their effect.

"Did Liam tell you that he got a hundred on his presentation?" She shifted foot-to-foot, choosing not to answer his question.

"He did. Hence the treat. I thought he deserved a celebratory cookie." He gestured to where her little boy munched happily and giggled with his grandparents.

God, Cassie is right. He is a Hallmark cinnamon roll. One she would not let herself take a bite out of.

"You look beautiful."

"Well, don't get used to it. It's for one night only, thanks to Willa. I'll be back to my normal pumpkin self come tomorrow," she chuckled, tugging on her necklace.

Eye's sparkling, he seemed to drink her in. "It's a good thing I like pumpkins...*a lot.*"

A crackling heat spread along her skin in the wake of his sweeping perusal. His wildfire gaze sparked at the base of her throat down to the simple silver crescent moon pendant necklace that dangled inches below her collarbone, inflaming the skin beneath the satin fabric of the dress, and blooming goosebumps along her bare legs.

Reminiscent of a starving man trying not to grab still-hot bread fresh out of the oven, his hands clenched and unclenched at his sides. For a moment, she imagined what it would be like to unleash his restraint. Those large hands trailing down to the small of her back and tucking her close. To press her softness against his hardness. To wet her parched lips with his taste.

She bit the inside of her cheek, battling the coiling tightness between her legs. "You're a good friend."

The muscles of his throat worked. "Friend."

It was all she could offer him, or anyone. There was more to consider than the desire buzzing through her bloodstream. There was the little boy sneaking a second cookie across the room. There were the friends laughing and clanking glasses. There was this man with his tempting sincerity. Her life here might be small compared to what she'd dreamed for herself, but it was hers. She'd given up so much of herself for the feeling of strong hands cupping her face and drinking her in like she was the only thing that mattered…the only thing they wanted to possess.

Never again. She took two steps back. "I should go. I'm not just a guest. I'm the help." Lips trembling, she pivoted and walked away from this man for a second time today.

CHAPTER THREE

"On Wednesdays, we wear pink." ~Mean Girls

Summer ran through her to-do list on the tablet in her hand. Raising her gaze, she sucked in the cool December air, and admired the romantic, outdoor winter-wedding scene.

A soft dusting of snow transformed the property into a romantic winter scene. White tents, wrapped in purple twinkle lights, took up the open lawn between the blue farmhouse and the little red barn turned living space. Rows of white chairs lined a purple carpet beneath the tent, facing a simple white dock, overlooking the now frozen pond. Bouquets of purple roses and unlit candles lined the dock's rail posts. The second tent rose behind the pond. Clusters of tables, draped in silvery tablecloths atop a temporary wooden floor, served as a barrier between the winter-ravaged grass and wedding guests. Thanks to Todd and Noah's help, Summer had secured enough outdoor heaters to ensure everyone would enjoy the wintry atmosphere without freezing.

While most couples would opt for an indoor setting for a

December day in Western New York, Clayton and Elle weren't most couples. The centerpieces, made up of paper bouquets made from the pages of their favorite Jane Austen novels, highlighted this. They had agonized over where to have their wedding until Clayton squeezed Elle's hand and said, "I knew she was my forever the moment Fitz barreled into her while she did yoga on the pond's dock. It's only fitting that's where we get married."

He'd been so right. It was perfect.

Her mom strolled up, looping her arm around Summer's shoulder. "Only you could transform a barren winter day into a fairy tale. This is stunning."

"It really is something," her dad whistled, joining them to take in the scene.

A small crew of staff had been hired for setup, but her parents had come to help with a few things. It was all hands on deck in preparation for this evening's festivities.

An uncontainable smile broke out on her face. "Thanks."

"I remember when you said you wanted to forgo college to plan parties. I was a little concerned. But look at this." Dad waved his hand.

She bit back the readied retort that she'd not gone to college to plan parties but to become an event planner. Tension spooled tight in Summer's muscles. When she'd told her parents she hadn't actually applied to college, but planned to move to New York City to pursue her dream of working in event planning, it hadn't gone well. There'd been shouts, slammed doors. Delayed mortification rose in her chest as she recalled hissing that she didn't want their small town lives.

She'd left three weeks later only to come home, almost ten years later, two months pregnant and broken. Her parents never once said "We told you so" nor reminded her of the mistake she'd made. They just enveloped her and soothed away the tears.

While they never pointed out the many, many mistakes Summer had made in her thirty-seven years, they did their best to direct her to new paths forward. Brochures for programs at Genesee Community College magically appeared upon the small desk pushed up against the window in Summer's bedroom. The bedroom that she'd lived in for the first eighteen years of her life and where she now lived, nine and a half years later.

God, I still live at home and my dad is about to lecture me about my career like I am a senior in high school again. She closed her eyes, readying for what she knew was coming.

"Just imagine what you could do if you took some business courses at GCC. Elle's Aunt Janet said she's taking a marketing class to help with the Village Rose's business. It starts at the end of January. See it's never too late to expand your knowledge."

"We could go back-to-school shopping," Mom added, her tone cheery.

"I should go check on the groom and then the bride." Summer said, trying to minimize the petulant teenage groan struggling to get free.

"The class would be—"

"Yeah. *We* should head home to take advantage of being alone," Mom interrupted, flashing a salacious smile at her husband.

Despite her mom's suggestive lilt causing Summer to cringe, she was grateful. As in-step as her parents were with each other, her mom had a subtle way to defuse moments like this. Either by focusing on the fun of it or by changing the subject.

"Oh, I do like the sound of that," Dad almost purred at her mom.

"You two." Summer shook her head at her parents.

"Oh hush." Mom made a dismissive gesture. "Everyone,

including you, could stand to have a little more *alone* time with someone."

Summer gaped.

"Todd is rather scrumptious with his bulky muscles. He reminds me of a shirtless hero on the front of a steamy Scottish romance novel. He's all mild-mannered, but I bet you he'd hoist you over his shoulder and toss you on a bed." Mom's eyebrows waggled. "You should let him toss you around a bit, or toss him around…I'm a feminist so I'm equal opportunity consensual tossin' around. In fact, your dad and I can watch Liam tonight if you want to stay out for some *tossin'*."

"Mom!" Heat flooded Summer's cheeks. "Boundaries! We've discussed this."

A furrow formed on Dad's brow. "I don't like the idea of anyone tossin' Summer around."

"I'm with dad on this one."

Mom blew out an annoyed breath. "I thought having an adult daughter meant we'd get to have these types of chats."

"No, thank you. I think I've been traumatized enough by your oversharing about Dad and your sex life."

"What are you telling the girl?" he gestured between them.

She ignored him. "Well, I only share to inspire you. You made me such a beautiful grandbaby, I'd love to have a few more. Perhaps one or two with red hair."

She pushed her mother playfully. "I'm done with you, woman. Dad, take your wife home. I'm going to go check in on the one and only grandbaby you'll have, and then do my job."

Mom sighed dramatically. "Where did *we* go wrong with you?"

Summer knew it was a teasing comment, but it stung, nonetheless. Her parents never expressed their disappointment, but she wondered if the brochures placed on her desk and casual comments about ways she could do more with her life were thinly veiled ways of saying, "You're not what we'd hoped you'd be."

Saying goodbye to them, Summer shuffled to the farmhouse. Kicking the light dusting of snow off her boots, she tugged them off and left them by the door. Clayton and his groom's party consisting of Noah, Nat, and Jerome, his partner at the vet clinic and Elle's cousin-in-law, claimed the farmhouse for their pre-wedding antics. Elle and her bridal party consisting of her longtime bestie Viet, Carmen, and Willa turned Elle's office/guest house in the little red barn into the bridal suite.

"Hi Mom!" Liam chirped, waving from the couch where he sat watching TV. Fitz, Clayton and Elle's plump pug curled beside him, and their muscular pit bull Lizzie, draped over his lap.

"Hey baby. Where is everyone?"

"Clayton and Jerome are making grilled cheeses."

She crossed her arms over her chest. "Shouldn't you be helping?"

"He is." Clayton strolled into the room carrying a tray of grilled cheese sandwiches, chips, and carrot sticks.

She tilted her head and cocked an eyebrow. "How?"

"Clearly he's wrangling the duo of evolved dire wolves that have claimed the couch," Jerome deadpanned, following Clayton with two bottles of beer and a juice box.

"We're eating in front of the TV?" It was funny how quickly the tone she'd heard coming from mom's throat so often as a teenager, now lived in hers. *God, I'm such a mom.*

"It's a bachelor party," Jerome said. "We're men. We're watching football and eating manly grilled cheese sandwiches."

"Yeah, it's a bachelor party. No moms allowed!" Liam puffed up, taking half the grilled cheese cut in triangles.

It was just how she cut his sandwiches. Warmth suffused

her, knowing that Clayton and Jerome knew how to cut Liam's sandwiches. It seemed like such a small thing to make misty happy tears prick her eyes, but the little things were always the most important. At least, that's what she'd experienced since that May day nine years ago after she'd given birth and held this tiny little person in her arms.

People had long been a challenge for Liam. He'd often struggled in social interactions. He'd avoid eye contact. He'd had difficulty understanding the unspoken cues that dominated most social exchanges. Sometimes he'd get overstimulated and shutdown or meltdown. The autism diagnosis helped her better understand how to assist Liam to navigate a world that could sometimes confound him. Hell, it confounded her.

For a long time, Liam's social network consisted just of her and her parents. A year and a half ago, she couldn't have dreamed of this scene. Of her son utterly comfortable in his own skin, surrounded by people who not just adored him but embraced him just as he was. So often, other parents wanted to "fix" Liam. They scrunch their faces and ask her if there was a pill or therapy that could make him "normal". She'd narrow her eyes and say, "He is normal."

What the fuck was normal, after all? Normal was a washing machine setting, not for people. If being normal meant Liam acted like she had in high school….no thank you. Her kindhearted son was perfect just as he was. She'd go mama bear on anyone who said otherwise.

"True, no moms allowed, but she's not mom now. She's the wedding planner, so she's allowed and must be listened to, or we'll make Elle unhappy." Clayton sat on the couch on the puppy-free side of Liam.

"Speaking as someone who married into that family you want to keep them happy." Jerome bit into a carrot.

"Alright, groomy, I'm off to the bridal suite to get ready with your intended. I expect you all de-bachelored and ready to go by four thirty." She smiled, looking around. "Where's Nat and Noah?"

"Kissing," all three groaned in unison.

"Natalie Joan, please extricate yourself from Noah. We have a tight schedule with the makeup artist and stylist!" she shouted, turning her head toward the foyer.

"They really are obnoxious." Clayton shook his head, sipping his beer.

Jerome's forehead puckered. "You've met Elle and you, right?"

"You're a pot, Jerome!" Liam pointed with his grilled cheese.

"Little man, did you just infer that I am the pot calling the kettle black?" he said in mock dismay.

Liam grinned widely.

"Nice burn." Jerome fist bumped the little boy.

"Oh, Liam. You might be spending entirely too much time with these lovestruck men." She shook her head, laughter rolling through her.

Burnt orange and amethyst painted the sky. Candles danced in the wintry breath that kissed Summer's cheeks. Heat lamps sheltered guests in an invisible force field of warmth as they sat beneath the radiant, twinkling lights. Snow-speckled pine trees draped in white lights shimmered at the edges of the property. The hum of instrumental love songs echoed in the evening air.

Summer stood at the back of the tent, scanning the scene with satisfaction. Everything was perfect. A mile-wide smile stretched across Clayton's face as he waited by the altar in a black tux with a purple and silver striped tie. Beside him, Noah nudged his ribs, whispering something to him, as they waited for the ceremony to begin.

"God, this is stunning." Todd stepped beside her. His woodsy scent enveloped her, his enticing warmth heating her skin. "You're amazing."

"Thank you." Pride swelled within her at his praise. She looked at the time on her iPad and brought up "If You Love Her" by Forrest Blakk. The melody glided across the property from strategically placed Bluetooth speakers.

Liam, who'd been practicing for a month, strolled, head high, in a miniature version of Clayton's suit and tie. Purple leashes were clipped to Fitz, who sported a purple bow tie, and Lizzie, who rocked a tiny silver starfish encrusted crown. Awed murmurs rose from the assembled guests as Liam marched down the purple runner leading from the little red barn to the pond's deck.

Reaching the front, Clayton high-fived her son before Liam took his seat in the front row beside Clayton's parents. Both puppies lowered to their haunches, settling at his feet.

"Our little guy did great." Todd's minty breath caressed the sensitive skin below her ear.

Our little guy? Was it that claiming of Liam, or the sensation of his breath like a promised kiss against her skin that stirred a longing within her. Imagine if Liam was their little guy and not…

She couldn't think about that. Not now. Not in the midst of all this love swirling around her. This was far too happy of a moment to be marred by the unhappy pull of the past. Not to mention to tarnish it with the thoughts of what would never be.

She nodded, watching the stately stream of the bridal party approaching the deck. As Carmen stepped onto the wooden planks and took her spot beside Willa and Viet, Summer cued up "Perfect" by Ed Sheeran.

Clayton's entire face lit with the first note of his and Elle's song.

Elle's cousin, Tobey, who was officiating, motioned for everyone to stand.

Clayton's gaze snapped to the porch of the Little Red Barn, where Elle emerged, her arm looped in her Uncle Pete's. Tears glistened in Pete's blue eyes and a heart-stoppingly big smile kicked across Elle's face as they strolled down the purple aisle.

Resplendent was the only word Summer could use to describe the bride. Elle's auburn waves were styled in a pinup inspired hairdo. A silvery starfish comb tucked into the silken strands. The dress, a mermaid silhouette framed her athletic body. Tiny gemstones along the bodice of her satin dress twinkled like a galaxy of stars in the glow of the setting sun.

With each step closer to the dock, Clayton's smile got a little bigger. Happy tears shimmered in his gray eyes.

Summer's heart swelled and tears pricked her eyes. A few twists of fate and she'd not be here. Elle had been her first friend and her first regret. Despite the forgiveness and regained friendship, that regret still reared its head from time-to-time, like Michael Myers refusing to die no matter how many times Jamie Lee Curtis took him out.

The music faded away as Elle stepped onto the dock. Weeping, Pete shook Clayton's hand before clenching his niece in a tight hug.

A lone tear dripped down Summer's face. Warmth enveloped her hand. Her eyes snapped to where Todd's large fingers had folded around hers. His green eyes remained fixed at the scene in front of them. She joined his stare, keeping her hand in his.

Clayton held Elle's hands in his. An unabashed smile covered his features.

"I've never seen someone so happy," Todd murmured.

"I know." She swallowed. "It almost makes you believe in happy endings."

"There's no such thing as a happy ending."

Her gaze jumped back to him.

"I don't believe in happy endings. There's nothing happy about an ending."

"What do you believe in?" she whispered.

"HEAs." He winked. "Happy ever afters."

A soft smile pulled at the corners of her lips. "Isn't that the same thing?"

"Not if you're doing it right."

"How do you know if you're doing it right." Her eyes remained fixed on his.

"I'll let you know when I get *my* HEA."

CHAPTER FOUR

"Don't have sex because you will get pregnant and die! Don't have sex in the missionary position, don't have sex standing up, just don't do it, OK, promise? OK, now everybody take some rubbers."
~Mean Girls

Music hummed through the tent. Between the heat lamps and crush of dancing bodies, the December chill was almost non-existent. Summer tapped her black dress boots, hidden below the long skirt of her purple velvet dress, against the leg of the table. She squinted in the blue light of the tablet, checking off the final items of her wedding to-do list. Couple married. *Check.* Photos of the couple beneath a canopy of snow covered trees bedecked in lights. *Check.* Slightly embarrassing toast by the best men. *Check.* Dinner served. *Check.* First dance. *Check.* Tearful Uncle/Niece dance. *Check.* Red velvet wedding cake cut. *Check.*

Outside of Lizzie stealing an unwatched piece of cake from one of the tables, the entire night had been perfect.

Satisfaction and a measure of pride bubbled inside her, as if Champagne fizzed through her bloodstream. She'd done it. She'd actually fucking done it. This was the first wedding she'd served as lead planner. In New York, she was just the assistant turning the vision of the planner into reality. She'd never had an actual plan to resurrect the skills she'd honed over ten years of event planning. It all came about by accident. At first, it was just helping Carmen out by volunteering for the annual Fall Fest planning committee last year. She'd not planned on doing it, but after Carmen lamented the last minute dropout of a few key committee members, Cassie had nudged her and volunteered her, saying, "Summer will help."

The next thing she knew, she was elbow deep in mums and pumpkin-theme decorations. What started as a onetime gig had morphed into helping with the village's annual Veteran's Day Pancake Breakfast, then the Christmas Market, followed by planning a few birthday parties for other volunteers' kids, and suddenly Summer had a business. She was being paid to plan parties and events. Now, she'd done a wedding.

Once again, her life had not gone as planned. *At least today had.* She looked at the final item on her checklist and smiled.

"Hey," she whined as the tablet was yanked out of her hands.

"Stop working," Todd chided with a soft laugh, moving the tablet away from her.

She reached, but he placed it at the far end of the table. "I need that."

He smirked. "No, you don't."

Her forehead creased with annoyance.

"First, I'd bet a hundred dollars you have your to-do list memorized."

She narrowed her eyes but said nothing.

"Second, it's time for you to take off your planner hat and put on your dancing shoes. You're also a guest at this wedding. You work too much."

"Says the man that spent last Sunday locked in his laboratory cooking up new witchy brews," she teased, leaning against the back of the chair.

His brow furrowed. "I don't know what to think of the mixed metaphors in that statement. Am I a mad scientist or a witch?"

"Warlock. Men can't be witches." Amusement curled her lips.

"Sweetheart, it's the twenty-first century. Men can be witches and women can be anything they damn well please."

A tiny thrill hummed through her. Was it the delicious way "Sweetheart" rolled off his tongue like hot caramel drizzled atop a sundae, or his veiled affirmation that she could be anything. Perhaps it was both.

"You should stop by my laboratory, as you call it, sometime. I'd love to show you what new concoctions I'm working on. I have a strawberries and cream ale recipe I'm experimenting with for the summer."

Adjusting in the chair, she twisted her body toward him. The flashing kaleidoscope of lights from the DJ booth brought out different shades in his green eyes. In the blue light they shined violet and a little wicked. The white light made them pop with a boyish brightness. In the red light their darker hue was reminiscent of a roguish hero from a romance novel.

Down, girl. She uncrossed and recrossed her legs. "So, how did you go from nerdy chemist to nerdy brewmaster?"

It was odd to think she'd never asked. Their friendship was still new. It had been little more than a leaf skating across the surface of a stream for much of the last year. There'd been rabbit hole conversations about favorite books or movies. Much of their interactions were buffered by Liam or their friends. She knew Todd was a good man with a good heart. That he'd left a job as a chemist in Rochester to work with Noah to open the Wine Down and the Farmer's Ale.

"It was my grandpa." A wistful expression covered his features.

"Old Chief Krueger?" She tilted her head to the right.

The Krueger family had a long history of police work in the county. Todd's grandpa had served as the village's police chief for almost twenty years. His father was the county Sheriff, and his younger sister Rose had joined the village's police force five years ago.

He shook his head. "No. My Grandpa Rice. My mom's dad."

Zach, Cassie's husband, was Todd's cousin. Grandpa Rice AKA Mr. Rice had been the high school chemistry teacher for Summer's parents and then Summer. He'd retired the year she'd graduated from high school. There'd been a big hoopla about it during the graduation ceremony where Carmen, their valedictorian, presented him with a framed periodic table signed by current and past students.

"I spent a lot of time with him as a kid, especially after..." he stopped himself, moving his eyes around the collection of happy guests dancing, sipping drinks, and laughing.

"After your mom?" She cringed. Who brings up someone's dead mom at a wedding? It was like being the cruel version of herself from high school, someone who'd pounce on any moment of weakness like a starved lioness. "Todd, I am so sorry. I shouldn't..."

His large hand covered hers, squeezing. "No. It's no secret that my mom died... And it's been a long time."

The memory of a fundraiser for Mandy Krueger's cancer treatment flashed in Summer's vision. Somewhere in the back of her closet may still be the pink *Team Mandy* T-shirt she'd worn at thirteen with fellow JV Cheerleaders from when they participated in the Relay for Life in honor of their favorite cheerleading coach, Todd's mom. She'd lost her battle with ovarian cancer the following year.

"I remember you coming to some of our cheerleading practices with your mom." A small smile lifted her lips.

Despite the cancer, Mandy, as she insisted the girls call her, coached them until she no longer could. At first it was just a silk scarf wrapped around her once vibrant red curls. Then it was a wheelchair. Then it was just a soft voice on a speaker phone wishing them good luck from her hospice bed.

"She loved cheerleading. She even made up cheers with the nurses at the hospital. God, it was so embarrassing. She'd drag me to your practices and competitions."

She nudged his shoulder with hers. "I don't think you minded too much. Especially when we rocked our short skirts to practice before a competition. I recall a smiling eleven-year-old watching us do cartwheels."

"Do you still have that uniform?" Devilment sparked in his eyes.

She swatted his arm with her free hand, trying not to marvel at its firmness. "Perv!"

A deep throaty laugh relaxed his features.

"So, you spent a lot of time with Grandpa Rice, then?"

"Yeah. When mom started getting sicker, he'd take me and Rose to his house to give Mom a break or, probably, to distract us from what was happening. He'd always cook up science experiments for us to do."

"Is that why you studied chemistry?" Her eyes went to where their hands were still joined. The rough pad of his thumb moved in lazy circles over her skin. Each stroke stoked a simmer in her blood.

"Yeah. I thought I wanted to be a teacher like him. To impact people the way he did…he still does. Ninety-two and he still teaches Sunday school."

"You impact people," she said, meeting his gaze. "You own two businesses that are reviving the main street in a previously dying town. Your witchy brews are attracting people to Perry. Not to mention that Noah and you have your hands in just about every community event or fundraiser in the village."

"Sure." Soft self-deprecation filled his tone.

"Don't do that." She went to pull her hand away to swat him again, but he held it tight.

"Do what?" His features turned playful.

"Put my friend down. I won't stand for it."

"Good thing you're sitting."

She rolled her eyes.

"Dance with me."

"Okay." The breathy answer slipped out before she had a chance to think better of it.

Before she could register what was happening, he rose and pulled her up beside him. The palm of his hand rested on her lower back, and he guided her toward the dance floor. Her skin sizzled with pleasure at the feel of his hand through the fabric of her dress.

This is a bad idea.

As if on cue, the fast-paced music slowed to a love song.

Great, the DJ is in on this bad idea. She worried her lower lip.

"Perfect timing." Amused wickedness glinted in his eyes. His strong hands settled on her waist, pulling her in close.

She should go. The catering staff were clearing the last of the discarded dishes from the tables, and she should check in with them. Or follow up with Todd's bartending staff to make sure they had everything they needed. There was an unnecessary text message to her parents to confirm that Liam, who had left two hours ago, was still asleep. There were clothes and makeup strewed across every surface of the bridal suite to clean up. There were so many other things she *should* be doing at this moment.

Instead, she was doing this thing she shouldn't be doing. She shouldn't be pressing in close to his firm chest. She shouldn't be resting her head against his shoulder. She shouldn't be drinking up the sensation of his muscular arms wrapped around her and his wintery, woodsy scent.

"You never told me how you went from chemist to brewmaster," she murmured, hoping the conversation would settle the pulsing urge to nuzzle in close.

"It's more fun to make beer than pharmaceuticals. Plus, I'm the boss. Who doesn't love being the boss. I know you enjoy telling me what to do."

Laughter bubbled out of her. "Smartass. How'd you get into beer, though?"

He pressed his head against hers. "Grandpa Rice brewed his own beer. When my mom died, I stopped talking to anyone. I pulled away from friends and things I used to enjoy. He made me go to the garage and sit with him while he brewed. At first, I just sat there quiet."

"You… Quiet?"

"Now who's being the smartass."

His smile warmed the side of her face.

"At first, I asked about how or why he was doing certain things. Then we started talking about other things. My father wouldn't approve of his eleven-year-old son making beer in the garage with his grandpa, so we kept it just between us. It was our secret, so I guess I felt like anything I said or was feeling was just between us. I love brewing both for the result and how people enjoy it, but also for the feeling it gives me when I'm doing it."

"What's that feeling?"

"Like I have the power to fix or create happiness in my hands. That no matter what life throws at me, I can make something good out of it." He nuzzled his nose into her loose locks.

"Do you really believe that?"

His hand stroked down her back. "Of course. I'm the former band geek dancing with the prom queen."

"I'm not the prom queen anymore."

"You're so much more. You've always been so much more," he whispered.

She tipped her head up. For a beat, their gazes joined in a

wordless dance that frightened her. She knew the steps but was too scared to dance them.

"I should…" she trailed off, pulling away.

He closed his eyes. "I know…you're working." Resignation underscored his words.

She opened and then closed her mouth. What could she say?

She pivoted and marched off the dance floor, past the rows of tables half-filled with guests, and out of the tent. Snow kicked up as she stomped across the yard toward the Little Red Barn. She didn't even know where she was going or what she was doing. She just knew she needed to get away. To get away from…

God what was she getting away from? Him? Her past? The look in his eyes as he looked at her? That look…fuck she could drown in the way he looked at her.

"Summer!" Todd called as he raced behind her. He caught her just as she reached the front porch. "Why are you leaving? Did I do something wrong?"

She opened the door and walked in. "Nothing. I just have things to do."

He followed her in. "This couldn't wait?"

He motioned around the room cluttered with the remnants of the bridal party getting ready. Empty champagne flutes sat on the kitchen counter beside a half-eaten box of chocolates. Four silk robes hung over the arm of the couch.

"Someone needs to clean this up." She plucked up Willa's makeup case.

"Why does it have to be you?"

"Because I'm the wedding planner." She placed Willa's makeup case back down, not knowing where it went.

"Or is it because if you are so busy cleaning up after or taking care of everyone else, you don't have to live your own life?"

She whirled, wagging her finger at him. "Don't fucking psychoanalyze me. We're friends but not that *kind* of friends."

"What kind of friends are we, Summer?" He stepped closer, heat darkened his gaze.

She raised her hands in front of her. "Stop!"

He jolted to a halt. "I'm not going to hurt you. I'd never hurt you."

"I know you wouldn't. At least, not like that. But something terrible will happen if you move any closer."

His right eyebrow ticked up. "What terrible thing will happen?"

"I'll kiss you."

A wry expression kicked across his face. "That doesn't sound terrible…not in the least."

"It would be."

"Hmmm." A low noise rumbled in his throat. "I've been told I'm not a terrible kisser. I have references."

Her pulse quickened. "I'm sure you'd be wonderful at it and even if you weren't you're smart, so you'd learn quick."

He took a tentative step forward. "The mad scientist in me thinks we should run an experiment. You know, determine if your theory is right."

Temptation tingled along her skin. Her breath shallowed at the idea of closing the distance between them. His full lips taking hers in first sweet, but then demanding kisses. The caress of his five o'clock shadow against her cheek. A squeak as he gripped her ass, claiming her. The gentle push of her back on to the couch and delicious heaviness of his body coming atop hers.

Stop! She shook her head. "I can't risk it if it fails."

"What if it succeeds?"

That was what she's feared the most. There'd been too many warning signs tonight. Her heart's skipped beat when he'd called Liam "our guy." Her skin's buzz at his touch. The knowledge that roasted inside her that if he kissed her, it wouldn't be terrible...not even a little.

"I can't," she croaked.

The playfulness in his eyes sobered to regret. "Won't... You won't."

"Can't or won't...it doesn't matter, we're...I'm not doing this." She glared.

"It does matter. Can't is something stopping you. Won't is you stopping yourself."

"What does it matter?"

"Because one I can live with and the other... I won't."

The resolve in his eyes almost knocked her over. They stood in a silent stare off. Neither backing down from their can'ts or won'ts.

His voice was quiet. "I'll go." He got up and turned, heading for the door.

"Todd." His name trembled on her lips. "I don't want to lose you as a friend."

The muscles of his back contracted with a heavy breath. "Goodnight, Summer." Then he walked out the door.

CHAPTER FIVE

"…I wish I could bake a cake filled with rainbows and smiles and everyone would eat and be happy…" ~Mean Girls

"Please, not so loud," Noah groaned, his fingers pressed to his temples.

"Too much fun last night?" Summer sipped her cup of tea, her eyes flicked between Noah's weary face to the restaurant filled with happy and some very hungover wedding attendees.

The brunch at the Sea Serpent, a restaurant and lounge along the quiet shores of the now frozen lake, was the last of the wedding shenanigans for the weekend. The happy couple would drop their fur babies off at Noah and Nat's before heading off to their weeklong honeymoon in England.

"Oh, my sweet hungover baby," Nat cooed, running her fingers across the dark stubble on his strong jawline.

"I told you, man, hair of the dog." A slightly buzzed Jerome beamed, holding up his half-empty Bloody Mary like an Olympian hoisting a gold medal. "Works every time."

Willa pointed to Nat. "What I don't get is how you're as fresh as a newborn's bottom when you went shot for shot with the rest of the groom's party last night. Besides our dear Jerome, who is still drunk, the rest of them look haggard. Hell, Elle said Clayton passed out on the couch last night."

Jerome's face creased. "Oh, man he missed out on wedding night sex. Poor groomy."

"Let's face it, they had sex long before then. Do you recall the twenty-five minutes when they disappeared between the dinner and cake cutting?" Summer said, clucking her tongue.

"Too loud," Noah whined.

Nat soothed her fingers into Noah's short dark hair. "First, I had the good sense to slam a Gatorade, half a bottle of water, and take two Advil before I went to bed. Also, unlike the rest of you, I'm still in my twenties." Nat preened, flipping her sandy locks over her shoulders.

"You'll be twenty-nine in March, so enjoy it. You have just over a year before this is you." Noah waved to his green-tinged face.

"Oh, he's so right. The hangover after my thirtieth lasted an entire week." Willa smeared jam on an English muffin.

"I'll take solace in the fact that I'll always be younger than you." With a bat of her long eyelashes, Nat leaned over and kissed the grimace on Noah's face.

"Old Man Wilson will enter his last year in his thirties in just a few weeks," Summer quipped.

"Don't remind me." Noah groaned once more. "Also, reminder that I *don't* want a party." He motioned with his fork between Summer and Nat.

Summer arched an eyebrow. "It's cute how you think you have any say in this."

Of course a party was in the works. For the last three weeks, she and Nat had conspired on a very non-secret surprise party on December 22. With the busy schedule of holiday parties and events that filled the month of December, his birthdays had long been intimate family dinners with his parents and the Owens, so Nat wanted to coordinate an obnoxious party for him.

"He is cute." Nat patted Noah's cheek.

"Ha!" Jerome barked. "That's what I love about Nat, she may look all pixie sweet but she's one feisty bitch. Then you toss in our reformed Regina George"—he tipped his head toward Summer— "and they are fucking unstoppable."

Summer cringed internally at his statement. Even Jerome, who'd not grown up in Perry, knew about Summer's past. In Perry, it often felt like who you were was who you'd always be. *I'll always be Regina George.*

Jerome's quip wasn't meant to needle her but, after the interaction with Amy on Friday and the weirdness with Todd last night, she felt raw. It didn't help that Todd had positioned himself across the room at a table with Elle's Uncle Pete and Aunt Janet.

Nothing happened last night, but so much happened. This morning when she walked into the brunch and found him beside Jerome, he merely nodded, mumbled a greeting and then made up an excuse to walk away.

The fact he was acting like a petulant child who didn't get the toy he wanted pissed her right off. If he was going to ignore her, then two could play that game. Now, if only she could get the obstinate corner of her eye to stop looking at him across the room.

"I don't think I like you calling my woman a bitch." Noah's forehead creased.

"*My woman?*" Laughter vibrated from Nat.

"That's some Alpha vibes from our dear cinnamon roll love god over there," Willa teased.

"You ladies and your romance novels." He sipped his black coffee.

"Also, as I mean it in the correct way and am part of the monthly mani/pedis brigade, I got the 'bitch' clearance from the Natster," Jerome said. The six-foot-seven, two-hundred and seventy pound wall of muscle, loved sipping on mimosas while pampering his tootsies as he called them. Each month he organized a mani/pedi outing for Elle, Nat, Summer, and Carmen. The only rule no husbands or boyfriends allowed, except for him.

"What's the proper meaning of bitch?" Noah asked, his brows linked in curiosity.

"Babe in total control of herself!" Summer and Nat hooted.

"Yes, queens!" Willa raised her champagne flute.

Noah grimaced. "Library voices, please."

"Oh, my poor baby." Nat made a kissy face.

"These two really could run the world." Jerome broke off a piece of croissant and waved it between Summer and Nat. "You should have them negotiate that deal with Maxwell's. I'm sure the buyer wouldn't be able to turn them down."

Summer's hackles rose. "Maxwell's?"

"They're a high-end grocery chain along the Eastern Seaboard. Their flagship store is in Manhattan," Noah explained.

"Did you ever shop there when you were living your *Sex and the City* life in New York City?" Willa asked, then sipped her mimosa.

"Uhh…a few times…yeah." Summer fiddled with the cloth napkin draped over her lap.

Nat tilted her head as if assessing Summer. *Not as if.* Summer knew her friend was studying the change in Summer's ease.

Fixing a pretend smile on her face she looked at Noah. "This is exciting. What's the deal?"

"It's not for sure yet. When Todd and I participated in the New York State Beer and Wine festival in October, the head buyer from Maxwell's was there. They want to feature local small breweries at their stores. Especially those are who are veterans, female, or BIPOC owned."

Summer merely nodded. A nervous jitter flashed through her limbs.

"The buyer is interested in possibly featuring a few Farmer's Ale brews at their flagship store and then, if sales are good, expanding distribution to other locations. It would mean amazing growth. We'd have to hire more staff and find a larger facility for making beer for mass production."

"Buddy, Todd and you are going to be beer moguls!" Jerome boomed, his deep voice shaded with pride. "You'll be like the Ben and Jerry's of beer."

"Head buyer? What's his name?" Summer schooled her features, trying not to show the anxiety pulsing within her.

"Vanessa Maxwell. She's the daughter of George Maxwell, their founder and CEO."

She let out a shaky breath, knowing all too well who Vanessa Maxwell was. She could almost picture the sleek black bob and whiskey-colored eyes made darker with disappointment.

"I need to go to the bathroom," Nat blurted. "Summer?"

Part of her wanted to stay put, but a larger part wanted to escape. An even larger part did not want to go with Nat because the moment they were behind the bathroom's closed doors, there'd be questions. So many questions.

"Bitches love to go to the bathroom together," Jerome chuckled.

Willa yanked the Bloody Mary out of his hand. "You're cut off."

"From the drink and your use of that word." Nat wagged a finger, standing up.

"Ah, boo." He pouted.

Summer was barely out of her seat before Nat grabbed her hand and tugged her toward the bathroom. Zigzagging through the white linen covered tables, they passed by the mix of still hungover and bright-eyed guests. The table nearest the entry to the dining room taunted her. Todd leaned back in the high back red chair, his green eyes focused on Janet, who sputtered and gestured with her hands about something. He'd retired the button-up shirts he'd worn for the rehearsal dinner and wedding in favor of a cerulean sweater that looked cozy soft. Like the ideal fabric to melt into while being snuggled up to on the couch.

No couch snuggles!

With each step closer to the table, she tried to avert her stare, but it was drawn to him like a bee to a rose. God, she wanted him to turn and look at her. Even more she was terrified what she'd do, if he did.

"Summer! Nat!" Janet crooned, stopping their forward momentum. "You girls aren't leaving, are you?"

"Nope. Just off to the ladies to gossip," Nat joked.

"I don't get you ladies and gabbing in the bathroom. Men's rooms are for silence and avoiding eye contact," Pete laughed. "Right, Todd?"

Todd just shrugged; his gaze fixed on his plate.

Really? Her blood boiled. The audacity of this man to be sullen because she'd set clear boundaries. Boundaries that were good for them both. Lines in the sand that would save either of them from getting hurt.

Narrowing her eyes, she crossed her arms over her chest. "*Some* men are good at silence and avoiding eye contact outside of the confines of the bathroom."

Both Pete and Janet's eyebrows cocked.

"We gotta go." Nat took hold of Summer's arm and yanked her through the entryway and down the long hall to the bathroom.

Anger blossomed with each step towards the door. How could he just ignore her? It's not as if she kissed him and then said, "Oops." She wasn't sending mixed signals.

Once they entered the quiet bathroom, Nat spun and placed her hands on her hips. "What is going on with you?"

"Nothing."

"Summer Joy Michaels, don't try to fool me. Remember I've perfected the 'I'm fine with a faux smile' schtick. Last night I saw Todd and you dancing and there were definitely sparks. Then suddenly you were both gone. Then he was gone and you were alone."

Her lips pinched. "I thought you were too busy sucking face and doing tequila shots with old man Wilson to notice my comings and goings?"

"Are there *comings* to discuss?" A salacious smile slanted her lips.

Summer groaned. "You're such a child sometimes."

"Seriously, though. The two of you have been on opposite sides of the brunch with a palpable tension. Not to mention you got all weird about their potential Maxwell's deal. What's that all about?" Determination shaded her gray eyes.

"Nothing happened with Todd." She let out an annoyed breath, turning to face the sink.

Nat shook her head and hit Summer with a disbelieving expression in the mirror. "But something *almost* happened?"

Stupid mirrors. She let out a low growl. And stupid best friends who see everything and don't let her crawl back into herself.

Nat softened her stance. "Whatever didn't happen seems to have affected you both. I know I'm allowing my best friend status to be intrusive, but...when you were dancing with Todd last night you looked happy. Like... really happy."

"I'm happy." The soft protest was punctuated by her very unhappy expression reflected in the mirror. Her lips turned down in a frown, her face creased with regret, remorse, and frustration.

"You're happy in a different way with Todd. You're lighter. You let this fun, flirty side out that you don't always let out."

She closed her eyes. "There was a moment last night where I thought… then I thought better of it."

"Why?"

"It won't work." She turned, facing Nat. "I'm too broken."

"Because of Max?"

It wasn't just the relationship with Max. It was easy for her best friend to think that was it. The truth was Summer was broken long before Max. Perhaps, that's why Max happened.

"I know you don't like to be pushed, but you pushed me to tell Noah how I felt, so turnabout is fair play, my beautiful bestie." She gripped Summer's arms. "You're not broken. You're scared, just like I was."

After seeing what she deemed an obvious mutual attraction and affection between Nat and Noah, Summer had encouraged her friend to go after the relationship. There'd been many underhanded and overhanded comments about Nat being in love with Noah and too scared to own the truth in her heart. Even after they'd started dating in secret, Summer had counseled her friend to be open about the relationship.

"You didn't let me hide and I won't let you hide."

"Nat." she begged in a pleading tone.

Nat had a deep desire to see the people in her life happy. Even if sometimes it meant prodding them to move out of the pasture that they'd so comfortably lounged in. Only there'd be no moving Summer. A quiet stubbornness took hold of her.

"Fine!"–she sloshed a breath— "I'll stop nagging about Todd, but why were you being weird about the Maxwell's deal? It wasn't just carryover from whatever is going on between Todd and you, was it?"

She closed her eyes and lifted her hand to her temple, rubbing away the dull but growing ache of frustration. "Max."

"What?"

She opened her eyes, meeting Nat's wide eyes. "Max is short for George Maxwell, Jr."

CHAPTER SIX

"**M**ax is Maxwell's?" Nat gaped.

Summer shifted foot-to-foot. She'd doled out tidbits about Max like breadcrumbs over the years. The only people who really knew about Max were her parents. She'd only ever told her parents, minus several parts that would ensure her dad did something that may end with him in prison for murder. Over the four years they dated, Mom and Dad had only met Max once, on a trip they made to the city. That had been early in the relationship. Before…

"Max? *That* Max?" Nat repeated, her tone becoming almost shrill. "The man who wasn't nice to you?"

Is that how she described it? Hearing her friend say it out loud somehow diminished what occurred between she and Max. Why had she said it in that way? Why did she not say it?

She forgets who I am and who she is. Who would people believe?

Max's caramel-dipped venom echoed inside her. He'd reduced her to less than a person with his insistence on referring to her in the third person.

Somehow his cruel words always came out smooth and controlled. The effect always left her dazed, reminiscent of waking up from a long nap and wondering if she was still in the midst of a nightmare.

He's not here. She swallowed down the hard lump in her throat. "It was more than not being nice."

Nat threaded their fingers. "Oh, Summer."

"Don't." Summer pulled away, turning to face the door. The dull sting of held back tears radiated behind her eyes.

"Noah and Todd won't make the deal with Maxwell's. They'd never—"

She whirled, her heart racing. "You can't tell them. You can't."

Few people knew about New York. About Max. Most of the village only knew that Summer had gotten pregnant and came home. Nobody knew who Liam's father was. Her parents were the only people who knew Max's true identity, and now Nat.

"I would never break your confidence. This is part of your story to tell, not mine." Nat chewed her lip. "But if we just told Noah that George Maxwell, Jr. is a bad guy, he'd not take the deal. No questions asked. You know Noah. He'll take the word of the people he loves and trusts without question."

"I won't be the reason this deal doesn't happen. You heard Noah, it wouldn't only expand their business but be an economic win for the village. Noah, Todd, Carmen, and so many others have dedicated so much of their lives to reinvigorate this town. This deal means jobs. It means tourism."

Nat raised her hand, cradling Summer's cheek. "But what does a partnership with Maxwell's mean for you?"

"It's not about me."

God, how very few times in her life she had said that.

Memories flooded in; of her as a teen, standing in girls' restrooms making everything about her. So much of her young life had been about her. About her wants and needs. Mostly her wants. Only in the last nine and a half years had she started thinking about something greater than herself.

"I want Liam to grow up in a place that offers resources. The more money that flows into this village, the more opportunity he'll have. Plus, Todd deserves this. If it was any other grocery chain besides Maxwell's, I'd be bursting with pride. He's so talented. The world deserves to taste his witchy brews."

The twinge in her chest softened. She'd teased him about his witchy brews at the wedding, but she was floored by his skill. The man could take flavors that didn't seem to fit and make them dance on your tastebuds. He'd take tried and true brews and elevate them in a way that made a person question if they'd ever truly had that taste before?

"You're doing this for Liam and Todd?" Nat arched a brow.

She waved her off. "Don't read into this."

"But what if the deal goes through and Max comes here?"

"Max is in line to take over once his dad retires. At least, that was the plan when we dated. CEOs in training aren't in the habit of visiting local breweries. Plus, he referred to anything west of Albany as dueling banjo territory. He'd never come here."

"What about Vanessa? She's his sister and the head buyer." Concern scrunched Nat's features.

"As department manager, she has a team of assistants that would come here. Also"–her mouth tightened into a firm line — "this may shock you, but Vanessa wasn't my biggest fan. She referred to me as Event Planning Barbie. She never thought I was good enough for her brother, so if she did see me, she likely wouldn't say anything."

It was the one time she was grateful for her past self's

behavior. Business-focused Vanessa, with her smart bob haircut and tailored black suits, hadn't warmed to Summer. Where Summer was about going to the latest trendy club with the fancy new handbag purchased by Max, Vanessa focused on Maxwell's expansion.

"If you think this is best, then I'll support you. I won't say anything to Noah." Nat fiddled with her gardenia pendant necklace.

"I know you hate lying to Noah, but I promise this is what's best for him…for the village." Summer placed her hands on Nat's upper arms, squeezing gently.

"This village has no idea of all you give and sacrifice for it."

Summer pushed back those threatening tears. "Don't saint me, Nat. It's just mean girl penance."

"You're not Regina George, reformed or otherwise. High school was so long ago. At some point, people need to get over it, you included."

"Says the woman who still bristles when she runs into Laura McKay because she beat her by half a point to become valedictorian."

Nat raised her hands in the air. "I still contend that she cheated. Those cupcakes she presented in home economics were so store-bought!"

A deep belly laugh eased Summer's tight muscles.

Nat let out a long sigh. "Whatever you want to do, I'm with you. You know that. I'm the Amy to your Meg. I've got your back."

Summer wrapped her arms around Nat, pulling her in. "Thank you."

"Don't you mean thank you, my best friend…love of my friendship life?" Nat teased.

"You ruin all our moments."

"You *love* it, and me."

She did. She really did.

"Now, did you drag me in here for that or did you actually have to use the restroom?" Summer asked, releasing Nat.

"Just for that."

"Alright, well head back. I'm going to use the bathroom since I'm here."

Nat's head cocked to the right. "Are you just trying to get me out of here so you can have a moment to yourself to process this and then figure out a smooth way to skip out of the brunch?"

"Yep." God, her friend knew her so well. Even without sharing all herself with Nat, she somehow still knew. They had an ability to read each other, even when the pages were written with invisible ink.

"Alright. I'll bounce and start with a cover about you having stomach issues."

"Natalie Joan, don't you dare insinuate that I have diarrhea!" Her mouth slackened with horror.

Nat's mouth quirked into a cheeky smile. "I won't insinuate, I'll flat out say that's what's happening." She sashayed toward the door.

"Bitch!" Summer jammed her hands on her hips.

"Now, now. You've joined Jerome in the 'Not Allowed to Use that Word' club." She laughed as she pushed through the door.

Once alone, Summer stood for a moment, facing the mirror. Somehow the image in front of her wasn't her of today but her of almost ten years ago. Perfectly styled platinum-blonde hair. Lips painted a deep red. A long sleeve red dress that stopped mid-thigh and clung to her once too-thin frame. The only sign that the put together woman in front of her wasn't as she appeared were sad eyes that almost sank into themselves as if terrified to face the world. To look at the faces of others who saw the truth hidden behind the layers of makeup and designer clothes.

"You're not that girl anymore," she whispered, allowing the image to dissolve.

The blonde hair had been replaced by wavy chestnut hair pulled in a high ponytail: a loose tendril pushed behind her ear. An oversized gray turtleneck sweater loosely hung over her fuller curves. Pumpkin Chapstick coated her lips more out of necessity than vanity. Her brown eyes were bright despite the wisps of sadness and regret that drifted within them. She was utterly transformed.

Summer splashed cold water on her face, the icy jolt pushing back the threatening tears. No tears today nor tomorrow.

Taking a paper towel, she patted her face dry. "You got this." She tossed it into the trash and turned to the door. Stepping out of the door, she collided with a firm chest. Tipping her head up, her breath caught. "Todd."

"We need to talk," he said, his chiseled jaw clenched.

CHAPTER SEVEN

"Cold. Shiny. Hard. PLASTIC." ~Mean Girls

He wants to talk? Anger seethed inside Summer.

He'd walked away from her last night and spent the entire morning ignoring her. Now, he stood in front of her in the long hallway off the restrooms and wanted to *talk*. His wintry, woodsy scent caressed her skin like murmured kisses.

Nope! Nope! We don't think about that. We're mad at him. She moved around him, putting space between them.

Reaching for her, his hand gently wrapped around her upper arm, halting her steps. It was the softest of touches. So opposite from large hands that had once gripped and hauled her back into a hard steel frame. The tender squeeze of her bicep akin to the wispy embrace of a soft spring breeze.

Her gaze dropped to his hand. *How could such large strong hands be so gentle?*

He let go of her, his jaw softening. "Can we talk, please?"

"Oh, I can talk." Annoyance wrinkled her features. "Can you? You're the one who walked away last night and spent this morning giving me the silent treatment like a sullen man-child."

His forehead puckered. "I wasn't giving you the silent treatment. I was giving you what you *think* you want, but not what you actually want."

Indignation simmered along her veins. "What does *that* mean?"

He stepped closer, the heat of his body twined around her blocking everything but the sensation of him…only him. His features brightened with the hint of a boyish grin.

"I think you know. You just don't want to admit it to me nor yourself."

Her pulse raced. All the protests disappeared. She merely stood drinking in the teasing determination that glinted in his eyes.

"Summer. Todd." Pete's laughter-filled voice shook her out of her trance.

She turned toward Pete and Janet, and their matching pair of knowing smirks.

"Hi." It came out like a yelp, as if she was a teenager again getting caught making out with Shane Peters on the front porch.

Only I hadn't been making out. Well, not with your mouth. The things she imagined doing to and having Todd do to her could make the most voracious reader of steamy romance novels clutch their pearls.

"Sorry to interrupt, we were just going to visit the restroom before we headed out." Janet's assessing gaze flipped between Summer and Todd.

If Summer thought Cassie was meddlesome with her love life, Janet was the Winston Churchill of matchmaking strategy. Elle's aunt had admitted during the wedding planning process that she'd specifically invited Clayton to Elle's welcome back BBQ last summer, not because he was her son-in-law's best man, but out of hopes of matching the two. Apparently, Clayton had asked one too many questions about how Tobey's cousin Elle was doing in California to not draw the attention of Perry's feisty Cupid.

"Unless you two would like one of the restrooms to *talk* more privately," Janet purred.

Summer's jaw slackened.

Todd snorted.

Pete tugged his wife's hand. "Leave them alone, Janet. Go take care of business. We'll race to see who gets out here first. Winner has to go start the truck and warm it up for the other."

"Oh, Petey-Pie, you know you'll be warming up the car for me." She sashayed to the door. "Summer, come see me at the Village Rose this week. Your dad wants me to talk to you about the marketing class I'm taking in January."

Summer's eyes narrowed as she watched Janet disappear into the ladies' room. Of course, her dad asked his dear cousin Janet to talk to her.

Pete shrugged and went into the men's room.

"Come with me." Todd took her hand, moving down the long hall.

"Where are we going?"

"To talk." He led them to a brown door labeled *Staff Only*.

Scanning the dimly lit hall he opened the door and pulled her in behind him. Their fingers remained linked as he shut the door and yanked on a cord dangling from a bare bulb, bathing the room in dim yellow light. A faint pine-cleaner aroma danced in the air. Neat shelves loaded with cleaning products, boxes of tissues, toilet paper, and paper towels lined the walls of the small janitor's closet, forcing them close together. The scant inches between them charged like the pull of a magnet, enticing her closer to the hard planes of his sculpted chest.

"We shouldn't be in here," she whispered, stepping back and running into the shelf, causing two rolls of toilet paper to tumble to the ground.

Todd's arms settled on her shoulders and guided her closer to him. "It's fine. The staff are busy with the brunch, nobody is going to interrupt us in here."

That thought ignited the smoldering embers in her belly. *Stop it, body, or I will polar plunge into the frozen lake to quell this unfortunate lust!* It had been so long since she'd felt hands exploring her skin. There was only so much a steamy romance novel and a vibrator could do.

"Talk." Her voice dripped with a foreign huskiness.

"First, I wasn't being sullen."

She made a *sure* face.

"Okay, maybe I was being a *little* sullen," he grumbled. "I just… I don't get you. I know you want me as much as I want you. I'm not blind. I see how you look at me."

"How do I look at you?"

He dropped his hands to her hips, tucking her close to his chest and dipping his lips inches from hers. "Like I'm the last piece of steak and you've not eaten in days."

The heated, minty taste of his breath caressed her lips in a prelude to what would come if only she'd say yes. How easy it would be to raise to her tiptoes, twine her arms around his neck, and close the distance between their lips.

"Fine," she said, breathlessly. "I want you. Are you happy?"

The corners of his mouth kicked up in that wickedly boyish grin of his. "It's a start." His arms banded around her back.

Every one of her muscles relaxed at his touch and every nerve ending sparked alive. *Fucking traitorous body! You're going into the lake.*

"I want you. You want me. We get along. I think…no, I know we'd be good together. I know you'd make me happy and—"

"You think I'd make you happy?" she scoffed.

She disappoints me time and time again. She closed her eyes at the unwanted memory marring this moment. Or, perhaps, it was a warning.

"You already do. Nothing makes me happier than bantering with you, getting lost in a conversation about a book, texting with you while we both binge the same show. The way you keep me on my toes."

She nibbled on the corner of her mouth. "You make me happy, too."

"Kiss me."

My move. Todd's intentions were clear, but she knew that his cinnamon roll nature would leave it up to her to close the distance she'd kept between them.

"I can't...I won't. There's too much at risk."

That boyish smile dragged down.

"There's Liam," she went on.

"I like Liam. You know that."

She didn't question how much Todd cared for her little boy and how much, in turn, Liam adored him. Since September, Liam had asked on three different occasions if Todd could be his mom's boyfriend. Each time, Todd had grinned, ruffling his hair, and saying, "It's up to your mom who she dates."

"Liam adores you."

"Then what's holding you back?" His right hand trailed up; his fingertips brushed her ear as he tucked that wayward tendril back. "I know you want this. Otherwise, you wouldn't be in my arms right now. You'd already have slipped away."

"Just because you want something doesn't mean you should have it." She swallowed thickly. "It's me. I'm too broken for a man like you."

"What does that mean? A man like me?" Concerned curiosity scrunched his features.

"You're a good man. You've always been. Hell, even when you were that trumpet playing kid with your rainbow of polo shirts tucked into ill-fitting jeans, I knew you had a big heart…a heart that I don't want to break."

"We both could have our hearts broken or break each other's heart."

"I don't deserve you." A small tremor quaked in her voice.

He bracketed her face between tender hands, his eyes searching hers. "You deserve so much more than me. You deserve everything."

She lowered her eyes, but the tender strokes of the pads of his fingers against her cheek guided her gaze back to him.

"Why do you think that, sweetheart? Is it because of who you used to be? That was almost twenty fucking years ago and you haven't been that person for a very long time."

"Time doesn't wash away what I did."

"No, it doesn't. Nothing washes the past away, but actions forge a future founded on forgiveness of each other and ourselves. I've watched you apologize to person after person. I've watched you be the person you were always meant to be. You're fucking amazing, Summer Michaels. You're funny. You're kind. You're talented. You're a fierce mama bear and not just for Liam, but for your friends."

She could wade into the loveliness of his words. Each syllable seeped into her skin with the comfort of his faith in her.

"It's not just that, though." His jaw hardened. "Liam's father. What happened?"

"Did Nat say something?"

He shook his head. "No, but you haven't dated anyone since coming back and you never talk about him."

The standard response to any question about where Liam's father was "He's not in his life." Most people left it at that, assuming that he hadn't wanted a baby. That the relationship ended because of her pregnancy. In many ways it had, but not in the way others assumed.

The sincerity that swam in his eyes coaxed the words out

of her. "His name was Max. We dated for four years and lived together for three of them. I loved him and thought he loved me, but... what we had wasn't love."

Why was she telling him this? She'd never told anyone, except her parents. After she'd come home over nine years ago, two and a half months pregnant and sporting both fresh and healing bruises, there was no hiding what had happened from them. They'd simply enfolded her broken body into their arms, whispering, "We've got you. You're safe."

Todd's long fingers caressed her cheeks. "I know I asked but if you're not ready to tell me, I'd understand. If you're ready, though, I promise to listen."

She leaned into him. Pressing her head against his chest, she listened to the soothing thump of his heart. Like the coziest of blankets, he held her close in his strong arms.

"I wasn't someone for him to love, I was something for him to possess. At first, I thought his constant checking in and desire to have me close was doting and sweet. He'd buy me clothes, pay for my gym membership, and to go to the salon. I thought he wanted to take care of me, but it was about controlling me. What I wore. Who my friends were. What I did. He'd monitor what I ate and make me weigh myself in front of him, saying I was an extension of him."

"What the fuck?" he muttered, holding her tighter.

She hadn't thought it would be possible to get closer. Somehow, it felt as if crawling inside Todd and making her new home within his heart still wouldn't be close enough. God, that scared her.

"It started slow. Little comments here and there. It was textbook. All the things you'd see in a *Lifetime* movie and wonder how the woman got herself into that relationship. Why she hadn't left at the first sign. It's easy to judge when you're not the one living it."

"Did he...did he hit you?" Todd's muscles tensed.

She closed her eyes. "No." How easy the lie slipped from her lips.

He let out a shaky breath.

"When I found out I was pregnant Max was in London on business. All I could think is what he'd do when he found out I was pregnant? Would he let me keep the baby?" Hot tears pricked her eyes. "If he would, what would our child's life be like? Max had made me quit my job a year after we moved in together. All the credit cards were in his name. He tracked all my spending and only gave me access to what he felt I needed. I packed a bag and bought a ticket to Los Angeles and took a cab, using his card there. I even booked a hotel out there."

"But you didn't go there."

"I made it look like I had. I used what little cash I had and took a bus to Rochester and then hitchhiked back to Perry. I didn't want to risk him finding out. He'd never come here. My parents met him once. Max didn't like them, so we didn't see them. I didn't come home. I let him isolate me…possess every inch of my life."

"No." The protest was gruff and almost a growl. "You didn't let him do anything. I know men like him. They know how to make you feel small. To make you feel like it's your fault. That you deserve their shitty treatment and cruel words."

Now her tears fell in earnest. She swiped at her eyes. God, she hated crying. Too many of her tears had been wasted on Max. On her past.

"So, he doesn't know about Liam?"

"No." She swallowed hard. "Do you think I'm wrong for hiding Liam? For not letting my son know his father?"

"No." His chin rested atop her head. "You are so strong, sweetheart. You were smart enough to protect Liam and you. Your heart was fierce enough to love again. Look at how deeply you love Liam. You say you're broken, but I disagree. He tried to break you, but your still fucking standing strong."

"You make me sound like Katniss Everdeen or Xena Warrior Princess." She let out a watery chuckle.

"They've got nothing on you." His fingers traced her hairline.

"I do want you, but I'm not ready," she murmured.

He pressed a tender of kisses against her temple. "I know, sweetheart. I'll wait. In the meantime, I'll be your friend. I promise I won't go all sullen man-child on you again." A tiny smirk curled his lips.

Their gazes locked. "You'll wait for me? What if you're waiting forever?"

"You're worth the wait."

Am I?

CHAPTER EIGHT

Cady: "Well, there must be something you're good at."
Karen: "I can stick my whole fist in my mouth, wanna see?" ~Mean
Girls

I t was a typical Sunday evening for Summer. Liam's cheerful hoots skipped into the kitchen from the living room. She'd left Liam sitting in front of the TV, his notebook filled with football stats scribbled in his neat handwriting atop his lap, and his eyes glued to both the action and the scrolling scores from other games on the screen. Dad lounged in the recliner, his slippered feet hung off the cushy edge of the footrest, the remote resting on his belly, and a lukewarm cup of tea in his hand.

Summer smiled contently as she stood at the counter, smearing peanut butter on wheat bread. After the brunch and unexpected moment with Todd in the closet, she'd nestled back into her normal Sunday routine. The final bits of homework reviewed, two rounds of Uno with Liam, which she lost, and a lively Sunday dinner where Liam debated her mother about how *very* wrong she was to claim that cats were superior to dogs. All of which led to now when Summer was making his lunch for tomorrow. All children, but especially Liam thrived with routine. Since returning to Perry, she'd admit, so had she.

While so much of her time with Max was regulated, there was a difference between that existence and the ebb and flow of her life in Perry. This was hers. She controlled it. She knew what to expect. Routine was the antidote to chaos, and more comfortable than feeling imprisoned.

Right now, it kept her mind from wandering back to that closet. To the feel of Todd's arms around her. The press of his lips against her temple. Of his wintry, woodsy scent that still clung to her sweater.

"You're drowning that bread in strawberry jelly," Mom laughed, as she walked into the kitchen.

Summer grimaced at the sight of the now-soggy bread covered in jelly, globs of stickiness dripping onto the paper towel below.

"Shit!" She scooped up the sandwich in the paper towel to toss it.

"One dollar!" Liam bellowed from the living room.

"That kid has bat-like hearing." Mom shook with laughter, holding up the swear jar and jangling it.

They'd started it three months ago after receiving a phone call from Ms. Liu, the school principal, that Liam had shouted "Fuck!" after being beamed with a ball during dodgeball. Dad thought the greater crime was that dodgeball was still played in PE. As a family, they agreed to nix the swearing in front of Liam. Anyone who swore had to put a dollar in the old pickle jar on the kitchen counter. Liam counted the money at the end of the month and then donated it to the county's animal rescue.

"You were miles away. Where were you?" Mom inquired, opening the cabinet and taking out two stemless wine glasses.

Summer tossed the ruined sandwich into the trash below

the sink and then washed her hands. "I'm here in the kitchen."

Mom's forehead creased. "And *who's* in the kitchen with you?"

"What does that mean?"

"Just that you had this starry look in your eyes that I haven't seen since you dated Shane in high school." She opened the fridge and grabbed a bottle of Riesling.

She scoffed. "Starry look? I was just thinking about the wedding and the brunch."

It wasn't a lie. What occupied her thoughts did occur at both events. She'd not filled anyone in on what happened in that storage closet. Although, she thought, Nat suspected. After wiping her tears with pilfered paper towels from the closet at the Sea Serpent, she and Todd made their way back to the dining room. The brunch was wrapping up, and the few remaining guests mingled at various tables, so Todd slipped into Willa's vacant seat beside Summer. Nat's eyebrow cocked, like an accusation, as her gray eyes remained fixed on them the entire time.

"It was such a lovely wedding. Liam had so much fun he conked out in the car on the way home last night." Mom popped the wine cork and poured two glasses.

A nine-year-old falling asleep in a car wasn't unusual but with Liam it was more the norm. Social situations, especially with big groups, drained his battery. Even with the different strategies they'd learned and implemented since working with the Autism Behavioral Specialist they saw weekly in Buffalo, situations like the wedding could overstimulate and zap Liam.

"Thank you for watching him last night and this morning," Summer said as she remade the sandwich.

They'd all been invited to the brunch but decided as a family that only Summer would go. After a weekend full of social interaction, Liam would benefit from some solo, quiet family time to recharge. Not all kids on the spectrum needed to disconnect, but Liam was a classic introvert. Solo time helped him recharge, so he spent most of the morning in his room reading some of his favorite books and the rest of the day with just the family.

"You also deserved a little grown-up fun after all the work you put into the wedding." Tiny crinkles etched the edges of Mom's brown eyes as she handed Summer a glass of wine.

"Thanks." Summer took the glass and sipped. The crisp liquid dripped along her bloodstream.

Mom combed her long fingers through her short brunette hair. "Did you dance with Todd last night?"

"Yes."

"Oh." She clucked her tongue. "So, there *was* a reason for that starry gaze in your eyes."

"Nothing happened." She focused on the sandwich.

You're worth the wait. His determined, whispered words buzzed inside her, countering that something *had* happened. Even if she wasn't willing to admit it.

"We're just friends," Summer said, doubling down. Whether to her mom or herself, she wasn't entirely sure.

"I always enjoy a friends-to-lovers story. You know your dad and I were best friends all through high school, and look at us. Friendship is the best foundation for a very happy part-nership."

A furrow settled on Summer's brow. "Drop it, Mom."

"Fine." She let out an exasperated breath. "Changing topics. You know several guests asked me if you had a website. A few were interested in hiring you for some events."

"It's fine to just give them my number, it's fine. That's the best way to get a hold of me." Summer slathered a smaller layer of jelly on a fresh slice of bread.

The idea that the event planning she'd done over the last year was an actual business was still a novelty. It had all come back into her life by sheer happenstance. Much like most of her life, this new career came about without a real plan. At least for *her* life. She'd made many plans for Liam related to his education and guiding him to be a man like her dad, and the other good ones she'd come to call friends in the last sixteen months.

Our guy. Todd's sweet claim of Liam bloomed warmly in her chest.

"Do you want me to make that? You're about to ruin a second sandwich," Mom chortled, pointing with her wineglass.

"No, I've got it."

God, she needed to get her brain de-Toddified. Had anyone ever occupied her thoughts this much? Max had, but not for the same reason. Much of the fixation with him in the last three years of their relationship had focused on how to avoid triggering the cruel side that lingered below the surface with him, like a crocodile ready to strike.

"Your dad and I think that you should get a website." Mom leaned against the counter.

"It's unnecessary. It's Perry, if someone needs me, they know how to find me."

"What if people not from the village want to hire you? With that Whatley fellow who's revitalizing the lake's waterfront to bring non-residents to the village. Residents with money that may want party planners."

One…two…three…breathe. Summer's jaw tightened. "Event planning…I do event planning, not party planning."

A dismissive expression swept across her mom's face. "Aren't they the *same* thing?"

"No." Summer let out a long breath. "I coordinate large scale events, not just parties."

How many times had she explained this to her parents? Neither of them got it. Party planning conjured images of hanging streamers and laying out cupcakes for children's birthdays or retiree's celebratory parties. Event planning was far more than a mere party. Events like the annual Fall Fest, which saw nearly one-thousand attendees invade the autumn-themed fair that took place in downtown each September, or the upcoming Christmas Market, required large scale coordination of vendors, decorations, security, marketing, permits, entertainment, sanitation plans, and all the logistics needed to make them work.

"Same difference." Mom flicked her wrist and continued, "Plus, *real* businesses have websites."

"It is a *real* business." The protest was so quiet, she'd wondered if she'd spoken it out loud.

Her mom placed her glass on the counter. "Honey, I know, and you've done a nice job. Your dad and I are so proud, especially considering just two years ago you were *just* a waitress. Now, you're a waitress/event planner."

Just a waitress? The words stung, causing a dull ache in Summer's chest that crept up into her throat.

What was wrong with being a waitress? Granted, she wasn't a nurse like her mom, but it was something she was good at. She enjoyed it. She had a good boss. She had regular customers who smiled because she knew how they took their coffee or made sure they got a few extra French fries.

"Is that why Dad asked Janet to approach me about the marketing class she's taking?" Summer slipped the completed sandwich into a zipper bag and pushed a little too hard along its seam to secure it shut.

"Your dad and I think the class would be good for you. It may help open some new horizons for you. To be—" her lips pinched "—We just want you to be open to…more."

The words "more than what you are" hung in the silence between them. That was the bottom line. Neither of them said it out loud, but it was as loud as her dad's cheering from the living room.

That realization pooled in Summer's belly, a bubbling,

queasy feeling within her. So often in her life she'd not been right. She'd always been missing something. In high school she lacked kindness. With Max she'd lacked strength. Since coming home, she'd lacked a good reputation. Standing in front of her mom's disappointed yet hopeful gaze, she felt utterly lacking.

"I'll talk to Janet," she breathed.

Mom folded her arms around her, pulling her into a hug. "I know we nag, but I'll never stop being your mom and wanting more for you."

But what if I'll never become the more you think I should be? She closed her eyes, willing her stiffened muscles to melt into the embrace.

"Goddamn run, you motherfucker!" Dad's voice boomed into the kitchen.

"Two dollars!" Summer and Mom yelled in unison.

"It's three. We said double for the F-word," Liam corrected nonchalantly.

Dad shuffled into the room; his face twisted with annoyance. Yanking his wallet out of his pocket, he pulled out a ten-dollar bill and tossed it into the jar.

"Dad, that's too much. You only owe three," Summer pointed to the jar.

"Down payment. The Bills are playing for shit," he muttered.

"Pop!" Liam scolded from the living room.

"Already paid." A laugh boosted his shout to his grandson.

"It boggles my mind that you teach impressionable teenagers with that *filthy* mouth of yours." Mom tutted, placing her hands on her hips.

"First, I'm the woodshop teacher so they expect it. We're the truck drivers of the teaching profession. Second—" he leaned in close, pressing a soft kiss to the corner of her pink lips "My dear Sharon, you *love* my filthy mouth."

"Gross!" Summer blanched. "Your daughter is standing right here."

"How do you think we got you?" He waggled his thick black eyebrows.

"Pop! The Dolphins just scored," Liam called.

His face scrunched. "I may need to go to the ATM."

Hours later, the soft white light of the lamp illuminated the corner of the couch that Summer nestled on reading the copy of *Jane Eyre* she'd checked out from the public library. The only sound was the furnace clicking on and off, knocking the chill of the early December night. She tried to lose herself in Jane and Mr. Rochester's romance, but her brain wandered to being cocooned by Todd's warmth in that closet. Fourteen years ago, if she'd been alone in a closet with a tall, muscular man with a boyishly wicked smile and piercing green eyes she'd have...

Desire tingled at her core with the deliciously dirty images that played in her vision. Strong hands slipping beneath her woolen sweater, heat lapping along her skin. A hot mouth consuming her inch by inch. Thick fingers unbuttoning her jeans and breaching the barrier between cotton panties and skin.

Skin on fire, pleasurable tension coiled in her core. Leaving the book on her lap, her hand slipped underneath the fleece blanket draped over her. Closing her eyes and sinking into the fantasy, her hands moved under the waistband of her pajama bottoms.

"Fuck," she gasped at the ping of her cell phone from the coffee table.

Jerking her hand back above her waistband, her eyes darted around the room. What the hell was she doing? She was in the living room. What if Liam woke up for a glass of water? What if Mom came down for a midnight snack? What if Dad shuffled in with a course catalog for GCC?

Pinching the bridge of her nose, she grumbled, "What is *wrong* with you?"

She reached for the phone, thinking it was Nat.

Todd: What part are you at?

A riot of butterflies cartwheeled in her stomach. Nibbling on her lip, her eyes snapped to the open book now resting on her knees. No more explanation was needed. She knew what he was referring to. He knew exactly what she was doing. Well, perhaps, not *exactly*.

Summer: Jane just agreed to marry Mr. Rochester.
Bride emoji.

Thanks to this being the third time Todd had read the classic Charlotte Brontë Gothic Romance, she wasn't worried about spoiling anything for him. Last week when they chatted in the children's section of the library while Liam picked his books, Todd had shared an affinity for all things Brontë. He'd been hooked since taking a Women in Victorian Literature course as an undergrad. He'd even offered to lend Summer some of his well-loved copies, complete with highlighted passages, notes in the margins, and dog-eared pages to his favorite parts. She'd declined to take him up on the offer until after she'd finished her first Brontë sister novel.

Summer's reading taste had long leaned toward modern writers. Especially those in the romance world. Give her a swoony historical or contemporary romance set in a small town with a dashing Duke or cinnamon roll hero any day. It hadn't been until the last few years that she'd started tackling some of the classics. "I'll be your Brontë reading buddy,"

Todd said at the library when she told him of her plan to tackle the Brontë sisters.

Happiness fluttered in her chest at that memory. There was something so sweet and a little chivalrous about his offering to do it with her. He hadn't mocked her for not reading it sooner. He exuded pure excitement to share this with her.

> **Summer: Although, there are hundreds of pages still to go, so I imagine it's not their happy ending, yet.**
> **Todd: There's no happy ending in *Jane Eyre*.**
> **Summer: I thought it was a romance?? *Shocked face Emoji*.**
> **Todd: It is. They get an HEA.**
> **Summer: An HEA is a happy ending.**
> **Todd: Not if you're doing it right. *Winky face emoji*.**

The temptation to know what he meant by that fizzed inside her. What was Todd's definition of a HEA? What would living his HEA be like? Could she be someone's HEA?

"Broken things don't work," she murmured, chiding herself.

> **Summer: It's late. Goodnight, friend.**
> **Todd: Goodnight, sweetheart.**

His words glowed like a dare. He wanted her. He'd wait for her.

Her fingers glided along the cell phone screen as if his lovely endearment was his stubbled cheek. "Broken things can be fixed." At least, she hoped.

CHAPTER NINE

"OMG! He said he'd wait for you?" Nat gushed, her hand atop her heart in a mock swoon.

"You're so obnoxious. Why are we friends?" Summer groaned, lamenting telling Nat about the conversation with Todd at the Sea Serpent.

She hadn't volunteered the story, but rather submitted to Nat's insistent questioning. The moment Summer walked into the Owens Family Clinic to set up for the weekly mutual aid group for parents of kids with disabilities, Nat had cornered her in the clinic's small conference room.

Over the summer, she and Nat had put together a proposal for a grant to establish remote individual and group mental health services. They'd been awarded the grant at the end of November but wouldn't have everything set up officially for a few more months. In the meantime, Nat had offered the clinic's conference room for Summer to host a group meeting for a few parents from the county she'd connected with through an online group. They met weekly to share struggles, celebrate successes, and offer support for how to help their children and themselves be successful in a world that wasn't always accessible to individuals with disabilities.

Mischief glinted in Nat's eyes. "You *love* me, but not as much as you love—"

Summer clamped her hand over Nat's mouth. "Stop! Or I'll tell Noah you want to watch the complete *Godfather* trilogy again."

Nat pushed Summer's hand off her mouth. "You monster! I think I'm still traumatized by that night. I just don't get his love for those movies."

"They're classics." Summer unwrapped a small fruit and cheese tray provided by Cassie, and placed it on the center of the table between snack-size paper plates and napkins.

"*The Princess and the Frog*, now that's a classic." Nat snagged a piece of cheddar from the tray. "So, how do you feel about Todd waiting for you? I mean besides the obvious that this is some swoony Austen-level shit?" She plopped onto a swivel chair and munched her pilfered piece of cheese.

A weird mixture of dread and thrill rose within her. How did she feel? Like a drunk bird flying in a hurricane, trying to find purchase anywhere. Confusion. Disbelief. Terror. Hope. Desire. A soup of emotion twisted and twirled inside her.

"I don't know how I feel." Summer sat in the chair opposite Nat.

Nat studied her. "I wonder if you know how you feel, but you just won't let yourself feel it."

"Excuse me?"

"I bet if you sat with these feelings for a bit, you'd know which one bubbles to the surface time-and-time again. Then you can ask yourself why you keep pushing it back."

"I think I liked you better before you started seeing a therapist." Summer lightly kicked Nat's shin.

"You know, in therapy you could explore these feelings and"—Nat's expression sobered— "and other things."

Summer leaned back and fiddled with the hem of her red turtleneck sweater. It had been four days since she'd started opening up about Max with both Nat and Todd. She hadn't spoken with either of them since then, but resisting the uncharacteristic impulse to share was difficult. Perhaps, it's why she'd succumbed so quickly to Nat's badgering about what was going on with her and Todd. Somehow just speaking the first few words of her story incited the urge to say more.

Nat, Elle, and Noah all saw therapists. While each shared that it could be painful and difficult at times, they all agreed that there was power in telling their stories. Each of them had gone through their own traumas but weren't broken by them. They'd put back together their hearts, opening themselves up to not just loving, but being loved.

They'd each begun healing. Could she do that as well? Push back the fear to love and be loved in return?

"Maybe you're right," she murmured, her eyes fixed on the blue and white-speckled floor.

Nat took Summer's hand. "I'm always right."

A *whoosh* of laughter fell out of her. "God, you're the worst."

"Sorry, it was getting too heavy in here and I know you like to keep it light before group." Nat smiled. "But…if you want, I can see if my therapist is taking on any additional tele-health clients."

It was time. She'd danced around this for years. When she'd first come home to Perry, there'd been very few options available to someone who didn't have health insurance and lived in an underserved rural community. That wasn't as much of an issue anymore. Summer had good health insurance thanks to Cassie. Mental health services would be more available in the village through the telehealth program Nat's clinic was establishing. All the excuses she'd once used no longer existed.

"I am not doing this because of Todd." Summer pointed a finger at Nat. "So, don't get all gushy-girl about this. I'm doing this because it's time for me to stop waiting *for me*. Todd may wait forever or give up when someone thirty pounds thinner without a son and years of emotional baggage waltzes into one of his businesses. Either way, this is about me."

Nat leaned closer, placing her hands on Summer's cheeks. "First, I know. You are a strong independent mama and the only little man you do anything for is Liam. Second, I have seen that exact woman saunter in and out of the brewery and wine bar, but that man only has eyes for you. He'll wait."

"It's not fair for him to have to wait for me."

"You never asked him to wait. That's his choice to make." Nat let go of Summer's face and stood up. "Also, as someone who had a man waiting for her, and she in turn for him, that first time you two kiss will be like Christmas morning when you unwrap a gift you've always wanted and never knew you couldn't live without."

Summer arched a brow. "What makes you think we'll be kissing."

"Oh, I give it 'til Christmas." Nat winked. "Remember, I'm always right." She tossed her sandy hair over her shoulder and sauntered out of the room.

After Nat left, Summer focused on readying the room. Their group wasn't large. Only four other parents, including Summer. Correction, it was two sets of married couples and Summer. She was the only single mom in the group.

"We brought homemade brownies," Felicia chirped as she strode into the room.

"By we, she means me as I was the only one who got up at four a.m., before my ten hour shift, to make them," LaToya, her wife, sassed playfully.

The Gomez-Williams lived in Warsaw, the next town over. Just like Perry the county was smaller. Everyone was connected to everyone. LaToya, a nurse practitioner, worked at the county nursing home with Summer's mom and her wife worked at Clayton and Jerome's veterinarian clinic.

Felicia batted her long dark eyelashes. "But baby, you're so much better at baking than me."

"It's a good thing you're pretty," LaToya teased, pressing a quick kiss to her wife's temple.

"Oh, thank God there's cheese!" Henry shuffled into the room and made a beeline for the snack tray. "Pelavi read an online article about the benefits of a vegan diet. She tossed twenty dollars of Tilamook into the bin, replacing it with vegan cheese." His smooth British accent twanged with pain.

"Oh no!" Felicia gasped; her brown eyes wide.

"Vegan cheese is an abomination," LaToya commiserated with a deep belly laugh.

Summer arched a brow. "Henry, I'm assuming Pelavi is meeting you here and will smell that cheddar on your breath."

"I come prepared." He pulled a small bottle of mouthwash out of his jacket pocket. "Spoils from work!"

There were only a few medical services in the village. Outside of Nat's primary care clinic, which she operated with her father, there was an optometry clinic and two dental clinics. One operated by Dr. Henry Williamson, and the other by his wife, Dr. Pelavi Gupta. Partners in life, but not in business. It was a classic enemies-to-lovers story for the two competing dentists turned husband and wife. Despite the deep love that sizzled beneath their relentless banter, which Summer thought was merely a very long form of foreplay, they'd kept their separate practices. Pelavi would laugh that while they shared a life, a dental practice was where she drew a line.

"How long do you think she'll stay vegan this time?" LaToya asked, taking the seat across from him at the conference table.

"Last time she went two weeks, so I figure I have ten more days." His dark eyes shined with beleaguered hope.

"Hi, Pelavi!" Felicia said in a cheerfully loud greeting, from the door where she stood guard.

Henry popped the rest of the cheese in his mouth, swallowing hard. With each click of heels down the long hallway from the clinic's reception area toward the conference room, panic seized his expression. He chased the cheese with the entire travel-sized bottle of Scope. Realization widened his eyes.

"Here," Summer chuckled, handing him a cup to spit into.

"Thanks," he gasped and then wiped his mouth with the sleeves of his sweater. "My darling." He rose; arms wide.

Lips ticked up in a grin, Summer discreetly tossed the cup in the trash. She'd empty and clean out the garbage after the meeting, so the cleaning service that took care of the clinic didn't have to deal with the spat-out mouthwash. The periodically forced veganism aside, Pelavi and Henry were deeply in love and doted on their three-year-old daughter, Nisha, who had Albinism. The same thing was true for Felicia and LaToya, whose adopted son Davey had Down syndrome. There was lots of playful bickering and verbal poking between both couples, but both were strong partnerships that dripped with love.

They were in this together. For one hour each week, Summer got to be in it with them. This unlikely fivesome made sense within the four walls of this room. All five were bound by their fierce protective nature for the good of their children.

Felicia scooped some fruit and cheese onto a plate. "Summer, I saw you dancing with Todd at Elle and Clayton's wedding."

Of course, Felicia had seen that. As one of the vet techs at Clayton's clinic, she and her wife had been guests at the wedding.

This town is too small. Summer shook her head.

"Todd?" Pelavi removed her red wool jacket, draping it on the back of her chair. "The sexy Prince Harry lookalike?"

Henry's forehead puckered. "*Sexy?*"

She brushed her long black hair behind her ears. "Don't be jealous; it's not attractive."

"How would you feel if I talked about that sexy blonde at the café?" He puffed up his chest. "She always gives me *extra* coleslaw."

She made a dismissive flick of her wrist. "Please, I'm secure enough to not be jealous."

"It helps that Laney is on our team." LaToya bit into a brownie.

"Also, Laney gives everyone extra coleslaw." Summer's face twisted in an apologetic expression.

Henry deflated with a pout. "There are far too many women in this group. I need a fellow man to have my back."

"Well, maybe if Summer starts dating the sexy brewmaster, he'll start coming," Felicia cooed, elbowing Summer's ribs.

What the fuck? She gaped. Their periodic comments about her being single was one thing, but were they seriously shipping her and Todd? *This town!*

"Felicia, you're making Summer uncomfortable," LaToya chided.

Summer gave her a grateful smile.

"Although, he is one fine cut of meat," LaToya said, saucily.

"Agreed." Pelavi and Felicia cackled.

Henry turned to his wife, arching a brow. "Meat? Thought you were vegan?"

Pelavi waved him off.

Summer just shook her head in mortification. "You shouldn't objectify him like that. We wouldn't like that if there were a group of men talking about one of us in that way."

"Heterosexual men have done this to women for centuries. Turnabout is fair play." Pelavi grinned.

"Preach!" Felicia cheered.

"Seriously, Summer, date this Todd! I need a man in this group." Henry tossed his head back dramatically.

"So do we, my dear," Pelavi teased, patting his cheek.

He leaned close and crooned, "There were no complaints about my masculinity this morning."

"Excuse me…" An unsure voice came from across the room.

Summer shifted her attention toward the door where Amy Whatley stood. Her red hair tied back in that low bun. Her expression uncertain as she looked between each of them.

"Is this the mutual aid group for parents of kids with disabilities?" she asked, worrying her bottom lip.

"Great, another woman," Henry grumbled, throwing his hands up.

Amy's brow furrowed. "Excuse me?"

"Ignore him. I do all the time," Pelavi clucked, her amber eyes twinkled with playfulness.

Henry bent close, whispering something in her ear that caused deep crimson to flush her cheeks.

Yep, it's definitely their foreplay. Ignoring them, Summer stood. "Amy…welcome."

As if just realizing Summer was in the room, Amy's uncertain expression morphed to frustrated disbelief. "Summer. I didn't know you were part of this."

"Part of this? Summer runs the group. She started it back in October to bring us together for our kids. Grab a seat." LaToya gestured to an empty seat across from Summer.

With a hesitant nod, Amy crossed the threshold. Like a slow motion scene from a film, she lowered onto the chair. As if waiting to make a break for it at any moment, Amy sat, spine straight, in her coat.

Pelavi shot Summer a "What is up with this woman?" look across the table. The beauty of this little fivesome is that none of them were from here. Henry grew up in London, but immigrated to the US for school and then made his home here. Pelavi had grown up in Buffalo. Both LaToya and Felicia were from Syracuse. With them all being close in age, if they had grown up in Perry they would have had first-hand experience with the Summer of high school. The Summer who lived all too well in Amy's annoyed gaze that stared back from across the table.

"Should we do introductions?" Felicia placed a gentle hand on Summer's hand.

Summer blinked. "Yes…good idea."

They went around the oval-shaped table for introductions. Each offered a little bit about themselves, and a lot about their kids. This was typical for their meetings.

The focus remained on their kids with sprinkled-in tidbits about their own wants and needs. About how Felicia was taking online business courses to open a pet grooming business in the next five years. How LaToya was obsessed with K-Dramas. The lively debates about paint colors and wall fixtures for the Dutch Colonial farmhouse the Gupta-Williamson's were remodeling. The group was animated when discussing book suggestions they'd received from Summer. It was something Summer appreciated about the group. While their kids were their foundation, it also reminded them – which they frankly needed frequent reminders of – that they weren't just parents.

Amy cleared her throat when it came her turn to introduce herself. "I'm Amy Whatley. My husband, Joseph, and I moved here from Boston. Our son's name is JJ and he's deaf."

"JJ? Does that stand for something?" Henry asked, leaning back against the chair's mesh fabric backrest.

"Joseph Junior."

Henry pointed a finger at his wife. "See, it's still a thing."

She rolled her eyes. "We were not going to name our daughter Henry. We've been over this. First, Henry is a boys' name. Second, *one* Henry Williamson in this world is quite enough."

"I thought we agreed not to gender our child?"

"Ignore those two." Felicia laughed and then gestured at Amy. "What do you like to do for fun?"

"I…" Amy's face pinched in consideration.

LaToya smiled brightly. "Oh, sometimes it's hard to remember we're not just parents and that we have interests outside of our kiddos."

"I like to read." It came out more like a question than a statement from Amy.

Summer understood this all too well. They all did. It wasn't until the last two years that she'd started to live a life outside of Liam. While her mom still teased and prodded her about needing more "adult time," Summer felt she'd come a long way. It first started with books from the library, next she joined a book club, formed a small but lovely friend group, and now this. Liam would always remain the leading man of her story, but she was starting to fill it with a rich tapestry of supporting characters. Of a best friend. Friends. Fellow parents. Colleagues. *Todd.*

Whatever role he ended up playing. He wasn't just a friend, but he wasn't more. He was something in-between. Something for the first time in a very long time, she was open to. To the idea of being more than just Liam's mom.

Felicia bumped her shoulder against Summer's. "Reading? Oh, you and Summer have that in common. She's our resident Belle."

"Belle?" Amy's eyebrow arched.

"You know from *Beauty and the Beast.* Just like Belle, she's always reading a book."

"Especially dirty ones," A salacious smile stretched across Pelavi's face.

Henry *tsked.* "Which you proceed to read once she lends or recommends them to you."

"I don't see you complaining when I get to the steamy parts."

Felicia snorted.

The stiffness in Amy's shoulders seemed to ease. She leaned back in the chair, unbuttoning her coat. "I like romance, too."

Summer allowed a small smile to lift her lips.

"Summer's turn to introduce herself!" Felicia commanded in her singsong sweet voice.

She waved her off. "No need. Amy already knows me."

"Oh, you two are friends?"

"No." Amy's denial was sharp.

Summer didn't blame her, despite the stinging sensation clogging her throat. They hadn't been friends. In fact, Summer wondered if she'd had any *real* friends in high school. None of the girls she'd called friends in high school were in her life now. None of the girls, all of whom still lived in the village, girls she'd held court in the school's cafeteria with, swapped books with her like Elle, or baked cookies with her like Carmen, or went on playdates to the park with she and Liam like Nat. None of them outstretched their arms and pulled her into tight hugs like Todd had done with Amy at the café last week.

"I knew her in high school," Amy offered.

"Have you stayed in touch since high school?" LaToya's assessing gaze jumped between the two women.

Amy shook her head.

"Then you don't know Summer." Felicia looped her arm around Summer's shoulders.

Warmth spread, pushing out that stinging in her chest. It was easy to forget who she was, when looking at a pair of eyes that mirrored back an image of her past. To Amy, who'd she'd been was who she was and, in many ways, to her Amy was still that lanky awkward girl from high school. Neither knew who they'd become.

"And I don't know Amy. I didn't know…really know her then or now. I'm sorry for that. I'm sorry for everything." Summer's gaze linked with Amy's.

The truth slinked through her. There was a reason the girls she'd called friends scattered in the breeze over the years; They did not *know* each other. Not really. Just as she'd known nothing about Amy outside of the superficial image presented to the world in a sometimes clumsy package.

She went on, "I'm Summer. My son, Liam, is on the Autism Spectrum. Like Pelavi says, I love steamy, romance books, but I'm getting into some of the classics."

Amy's mouth curved into a tiny, but present smile. "So, what happens in this group?"

CHAPTER TEN

"There's a 30% chance that it's already raining!" ~Mean Girls

Snowflakes glittered in the glow from the streetlamps. The effect seemed to ensconce the clinic's parking lot in a shimmer of fairy dust. Fresh snow kissed Summer's cheeks as she held the clinic door open for the remainder of the group. Henry and Pelavi had already headed home to relieve the babysitter, but Felicia, LaToya, and Amy remained behind to help with clean up.

A red-cheeked Felicia skipped out, holding an empty plate, her wife shuffling behind her. They'd split the remaining brownies between the attendees to take home for their kiddos and themselves. Summer had even snagged a few and they were stashed in a Ziplock bag in her purse.

"It was a great meeting tonight," Felicia gushed.

It had been. After Amy's initial tension, the group eased her into something akin to almost comfortable. Halfway through the meeting, she'd even removed her coat. There were even a few smiles and one honest-to-god snort of laughter.

"I love the list of accessible kid-friendly activities that you put together. I think we'll check out that Christmas puppet show at the children's theatre downtown." LaToya folded her arms around Summer and squeezed tight. "See you next week."

"Next week." Summer released her.

Next, Felicia wrapped Summer in a long hug. "Seriously, you should *totally* hook up with that Todd. Get on that dick stick, lady."

"Oh, my god!" A nervous laugh escaped.

No matter how hard she tried to maintain the professional atmosphere of the group, during the last fifteen minutes, the conversation wandered back to whatever was happening between her and Todd. Granted, she was still trying to figure it out, but the rest of the village occupants seemed to have lots and lots of opinions. Amy's pinched lips and narrowed eyes clearly communicated her unfavorable thoughts of her old friend dating Summer.

It had been so long since she'd thought of dating anyone, but over the last few months of the developing friendship with Todd, her brain meandered more and more around the idea. Not just of dating someone, but specifically *him*. The more time she spent with him, the more he occupied her thoughts. The dashing heroes from her romance novels all morphed to a tall man with coppery red hair and a tiny scar over his left eye, especially during her private time with her vibrator. Lord, those green eyes sparkled like emeralds played on repeat in her fantasies.

"Leave her alone," LaToya tutted, taking her wife's hand and tugging her toward their Jeep. After helping her wife into the passenger's side, LaToya walked around the front. Before opening her door, she turned, facing Summer. "I told her to leave you alone, but she's not wrong. I'd be the first to say you don't need someone else to complete you or to make you happy, but"— she gazed at her wife in the jeep— "life is so much better when it's shared with the right person. I know something about letting one's past hold you back from the beauty of the today and the hope for tomorrow."

Summer blinked.

LaToya had shared a few weeks back about her and Felicia's story. A few months after the birth of her daughter, Darci, LaToya's first wife Maria died in a car accident. Five years later, she met Felicia at a friend's birthday celebration. For so long she'd not been open to another relationship outside of a casual hookup, believing she'd had, and lost, her one great love.

"I almost gave up the life that I have now because I was scared that I would lose it again, or that, for some reason, I didn't deserve a second chance at happiness." LaToya's expression grew thoughtful. "Whether it's Todd, someone else, or nobody… I hope you let go of whatever is holding you back. You deserve to be truly happy."

Not knowing what else to say or do, Summer just nodded. There'd been no great love in Summer's life. For a few months during their first year of dating, she thought Max could be. The delusion of it clung, keeping her in the relationship far longer than she should have stayed. With clearer vision looking back she knew it was never love. Had Summer ever been in love? Had she ever been loved by anyone besides her parents, Liam, and Nat? The word no echoed within her aching heart.

The creak of the driver's side door snapped Summer's focus back to LaToya.

"Also, while I'm not an expert on the dick stick, I can testify that going to O-town does do wonders for your disposition." LaToya's big smile slanted into a salacious grin.

"Good lord!" Summer snorted as a cackling LaToya jumped into her vehicle.

"I see Perry hasn't changed *that* much." Amy's tone was dry as she walked out of the clinic.

Shutting the door behind her and locking it, Summer

shook her head. "Nope. Everyone is still up in your business."

Adjusting the strap of her leather purse, Amy stood in front of Summer. An awkward beat stretched between them. The crunch of snow beneath LaToya and Felicia's wheels was the only sound in the now almost deserted parking lot. Two very different vehicles stood watch, as two very different women stared at each other. The candy-apple-red SUV, already remote started, hummed quietly, warming itself and waiting for the chic woman in her black London Fog coat that hugged her slender frame. On the opposite end of the spectrum, Summer's not-yet started, rusty, Chevy Cobalt, sat cold. Summer was thankful for her puffy, four years-old, Columbia jacket which would keep her warm, even as it accentuated her squishier physique.

"I'm glad you came tonight. I hope you found the time was helpful." Summer slid her sneakered feet across the snow-covered sidewalk leading into the parking lot.

"It was a good meeting." The corners of Amy's lips tugged up, softening her harsh expression.

Summer nibbled on her lip. "I hope you'll come back."

Amy nodded.

"And bring Joseph. Henry would love to have another guy in the group."

A firm line hardened her features. "We'll see." Amy turned. "I should go."

"Amy, wait."

She pivoted, facing Summer. "Are you going to apologize, again?"

Was she? Had that been what she was about to do? It would be the third apology since first seeing Amy almost a week ago.

Nothing washes the past away, but actions forge a future founded on forgiveness of each other and ourselves. Todd's words filled her with an unexpected confidence.

"No." Her brown eyes locked with Amy's blue ones.

Summer was done apologizing. She'd made her amends. Moving forward, once the apology was made, she'd focus on living in the now. Cruel Summer belonged in the past. There'd be no living with the phantom of whom she'd been. Not anymore. If she wanted to be seen as who she was rather than her past self, then she needed to stop living in her own shadow.

"I do hope you come back to group," she offered with a small smile.

Nodding, Amy turned and walked to her SUV and got in.

As Amy pulled away, Summer let out a long breath. The wet snow made the pavement slick, so she shuffled carefully to her car, wishing she'd worn boots. She'd come straight from the café, so she was still in her sneakers. Getting in the car, she slipped her gloves into her pockets and rubbed her hands together, hoping the friction would warm her chilled fingers. Grabbing her keys from her purse, she pushed them into the ignition and twisted.

Nothing.

A furrow wrinkled her forehead. "Fuck." She turned the key again, but the vehicle didn't start. "Great," she groaned, resting her head back and closing her eyes.

No doubt the battery had given up the ghost. Whenever the temperature dipped below thirty degrees, it always did this. Regret filled her at deciding to postpone dropping the car off to have its battery replaced until after this weekend's Christmas Market.

Summer grabbed her phone. It was just ten o'clock. After putting Liam to bed hours ago, Mom and Dad were likely already tucked into their own warm bed. Dad would happily come get her, but she hated the idea of disturbing his sleep. They'd already done so much for her today, taking Liam to his appointment with the behavioral specialist in Buffalo so Summer could meet with Carmen at the café, after her shift, to finalize details for the Christmas Market. They took on homework duty and watched him tonight, so she could go to group.

As much as her parents drove her nuts with their prodding about her career and lack of a love life, she was so grateful for them. It wasn't just their support with all things Liam-related, but how much they doted on and adored him. Sometimes she thought they saw him as their do-over kid. His big heart and gentle nature was so opposite her. At that age, she'd already showed glimpses of her future self with temper tantrums about getting the most fashionable Barbie.

Not wanting to drag Dad out of bed, she slipped her cell back into her purse and got out of the vehicle. "Guess I'm walking," she grumbled.

One of the beauties of Perry was that nothing was too far for a walk. Granted, she lived across town near the high school, but the walk was only twenty-minutes. Even in twenty-five degrees and wet snow, it was doable. She just wished she'd worn boots.

The normal magical quality of Perry at night, with its blanket of twinkling stars, dissolved away by wet flurries. Still, the way snowflakes danced in the lights from the sleepy village's houses, bedecked in Christmas decorations, reminded Summer of something out of a holiday fairytale. Not every neighborhood radiated with the glow of red, green, and white, but like unexpected Christmas fireworks, there were bursts of holiday splendor on each street. Downtown, though, transformed to a living replica of a cheesy Hallmark movie during the month of December.

A smile curled her lips as she reached the start of Main Street. After ten on a Thursday night, the central business district was already fast asleep with every storefront closed until tomorrow. Decorations illuminated the rows of late nineteenth century brick and cement buildings. Iron lamp posts along the street featured lit garlands. Each business's front window was filled with a mix of miniature pine trees covered in twinkle lights, vibrant red poinsettia in gold buckets, or lit Santa Clauses. Holly and wreaths adorned with fat red ribbons hung on each business's front door. Todd and Noah's wine bar was like an explosion of Christmas with its candy cane-draped fat pine tree taking up the center of the front window. Despite having closed at nine-thirty, the tree remained lit, illuminating the bar in soft light.

She knew their brewery around the corner featured another obnoxiously large tree. Their little friend group helped the guys decorate it the Sunday after Thanksgiving. Jerome's surprisingly deep bass voice led them in an impromptu Christmas singalong while they snacked on leftovers from everyone's turkey day meal and drank Todd's pumpkin ale and mulled wine to welcome the holiday season. Like it was nothing at all Todd hoisted Liam up on his shoulders to put the star atop the tree. The memory warmed her against the icy December night.

Turning down Covington Street, she left behind the brightly lit Main Street. Darkness, with snatches from a few scattered front porch lights and decorated houses, filled the neighborhood. The snow flurries were coming harder now, dampening her clothes, skin, and hair, cold soaked into her bones. It was funny that the snow could leave you as teeth-chattering wet as a rainstorm.

Turning down Leicester Street, she lamented the decision to walk but it was too late to turn back now. "Only ten more minutes."

A sole streetlamp illuminated her path as she walked down the darkened street. Like a beacon, the glow of pink from a house at the end of the street, called to her. Reaching the house, she stopped. It was a simple, lovely two-story blue house with white lattice along its sides and a steeply pitched, gray roof. Lit pink candy canes flanked the snow-dusted walkway leading to the oversized porch. Pink string lights crisscrossed white pillars, reaching up and outlining the porch roof's perimeter.

She chuckled, fixating on the fat evergreen tree adorned in pink Christmas lights, ribbons, and a pink star on its top. "That's a lot of pink."

There was something sweet about the dreamy Barbie's Christmas cottage décor of the house. Summer scanned the quiet neighborhood. None of the other houses appeared decorated or, if so, had already turned their lights off for the night.

A flash of white fur trotted by the house's front bay window, drawing her attention. Summer's breath caught in realization of whose house she stood in front of. Beyond the Christmas tree that dominated the front window, a muscular figure came into focus. He sat on a large couch, his face twisted in concentration, and a book on his lap.

"Todd." It was almost a gasp.

As if he heard her, he looked up. His green eyes met hers through the barrier of windowpane between them. A wordless conversation seemed to flow. The bewilderment glinting in his eyes telegraphed confusion for why she was standing on the sidewalk outside his house staring at him at a quarter after ten at night.

"I look like a stalker!" she squeaked. Horrified, she pivoted quickly to leave, but the slick snow and her sneakers had a counter suggestion. "Crap!" she yelped as she went down.

With the grace of a newborn deer, she slipped and fell into the snow. She landed on her back on a snow pile where soft grass had once been.

"So, embarrassing." She closed her eyes. "God, I hope he didn't see that."

"Summer!" The slam of a door accompanied Todd's worried shout.

"*Great*, I'm not just a stalker but a clumsy one," she mumbled to herself.

"Are you okay?" Todd's hands grasped her arms.

Blinking her eyes open, her gaze met his concerned one. Todd hovered over her, squatting on his haunches. The image of his strong body above her pulsed a tingle at her core, heating her chilled skin.

She swallowed thickly. "Just mortified."

A warm smile washed over every inch of his chiseled face, softening that strong jawline and igniting a spark in his eyes. "When I wanted you to fall for me, this isn't exactly what I had in mind."

She rolled her eyes. "You're hilarious."

"Let me help you." He gripped under her arms and lifted her to a seated position.

The tender caresses of his hands checking her body for injury sent fevered liquid seeping along her bloodstream despite the layers of cold and damp clothes. Along her arms. Up to her shoulders. Stroking over the wool cap on her head and into the now wet strands of her low ponytail. Reaching her face, the warm pads of his fingers brushed across her cheeks. The soothing touch of his skin against hers drew a contented sigh from her.

Somehow, his touch dulled all feelings of discomfort. The ache from where her butt had slammed against the ground was a mere wisp of hurt. The shiver cascading along her limbs was now a tickle. The embarrassment that heated her cheeks was…well, that was still very much present.

"You're shivering, let me warm you up." His hands rubbed on her arms.

Warm me up? The spot between her thighs clenched at the idea of how many ways he could warm her up. The many, *many* ways she'd fantasized while alone in the shower this morning, the steam cocooning her while her hands trailed down her slick skin wishing they were his.

Fuck, even the cold moisture of the snow, soaking her clothes, wasn't cooling down her lusty lady bits. She'd never been like this. Something had shifted since that moment in the closet. Every inch of her had sparked awake with need… with want.

You need to get a grip.

"Can you stand?" he asked.

She nodded. "Yeah."

Taking her hands, he helped her to her feet.

Dusting her backside off, she winced. "I'm soaked."

"Yeah. Let me get you warm and dry. Come on." He placed his hands on her shoulders and guided her into the house.

Heat and a tail-wagging Sheba greeted them. Summer bent, scratching the huskie's silky white fur. "Hello, lovely girl," she cooed, enjoying how Sheba melted into her touch.

Since being introduced to Todd's three-year-old rescue pup in September, there'd been several planned and unplanned playdates at the park. Liam and Sheba were equally enamored with one another. In fact, Liam had asked on three different occasions for Todd to be his mom's boyfriend so he could play with Sheba all the time.

"Let's get you out of these clothes," Todd said, as Summer rose.

"Excuse me?" Her mouth dropped open.

"Someone's mind is in the gutter." The husky laugh rumbling in his throat almost zinged across her body.

Stop it, vagina! She looked away from him.

"Let me get you dry clothes. You can change in the down-stairs bathroom, and I'll toss your wet clothes into the laundry and make you some tea to warm up."

"This isn't necessary. I can just head home. It's not far."

He looked out the small window at the top of the door. "Where's your car?"

"Ah…" She shifted foot-to-foot. "…the clinic parking lot. It wouldn't start, so I was walking home."

A hardness tightened his jaw. "You were walking home alone…at night… in the middle of a snowstorm?"

"It's just flurries," she protested with a dismissive wave.

The creases in his forehead deepened. "Next time *you* call me."

"It's late."

"*Exactly.*" He let out an exasperated breath.

"You're being a little alpha male right now." Eyes narrowed; she folded her arms over her chest.

"What would you say if Nat had done this?" His left eyebrow ticked up, calling attention to that tiny scar above his eye.

She frowned. *Stupid logic.*

"Check and mate."

CHAPTER ELEVEN

---

*"At your age, you're going to have lots of urges. You're going to
want to take off your clothes and touch each other. But if you do
touch each other, you will get chlamydia…and die." ~Mean Girls*

I*'m sans panties in Todd Krueger's bathroom. Correction. My
snatch is commando in Todd Krueger's pajama bottoms.* Wide-
eyed, Summer gaped at herself in the mirror.

How had tonight gone so far left? Right now, she should
be curled up, in her *own* pajamas, finishing the last few chap-
ters of *Jane Eyre*. She shouldn't be in his flannel pajama
bottoms, the fabric soft against her naked skin, her nostrils
full of his wintry-woodsy scent that clung to the white
Henley he'd lent her. Thank God, her bra survived the
soaking snow. Going commando in Todd's clothes was one
thing, but running around his house braless was a bridge too
far for her to travel tonight.

Unwrapping the fluffy towel she'd used to dry her hair
she scooped her pile of wet clothes up and tucked them in it.
The clothes pile in her arms, she opened the door. Todd stood

on the other side with a lopsided grin stretched across his face.

Heat crawled along her body following the sweep of his gaze down her figure. His eyes stopped at her bare feet then lifted back to her face. Desire flickered in those green pupils. Having a man lather attention on her feet had never done it for Summer. But at that moment, her belly clenched at the idea of Todd's strong hands massaging the arch of her foot and sucking on her recently pedicured toes while his hands moved up her calves.

You need to stop! She bit the inside of her cheek, fighting the growing arousal slickening between her legs.

"Are you warm enough?"

She nodded.

His gaze moved back to her feet. "Here." He took off his slippers and bending down, he twisted them around until they lined up with her toes. "Put these on. The hardwood floors can be frigid."

"What about you?"

"I'm wearing socks. Plus, I have spares. I'll grab an extra pair." He straightened back to his full height.

"Thank you," she said, pushing into the slippers. They were twice her size but somehow felt like the perfect fit. Her toes curled happily inside the warm suede cocoon.

"Let me take this." He took the clothes bundle away from her.

"I can do it." Her voice was a little high-pitched as she grabbed for the clothes.

But he was quicker. "I got it."

Oh my god, he's going to see my very un-cute granny panties. Her heartbeat ticked up. "Please don't look. Just toss them in."

Amusement tugged at his mouth. "As you wish. Let me blindly toss these into the wash. Why don't you make your-self at home in the living room?"

"Okay," she murmured. She padded away from him down the long hallway.

Black framed photos of Sheba dotted the robin's egg-blue walls. In some, she was a puppy; tongue lagging from a big smile as she lay on a blanket at the park. Another showed her fully grown and jumping into a pile of leaves; swirls of red, gold, and brown flipping into the air from her impact. Each picture told the story of a very well-loved and cared-for puppy. Seeing them sent warmth through Summer's body.

Reaching the living room, she spied the apple of Todd's eyes curled atop an oversize bed beneath the Christmas tree. It was just one of many dog beds around the house. Summer had spotted another one in the nook in the kitchen when she'd walked past it to change in the downstairs bathroom. It was silly that his doting nature with Sheba caused a wobble in her knees. His adoring puppy-dad ways spoke of an atten-tive and thoughtful man.

If he's like this with a dog imagine... She shook her head. She couldn't allow her thoughts to wander down that thread.

Arms wrapped around her middle in a hug, she scanned the room. A burgundy sectional couch sat opposite a large flatscreen. Tall black bookshelves filled with books and several silver-framed photos flanked the TV.

Summer picked up one of the pictures. It was a candid shot of a woman in a pink dress and a little boy dancing. Vibrant, but wild, red curls tumbled down the woman's slender shoulders. Her effervescent smile beamed at the spikey-haired, carrot-topped little boy bowing and holding out his hand to dance.

"That was at my Aunt Jody's wedding."

Startled, Summer swung around, the frame clenched to her chest.

"I didn't mean to scare you." A roguish yet apologetic, smile covered Todd's face.

"I didn't mean to snoop," she countered, cheeks flushed.

"It's not snooping when I have it out for anyone to see." He sauntered closer, taking the picture from her. Wistfulness shimmered in his eyes as he looked at the photo.

"She is so beautiful."

He looked from the picture to Summer. "She was."

"Pink." Summer's gaze drifted to the Christmas tree. "All the pink, it's for your mom."

It was her favorite color."

"She always wore pink. Even when we needed to rock our Perry pride with blue and gold during games and competitions, she'd wear a pink ribbon in her hair."

The memory rose of Mandy's crimson curls tied up in a pink silk ribbon. A variety of silk scarves in different shades of pink replaced that ribbon once Mandy lost her hair, but she never lost her "blush" as she called it.

His mouth lifted into a sad smile. "I remember all the cheerleaders wearing pink ribbons in their hair for games to honor her the year she passed."

"It let us feel like she was still there cheering us on."

"They all stopped wearing the pink ribbons the following year, but you never did. It was like everyone else forgot about her, but you didn't. Each time I'd see that flash of pink in the sea of blue and gold along the sidelines at football games it was like she was still there."

The year after Mandy died the cheerleaders reverted to the blue and gold ribbons. It hadn't been a conscience decision. There'd been no proclamation from the new coach. For some reason, going back to the team colors felt wrong to Summer and she never made the switch. She'd been accused by the new cheer coach and some of the other girls on the team that she was just trying to stand out. She never corrected them on their assumption and just let them think what they wanted about her. *They did anyways.*

Todd's gaze wove with hers. Something fluttered in her chest.

"Thank you for not forgetting her." His fingers curled tight around the photo's frame.

The intensity of his grateful stare caused a stutter in her breath. Breaking the eye contact, her gaze flicked to the twinkling lights zigzagging the pine branches. "That's why you have all the pink...so you have your mom again for Christmas."

"Mom always had pink lights on the tree, but after she died—" Remorse and a twinge of anger shaded his stare. "We had them for the first Christmas after but then...my dad said it was time to move on."

"That's bullshit," she snapped, annoyance flamed inside her.

How could a father say that to a grieving boy? Todd was eleven and his little sister, Rose, was seven, when their mother died. Part of her wished she'd known this. That she'd done more than just wear a pink ribbon in her hair. She had been only thirteen, what could she have done? *More than what you did.* Regret swirled in her belly.

He shrugged. "That's my dad."

She'd had little interaction with Sheriff Jeff Krueger in her thirty-seven years. As much of a mean girl as she was in high school, she'd not gotten into trouble. Interactions with Sheriff Krueger had primarily been when he'd pick up his wife from cheerleading practice, at village events, or if he'd come to the school to speak to them about not drinking and driving. Since coming home, she'd had even fewer interactions outside of him dropping in to pick up a cup of coffee and breakfast sandwich at the cafe.

What she did know was that each time his name was mentioned, Todd's demeanor would shift. He'd get quieter. A slight bristle seemed to take over his usually relaxed form. She'd never seen Sheriff Krueger come into the wine bar or brewery, even on special occasions. He'd not been among the supportive smiles of friends and family at the brewery's grand opening.

"Asshole," she muttered, not keeping her thoughts quiet.

"I don't want to talk about him," he said, reaching around Summer to place the frame back on the shelf behind her. His body heat lapped along her skin despite the barrier of his clothes on her.

The proximity of their bodies made breathing difficult. Her pulse quickened. How easy, yet difficult, it would be to eliminate those inches. To move her head just a little to the left and feather kisses across his jawline, the scratch of his stubble against her lips. To curl her fingers into the cotton of his T-shirt and pull him against her.

"Amy came to group tonight," she said breathlessly, yanking herself away from those alluring but very wrong impulses.

"How'd that go?"

She let out a humorless laugh. "We won't be braiding each other's hair anytime soon, but I think we'll end up casually indifferent acquaintances. I mean, she spoke to me and didn't look like she wanted me to fall into a black hole…which is progress."

"Braiding each other's hair? So, that's what ladies do when they hang out." He smirked.

"Oh yeah," she crooned, walking past him. "That and having sleepovers complete with pillow fights in sexy jammies and practice kissing each other." With a cheeky grin, she sat on the couch.

That left eyebrow of his ticked up. "Wanna sleep over?"

She grabbed a plush pillow from the couch and flung it at him. "Perv!"

Catching it, he flashed a wicked expression that caused her stomach to swoop.

"I was promised tea." Was she batting her eyes? *Yep, I am.*

"As you wish." He bowed.

While Todd made tea, she shot a quick text to Mom and Dad to let them know she would be home later than normal. They both kept their phones on silent at night, but just in case they woke up she didn't want them to worry. She didn't have to tell them what she was doing, because that would open up way too many questions from them tomorrow. Somehow, she'd fallen into a vortex and was a teenager again breaking curfew to be with a boy.

You need to move out soon, she thought as she unfolded the fleece blanket flung over the corner of the sectional and snuggled into it.

A few minutes later, Todd returned with two steaming mugs of tea. Handing her one, he settled on the couch beside her.

"Why were you peeping in my window?" he teased.

She almost spat out her tea. "I wasn't peeping. I was..." Her nose crinkled. "Well, I wasn't *intentionally* peeping. I was looking at your decorations."

"Likely story."

She swatted his chest and tried not to revel in the taut muscle under her hand. "Shut up." She placed her mug on the coffee table and grabbed the book that he'd discarded there. "So, what were you reading before I—"

"Fell in front of my house after getting caught peeping in my window." He chuckled.

"You should be *so* lucky."

"That I would." His rich, deep tenor sent electricity zinging through her.

Biting her lip, she flipped the book to examine the front. "Are you reading Elizabeth Lake?" she squealed.

He grabbed the book. "You're not the only one that enjoys rogue dukes and feisty heroines."

This writer was one of her favorite historical romance authors. Glee thrummed through her. "This is a good one. What part are you at?"

One of the first real conversations they'd had was book related. It was in May when she was organizing the grand opening for the brewery. While waiting for the DJ, they got lost in the pages of that month's book club selection. Elle had chosen a retelling of *Pride and Prejudice* that took place at a burlesque club in New York City. Todd wasn't in book club but was a voracious reader, so they went down a book-related rabbit hole. An hour later, she *tsked* that she needed to get back to work and he just winked saying he'd buy the book so they could talk about it.

A week later, he showed up at Cassie's for lunch, book in hand with highlighted passages. Between serving tables and her quips for him to get a life they dissected their favorite parts. It was the start of many conversations about books, TV, movies, and anything. She'd admit that he was one of her favorite people to get lost down a rabbit hole with.

"He's just offered her a marriage of convenience to get her away from that evil Marquis."

She yanked the book back, opening to the page his bookmark was tucked into. "He's so dashing," she gushed, reading the young duke's dialogue.

"He's guided by love which can turn the most un-dashing man into a smooth talker."

"It probably helps that he's also handsome and a rich duke," she snarked.

"See I knew I was doing something wrong." His fingers brushed against hers, taking the book back.

She turned, their gazes locking. Heat bloomed in her. "What are you doing wrong?" She swallowed thickly, realizing there was absolutely nothing this man was doing wrong.

"Not being a handsome duke." The huskiness in his voice caused shivers along her spine.

"You're a handsome brewmaster." She lifted her hand to cradle his cheek. Her fingers glided across the rough stubble.

His eyes closed. "Summer."

"Todd." The breathlessness of his spoken name dripped with needy desire.

The want in her belly sparked embers of a coming fire across every nerve ending. There was no fighting this anymore. Tossing the blanket aside, she crawled into his lap, straddled him and clamped her hands on his cheeks.

He let out a quiet groan.

"Am I too heavy?" she worried her lip, moving to get off him.

Hands tight on her hips, he held her in place. "That was a happy groan. A *very* happy one."

The crackling air between them was reminiscent of the sky before a lightning storm. He trailed his hands along her sides. Her fingers curled into his shirt. Their breaths grew ragged as they remained staring at each other, neither closing the distance.

She wanted this so bad. Longing simmered in her veins. The dryness of her mouth begged to taste him. To glide her tongue over his. Every cell in her screamed for his touch.

His fingers threaded into her now dry hair. "You're not ready yet, sweetheart."

"What makes you say that?"

His hands moved to her cheeks to stroke along her soft skin. "Because you would have kissed me already. I know you. When you're ready to do something, it happens."

"You could always kiss me, first."

He shook his head. "We both know you have to make the first move."

Lips puckered, she almost pouted. "But I want you."

"I know sweetheart." He chuckled. "And I want you very much...I think you can tell that."

"Then take me," she commanded, rubbing her heated core against him, delighting in the proof of how much he wanted her straining against his sweatpants.

"Fuck," he let out a low moan.

Was she really rubbing herself against him like a cat in heat? *What the fuck am I doing?* Mortification flushed her cheeks. "I'm so sorry." She stilled the motion of her hips and moved to get off him.

His grip on her waist kept her secure to him. "Nothing to apologize for, sweetheart."

"Easy for you to say; you're not the one embarrassed *and* sexually frustrated."

"Is this sexual frustration in general or a specific want?" His left eyebrow arched.

What was it about that left eyebrow that got her? Were eyebrows erotic? Somehow, his left one was the sexiest thing on a man that already dripped with sex appeal.

She raised her hand to his eyebrow, tracing it. "It's specific to you. Nobody has fired up my lady bits like you in…God, maybe ever. It's not like I haven't been sexually attracted to other men before, but…"

His arms banded around her back. "Let's not talk about you wanting other men while you're straddling me."

She giggled. When was the last time she'd giggled? "I want you very much," she admitted. "Like I think about you way more than is appropriate. I look forward to you coming into the café every day and on the days you don't I'm a little sad."

"Come here." He repositioned them to lay on the couch. His muscular arms cradling her against his chest. "I'm a little sad on the days I can't have lunch at the café or the days you're not working."

"I'm sorry I can't or won't—I'm not sure which—kiss you."

He nuzzled his nose into her hair. "No apologies. This is progress. You're letting me hold you and you haven't insulted me yet."

"Give it ten minutes…you're likely to do something stupid."

The rumble of his deep laugh vibrated along her back. God, she loved that feeling. The musicality of his laugh was one thing, but to have the sensation pulsate through her buzzed a happy tipsiness in her veins. She could get drunk off his laugh.

This man both calmed and unnerved her in all the best ways. Why was it so hard to close the distance? To give in to the feelings that she had for him?

Fucking past. She fiddled with the string on the pajama bottoms she wore. For almost ten years, she'd been shackled to her past. The cruel and uncaring teenage Summer. The reckless Summer from her early twenties, falling for a handsome prince who hid a villain. The broken woman she'd been in her late twenties as she escaped. Only she'd not escaped. In so many ways, she was still imprisoned by her past, taking away the freedom to embrace today and tomorrow. Of embracing this good man who lay beside her, his strong arms folded around her. It was just as LaToya warned, if she didn't let go of yesterday there'd be no promise of a tomorrow.

Twisting, she faced him. "Why me?"

Confusion wrinkled his forehead. "Why you?"

"Why do you want me? Have you seen yourself? They call you the sexy brewmaster around town."

A wry expression broke across his face. "Do you think I'm a sexy brewmaster?"

She swatted him. "I'm being serious. You're successful. You're kind." Her lips tugged up into a bashful smile. "You're sexy with all your muscles and that face of yours. You could have anyone."

"And I want you."

"*Exactly!*" She huffed with a self-deprecating laugh.

"Don't do that." His tone stern.

She arched an eyebrow.

"Don't put down my friend; I won't stand for it."

Happiness bubbled in her chest as he repeated her words from the wedding. "Good thing you're lying down."

He brushed a tendril of her hair behind her ear. "Good thing." The warmth of his breath caressed her skin, teasing her with what to expect if she'd close the distance between them. "I told you this already, but I'll tell you every day until you believe it and even then I might just keep telling you all the reasons I like you because I never want you to forget how amazing you are. Nobody makes me laugh or keeps me on my toes like you. You're kind. You're a supportive friend."

She snorted a little.

"You're smart as hell. I could spend hours talking to you about books and anything else. God, you're so talented. Look at what you did for Elle and Clayton's wedding. I know this weekend's Christmas Market will be just as stunning. No matter the chaos happening around you, you bring the calm."

"Todd."

Undeterred by her quiet protest, he went on. "Every time I see you, I think my heart stops, because you're so fucking beautiful. Even now, hair all messy and in my clothes, all I can think is how gorgeous you are and how I very much want you to always wear my clothes. Like I'm going to drop off a box of my T-shirts for you to we—"

She pressed her lips against his. Slow…so slowly she took his full lips in a tentative kiss reminiscent of those first few pedals of riding a bicycle without training wheels, figuring out the pace and hoping to not fall. At first, he made no movement. His hands remained motionless at her sides and his mouth didn't kiss her back. She experienced a moment of fear that she was doing it wrong or that the actuality of kissing her had scared him out of his wanting of her.

"Summer." He pulled away, his eyes searching hers.

Nodding, as if he saw what he was looking for, he leaned back in, capturing her lips in a consuming kiss. His hands wove into her hair, pulling her deeper into his embrace. Licking the seam of her mouth he coaxed her open. The slick heat of his tongue slid across hers. The taste of the peppermint tea he was drinking filled her.

"Todd," she moaned as his mouth trailed kisses down her jawline to the column of her throat.

"Is this okay, sweetheart?" he murmured, sliding his hands beneath the hem of the Henley.

"Yes." Her breath caught as his fingers skimmed across her belly.

"You're so goddamn soft." He kissed her jawline. "You always smell like strawberries and cream."

"It's the body wash I use." She gasped as his fingers moved down, playing with the string of the flannel pajama bottoms she wore.

"You mentioned being sexually frustrated." He untied the string. "As your friend, I'd like to help you. Is this okay?" He dipped a finger beneath the waistband.

"Very okay." Goosebumps cascaded across her skin.

His thick fingers crawled down. Wickedness shaded his eyes almost black. His fingers ran across the small tuft of hair at her core. "It was killing me knowing you were wearing my pajama bottoms with no panties. The idea of something that I wore touching this"—his fingers slid along her slick center causing her to buck against him— "was destroying my resolve to not kiss you the moment you walked out of the bathroom."

"You said you wouldn't look at the bundle of clothes." She moaned with the first slow flick against her clit.

"I didn't." His deep voice grew growly. "I always keep my promises."

"How did you…know?" she stuttered, pleasure tightening with his lazy circles.

"Your nervousness about me with your clothes was the give away." He bent close, nipping at her earlobe.

With languid strokes he circled that throbbing bundle of nerves. Biting her lip, she tried to stamp out the needy moan begging to come out.

He applied a little more pressure. "No need to be quiet, sweetheart. It's just us and Sheba and she's fast asleep under the tree. You make all the noises. Let me know if you like –" he pressed a little harder "—what I'm doing."

"Oh, god," she whined, writhing against him. The building pressure blazed like wildfire inside her.

"Tonight, I'll touch you but one day, very soon, this will be my tongue tasting you. Rolling and sucking your clit. Drinking up your sweetness." He moved his fingers between hard and light caresses, taking her to the edge and bringing her back again.

Summer's nails dug into his shoulders. Her hips moved against his working fingers, searching for relief. "Todd, please."

With her needy whimper, a rakish smile pulled at the corners of his lips. "Please, what sweetheart? Tell me what you want."

"More… I want more," she panted, tugging the pajama bottoms down to her knees.

His eyes looked down to take in her nakedness. "Such a pretty pussy," he purred, sliding a finger down her wetness and pushing it inside her.

"Todd!" she cried, spreading her legs wider.

"You feel so good sweetheart. So warm and wet for me. So tight." He nipped at her lips. "If you feel this good with my finger I don't know if my dick will be able to handle you."

She clenched around him. "Oh!" Any effort to form words was useless. Her hands gripped at his shoulders while her hips rocked under his ministrations.

"You like it when I praise you, don't you?"

She just panted in response.

"Like I said, I'll tell you every day why I like you. Now,

relax and let me show you. Let me make you feel good, sweetheart."

Alternating between hard and soft pressure on her clit, and slow deep pumps of his finger inside her, he devoured her mouth with kisses. His mouth claimed each moan and whimper. The pressure built; tension coiled across every inch of her body. The tightening sensation inched closer to release. Pushing a second finger inside her, he crooked his fingers, finding that spot on her inside wall.

"Fuck!" she screamed with the wall-slamming effect of her orgasm.

Todd's fingers continued working, allowing her to ride out her release. As the aftershocks of her climax slowed, her hips settled.

He leaned in and pressed a kiss to her sweat-dampened forehead. "Was that okay, sweetheart?"

Her laugh was breathless. "So okay."

"Good. That was for us. But this is for me." He removed his fingers, bringing them to his lips and sucking each one. "Just like I thought, sweet. Like strawberries and cream."

She swatted him. "You're so obnoxious."

"You have no idea how obnoxious I can be when it comes to you." His big smile pressed against hers. The salty-sweet taste of her release clung to his lips.

"Well, let's find out." Her hands moved to the waistband of his sweatpants.

Gently wrapping his fingers around her wrist, he guided her away. "Not tonight, sweetheart."

Rejection burned in her throat. "Okay." Summer yanked up the pajama bottoms and wiggled to get off the couch.

"Nope." He held her in place beside him. "Not like that. Trust me, I fucking want you so bad. I want to scoop you up, take you into my bedroom, and spend the rest of the night learning all the different ways to make you cry out my name. But we need to take this slow."

"You just fingered me on your couch." Her forehead puckered.

"Yes, but I did it slowly." He smirked. "I know this doesn't make sense, but this was a big step for you tonight. I have a feeling you're going to freak out just a little bit in the morning and I don't want to push this too quickly. You're important to me. I want to do this right."

Despite the lingering residue of rejection, she smiled. "Like taking me out on a *real* date with candles and flowers?"

"Yes." His boyish grin stole her heart. "Summer Michaels, will you go out with me on a *real* date?"

She gnawed her lower lip, but it was just for show. Despite the worries that twirled within her, it was a yes!

CHAPTER TWELVE

*"I'm not like a *regular* mom, I'm a *cool* mom." ~Mean Girls*

The cell phone's alarm rang through the room, jolting Summer awake. With a whiny groan, she plucked it off the bedstand. Morning had come far too early, even with bypassing her usual five a.m. wakeup, allowing herself to sleep until seven today. Due to this weekend's Christmas Market she'd only be working the lunch shift instead of opening the café with Cassie for breakfast.

Most mornings, she'd leave just after waking Liam up. But whenever she didn't work the breakfast/lunch shift, she liked being part of his morning routine before school. Dad, who worked at the high school, usually walked or dropped Liam off, depending on the weather.

A message notification flashed on her phone's screen. Todd. Happiness fluttered along her nerves. Had it been a mere six hours since he'd walked her home? After what she had dubbed the "couch incident," there'd been a little more kissing, a lot more holding, and even more talking before she cleaned up in his bathroom and changed into her freshly laundered clothes. He offered to drive her home, but she said she'd walk. Naturally, he wouldn't let her do that so he grabbed Sheba's leash and the three of them walked the ten minutes to her house. The way he'd shifted foot-to-foot at her front door before he'd said, "Goodnight" with a tender press of his lips to her forehead was a little reminiscent of a high school first date. Although, it wasn't their first date. That would be tonight.

"I'm going on a date with Todd Krueger," she murmured, a little starry-eyed and a lot disbelieving.

Swiping open the phone, she turned off the alarm completely and brought up her messages.

Todd: Good morning, sweetheart. Look in your driveway.

Confusion lined her forehead. Pushing off the blankets she jumped out of bed and padded to the window. Her bedroom overlooked the side of the house where the driveway was. Parked behind her dad's SUV was her car.

"What?" Her lips quirked.

Summer: What did you do?
Todd: Well, good morning to you too. *Smirking emoji.*

The eye roll wasn't as large as the smile that kicked across her face.

Summer: Good morning, what did you do? *Eye roll emoji.*
Todd: Before Noah and I went to work out this morning, I got him to help me jump and move your car to your place. It should be okay to drive, but Ryan at King's Garage said they can replace the battery over the weekend. If you need a car, you can use mine.

**Summer: God, I forgot Noah and you go to the gym
at five a.m. most mornings.**
Todd: *Muscle man GIF.*

She snorted.

Summer: You didn't need to do all that for me.
Todd: I'd do anything for you.

Her stomach jumped at his flirty sweetness.

Summer: Did you tell Noah what happened??
Todd: I never finger and tell.
Summer: *Middle finger emoji.*
Todd: Is that a request for a repeat performance?
Smiley emoji.

*This man! Was it possible for your butterflies to swoon while
your vagina clenched?* She'd never experienced the dual sensation of simultaneous swooning and horniness.

**Todd: I told Noah I ran into you last night while you
were walking home. Kept it very G-rated.**
**Summer: Thanks. It's not a secret. Like he's going to
know as soon as Nat knows and let's face it...you've
got about five hours before she knows.**

She'd seen enough secret dating to last a lifetime. Nat and
Noah's relationship had bloomed in secret for well over a
month. After pushing her friend hard to be open about the
relationship, despite the fear Nat had about Clayton's reaction, it didn't seem right to keep this a secret.

Although, she did want to keep it a little quiet. She had
Liam to think of, so they'd discussed last night to keep it low-
key around her parents and him until they figured out exactly

what all this meant. If this ended with her heartbroken, she knew she could recover. But she wasn't sure how Liam would react to Todd being part of their life and then gone. That was perhaps the scariest aspect of this entire thing. She didn't want to risk their friendship, but she also didn't want to not, *not* risk it.

Summer: See you at lunch?

She knew it was a little greedy to want him to come to the café for lunch when she was going on a date with him that night. It was akin to a kid asking for caramel sauce atop a delicious piece of warm apple pie already covered with a giant scoop of vanilla ice cream.

Just as she went to type that it was totally okay if he didn't come to the café for lunch today his response filled her screen.

Todd: Try to keep me away. *Winky face emoji.*

A happy giggle left her lips. Summer clamped her hand over her mouth. *Seriously? You're not sixteen.*

Placing her phone on the bedstand, she grabbed the oversized Bill's sweatshirt flung over the chair in front of the small desk in the corner and pulled it over the Henley – Todd's Henley – she'd worn to bed. She may have nicked it from his place like the crush-sick teenager she was acting like. In her defense, her sweater hadn't dried completely, and they were walking home. Yeah, that was the story she was going with.

The sound of the TV drifted upward, as Summer headed downstairs. Most mornings, Dad was up by five a.m. to start his two and a half hours of news watching while he got ready. Even in the summer, he'd get up to watch the local news over several cups of coffee.

"Morning." Summer waved, walking past the living room.

"Morning, Summer Joy." Dad's dark eyes twinkled over his *World's Best Grandpa* mug.

"Morning, Mom," Liam chirped over his cereal from where he sat at the coffee table.

Arms crossed over her chest she arched an eyebrow. "Breakfast in front of the TV."

"Uh…" Dad's brow furrowed. "It's for school."

She looked unconvinced.

"He's learning current events."

"I am?" Liam's face scrunched.

"Kid, work with me," he muttered.

Summer shook her head and laughed. "This one time." She pointed to her dad. "But you're in trouble, mister." She shuffled into the kitchen.

"I told him he was going to get in trouble." Mom sat at the kitchen table and lifted her head up from her e-reader with a chuckle.

Summer opened the fridge, grabbing the jug of orange juice. "What are you reading?"

"That romance about the demon who turns into a dragon that all the nurses from work are drooling about."

Grabbing a glass, she poured some juice. "The one by Kimberly Lemming? That's a good one."

Mom fanned herself. "That scene on the island. I may have to take your dad on a weekend getaway soon."

"Gross," she groaned.

"Don't be prejudiced. People in their sixties can have very active and fulfilling sex lives, especially when their hips are in as good of shape as mine and your father's," she retorted.

"Yes, but they don't need to speak about it in front of their adult children. I was traumatized enough by the ballroom dancing phase you went through four years ago. I don't think I'll ever recover from seeing Dad twerking in that sequin-studded suit."

"He did look good in that."

"I look good in everything. Especially these sexy chinos," Dad drawled as he strutted into the room.

Summer shook her head. "You two."

"Are we embarrassing *our* daughter?" he teased, shaking his butt and dancing over to his wife. "But I can't help it. These hips can't be contained." Dad teased, gyrating his hips saucily…

Giggling, Mom slapped his butt. "Stop or I'll take you upstairs and you'll be late for work."

"Yes, please." He placed kisses on her neck that made her squeal with laughter. "My beautiful wife is a nurse, so she can write me a note for being late."

Horror aside, joy swirled within Summer. The love between her parents seemed effortless and endless. While there'd been fights and arguments over the years, they were happy. No relationship was perfect but she imagined her parents were about as close as one could get. They loved each other, but they also liked each other. At the end of the day, they were best friends.

I'll always be your friend, even when I'm more. Todd's promise lingered inside her. Bent close, his lips inches from hers, he'd whispered that to her last night while they remained curled together on the couch before the ding of the dryer pulled them apart, signaling the end of their night.

Tonight, she'd take the first steps toward something more. She just needed to secure a babysitter.

"If you two could cease acting like horny teenagers for five minutes, I have a favor to ask." Summer cleared her throat.

Placing one last kiss on Mom's lips, Dad straightened. "What can we do for you, the living, breathing product of our love?"

"Eww." She blanched. "Anyways, would you be able to watch Liam tonight? Mom, I know you will be on second shift, so you won't be home until eleven, but Dad, would you be able to? I'm sorry to ask, because I know you watched him last night and will be doing the heavy lifting over the weekend because of the Christmas Market."

"Summer Joy, it's never a heavy lift. He's our grandson," he assured.

Her fingers wrapped tighter around the juice glass. "I know, but you do a lot for us, and I don't want you to feel taken advantage of."

Dad's eyes narrowed. "Stop that. You're not taking advantage of us *at* all. You're a good mom. You're a good daughter."

Unexpected emotion formed a lump in her throat.

"Plus, it will be boys' night." He smiled widely, rubbing his hands together. "Liam, you want to have pizza, make root beer floats, and watch *Fast and Furious* with Pop tonight?" His head tipped toward his grandson, who walked into the room carrying his empty cereal bowl.

"It's Friday…we have to have a fish fry," Liam countered, placing his bowl in the sink.

"But it's boys' night." Broad chest puffed up, Dad gestured around the room as if a gaggle of men stood there waiting to engage in manly activities. "That means boys' night rules, remember?"

Liam thrived with routine and seldom liked to deviate from it. Sometimes, changes to a plan could cause anxiety and even mini-meltdowns. To counter this, they'd developed a series of rules, helping him navigate changes. If he knew what to expect, it was easier for him to recalibrate.

"Blanket fort?" Liam beamed.

"Blanket fort!" Dad high-fived his grandson.

"Alright, manly men, you need to get going or you'll be late," Mom tutted.

Summer grabbed Liam's lunch bag out of the fridge. "Go put this in your backpack and get ready." She bent to kiss his forehead.

"I'm not a baby," he grumbled.

"But you're my baby," she cooed, peppering him with kisses.

Wiggling away from her, he mumbled, "You're so embarrassing." Then walked out of the room.

"See, not so fun when you're on the opposite side," Dad clucked.

"Ha!" Summer grabbed her juice from the counter. "Thanks for watching him tonight, Dad."

"What are you doing tonight, honey?" Mom asked as she poured sugar into her tea mug.

"Just a few things I need to get done." Shrugging, she sipped her juice.

Dad cleared his throat. "Would these things be Todd Krueger?"

Summer spat out her juice.

"That's a yes." Dad boomed with a deep laugh.

"How?" she gaped.

"I heard you come home last night and when I looked out the window, I saw Todd walking away. Then this morning, I saw he and Noah dropping off your car around six this morning. Now you need a babysitter." Dad ran through his litany of observations with a smug smile on his face.

"We did the math." Mom handed Summer a paper towel. "Plus, it doesn't take a genius to see that man is smitten with you."

She arched a brow. "Smitten?"

"And I think you're a little smitten with him."

She fought the heat flushing her cheeks.

"He's a nice man. You deserve nice." Dad looped his bulky arm around her, tucking her into his side. "I liked him when he was one of my students and I like him now. He's respectful to your parents. He's good with Liam, but more importantly he's good with you."

Tears pricked at her eyes. "I know my judgment in the

past about men wasn't..." A lump choked her ability to speak.

He pressed a kiss to the top of her head. "Oh, Summer Joy, that wasn't your doing. I hope you know that. If I ever see that Max, I'll—"

"Pop!" Liam screamed from the foyer. "We're going to be late!"

"Be right there, bud," he shouted.

"It's okay. We'll never see him."

"Good, then I don't have to go to jail." A weak smile curled his mouth. "I love you, Summer Joy."

"I love you, too." She sniffled, burying herself in his embrace.

Mom's arms came around her. "No hugs in the kitchen without me."

Sandwiched between her parents, Summer let a few tears tumble out. They may nag. They may embarrass her. But they were always there. Even when she didn't allow them to be.

A year into the relationship with Max her parents had visited New York City. They'd had lunch at an upscale French restaurant. Max oozed with charm and picked up the bill, but her dad was uncharacteristically icy to him. Never one to mince words, Dad told Summer he didn't trust Max. "He's too slick," he'd warned, standing outside the restaurant. Believing she was in love she argued with him. Later, Max held her, telling her they just couldn't accept her big life with him. That they were small. Little by little, she ate up his poisonous words allowing them to create a divide between her and her parents.

"I'm sorry I didn't listen to you when you tried to warn me about him," she croaked.

"None of what happened was your fault," Mom reassured, squeezing her tighter.

"Pop!" Liam bellowed.

He released her, stepping back. "Bud, count to one hundred in Spanish and then I'll be there."

"If I had listened to you back then I wouldn't have him." She swiped at the tears in her eyes. "Max was both the worst and best thing to happen to me because I got Liam. No matter what, I can't regret my choices because it brought me him. I just wish I hadn't pushed you away like I did."

"That's the past." Mom looped her arm around Summer's middle. "We have each other now."

Dad placed a hand on her shoulder and squeezed tenderly. "We'll always have each other."

"I'm sorry for getting so emotional." Summer looked between both her parents. "I know I have a lot of feelings to work on. I'm not going to pretend that this isn't a little scary and a big step. Nat is talking to her therapist to see if they can take me on to help me work through some of this. It's time for me to do the work to put the past where it belongs…in my past."

"I'm so proud of you, Summer Joy." He bent and kissed her forehead.

"*Noventa, nueve y cien.* Pop!"

"Coming, bud." His face wrinkled. "God, that kid counts fast."

"And in Spanish." Mom's face lit with pride.

Hours later, Summer leaned over the metal counter at Cassie's Cafe, filling small plastic souffle cups with ranch dressing. The closer the clock inched to one-fifteen the more anxious excitement buzzed inside her. Most Fridays, Todd and Noah didn't come in until then for lunch in order to eat with Nat. Since the Owens Family Clinic was open Saturday mornings, they closed around twelve-thirty on Friday. By the time Nat wrapped up signing orders and charting, she'd meet the guys for lunch after one.

The lunch rush slowed after one-thirty, which in turn allowed Summer to sometimes take her lunch break with them. If she still had customers, she could still linger a little bit longer at their table.

She, of course, was not thinking about this as she forgot the salad dressing and had to come back to fill them for table two. Todd's mouth slanted into that boyishly wicked smile hadn't occupied her thoughts when the cups overflowed with ranch. Certainly she'd not been daydreaming about that sexy scar above his left eye as she wiped the puddles of dressing from the counter. No way was she at work fantasizing of strong hands gliding over her curves as she refilled the cups. *Nope*, none of that clouded her brain.

"French Fries and Wedge Salad is here!" Cassie crooned, sauntering into the kitchen. "He's got Veggie Burger and little Ms. Let Me Ask About Today's Special But Still Order The Salmon Salad with him."

Summer's heart thumped. She wasn't sure if the cheetah-like cadence of her heartbeat was at the idea of seeing Todd after last night or seeing Nat. She'd not texted nor called Nat about the couch incident. Mornings were always jam-packed at the clinic. At least, that's the excuse Summer told herself for not yet letting her best friend know that she'd crossed the borders of the friend zone with Todd.

Where they were now, she had no idea. This was uncharted territory. It wasn't just the idea of being out of practice with dating, but that this somehow felt so different than anyone else she'd ever dated. This thing—whatever it was with Todd—was more than the crush-drunk butterflies that bashed around in her belly.

"I sat them in Laney's section," Cassie announced.

"What?" Summer jerked, dropping one of the cups of

ranch dressing which tumbled to the floor. "Shit!" She winced.

Eyes twinkling with mischief, Cassie pointed. "I knew it!"

"Knew what?"

"Admit it, you are totally into Todd Krueger." Cassie waggled her eyebrows, placing her hands on her shapely hips.

Heat flamed in Summer's cheeks. God, she wanted to be cool about this. To roll her eyes. To flick her wrist. To scoff. Instead, she blushed like a thirteen-year-old girl after the boy she likes winked at her across the school cafeteria.

Zach perked up, flipping a burger on the grill. "Of course, she is. Women *can't* resist the Rice men. You couldn't resist me." He beamed at his wife from across the kitchen.

"Don't remind me. I'm still not a hundred percent convinced you didn't get a witch to put a love spell on me," she snarked with a playful smirk. Turning her amber eyes back on Summer, she grinned. "Have you succumbed to the charms of a Rice man?"

"Ha!" Zach huffed a laugh. "You admit it was charm and not witchcraft."

Cassie ignored him.

"Todd's only half Rice," Summer countered, pretending that her non-answer had not just confirmed Cassie's accusation.

"And you're *one hundred percent* into both halves of him."

A nervous laugh vibrated in Summer's throat. Grabbing the tray full of ranch dressing, she then headed toward the kitchen door, not addressing Cassie's knowing expression. Pushing into the dining room, Summer's steps halted. Noah, Nat, and Todd sat at table three. Her section. Clearly Cassie had been playing a little matchmaking subterfuge. Noah and Nat's backs faced her in the small four-person booth along the front windows, but Todd's handsome face was directed right at her.

Sunlight cascaded into the café through the large front windows. Todd's red hair almost shimmered in its brightness. His sparkling green eyes drifted to her. A large smile belted across his face and stole her breath. The man was gorgeous. As if an artist had sculpted him out of marble then painted him with the most vibrant of colors. Even that tiny scar somehow made his perfection just a little bit more.

Those already too-active butterflies which had fluttered wildly in her stomach went into overdrive. All the cliches slammed into her. Quickened pulse. Hitched breath. Clenched belly. Dry mouth.

You are the girl you used to make fun of. She bit her lower lip.

Sucking in a breath, she crossed the room. After dropping off the salad dressings at table two she slipped the tray under her arm and scooted to table three.

"Hi," Todd greeted, his entire body seeming to smile.

"Hi," Summer's voice came out a little breathy.

Their gazes tangled in a long embrace.

An urge to bend down and press a quick kiss to his lips or slide in beside him pulsed within her. Alongside a jittery urge to act as if nothing had changed; like everything was as it had always been between them. The feeling was reminiscent of being the rope in a fierce game of tug-of-war. Half of her wanting to claim him in front of everyone. The other half wanting to hide.

"Summer." Noah's baritone snapped her out of her staring contest with Todd.

"Hi," she said, her voice high-pitched. "Noah. Nat. Hi."

Nat's mouth curved up. "Summer."

Summer's forehead creased, taking in the stunted greeting from her friend. Where was the tackling hug? Where was the giddy greeting?

Summer pointed at Todd. "*You* told her!"

He raised his hands in defense, shaking his head. "She figured it out."

Eyebrow arched, she eyed Nat.

Amused smugness glinted in her eyes. "The fact that you think I wouldn't put two-and-two together is a real shame. You should know I'm brilliant."

"How?"

"Noah mentioned going with Todd to jump your car this morning. Then one of my patients mentioned looking out their front window last night and seeing Todd and you walking together after midnight." A smug smile pulled at the corners of her lips. "I believe they gasped 'how scandalous'."

"Small towns," Summer muttered. "How is it you two snuck around for over a month without getting found out when you first started dating and *we're* caught within thirteen hours?"

"We're stealthy," Noah drawled, wrapping a muscular arm around his girlfriend.

"You're not *that* stealthy, Prince Charming. I caught you pressing Nat against the side of the Wine Down in a hot and heavy make out session within the first five minutes of your courtship." Todd smirked.

"Courtship?" Summer chortled.

"OMG! This is really happening! You're dating!" Nat's loud squeal caused Summer to jump back and the chatter at the other tables to hush or stop completely. Even if it wasn't a small town with everyone's interest piqued by two people they knew dating, the joy radiating from Nat was a beacon for everyone's attention.

Summer shook her head. "Great, now the *whole* town knows."

Her face twisted in apology. "Sorry…This is huge news. You are really dating each other?"

"Well, we're going on *a* date tonight."

Todd's hand brushed her arm, resolve in his emerald eyes. "A first of many dates."

Leaning into the touch of his hand and promise of his words, a big smile lifted her lips.

"OMG! OMG! Oh my God!" Exuberant joy, reminiscent of a child bouncing in their seat when needing to pee on a long road trip, vibrated from Nat. "Where are you going for your first date?"

"Were you this excited for our first date?" Noah pressed a kiss to Nat's cheek.

Summer tilted her head. "I don't know where we're going."

They hadn't talked about what they'd be doing tonight. Todd had only said he'd plan it and to meet at his place at six since picking her up at her place would raise some questions for Liam and her parents. Although, after this morning, they now knew but would likely make a pickup awkward. The image of her parents' waggled brows, them cooing something inappropriate halted any delusion of having Todd pick her up at home.

"What?" Shock contorted Nat's face. "You haven't told her? She needs time to prep. What does she wear? A lady needs time to gussy up."

"Gussy up?" Summer snorted. "I don't even think my mom uses that term."

"Summer will be beautiful in whatever she wears." Todd's gaze swept down her figure appreciatively, causing her tummy to flip.

"Smooth," Noah crooned.

"Aww." Nat covered her heart with both hands. "That is *very* sweet but also you know nothing about ladies."

"It's a surprise," he insisted.

A determined furrow lined Nat's brow. "Challenge accepted."

Summer and Noah shook with laughter.

"On that note, I'll put in your orders while Nat interrogates Todd," she said, taking out the ordering pad from her apron pocket and jotting down their usual order.

"Wait! You don't know what I want." Nat's lips pursed, tipping her head to Summer. "What are your specials?"

"Today's special is a salmon salad and tater tots," Summer deadpanned.

"Ooh, I'll take that."

Laughing, she pivoted and strode to the kitchen door. Once at the door, she looked over her shoulder to find a pair of emerald eyes gazing at her from across the room. Nat's barrage of questions filtered through the café, but his eyes remained focused on Summer in a silent conversation. The tic of his eyebrow telegraphed that it was just them. That despite the prodding of their well-intentioned friends and some nosy village residents, that they were in this together. That even if they were taking steps into unknown territory, he was still her friend. Which was perfect because she knew a friend was needed to lean on right now. Fear and excitement swirled in her, but she'd keep going.

With one last nodding smile, Summer turned and pushed into the kitchen. Like a puppy that had snagged a fallen piece of steak, the entire staff of Cassie's Café beamed, greeting her with loud claps. Clearly Nat's squeal had made it to the kitchen.

"Rice men are irresistible," Zach hooted and high-fived his wife.

CHAPTER THIRTEEN

"You're a regulation hottie." ~Mean Girls

For the second time in a week, Summer had been forced into a makeover. Despite her protests that she had a cute sweater to wear for tonight, Nat, after badgering Todd for the details of what tonight's date entailed, announced they were going shopping.

"Pick her up at our place at six," Nat ordered, pulling Summer towards the café's front door.

Laughter lit Todd's face.

"I still have an hour in my shift," Summer protested.

"Nope, you have a date to get ready for. You're relieved. Hot Stuff over there can cover your tables." Cassie tipped her head at Noah. "Ready to don a Cassie's Café apron?"

Noah winked. "You got it."

"How do you feel about wearing *only* the apron?"

Todd slapped a frowning Noah's shoulder. "Check it out, Prince Charming, finally someone who understands what you bring to the table."

"Pretty sure that violates all kinds of labor laws," he warned.

"Cassie has a very loose interpretation of HR rules and regulations," Summer snarked. "Slow down, She-Hulk. I need my jacket!" She pulled against Nat's forceful tug toward the door.

"Here you go!" Laney emerged from the kitchen, tossing Summer's purse and jacket into her arms.

Almost four hours later, Summer sat on Nat and Noah's bed, while Carmen brushed highlighter over her cheeks. The bat signal had been sent to the mani/pedi crew's group text, demanding reinforcements for Project First Date. Although Jerome had dubbed the session *It's about fricking time* on their message thread.

Nat took care of the outfit, making Summer try on far too many dresses at the small boutique she dragged her to in Geneseo. She also made her buy some sexy lingerie, which Summer didn't protest too much about. Carmen, whose dark brown hair fell in thick waves similar to Summer's, was on hair and makeup duty.

"You have such lovely skin," Carmen cooed, swiping purplish-pink lip stain across Summer's lips.

"I still think red lipstick. Red screams *'come here, boy.'* I mean, if I wore lipstick, I'd do red for a date," Jerome drawled.

Carmen *tsked*. "Red lipstick isn't for first dates. It's for the date when you're ready to have sex."

The corners of his lips lifted into a wry grin. "Well, the pink on Summer's cheeks may indicate that she's ready for red lipstick...lots of red lipstick."

Ignoring the heat creeping up her neck at the idea of sex with Todd, she cleared her throat. "What exactly is *your* function here?" She gestured to where Jerome's large body was folded into a black leather chair tucked in the corner.

"Moral support," he said through a mouthful of chips.

A strange sense of déja vu crept up in Summer's chest. Prior to last Friday, the last time she'd got ready for a date with a group of friends had been in high school. Even then, it hadn't been like this. Getting ready for school dances with her girlfriends had been consumed by an unspoken competition to be the cutest girl in the room. There were little under-handed comments and backhanded compliments tossed amongst each other.

None of *that* existed here. The presence of competition had been replaced by support and kinship, and she discovered she liked the way that enveloped her. While the three were helping Summer get ready, it was about all of them. They offered support to Jerome, who shared that he and Tobey had applied to become foster parents. Each person here had cooed over photos of Francisco, Carmen's now one-year-old son, and helped strategize her forthcoming bid for a third term as village mayor. There was chatter about Noah's birthday party next Thursday.

These are real friends. The warmth of belonging settled within her.

"All done," Carmen announced, stepping back to admire her work.

"Gorgeous!" Nat moved in beside Carmen.

Summer stood, unable to see her reflection in the mirror with her friends circled around her.

Jerome rose, the bag of chips still in hand, his large choco-late eyes sweeping down her figure. "When Todd sees you in that, he'll be sporting the male equivalent of red lipstick."

"Gross!" Summer and Carmen groaned in unison.

Smirking, he shrugged.

"Check yourself out." Nat stepped aside and motioned to the full-length mirror hung on the back of the closed door.

Breath *whooshed* from Summer's lungs. Last week's makeover felt like a performance. Summer had been pushed into a tight red dress with the red lipstick Jerome advocated. It had been fun but was reminiscent of playing dress up. Of being who she'd once been and had never quite felt comfortable as despite the shark-like confidence that shimmered at the surface.

Now, the image in front of her seemed more her. Even if it wasn't the jeans and sweater she typically wore, this was her. A version of herself she'd not seen in a long time or, maybe, had never seen. The reflection in the mirror wasn't the over-done blonde of the past, nor the plain chestnut-ponytailed-hair version of herself of today. Looking back at her was…her.

The clothes, makeup, and hair style didn't replace Summer as much as they accentuated her looks. Silver hoop earrings shimmered from loose glossy waves of chestnut framing her face. Light-pink hued her lips and cheeks. A navy, scoop-neck sweater dress hugged her breasts but flowed loosely over her curves to create a flattering silhouette. The argyle-patterned dress stopped just below her knees. Black tights were paired with sensible but cute, knee-high, chunky-heeled black boots.

"One last thing," Carmen said, heading to one of the large tote bags she'd brought with her and tossed atop the bed. "I'm on strict orders from Elle to put a pic of your date outfit into the group chat and to make you wear this."

Elle had been on the group text. Despite the time difference in London and being on her honeymoon, she'd responded immediately with a barrage of excited-face emojis that made Summer do a double take at the message thinking it was Nat and *not* the generally more reserved Elle.

Carmen unfolded a red wool peacoat, handing it to Summer. "Elle bought it for your Christmas present, but insisted you get it early."

"What?" Summer gaped at the coat. "This is *too* much."

"Nope." Carmen pulled out a white cashmere scarf, gloves, and hat set, handing them to Summer. "This is too much. You know Elle, her love language is gifts. She said for me to remind you that she retains bridal privilege 'til she returns on Sunday, so you have to just accept the gifts."

Summer's heart squeezed. *How is this my life?*

Twenty years ago, when she'd gotten ready for the Winter Ball, her senior year, with her *friends,* she'd thought her life was perfect. She would be crowned Winter Ball Queen that night. She'd lose her virginity to Shane. She'd already hatched a plan to say goodbye to Perry after graduation and go on to live her big life. Only she had no idea that her big life was here all along with people she'd never expected to become the stars making up her galaxy. People like Carmen and Elle, whom she'd tormented at that very same dance, who'd so graciously embraced her now. People she'd never expected to come into her life, like the big-hearted Jerome. People like Nat and Todd whom she'd never paid a lot of attention to, but who'd joined her parents and Liam to become the most important people in her life.

"Thank you…" Emotion threatened to steal her words.

"I brought you condoms!" Jerome blurted.

"What?" Carmen spun, poking him. "Why are you ruining our little moment?"

He motioned to Summer with the bag of chips. "She looks like she may cry, and we don't want to undo that stellar makeup job."

"But condoms? It's only their first date."

Nat snorted. "I brought her condoms too."

The doorbell rang, followed by the puppy barks of Tink, Nat's five-month-old golden retriever.

"He's here!" Nat squealed.

"Alright, gorgeous, we're going to go downstairs so you can make your grand entrance and I can help Noah harass Todd about his intentions with *our* Summer." Jerome beamed. "Come on, ladies, let's go get a front row seat to watch Todd lose his mind."

"More like his heart." Carmen winked and then followed Jerome out the door.

"I think he already has," Nat cooed and walked out of the room and closed the door behind her.

With a deep breath, Summer scooped up the gifts from Elle and headed down. The teasing questions of her friends drifted up the spiral staircase to the second floor. Pausing on the landing, she listened to Noah's already husky baritone deepen as he asked, "Will you have her back by curfew?" and Todd's snarked reply calling Noah "Old Man Wilson."

The lighthearted banter coursed inside her. Happiness seemed to be her default emotion lately.

Taking the first step, she moved her way to the first floor. Until Todd came into view. He sat in an oversize armchair in the living room directly across from where Noah sat, Nat on his lap, and Jerome chomping on Doritos beside him on the couch. Annoyed laughter crinkled his face as their friends took turns harassing him. Carmen leaned on the chair's armrest; phone aimed to take pictures.

"I expect you to act like a gentleman," Noah drawled with a playful shade of warning in his voice. "No funny business."

"Was what I heard going on in the brewery office yesterday gentlemanly, Prince Char…" Todd's words faltered as his eyes met Summer's.

Warmth bloomed in her chest. Her lips tugged up in a big smile with each step closer to the first floor.

As he stood, an equally large smile stretched across Todd's face. A pale-blue sweater hugged his broad chest and his gray slacks molded over his muscular legs. Heat flashed in his green eyes as he swept his gaze over her, which caused her belly to clench.

He moved to the bottom of the steps, meeting her. "You're so pretty, sweetheart."

She'd been called beautiful, sexy, hot, and gorgeous before. From the age of fifteen until twenty-eight, they'd been common labels bestowed upon her. She'd never been called pretty. Maybe it was the sincerity that swam in his eyes.

Maybe it was the fact she'd never been called pretty before. Maybe it was just because it was Todd, who had somehow burrowed himself into her heart.

It's that and so much more.

"Thank you." She took his outstretched hand, and a tingle zinged along her skin.

Threading their fingers, he smirked. "I'm sorry."

"Why?"

"For being impatient." Banding his arms about her back, he pressed her in close and captured her mouth in a toe-curling kiss.

The gushes, hoots, and whistles of their friends broke their kiss.

"Dude, you're supposed to wait 'til the end of the date," Noah chided with a laugh.

"See." Carmen elbowed Jerome. "She didn't need the red lipstick."

"Yeah, but they may need the condoms," Jerome quipped.

After leaving Noah's, they linked their fingers, only letting go to get into the vehicle. As Todd steered his SUV along the thruway, he reached across the console to weave their hands together.

Whenever he needed to put his hand back on the wheel, he'd lift their joined hands and press a gentle kiss to her knuckles before letting go.

"Where are you taking me?" she asked as he steered to the exit for Hamburg.

They'd been in the car just about an hour. At first, she thought he was taking her to dinner in Buffalo, but they sped past that exit.

Mischief crinkled his eyes. "We're almost there and it's a surprise."

They pulled into the village of Hamburg. Like Perry, the small town outside of Buffalo had revitalized its downtown. Christmas lights twinkled in the windows of boutiques and cafes tucked into downtown's assortment of brick buildings. Wreaths strung with colorful lights hung from iron lamp posts lining the main street. An oversize pine tree radiated with lights and ornaments at the village's center.

Locating an empty spot along the village's main drag, they parked. Todd jumped out and jogged around to the passenger's side. Taking her hand again, he guided her down the snow-frosted sidewalk toward a white brick building.

"Did we drive an hour to go to a bookstore?" She arched an eyebrow, taking in the green shingle with *Merit Badge Books* in gold script. "You realize there is a bookstore in Perry, right?"

"Come on, smartass." He chuckled.

Once inside, cloves and cinnamon scents drifted in the air from carafes of hot cider positioned beside the register. A set of stairs led to a cozy seating area on the shops second floor. Pine bookshelves and small tables loaded with books filled the first floor. Summer's gaze was drawn to the heart-shaped sign pointing to two stacks solely dedicated to Romance. It was larger than the single shelf of romance novels at Cow Tales, Perry's bookstore.

"Oh, my goodness," she squealed, admiring the bookshelf dedicated to historical romance.

He pulled her away from the kaleidoscope of colorful book covers. "Not yet, that's not the surprise."

"But..." A slight pout covered her face as he moved them to the second floor where rows of chairs were set up.

"What are we..." Summer's breath caught at the sight of a large cardboard poster atop an easel at the start of the chairs that read *Elizabeth Lake Reading & Book Signing*. Eyes wide, she looked at him. It was one of her favorite historical romance authors. The very one who wrote the book he'd been reading, and they'd been discussing minutes before the couch incident.

Smirking, he nodded. "When planning this date, I googled 'historical romance-themed dates in Western New York' and came upon this event for one of your favorite authors."

She blinked. "You googled historical romance-themed dates?"

He rubbed the back of his head. "I know it's a little cheesy, but I wanted something special for you. Not just the standard dinner and a movie thing. Not that I don't want to do that with you. I want to do *all* the things with you. All the special and un-special things. I just wanted tonight to be different, because…it feels different with you." A boyish smile lit his face.

She shook her head. "I'm sorry," she said, brow creased.

His eyebrow cocked.

Closing the distance between them she wrapped her arms around the nape of his neck and lifted to her tiptoes. His smile was mere inches from hers. The minty freshness of his breath placed ghost kisses against her lips. With a large grin, she captured his mouth.

Nibbling her lower lip, he coaxed her open. The wet heat of his tongue glided across hers, deepening their kiss. His grip on her waist tightened, pulling her flush against him. The first embers of fire sparked in her belly and simmered in her bloodstream.

Slowing the kiss, Todd pulled only scant inches from her lips and grinned. "I was told we're supposed to kiss at the end of the date."

"You fingered me on your couch before we went on our first date, so clearly all the dating rules of etiquette have been ignored," she quipped.

"I'm going to enjoy breaking all the rules with you." He nuzzled his nose against hers.

CHAPTER FOURTEEN

"Coach Carr, step away from the underage girls!" ~Mean Girls

The gentle hum of pop music wafted through the small bistro located down the street from the bookstore. After they'd listened to Elizabeth Lake read the first chapter from her latest Regency romance, he'd taken her to dinner. Well, after he'd purchased three copies of the book; one signed for her to keep, one for her to read, and one for him to do a buddy read with her.

"I don't think a date has ever bought me books before," Summer mused as she ran her fingers over the smooth red linen tablecloth.

"I know it's not flowers." He almost looked apologetic. "But I did get the candles and dinner part right." Winking, he gestured to the flameless tealights in sea glass candleholders on the center of the table.

She scoffed and then offered a cheeky grin. "Who needs flowers."

He arched a brow.

"Just teasing." She reached across the table and took his hand. "You got so much right. It's perfect."

It really was. Other good, even great, dates littered her past. There'd been the time Shane, her high school boyfriend, had taken her on a romantic picnic – complete with a checkered blanket and wicker basket – at the base of the waterfalls in Letchworth Park. There'd been the time Max, early in their relationship, took her sailing on his family's yacht off Martha's Vineyard. She wouldn't pretend they weren't good but nothing those other men had planned compared to this one. Both had been sweet, but not her. At the time, Summer wasn't and still wasn't an "outdoors girl" and she got seasick. She'd just smiled and pretended it was romantic, because they expected that reaction.

This was none of that. The thought Todd put into tonight's date wasn't just about what would be considered romantic or date-worthy, but what was worthy of *her*. The sweetness of this man made her head swirl as if she'd guzzled the glass of Riesling in front of her rather than just taken two small sips.

"Although, I should have gotten a reservation at the fancy place down the street instead of taking you to a pizzeria." His face scrunched.

Her lips pursed. "First, it's an Italian bistro *and* pizzeria."

He smirked.

"Second, I love pizza and am excited to get something besides just cheese or sausage and mushrooms."

"Why just those toppings?" His thumb skated across her hand.

"Liam only likes cheese. My parents like sausage and mushrooms."

"What do you like?"

"Ham and pineapple."

Mock horror filled his features. "And here I thought you were perfect."

She kicked his shin. "Don't be Judge Judy about this, Mr. Drizzles Honey On Pizza."

"It's delicious." His mouth curled with playfulness. "I hadn't realized you were paying attention to my pizza eating habits."

She bit her lip. "Not like that. I'm not a stalker."

"Says the woman I caught outside my window last night."

She kicked him again.

He pretend-winced.

"You've just mentioned it a few times that you make homemade pizza with spicy sausage and honey drizzle."

"I make excellent pizza." He leaned back against the plush, leather booth.

"Perhaps, I'll let you make it for me sometime." She batted her eyes.

"Monday."

She arched an eyebrow. "What about Monday?"

"Let me make you dinner Monday. It can be our second date or…"

"We haven't even finished our first date," she giggled.

"What happened to breaking all the rules with me?"

Would her belly ever cease flipping because of this man? Just when she thought she was acclimated to being with him, he'd say or do something that made dopey giddiness flutter inside her like a crush-drunk teenager.

Her head tilted. "What was the 'or' about? The 'second date or' that you started to say?"

"Well, if you don't want it to be a second date, then maybe it can just be a friendly dinner with Liam, you, and me." He stopped, seeming to consider his words. "I know we're not telling him we're dating yet, but I thought it might be a good idea to do things together just the three of us. I want to give us a real shot and that means Liam getting comfortable with the idea of me being part of your lives *and* you being comfortable with it. That means the three of us spending time together."

Still holding his hand, she leaned back.

This was the complicated bit. It wasn't just her life which would be impacted by a relationship with Todd, but her son's. She had no fear about Liam spending time with Todd. Since becoming reacquainted with him at Elle's Uncle Pete's fiftieth birthday last summer, this wonderful man had been a fixture in their life. Especially after she'd planned the brewery's grand opening in May. Over the last seven months, their casual hellos and chats had bloomed into a friendship that included many interactions between Todd and Liam. There'd been planned and unplanned playdates at the park, reading together at the library, dinners, and parties.

The fear she felt stemmed from the change of having a fifth person added into the little foursome that was her, her parents, and Liam. Would Liam embrace Todd in this new capacity? And if he did, what would happen if Todd was no longer in that role?

It's not just my heart at risk.

Her eyes drifted around the room, dropping on a little boy giggling with a man. His sweet face lit with laughter as the man talked to him. The memory of Liam's brown eyes shimmering with excitement while Todd helped him draft the script for his presentation about dogs flashed in her mind's eye. The same excitement was mirrored in Todd's green eyes, his neat penmanship scripting the words Liam should say in his notebook. The memory twisted and turned within her.

"Hey." The low timbre of Todd's voice pulled her attention back to him. "No pressure. When you're ready, or when you think Liam is ready, I'm ready." His nose crinkled. "Perhaps, I need a thesaurus. That's a lot of use of the word ready."

Amusement lifted her lips.

Appearing in front of them, the server drawled, "Are you folks ready to order food?"

"Ready?" Todd's left eyebrow ticked up, punctuating the playfully wry grin sweeping across his face.

God, what was it about that left eyebrow that ignited her nerve endings? Some women were done-in by corded forearms. Some by chiseled jawlines. Some by tight butts in fitted jeans. That eyebrow of his underscored by that scar featured in her fantasies each night.

"I'm ready," she said, laughter coating her words.

"We'll have the Hawaiian pizza and antipasto salad to share." Smirking, he tipped his head to Summer. "Anything else, sweetheart?"

Summer bit back the blooming smile. "Nope."

The server nodded then walked away.

"I thought you didn't like ham and pineapple."

"I never said I didn't like it. I just question the validity of its existence."

She vibrated with laughter.

"However, someone reminded me that men in honey houses shouldn't throw shade. I've never actually had ham and pineapple on my pizza. Since you're finally giving me a chance, I can give ham and pineapple a chance."

She raised her glass. "Here's to taking chances."

"Taking chances"—he clinked his glass of red wine against hers— "and breaking all the rules."

Warmth coursed through her bloodstream. She could blame the wine but knew it was a hundred percent the Todd effect. Even before she'd opened herself to the possibility of something with him, he'd had this impact on her. Nat had seen it long before Summer allowed herself to even glance his way. For months, her best friend teased and pushed her to admit to the growing crush she had on him. Her parents soon jumped on that bandwagon. Even Liam had asked Todd to be his mom's boyfriend.

"You got quiet." His eyes captured her gaze. "What are you thinking?"

She thought about lying. About shrugging and saying she was lost in her to-do list for tomorrow's Christmas Market. But she'd held so much of herself back with him. The inclination to keep her thoughts tucked inside was smashed by the pull to open herself more to him.

"Just how everyone else saw this"—she motioned between them— "before I was willing to admit what was between us. Even Liam."

"He's a smart kid."

"I love how good you are with him. How all you guys are. Even though Max wasn't the father I wanted for Liam, I worry that I took that from him. You know the father/son relationship." She let out a long breath. "I know he has my dad, but he's not *his* dad."

"The father/son relationship isn't all that it's cracked up to be." An iciness chilled his voice.

Summer reached across the table, linking their hands. "I'm the last person to force anyone to talk about the things they don't want to talk about, but if you want to—" she squeezed his hand— "I want to listen."

He raised their joined fingers to his lips, pressing a tender kiss to her knuckles. "I know, sweetheart."

He didn't need to say it. Nodding, she changed the subject. Everyone needed to walk their own path of unveiling themselves. Dad always said people were croissants to be enjoyed one layer at a time. There was more to Todd than his snarky, carefree, flirty layer. Just as there was more to her than the standoffish, guarded veneer.

We'll peel back each other's truths one layer at a time. She held his hand just a little tighter.

The bistro crowd thinned. Only two other customers remained among the red linen-covered tables. Light pop music from hidden speakers danced through the room. Three slices of Hawaiian pizza and an empty salad bowl sat between them. Their glasses of wine had been replaced with a diet cola for her and ginger ale for him. Effortless conversation flowed. Despite the occasional butterflies and heated cheeks, contented easiness sighed along her limbs.

"I'll admit," he said, wiping the corners of his mouth with the red cloth napkin. "I'm glad I gave ham and pineapple a chance."

"See! You should always listen to me," she boasted, unwrapping one of the handwipes from the table and cleaning her hands.

A throaty laugh rumbled from him; the sound sending a giddy zing through her.

Summer leaned back against the plush booth, allowing the happiness thrumming inside her to soak in. The first bars of Forest Blakk's "Fall into Me" filled the room.

"Oh, I love this song," she gushed.

Mirth sparkled in his eyes. "Dance with me." He stood and held out his hand.

Looking around, she opened her mouth to protest but stopped herself. The Summer of the past wouldn't have done this. She'd be embarrassed or concerned about what others would think. She'd be scared about what this meant.

I'm not her anymore. I'm me. Taking his hand, she allowed him to guide her into his arms. In the flickering light of the flameless candles, they swayed to Forest Blakk's caramel-smooth voice. On full display to the smiling gazes of the elderly couple at the other table and the teenager sweeping the floor, she leaned into him and this moment.

"I'm glad I gave you a chance." She pressed into his warm embrace.

Mouth inches from her ear, he whispered, "See. You should always listen to me."

A soft giggle left her lips. "You silly man." She closed her eyes and rested her head on his shoulder as they danced. "Thank you for giving *me* a chance."

The SUV slowed to a stop in front of Summer's house. Her car, which had been returned by Nat and Noah earlier in the night, took the last spot in the driveway. Instead of letting the vehicle idle, Todd shut it off. The boxed-up leftover pizza and her books sat in his backseat.

"Thank you for tonight." She knew she should say goodnight and slip out. It was late. She had to meet Carmen by eight a.m. to set up for the Christmas Market. Logic pushed her to get out of the car but, like an obstinate child, every cell in her body refused to move. "I had a really good time."

Moonlight and the rainbow of Christmas lights wrapped around the front porch illuminated his handsome face. Outside of her house, darkness engulfed the sleepy neighborhood. No doubt, her parents had left the lights on for her.

Laughter fell out of her.

He quirked that sexy left eyebrow. "What?"

"I'm thirty-seven-years-old and my parents left the front porch light on for me like I'm a teenager." She leaned her head back against the headrest. "I really do need to move out."

"Do you think about that? About Liam and you moving out?"

"Sometimes." She sighed. "Between what I make at the café and from event planning, I could afford a two-bedroom apartment. But..." The words ceased as she looked at the house.

He sat quietly, waiting for her to go on.

"Whenever the topic has come up, I say it's because of Liam. Part of that is true. I feel guilty that I've already taken so much from him. I don't want to take *them* from him."

He reached across the console and folded her hands in his. "I don't know Max, but I know you. If you felt it was a greater risk for him to be part of Liam's life than for Liam to not know him then I trust your decision. You're a fiercely protective mom. Sweetheart, you've taken nothing from Liam. You've given him everything. And if that isn't enough, you've filled his life with your parents and a team of adults that has his back…and yours."

Squeezing his hand, she swallowed the hard lump in her throat. "Thank you."

"You said Liam is the reason you tell people why you don't want to move out but what's the real reason?"

"It's me. When I left for New York, I pushed them away. Especially when I was seeing Max. I didn't really talk to them or see them for three years until I showed up pregnant. I feel guilty about that but that's not why I stay. I'm safe with them. No matter who I was in my past and what I did, they've never stopped loving me."

"I don't think moving out will stop them from loving you." A warm smile curved his lips.

"I know." She returned his smile. "I'm still conflicted. I love living with them but at moments like this I wish I didn't."

Flirtation sparked in his expression. "A moment like this?"

"One where I'm in a vehicle after a very perfect first date waiting for my date to make his move." She blinked, then blinked again.

He turned his gaze to the front porch and then back to her. "You don't think they're looking out the window at us, do you?"

"Why? Are you scared they'll see you try to make a move?"

"I like your dad, but he was the only teacher in high school who scared me. I swear he'd laugh maniacally as he pushed boards through the table saw in the woodshop. I couldn't watch *Dexter* without thinking of your dad."

"So, you're *not* going to make a move then?" She arched an eyebrow.

"I didn't say that." His voice was a low rumble.

"Then make your move." The request was breathy.

With a playfully wicked smile, he leaned over the console and pulled her in close. Lips inches from hers, his hot breath teased her. "It's you're move," he rasped.

"Tease," she purred, taking his mouth. The deep kiss was devouring, as if she was a woman starved. As if each kiss with him prior to this had been small nibbles unable to quell the hunger that coursed in her for him. Without breaking the seal between their lips, she crawled into his lap.

"Why hello there," he said with a flirty lilt as she straddled him.

"Hello to you."

Smiling, they stared at each other for a beat. Their panting breaths fogged the windows. His fingers wove into her loose tendrils. He brought her mouth to his in a slow, tantalizing kiss. Opening to him, his tongue found hers in a languid dance. Heat tiptoed up her spine as his hands glided down her body.

"I need to get my own place," she whined.

His hands gripped her ass, making her squeal. "Why Summer Michaels! Did you want to invite me in for a very adult sleepover?"

"Yes." She rubbed herself against him, enjoying the feel of his growing arousal beneath her heated core. "Complete with sexy jammies, pillow fights, and practice kissing."

"*Mm hm.*" His lips kissed along her jawline. "No sexy jammies required for the games I have in mind for our sleepover."

Her core clenched.

His hands tightened on her rear and he pressed her harder against his erection.

A loud gasp escaped her lips at the friction sending a

delicious tingle between her legs. As if she was his last meal, his mouth almost devoured hers. Grinding against him, her internal thermostat inched higher. The friction from his hardness hit her just in the right spot. Pressure built. His lips coasted up the column of her throat and along her jawline.

"Take what you want, sweetheart," he murmured, his hands urged her to move against him. "This is just a teaser."

The pressure coiled tighter and tighter until…

"Oh!" She whimpered with release.

"Oh, sweetheart." He placed a gentle kiss on the center of her forehead.

"So much for taking it slow." She breathed. "What is wrong with me? I've literally crawled onto your lap and thrown myself at you *twice* in the last twenty-four hours."

"I'm not complaining." He brushed her hair behind her ears. "I could get use to giving you nightly orgasms. In fact, what are you doing this time tomorrow?"

She swatted his chest. "Perv."

"Says the woman who is straddling *my* lap."

A loud knock on the window startled them. Jerking, both their heads turned to the fogged image of a man knocking on the driver's side window. Not a man but…

"Mr. Michaels." It was almost a gulp coming out of Todd as he rolled down the window.

Crossing his arms over his broad chest, one thick eyebrow cocked. "I see from the way my daughter is straddling you that the date went well."

Summer's jaw slackened.

Todd swallowed hard. "Yes."

Dad's gaze jumped between Summer and Todd. "Son, how'd you like a tour of my woodshop? I can show you my woodchopper."

"Dad!"

"Brian, I told you to leave them alone," Mom bellowed,

standing on the front porch wrapped in a fluffy red robe. "I'd like more grandchildren."

"Mom!" Summer's eyes widened.

"I'd prefer they're *not* conceived in a vehicle parked in front of the house," he shouted back.

"I need to move out," she groaned, and hid her flaming face against Todd's chest.

CHAPTER FIFTEEN

"Your face smells like peppermint." ~Mean Girls

The aroma of honey-glazed nuts danced in the late afternoon air. Vendor tents adorned with lit garlands filled main street. Shoppers with large tote bags embossed with *Christmas in Perry-dise* ambled along the downtown streets. Music waltzed around the event thanks to the busker wearing a Santa hat. It was all something out of a sappy holiday movie.

Pride bloomed in Summer's chest. This year they'd expanded the size of the annual holiday event. Nearly a hundred artisans had taken over downtown. Each business offered holiday-themed treats, activities, and wares. A puppet show version of *A Christmas Carol* and *How the Grinch Stole Christmas* was performed throughout the day at the art council. The Wine Down offered mulled wine. The brewery had special six-packs of their holiday brews. Even Cassie's Café had a curbside stand selling Zach's famous pumpkin chili made with his secret ingredient, Todd's pumpkin ale.

Consulting her iPad, Summer marked off, *Check on Vendors* from her to-do list. Throughout today, she and Carmen agreed to take turns checking in with vendors, volunteers, and the parade of musicians performing at various spots across downtown.

"I can't believe I pulled this off," she whispered as satisfaction washed over her.

The doubting Thomases had been in full force when she and Carmen proposed expanding the event from a mere dozen vendors at the local high school to a large outdoor market in downtown. The village board worried an outdoor event in the unpredictable December weather of Western New York wouldn't work. *What if it sleets? Would anyone want to come to Perry to shop for Christmas? Where will they park? What about ice?* Each reason to say no, she and Carmen twisted to a yes.

Slipping her tablet into her tote, she moved through the market toward the main staff tent. Her eyes caught on the bakery's front window. Adults and children huddled around old fashioned farm style tables, piping bags filled with colorful frosting and an array of sprinkles between them, ready for cookie decorating.

Liam sat beside a dimple-cheeked, copper-haired little boy. His forehead wrinkled in concentration. Her dad stood behind him talking to Noah and munching on a cookie. Beside Liam, Todd grinned as he said something to him. A big smile erupted on Liam's face as he held up his decorated gingerbread masterpiece to show Todd.

Summer's hand rested on her heart, letting all the feels in her chest bloom.

"He's so good with him." Nat's singsong voice snagged Summer's attention.

"You should wear a bell," she muttered, turning to face her friend.

A sassy grin on her face, Nat shook her arms jangling the bell charm bracelets on her wrists. "I am!"

"You're too much."

Slipping her arm through Summer's she cooed, "I think I'm just the *right* amount." She turned them to face the bakery. "Look at our very sexy men surrounded by a gaggle of children. Don't tell my mother, but I think my ovaries may combust." She pointed at Noah, who for some unknown reason was being tackled by three younger boys, while Todd appeared to cheer them on.

Summer smirked. "The bar is *so* low for men. I highly doubt if we were the ones in there that Todd and Noah's male version of ovaries would be combusting."

"First, they're called testicles," Nat deadpanned.

Summer's nose scrunched. "Ugh, this is why you're the doctor."

Nat bumped Summer's hip. "Second, Noah would be very turned on by that. I think he'd happily put a baby in me at any moment."

"Have you two been talking more about it?"

"Yes… I know he's my forever person, but"—Nat worried her lip— "is it too soon? We've only been together since August, and we just moved in together."

"At that rate, it's a wonder you're not married and knocked up already," she quipped.

"Hardy har har," Nat scoffed.

Summer squeezed Nat's arm. "Seriously, though. Take the relationship at your pace. If you want that man to put a baby in you and he's game, go for it. If you want to wait and he's supportive, then wait. All that matters is that Noah and you are on the same page. Everyone has to do things at their speed. Even if it is at the speed of sound."

"Thanks." Nat's lips tugged up with mischief. "You didn't correct me when I said *our* men. So, Todd is your man?"

"Yes." The casual utterance sounded almost the way a child's would if his hand was caught in the cookie jar.

Although, he's been the one with his hand in my cookie jar. Her face burned so hot, she was certain the memory may be visible in her heated features.

"Yay!" Nat squealed. "You must tell me everything about the date. How was it?"

Flicking her gaze between the bakery where Todd now led a team of children, including Liam, in body slamming Noah, and back to Nat, she sighed happily. "Amazing. He took me to a bookstore to see Elizabeth Lake read from her new novel and bought me one book to get it signed and another to read."

"*Swoon!*"

A goofy grin anchored her lips. "He bought a copy for himself, so we can do a buddy-read."

Nat slapped her hands on her chest. "It's like how Noah is doing a buddy-watch of *Gilmore Girls* with me, and Tobey's taking salsa dancing classes with Jerome. These men of ours. What do they put in the water in Perry?"

Their small friend group really did have a gaggle of ridiculously sweet men, who adored their partners. Carmen's husband, Mathew, doted on his wife. He'd show up to drop off her favorite hazelnut latte when they'd had late night planning sessions for village events. Clayton sent Elle flowers every Friday. There'd even been a picture of her on social media with a bouquet of carnations while she and Clayton wandered through Portobello Road Market in London. The ladies and Jerome were equally sweet to their men.

My man? That thought swirled inside Summer. Since August, she and Todd had been the only single ones in their little group. It was strange to count herself among the taken ones, especially since they'd only been on one date. Was she taken? This was all so new, a little overwhelming, and a lot exciting.

"I can honestly say it was the best date of my life," she admitted.

She'd barely slept last night as she relived each moment

of the date with him. The feel of his fingers threaded in hers. The musicality of his laugh. The effortless conversation. The press of his lips against hers. It was perfect and it was terrifying. It had been years since she'd allowed herself to get lost in not just the idea of someone else but the idea of being an *us*.

"OMG! Will there be a second date?"

"Well…" she drew out the word.

Brows knitted together Nat turned to Summer. "Please, tell me you're not going skittish rabbit on him, already?"

"Nothing like that." Her lips pursed. "Also, thanks for the unwavering support, bestie."

"Sometimes being a good bestie is telling your friend when they are allowing their past to dictate too much of their now and steal away the hope of the future."

"Wow," she gaped. "I thought I was the no-nonsense one?"

Waving her free hand, Nat made a *pfft* sound with her mouth.

"Anyway, I'm not running scared. Although, I am scared." That, she could admit to herself and to her friend. "I want a second date. I'd like more than that."

"Then what's the problem?"

"He's offered to cook for me Monday."

"That monster!" Nat exclaimed with mock-horror.

"Smartass." She rolled her eyes. "He gave me the option of it being our second date or, if I wanted, I could bring Liam."

"Like a family date?" Nat gushed; her eyes wide.

That was exactly the concern. For Summer, this blossoming relationship with Todd wasn't like Nat and Noah. There was no discussion of potential future children because there was an actual child in the mix.

"It's not just us becoming a couple. That's part of it, but it's also about becoming a…"

"Family," Nat filled in the word that lingered in Summer's throat.

"I mean, it's too soon to even think, right? We just started dating, but I'm a package deal. I can't just think about me. I have to think of my son."

Tipping her head towards the bakery, Nat elbowed Summer.

A cheering Liam sat on Todd's shoulders. Her little boy raised a belt over his head like a *WWE* wrestler. Big smiles beamed from both their faces. The two were completely at ease with one another. For any outsider, they looked the part of father and son.

Nat leaned her head against Summer's shoulder. "Someone wise once told me relationships go at their own pace. I think that stands true for friends, couples, and families."

"I hate you when you use my own advice against me," she grumbled, pressing in a little closer.

"You *love* me."

She let out a loud sigh. "I do."

Tents had been lowered and tables were folded away. The last of the vendors packed up their remaining stock. Volunteers roamed the now-deserted downtown, cleaning up discarded trash. Most businesses were closed for the night except for the brewery and the wine bar.

"Why don't you head to the Wine Down. I'll finish up," Summer offered, watching Carmen rub her hands together in the frosty night air.

The Wine Down would remain open for a private event for the Christmas Market volunteers. As president of the small business association for the county, Noah offered to sponsor free food and drink for all volunteers. Just a small thank you for their work. Besides the cheese boards the wine bar offered, they had food delivered from Daryl's, the village's local pizzeria, and several platters of cookies from the bakery.

"Are you sure?" Carmen looked around the disappearing market.

"I got you, Madam Mayor." She winked. "You deserve a break."

Carmen opened her mouth to protest.

But Summer raised her hand. "Nope. Go get warm. Plus, the volunteers need to be greeted by our fearless leader."

"We're a team. None of this would have happened without you."

Despite the nip in the cold breeze, warmth cascaded across Summer's limbs. It was strange to think that she and Carmen Herrera-Fischer were a team. In high school, Summer had teased Carmen, whose fashion was more European chic and less Abercrombie & Fitch which had been favored by the more popular girls. Somehow, Carmen was able to forgive and see Summer for who she'd become rather than who she'd been. Over the last year, the two women had formed not just a strong working relationship, but a close friendship.

"Listen. Modest Melly, scoot." She gestured toward the wine bar.

Carmen placed her hands on her hips. "Only if you admit that you are just as responsible for this. I couldn't have done any of this without you."

"Like you said; we're a team."

Wrapping her arms around Summer, Carmen tucked her in close. "We're badass bitches."

She snorted. "Did you swear?"

"I blame Elle, she swears like a sailor." Grinning, Carmen pulled away. "I'll see you in there. We need to celebrate *our* victory."

"You got it."

As Carmen walked away, Summer wandered along the street, helping vendors load boxes into their trailers and trucks. The last of the vendors loaded, she checked on volunteers and relieved them for the night.

Sucking in the wintry air, she took in the scene. The once bustling downtown had transformed back to its standard sleepiness for a Saturday after ten p.m. It was a few days before the solstice and exactly seven days away from Christmas. The lingering scent of glazed nuts, the twinkling Christmas lights, and the radiant glow of people celebrating made this moment perfect.

"Done," she whispered and checked off the last item on her to-do list.

Looking up, her eyes wandered toward the now closed bakery. The glow of white Christmas lights encircling the front window lit the quiet bakery. Just a few hours earlier she'd watched Todd and Liam together through that big window. Like it was a television show of a potential future of her, her little boy, and Todd.

Could we have that? The question taunted her with a promise of a future ready for her to reach out and grab if only she would.

"Summer Michaels!" An almost shrill voice interrupted her thoughts.

Turning, she saw a barely five-foot tall brunette striding toward her. "Janet."

"You were supposed to come talk to me about that class I'm taking. I saw you walk past the florist shop three times this week, but *you* didn't stop in. Your dad and I chatted about it today when I saw him at the bakery." She propped her hands on her hips.

Crap. She'd completely forgot about telling her parents that she'd speak with Janet about the marketing class at GCC.

"I'm so sorry, Janet. I..." Should she tell the truth or lie?

Janet's face softened with a warm smile. "You were busy

with this shindig and"—she leaned in, as if telling a secret—"and going on a date with Todd Kruger."

Small towns. A furrow notched her brow.

"Pish-posh," Janet said with a dismissive wave of her hand. "There's very little that happens in Perry that I don't know about."

"I'm sorry. I'll come in this week."

"You best." She wagged a finger at her. "You're such a smart girl. This market was huge for the village. I think you'd get a lot out of the class, but more importantly, I think you'd have so much to offer the class."

Janet's compliment nearly stole Summer's breath. When both her parents spoke to her about taking classes, it was all about what Summer would get out of it. How it would help her live up to her potential. Janet made it sound less about Summer being deficient and more like her having everything to give.

"Plus, we could be study buddies." A wide grin lit Janet's face.

"Thanks." She swallowed the lump that had formed in her throat. "I'll stop by this week."

"I'll be at the shop every day but Monday. Clayton and Elle fly back in early Monday morning. Pete and I will be picking them up."

"Okay." She nodded. "Are you coming to the Wine Down?"

"Threaten me with a glass of wine…yes please." Janet took Summer's arm and shuffled to the wine bar's front door.

Walking into the bar, heat caressed Summer's cheeks. Laughter and chatter filled the large open room. After a quick hug Janet strolled to her husband, Pete, who leaned against the bar talking to Carmen and Mathew. Summer scanned the room, but didn't spy Todd. Likely he was at the brewery. It was the only other business, outside of the VFW, open past ten on a Saturday night.

Making eye contact with Nat, who worked the bar with Noah, she mouthed *Todd?*

Nat's eyes sparked with delight, and she mouthed *His laboratory.*

Nodding, she pivoted and walked out. Nat would explain to Carmen, who would understand. In this moment of victory, Summer wanted Todd there. Like a magnet drawn to its other half, she walked down the street and ducked inside the brewery. With a quick wave to Laney, who sat extra close to Ana Singh at a table in the corner, she moved through the room and down the back hall that led to the basement.

The wood door creaked as she eased it open and started down the stairs. Shutting it behind her, she descended the narrow stairs. When the guys first bought this place, it had a cement basement typical of the mid-Nineteenth century buildings that lined the downtown streets. Reaching the bottom step, she came to the renovated space. The basement was split into two sections. A large open space with barrels and kegs where they stored and brewed. Shelves filled with cans and bottles of beer and cider covered exposed brick walls. On the right, there was a small office with a yellow door. That's where Todd created his recipes. She'd called it his laboratory since he'd first shown her it while planning the grand opening.

"Hey." Entering the office, she shucked her coat off.

Todd sat at his desk hunched over a computer. A stack of papers beside him. He looked up and joy glinted in his gaze. "Hey, sweetheart."

She hung her coat on the hook by the door and turned to him. "I didn't see you at the Wine Down." She crossed the room.

He swiveled his chair, flirtation playing on his lips. "Miss me already?"

"*Maybe,*" she said, wiggling her hips.

He reached out and pulled her onto his lap. "Well, I missed you."

"We'll break your chair."

He pressed tickling kisses to her neck. "I'll get a new chair." He nuzzled into her hair. "God, you always smell so good."

With a breathy giggle she melted into his body. His firm chest pressed against her back and arms cocooned her in a sense of safety, acceptance, and a word she'd not let herself think. It was too soon for even a glimmer of that word. She knew that, and so did the skittish rabbit that Nat accused her of being.

Moving her gaze to the desk, her eyes focused on the stack of papers. On the top sheet an image of a beer bottle with the words *Summer breeze* over a small field of strawberry plants. She picked up the illustration. "What's this?"

"The bottle design for our summer brew."

Her eyebrows knitted. "Shouldn't breeze be capitalized?"

"No. You only capitalize proper names."

"But summer is… Todd." Her eyes wide.

He shifted in his seat, resting his chin in the crook of her neck. "It's named for you."

"This is the beer you mentioned at the wedding. The one that tastes like strawberries and cream."

He'd said she always smelled like strawberries and cream. Realization washed over her. He'd been working on this long before their first dance at the wedding, the couch incident, or last night. Each brew at the Farmer's Ale was named after something or someone important to Todd and Noah. She knew Todd was working on a special cider for Valentine's Day that Noah wanted to be inspired by Nat.

"I've never pretended to be cool about how I feel about you," he murmured.

Setting the paper down, she nodded. "Naming a beer after me is a big deal in your world."

"Sweetheart, I'm all in. This isn't just a casual fling for me. I want a future with you. I won't pretend otherwise."

Her heart stuttered. "A future? What happened to taking it slow?"

"I said I want a future with you. I didn't say it needed to happen now. I'm okay with going slow...as long as we're going somewhere."

A small smile curved her lips. "Does that future still include you making homemade pizza on Monday?"

"Of course."

"Great." She twisted her head and met his stare. "What time should Liam and I be there?"

CHAPTER SIXTEEN

"Calling someone fat doesn't make you any skinnier. Calling someone stupid doesn't make you any smarter. And ruining Regina George's life definitely didn't make me any happier." ~Mean Girls

"Mom!" Liam's shout skipped up the stairs. "I'm ready."

Shaking her head, she descended to the first floor. "Mr. Impatient."

Snow had blanketed the village overnight, making it perfect for Sunday afternoon sledding behind the high school. The three giant hills that made up the soccer, baseball, and softball fields had been the number one winter hot spot for the village's kids since Summer's parents were little. Winter weekends—the only time children voluntarily went to school—featured sled-dragging kids trudging up each hill. The bravest started at the top with the goal of getting enough momentum to coast down all three hills, reaching the bottom without stopping or tumbling off. As little girls, she and Elle had stayed out sledding until their noses burned from the whipping cold wind, it was always the best way to spend a wintry day.

After being tied up with work and the date with Todd, Summer thought both she and Liam deserved the treat of an afternoon of play together. It was important to her to spend as much time with him as possible. While she understood it was necessary to have her own life—something her mother and father stressed—guilt still nibbled when she was gone more than normal. She'd missed three bedtimes this week and that didn't sit right with her.

"No gloves," she said, reaching the bottom step.

"They're in my pocket," he grumbled and yanked them out of his pocket to put on.

Grabbing her jacket from the hook by the door, she tugged it on. "Are we forgetting anything?"

His face wrinkled. "Nope."

"Are you sure?" She arched an eyebrow.

"My tube!" he exclaimed. "Pop! Where's my tube?"

"Garage." Dad's deep voice floated in from the kitchen.

Placing a thermos of hot chocolate and several disposable cups into an oversized tote bag, Summer met Liam in front of the garage. The house was just a few streets down from the high school allowing them to walk to meet Henry, Pelavi, Felicia, and their kiddos. LaToya was working at the nursing home so she'd miss the playdate.

Snow crunched beneath her boots, punctuating the quiet between them or, perhaps, it just felt like that because she wanted to talk to Liam about dinner with Todd on Monday. Why was it scarier to tell her son about dating Todd then actually dating him? Did she want to tell him they were dating or just that they would be having dinner with a friend. This wasn't unusual. There'd been many dinners at her friends' places over the last year.

Although, this isn't a friendly dinner, she reminded herself. It wouldn't be like veggie chili Sundays at Noah and Nat's, or a BBQ at Clayton and Elle's. It wasn't just pizza but a dress rehearsal for what could be if the future that Todd spoke of happened.

"Baby, what do you think about Todd?" she blurted.

"He's cool." Liam stopped, looked both ways, and took her hand before they crossed the street in front of the high school.

He teetered between becoming a little man and still being her little boy. Over the last year he'd started asserting his independence and pulling his hand away when they walked, but still took it each time they crossed the street. Liam said it was because her dad told him gentlemen take ladies' hands when crossing streets, but Summer hoped it was because he was still the little boy who wanted his mom when doing things still a little scary.

"You like him?" She squeezed his hand.

Nose crinkled; he looked at her. "Yeah. Why?"

"Well…" she clucked her tongue "He's invited us for dinner Monday. He's going to make homemade pizza." God, she was a chickenshit. Why did telling Liam about the potential of her and Todd scare her? She knew he adored Todd.

"Will Sheba be there?"

"Since she lives at Todd's house I'd imagine so."

"Cool," he said, dropping her hand once they reached the sidewalk in front of the high school.

She could see the frowny face emoji flash across her heart when he released her hand. It was the perils of parenting. Her mother teased her about this. Moments like this she regretted every "God, I'm not a child" retort she'd thrown at her parents from the age of twelve until…probably now.

I'm going to hug my mother and father when I get home.

"I can practice my sign language with Sheba," he announced as he trotted down the snow-covered sidewalk.

"Your what?" Confusion lined her face.

"Nat and Todd are teaching me to sign," he explained,

pulling the tube around the orange brick building toward the trio of hills.

Summer knew that both Nat and Todd knew how to sign. Nat learned American Sign Language in undergrad and used it with patients. Todd's grandmother, Mrs. Rice, who passed several years back, had been deaf so he'd grown up signing. When he'd adopted Sheba, who was also deaf, he used various signs and touches for her commands.

"You didn't tell me you were learning ASL," she said, a little pang of sadness in her chest.

Had it already begun? Was he already having a whole life without her? He was learning a new language and hadn't mentioned it.

He shrugged. "It's not a big deal. I just started learning a few weeks ago."

"Why did you want to learn?"

"My new friend knows it and if I learn, then I can talk to him. Also, it's cool."

"New friend?"

"JJ. He moved here a few weeks ago."

JJ? *Amy's son?* Realization zinged through her. The image of the copper-haired boy who'd sat beside him at the bakery flashed in her vision. "Baby, was JJ decorating cookies with you yesterday?"

"Yeah. He's cool, even if he likes the Patriots."

"The Patriots?" She guffawed. "What would Pop think of you hangin' with a New England fan?"

"Pop shouldn't discriminate."

"Agreed." Happy pride curled her mouth. "I'm glad you have a new friend."

She only hoped her relationship with Amy wouldn't impact this. Liam had struggled to find his place in school. He was bright but challenged in social interactions, making it difficult for him to make friends. She also worried that some of the parents who had known Summer all too well in high school had left Liam off birthday invites because of her.

Reaching the base of the hill, they spotted Pelavi, who stood shooting a video on her phone of Henry and their little girl, Nisha, sliding down the smallest hill, which they'd dubbed the bunny slope. Felicia knelt to the side, building a snowman with her son, Davey.

"Liam!" Davey jumped up and bounded to Liam.

Both Nisha and Davey were four years younger than Liam. Despite getting to the age of being too big for some of their games, he always indulged them. His tender heart was her biggest source of pride as a mother.

"I brought hot chocolate." Summer hoisted her bag up.

"You're a goddess! Please tell me it's made with real milk," Pelavi hooted.

"I see the veganism didn't last," she teased.

Hot chocolate was sipped between each adult racing down the bunny slope with the kids until Nisha and Davey lost interest. Their focus fixed on the construction of an army of snow people in-between tossing snowballs at Henry after his wife urged them to "get him!"

"JJ!" Liam grinned, signing as a little boy in a blue Columbia jacket and Patriots knit hat ran over to him.

A big smile swept across JJ's rosy face. He looked exactly like his mom with a pair of icy blue eyes. Signing something he tipped his head toward the larger hill.

"Mom," Liam twisted towards her. "Can I go sledding with JJ on the bigger hills?"

She nodded. "Sure. Just make sure you stay where I can see you."

Grinning, he grabbed his tube and ran up the hill with JJ.

"Is that Amy's son?" Felicia sipped her hot chocolate.

"I think so," Summer offered.

"It must be, because there's Amy." Pelavi gestured and

waved toward a group of three other women standing on the other side of the field. "Looks like she's with the *cool* moms."

Just like in high school with their cliques, the parents functioned in the same way. There were several factions of parent groups. Amy seemed to have fallen in with the cool moms. Women married to well-to-do spouses who showed up at school events with designer bags. The common thread binding the cool moms, besides their bank accounts, was that they didn't like Summer. This was due mainly because of their ringleader, Erica, the new queen bee and Summer's former high school frenemy. The old friend/rival had been the first to whisper behind Summer's back. Each time she came into Cassie's Café she'd ask with a serpentine smile how Summer was holding up as a *single* mom.

"It can be hard moving back. I'm glad she's made friends." Summer's gaze caught on Amy sitting quietly among the group of clucking women.

"I prefer the uncool moms' club," Felicia teased, hip-checking Pelavi and then Summer.

"I beg to differ. We're the *hot* moms club," Pelavi tossed her long dark hair over her shoulder.

All three women laughed.

"Speaking of hot; did my eyes deceive me last night or did I see you walking hand-in-hand with Todd Kruger outside the brewery?" A coy expression covered Felicia's face.

"This town," she groaned.

"Todd Krueger!" Pelavi squealed.

"You ladies okay?" Henry popped his head up from the snowman he was making.

"Girl talk." Pelavi waved her hands dismissively.

His face scrunched. "Seriously, we need another man in this group."

"Oh, don't worry. Summer is working on that," she crooned.

"I approve!" He saluted. "Carry on, ladies."

Heat flamed in Summer's cheeks.

"So, I take it from the blush on your cheeks that you've exited the friend zone with the village's sexy Prince Harry look-a-like." Speculation sparked in Pelavi's brown eyes.

"We are seeing each other," she offered, each word uttered carefully.

"Is he a good kisser?"

Summer sipped her hot chocolate, not answering.

"I knew it!" Pelavi fanned herself.

"Have you two went on a date, yet? We need details!" Happy crinkles kissed the edges of Felicia's eyes.

Blushing, Summer gave them some details leaving out the sexier bits. Well, maybe not all the sexy bits. Pelavi was like a dog with a bone about getting the juicy details.

"He's making you and Liam dinner? Adorable!" Felicia pressed her hand to her chest.

"A man who can cook is a keeper!" Pelavi's gaze jumped to her husband who lay on the ground making snow angels with Davey and Nisha.

"Have you told Liam that you two are dating?" Felicia asked.

Summer's gaze flicked to Liam who trudged back up the hill with JJ in tow after their third pass down. "No. I'm not sure when to tell him."

Felicia nodded. "Dating with a kid is tricky. LaToya's daughter was seven when I came into the picture. We were dating six months before she introduced me."

"Yes, but Todd already knows Liam and they like each other. We saw them at the bakery yesterday," Pelavi offered.

"I've never gone on a date, let alone dated someone since before Liam was born." Summer looked between her friends and her son. "This is a big change for him."

"It's a big change for you," Pelavi countered.

Felicia shuffled her feet in the snow. "Have you not told

Liam that you're dating because you're scared it makes it real?"

Summer avoided the empathetic but determined stares of her friends.

"Protecting your son is one thing, but are you using him to protect yourself?" Pelavi's words hung between them like a mirror showing Summer her unspoken truth.

Summer closed her eyes. Was that what was happening? Was she using her son as an excuse to continue to hide? Dating as a single parent had its challenges but wasn't unheard of. LaToya had done it. The village was littered with blended families. For years, she'd used Liam as an excuse not to date. Now, was she using him as a reason to not fully embrace a relationship with Todd?

"Part of why LaToya held off on introducing me as her girlfriend to Darcy was because it made it real for her. She was letting go of her past life and embracing one with me," Felicia said.

"I want to let go of my past," she admitted, opening her eyes. "I'm taking baby steps."

The past week had been peppered with steps she'd taken to free her heart from the past. From Max. From who'd she'd been in New York and who'd she'd been as a teenager. It wasn't just the kiss and date with Todd moving her forward but asking Nat to talk to her therapist about possible openings. Yesterday, Nat gave Summer her therapist's contact info saying that Dr. Horin would have openings after the New Year, and to call on Monday to schedule an initial appointment.

"We're not trying to pressure you to do something you're not truly ready for. Please know that." Felicia placed her gloved hand on Summer's shoulder. "But like you said… baby steps. We always talk about change being hard on our kids, but I think it's harder on us. We tell our kids to be brave and do scary things. We need to remember that we need to be brave, too."

Summer blew out a long breath. "Why do I have smart friends?"

Pelavi *tsked*. "Smart and hot friends."

They chuckled.

"Liam!" Davey shrilled pointing wildly at the hill.

Summer snapped her eyes to the top of the hill, where Liam was on top of a little boy while another flung a snowball at him and shouted.

"Liam!" Eyes wide, she screamed and took off.

"Henry!" Pelavi shouted at her husband, who jumped up and sprinted alongside Summer toward Liam.

Heart roaring, her feet pounded against the hard snow. Breath raced out of her with each inch closer.

"Freak!" The other little boy launched himself at Liam, tackling him to the ground.

"Get off him!" Summer shouted, reaching the top of the hill.

Ignoring her, the little boy raised his balled-up fist and slammed it into Liam's face.

Henry grabbed the little boy and pulled him off Liam. "Stop!"

"Let go of me!" The little boy's arms punched, and legs kicked.

Summer fell to her knees beside Liam. "Baby, are you okay?"

He sat up, tears brimming in his eyes, and glared at the little boy struggling in Henry's arms. "Take it back, Xander!"

"Take what back?" Summer asked, eyebrows knitted in confusion.

"What is going on?" Erica demanded, reaching them, her voice breathless. "Let go of my son."

Summer looked up to see a stern-faced Erica, hands on hips, standing in front of Henry.

Henry plopped the boy on the ground, who immediately ran to his mother. "I was pulling them apart. He was attacking Liam." He pointed to the fat lip forming on Liam's mouth.

Erica's brow pinched. "Xander, is that true?"

"He pushed Jason." Xander scowled, pointing at Liam.

The other boy, who Summer assumed was Jason, stood looking between Liam and Xander. "He just pushed me for no reason," he said, face scrunched.

"That's not true!" Liam hissed, anger vibrating through him.

"Baby, what happened?" Summer placed her hand on his arms to soothe him.

"They—"

"We were just playing and then Liam tackled Jason," Xander interrupted Liam.

"I'm not surprised. Just like his mother, he's a bully," Erica sneered.

Summer blanched, not at being called a bully but at the idea of Liam being labeled as one. She knew all too well who she'd been in school. She'd never shrink away from that truth. But Liam was nothing like how she'd been.

"I'm not a bully! He's lying!" Fat angry tears rolled down Liam's red face. "They were calling JJ names and throwing snowballs at him."

"Were not!" Xander snapped back, a defiant expression on his face. "Right, Jason?"

Quiet, Jason shifted foot-to-foot.

"Lies. I don't even see JJ here." Erica scanned the top of the hill.

Summer gazed to the bottom of the hill where Amy knelt in front of her son signing.

"My son doesn't lie." Summer wrapped her arms around him.

"Sure. Just like he doesn't attack other children." Erica crossed her arms over her chest.

"They were picking on JJ." Liam's lip quivered. "They called him the R-word. You said to always stand up for others."

"That's rich coming from *your* son," Erica snarled.

Schooling her features, Summer ignored Erica's vitriolic comment. "That's right baby, but we don't hit. Even when someone is saying mean things, we never hit. We get an adult."

"But they threw snowballs with rocks in them at JJ's head," he said, wiping tears from his eyes. "They hurt him."

"They what?"

"I'm not listening to this. Boys, let's go." Erica motioned to her sons. "He's a liar and a bully just like his mom."

"He's not, and neither is she," Amy seethed, reaching the top of the hill with JJ at her side.

"Excuse me?" Erica spun; one blonde eyebrow arched.

"JJ told me what happened. Xander and Jason were calling both boys names and then threw snowballs at JJ when his back was turned. Luckily, they have shitty aim and the rocks hit his back and not his head." Her icy blue eyes narrowed to slits. "Apparently they've done this a few times at the school thinking it's funny that he can't hear them."

"This must be a misunderstanding. Xander and Jason would never do something like that." Erica gestured at JJ. "He must be mistaken. He can't even hear… How does he know what was being said?"

Face scrunched in defiance, JJ signed.

"Liam told me, and I can read lips," Amy interpreted.

Shock slackened her features. "It's not true."

"It is," Jason said, his voice quiet. His dark eyes darting between a glaring Xander and everyone else.

"Go on," Henry encouraged.

"They're telling the truth, mom." He looked up, lip trembling. "I'm sorry, Liam. I'm sorry, JJ. We shouldn't have done that."

Signing, JJ nodded.

"Thank you for apologizing and telling the truth," Amy interpreted.

"I'm sorry I pushed you," Liam said, standing up and putting his hand out.

Jason cautiously took the outstretched hand and shook it.

"Is this true, Xander?" Erica looked at her other son, red crawling up her neck.

The boy said nothing.

"I think you owe JJ an apology."

"Sorry," he muttered, looking down at his feet.

"You have to look at him when your speaking, so he can read your lips." A stern expression was fixed on Liam's face.

Summer's heart squeezed at the fierce protectiveness in her little boy's eyes. Todd called her the mama bear-est of mama bears and today her little cub showed that he could take care of himself and, more importantly, others.

Xander blew out an annoyed breath and looked up. "Sorry, JJ."

JJ signed.

"Thank you," Amy interpreted. "Also, apologize to Liam. JJ says you are always calling him names in school."

"What?" Erica's eyebrows almost reached her hairline.

Xander's stare moved to the ground. "Sorry."

Amy glared at Erica. "And you owe one to Summer."

What? Summer gaped.

"We need to be an example for our children and what you said to her was unkind. She's raised a kindhearted little boy. She's not who she was in high school. None of us are, including you. I always thought you were the *nice* one of the cool girls. But now, I wonder."

Reminiscent of gunslingers at high noon, Amy and Erica stared at each other; neither backing down.

"It's fine." Summer cleared her throat.

Summer knew the expression on Erica's face all-too-well. It was the look of someone who knew they were wrong but was unwilling to admit it. That expression had stared back in the mirror so much throughout Summer's life. She knew better than anyone the time it took to face that look and what it meant about oneself.

Red faced, Erica adjusted her purse. "Xander, Jason, let's go."

While Erica stomped away, her boys following behind her, Summer knelt and scooped up a clump of snow. "Here baby, let's put this on your lip."

Liam winced as she pressed the snow against his lip.

"I know," she soothed. "Why didn't you tell me about Xander picking on you in school?"

He shrugged. "It's not a big deal."

"It is a big deal."

"I told Pop. He said haters gonna hate."

She snorted. "What?"

"Plus, you said to not let people tell you who you are but to be who you are."

"And you're someone that stands up for others," Amy cut in, admiration lit her features. "Liam, thank you for defending JJ. You're a good friend." Amy signed as she spoke.

Liam handed the snow back to his mom and signed as he said, "He's my friend. That's what friends do."

"You sign?"

"He's learning." Summer grinned. "Todd and Nat are teaching him."

"JJ told me about his friend who was learning to sign. I just didn't put two and two together that it was Liam."

After Henry checked out Liam's lip and proclaimed that in his medical opinion the kid needed to floss more, he gave the all-clear.

Back at the bottom of the hill, Liam and JJ sat on their

sleds, an ice pack from Felicia's first aid kit on his lip, as Davey and Nisha buried Henry in snow. Cackling, Felicia and Pelavi helped the kids. Summer and Amy stood a few feet away, sipping on the remainder of the hot chocolate.

"So, Todd is teaching Liam sign language?" Amy asked.

"And Nat," Summer added, playing coy.

"But Nat isn't the one who half the village is in a gossip frenzy about."

Summer pinched the bridge of her nose. "This town."

A soft laugh fell out of Amy's mouth. "It is one of the downsides of Perry."

"That and dealing with the people you hated in high school."

"Or the people that hated you."

"I never hated you." Summer's gaze met Amy's. "I think the only person I truly hated in high school, well besides Erica, was myself. When I went into seventh grade, I made JV cheerleading. The older girls took me under their wing. Soon, I learned to stay their friend meant acting like them. Once I started…" Shaking her head, she let out a hard sigh. "I guess it seemed easier to keep playing the role of the mean girl. It doesn't excuse my behavior. It's taken me years to understand it myself and I'm still working on understanding who I was so I can avoid going back."

"For the record, I didn't hate you in high school."

Summer's right eyebrow cocked in disbelief. "But I was the worst!"

"You were." A quiet laugh filled the air. "But you had these moments where you'd do something unexpected. Like the time you defended the marching band when rival football players mocked us during a homecoming game, or when you called a bunch of guys picking on Todd, when he was a freshman, what was it? Oh yeah—dickless wonders. I liked *that* Summer."

"I didn't realize anyone noticed." She raked her teeth against her lower lip.

"You were the prom queen...everyone noticed what you did."

"I'm not the prom queen anymore."

"No, you're way better than that." Amy tipped her head to Liam, who now leaned in the snow helping Nisha cover her dad's feet. "You're a hell of a mom."

"He's the best thing I've ever done." Pride bubbled inside her. "You know, you're a pretty amazing mom too." She gestured to JJ who made snow angels with Davey.

"Maybe Liam and you could come over for a playdate over the Christmas break."

Summer beamed. "I'd like that."

"So would I." Amy reached out her hand just as Liam had done with Jason and Summer took it.

CHAPTER SEVENTEEN

Summer stretched out on the bed with Liam snuggled into her, while she read aloud a chapter from *Charlie and the Chocolate Factory*. Most nights, he'd read to himself before bed but after all that happened today, he'd asked her to do it.

Curled up in her arms, he was still her little boy. Although today Liam showed her that he was the little version of the man that she hoped he'd grow up to be. A man who was loyal and protective of the people he cared about. A man who defended others. A man who could apologize for mistakes. A man like her dad. Like the other good men in their lives. Men like…

Todd.

Finishing the chapter, Summer closed the book. "Baby, you like Todd, right?"

"Yes." His face wrinkled. "Why are you asking me this again?"

Time to be brave. She sat up straighter. "You know how we're going to have dinner at Todd's tomorrow?"

"Yeah, because he's your boyfriend."

Blinking, her mouth dropped open. "Excuse me?"

"You're boyfriend and girlfriend. I overheard Pop and Grandma talking yesterday about you going on a date with Todd on Friday night."

Technically she wasn't sure if Todd was her boyfriend. They'd only been on one date. They hadn't discussed labels. Just a promise of a future, which one could infer meant he *was* her boyfriend and *she* his girlfriend. Clearly a conversation was needed, but as smart as Liam was, she doubted she had the emotional bandwidth to explain the intricacies of what constituted dating someone versus being in a relationship.

Hell, I don't even know if I can explain it to myself.

Shifting in the bed, she looked at him. "How do you feel about me dating Todd?"

"It's okay."

"Are you sure? Because if you aren't..." She didn't allow herself to complete the sentence, but if Liam wasn't okay with this, she'd walk away. No matter how she felt about Todd, her son was the priority.

"I like Todd. He's nice and fun. He's got Sheba. Plus, he looks at you how you're supposed to look at a girlfriend."

"How's that?"

"Like how Pop and Grandma look at each other. All gushy and stuff." His nose scrunched up.

Laughter rumbled in her chest.

"He makes you happy and I want you to be happy, Mom."

She folded her arms around him, tucking him into her chest. "But I am happy, baby. I've got you, Pop, and Grandma."

"And Todd." He snuggled in. "I know you're happy, but I want you to be happy like Nat and Noah, or Elle and Clayton."

Her heart almost ached with the love she had for her little boy. In that moment, she knew the hesitation she'd felt about telling him had nothing to do with Liam not accepting Todd's role in their lives. Empathy and kindness radiated from her son. All he wanted was for her to be happy. And she realized the only barrier to her happiness had been herself. Felicia had been right; she'd used her son as an excuse to avoid her feelings for Todd.

"I love you so much, baby." She kissed the top of his head.

"I love you too, Mom." He yawned. "Does Todd being your boyfriend mean I get more time with Sheba?"

"I think the only reason you want me to date Todd is because of Sheba." She stood and clicked off the bedside lamp.

"I want a dog. If you two get married, would Todd and Sheba live here? Sheba could sleep in my room."

She shook with laughter. "One step at a time, baby."

She shuffled out of his room and shut the door behind her. Pulling her phone from her back pocket, she pulled up her messages app. Fingers hovering over the last message with Todd, her eyes flicked between the phone and the grandfather clock at the end of the hall. It was eight thirty. The brewery and wine bar both closed at seven on Sundays. He'd likely be home by now.

Nibbling on her lower lip, she crossed the hall to her room. "You're crazy," she whispered as she changed out of her pajamas.

She loosened her long chestnut hair from its low ponytail and brushed it out. In front of the mirror on the closet door, she swiped pink lipstain across her lips. With a quick spritz of perfume, she tiptoed downstairs where her parents sat in the living room watching reruns of *The Office* on TV.

"You're dressed." Dad's brows shot up, his tone questioning.

"Yeah." She smoothed down her hair. "I was thinking of going for a walk before bed."

A knowing gleam sparked in Mom's eyes. "Walking anywhere in particular?"

She grabbed her coat off the hook in the foyer. "Just around."

"Mm hmm." Mom smirked.

"Use a condom." Dad shook his head.

Mortification flamed in Summer's face.

"Brian!" Mom tossed a throw pillow at him. "Don't tell her that. I want more grandbabies."

"Fine." His face scrunched. "Summer Joy, go ahead and pull the goalie."

"I don't know about you two sometimes." Grinning she shook her head. "So, I'm just going to say I love you both and I'll be home later."

"Have fun!" Mom cooed as Summer headed out.

Six minutes later, she spied the pink light radiating on the corner of Todd's street. Unlike the other night, the entire street glowed with Christmas decorations. Standing in front of his house, her cheeks flushed from the power walk and the kiss of the icy night air. Despite the chill, heat cascaded within her. Running up his steps, she knocked on the front door.

A few moments later, the door swung open. Todd appeared in faded blue jeans and a fitted black T-shirt. That sexy left eyebrow of his ticked up with seductive confusion. Well, at least it was seductive to her.

"Liam knows we're dating," she blurted.

"Come in." He stepped to the side, motioning for her to enter.

She walked into the house, turning to face him.

"How did he take it?"

"He's cool with it. He likes you and he especially likes Sheba."

He sloshed out a breath that sounded relieved.

"Although, he thinks you're my boyfriend." She fiddled with the red buttons on her coat. "Are you my boyfriend?"

Oh my god! What am I doing? Was she really asking this? Who was she? She'd not even done something this silly as a teenager. She'd never run after boys; they'd run after her. *He's not a boy. He's a man. My man.* That claiming thought surged certainty inside her.

"I want to be your boyfriend." He stepped close, the furnace of his body caressed every inch of her.

"I want to be your girlfriend."

Unbridled joy covered every inch of his face. "Then I'm your boyfriend."

"And I'm your girlfriend."

He reached for her, pulling her in.

"Wait." She placed her hand on his chest. "Can I use your bathroom first?"

Face scrunched, he let go of her. "Okay."

Leaving her coat on, she slipped out of her boots and shuffled to the bathroom. There she took off her coat and hung it on the hook on the back of the door. With a reassuring look in the mirror, she unbuttoned and pushed down her jeans. Taking off just about everything except that one thing she knew would drive him wild, she examined herself in the mirror.

A chill zipped from the hardwood floor into her bare feet, up her naked legs, and tightened her pebbling nipples, which were visible through the one article of clothing she wore. Tiptoeing down the hall, she entered the living room where Todd stood, his back to her, staring at the tree.

She cleared her throat. "I'm ready for my boyfriend to kiss me now."

Todd turned, his breath catching. Heat flashed in his eyes.

"Does my boyfriend approve?" She batted her long eyelashes, running her hands down his Henley on her body which barely went past her ass.

The muscles of his throat worked. The sweep of his gaze

along her body ignited every nerve ending into raging bonfires.

"So fucking approve." He crossed the room, pulled her into his arms, and claimed her mouth in a hungry kiss.

His strong hands trailed down her soft curves. As if the first strike of a match, her body flickered awake with need. Lava pooled in her belly and needy heat burned in her veins. His tight squeeze of her ass elicited a giggly moan from her.

"What are you wearing under this?" he asked between fevered kisses.

"Nothing," she breathed.

"Fuck," he groaned.

She looped her arms around his nape. "Extra clothes would only get in the way for what I have in mind for tonight."

He slipped her hands off him. "Oh, sweetheart." He bent down and hoisted her onto his shoulder "I'm taking you to my bedroom."

She giggled. "Will you be showing me all the ways you're going to make me scream your name now?"

He playfully slapped her ass, making her squeak. "Tonight will just be a warmup."

Like she weighed nothing, he carried her up the stairs and down the hall. Past the four doors that led to the end of the corridor.

"How many bedrooms is this place?"

"Three and a bathroom." He opened the door at the end of the hall, carrying her inside. "There's also an ensuite bathroom off the principal bedroom."

With a quiet click, he hit the switch, bathing the room in soft white light. Crossing the room, he paused and lowered her to her feet in front of the king-size bed draped in a thick evergreen comforter. The bedroom was simple, but cozy. An old wingback chair sat tucked in the corner beside a small table piled high with books. Landscape photos in rustic wooden frames dotted the tan walls.

"Do you want a tour?" His hands dragged down her sides. "Or do you want me to spread you out on this bed and taste you?"

Goddamn, this man. Her core clenched.

Moving his hands to the hem of her shirt, she guided him to raise the fabric up. The cool air licked against her bare skin when he pulled the Henley over her head. Dropping the shirt to the floor, he stepped back. His eyes roamed across her naked form. Breath growing ragged, she took in his darkening eyes as they surveyed her.

It wasn't the body she'd once had. Her once-toned physique had softened. A small squishy swell had replaced the flat stomach she used to spend hours in the gym and barely ate to have. The perky breasts of her twenties were now rounder and sagged just a bit, despite what Nat said. A thin scar ran across her abdomen from the complications with Liam's birth.

He moved close, raising his hand to her cheek. "You're so beautiful, sweetheart."

She placed her hand atop his, moving it down her body. "Touch me, Todd."

With an almost reverent kiss, his hands coasted along her bare skin. Those rough, but gentle, hands praised her with their touch. He trailed kisses down her neck, along her collarbone, moving lower to flick his tongue against the taut pink nipple of her left breast. He nipped and then took the bud in his mouth.

Head tossed back; she arched into his hardening sucks. A throaty moan sighed out of her. Arousal slickened the spot between her legs. His lips moved to her other breast, and the rough pads of his fingers touched her outer thighs.

Kissing down her body, he fell to his knees in front of her.

Like an acolyte, he peered up at her through hooded lids. "Sit on the edge of the bed, sweetheart."

The gentle command in his voice both soothed and set her on fire. She could give herself to him completely, knowing that with him she was safe. He'd take charge but he'd never control. He'd claim her but never own.

She sat. Her eyes meeting his.

His hands gripped her thighs pushing her legs wide. "This pretty pink pussy." His index finger ran along her center, making her shiver with need. "You're so wet."

"Todd," she whimpered with want.

With a wicked grin, he eased her back on the bed and lifted her legs. Pressing chaste kisses along her inner thighs, he teased closer to her core. Desire threatened to engulf her. Her skin blazed with each soft press of his lips.

A slow lick over her center made her moan. "Oh, Todd."

"Fuck... You're the best thing I've ever tasted." His tongue found her clit, flicking it with soft licks.

Back bowed, a delicious pressure coiled in her belly. Her hands moved to her breasts pinching and rolling her nipples as he worked her. Looking up at her, he let out an appreciative groan at her fondling of her breasts. His mouth fluctuated between gentle licks and hard sucks pushing her closer to the edge. Tapping a finger at her entrance, he pushed it in. Pleasurable tension wound within her. Finger crooked, he hit that secret spot inside her again causing her muscles to beg for release. He pumped in rhythm with his licking tongue and sucking mouth against that sensitive nub.

"God... Todd!" she cried as release ripped through her.

Todd remained focused. Lapping her up, he guided her through her climax. Falling back on his haunches, a smug smile stretched across his face. "That's one, sweetheart," he boasted, standing up.

"Aren't we cocky?" she panted, lifting herself to her

elbows. "I see there's good reason." Her eyes darted to the bulge straining the front of his jeans.

He looked down and then back at her with an almost boyish smirk that both stole her heart and flooded her with wantonness.

She rose, taking the hem of his T-shirt and pulling it over his head. Her hands skated along his defined torso, delighting in the clench of his muscles at her touch. Licking her lips, she unbuttoned his jeans and pulled the zipper down. Stepping back, Todd pushed down his jeans and then his red boxer briefs.

Summer stepped closer and wrapped her hand around his impressive length. "You have such a pretty cock," she purred.

He burst out laughing.

"What?" She arched an eyebrow. "You said my pussy is pretty... And this is one"—she pumped him twice—"pretty cock."

A throaty moan rumbled out of him. Taking her wrist, he ceased her movements. "I need to be inside you."

"Condom?"

After a tender kiss to her shoulder, he moved to the bedstand and pulled out an unopened box of condoms.

"Are those new?"

"I bought them after Thursday…just in case." An eager smile curled his lips.

"You really are cocky?" she teased, crawling onto the bed.

"Says the woman that straddled me twice in a twenty-four- hour period and then emerged from my bathroom wearing only my shirt."

"You loved it." She got on all fours on the bed, looking over her shoulders with a sultry expression.

"Is that an invitation?"

She wiggled her backside. "Is this how you want me?"

Not answering her, he rolled on the condom. Like a prowling lion he got on the bed and crawled toward her.

Kissing her spine, his hands moved along her body. Brushing her hair to one shoulder, he kissed up her neck.

"Not this time. I want to see your eyes when I fuck you for the first time," he whispered in her ear.

Need boiled over in her belly. Raising on just her knees, she covered his mouth with hers in a deep kiss. Shoving him back down on the bed, she moved on top of him.

"You seem to enjoy me straddling you." She positioned herself over his cock. Taking him in hand, she guided him inside her. The sweet stretching ache moved through her as inch by inch she took him.

"Summer," he groaned, head rolling back against the bed.

"As good as your fingers?" The teasing comment was breathless.

He gripped her hips, moving her in a languid motion against him. "So much better."

"Agreed," she breathed.

With each rock, he thrusted his hips, surging deeper inside her. Placing her hands on his chest, she rocked harder against him. Their hips moved in tandem, chasing pleasure.

"Ride me, sweetheart," he growled.

His hands moved up to cup her breasts. Pleasure built with the rhythmic pace of his thrusts and mix of gentle rolling and hard pinches of her nipples. Familiar pressure spooled tight in her core. His hands moved back down her body, one gripping her hip and the other slipping between them. The first lazy circle of her clit ripped loose her orgasm.

As her cries of his name filled the room, he flipped her onto her back. Resting her legs high on his hips, he drove deeper, extending her pleasure. Her fingernails bit into his back. The pleasure was too much.

"Todd!" she whimpered.

"Come again for me, sweetheart." Teeth gritted, he pumped harder.

Her body taut with wanted release. Twining tighter and

tighter, her pelvic muscles clenched around him. She screamed his name. The pleasure thrumming through her.

Riding out her orgasm, she clung to him. His darkened eyes fogged with need. His focused thrusts grew uncoordinated and chaotic as he chased his own release.

"Take what you need, baby," she rasped, repeating his command from Friday night.

With one last deep drive, he shook with climax. Panting, he collapsed atop her. The delicious heaviness of his body on hers tethered her to this moment. The sensation of belonging filled her. Both, of him belonging with her and she with him. Not *to* each other, but *with*.

Lifting his head, his eyes faded back to their normal emerald green, he met her gaze. His hands threaded into her sex-rumpled hair. "What are you thinking, sweetheart?"

"That if that's the warmup, I don't think I'll survive the actual show."

CHAPTER EIGHTEEN

Hot water licked across Summer's slick body. The aroma of peppermint from the bodywash Todd lathered her with infused the steam that bellowed around them. Pressed against his firm chest, she closed her eyes and sank deeper into him.

She could have floated away. A lightness that she'd not experienced in such a long time bloomed in her chest. The fear that had held her back seemed to wash down the drain. Every excuse to hold back from this man—from this relationship—was gone.

"We had sex tonight," she said.

"That we did." His smirk was audible.

"Really good sex." Her brow puckered. "Like you're *really* good at sex. How did you get so good?"

A chuckle huffed out of him. "Well, I've had a long time to think about the things I wanted to do with you."

"How long?"

He rinsed the soap off her body. "I won't pretend that I didn't have some fantasies about you in school but—"

"Did you spank it to thoughts of me when you were a teen?" she interrupted, laughing.

"I think you underestimate how good you looked in your cheerleading uniform in high school." He squeezed her rear.

"Perv," she teased with a wiggle of her butt against his growing length.

His hands moved to her hips, pressing her tighter against his hardness. "As good as you looked then, nothing compares to how pretty you look now." He kissed the hollow below her ear.

"You're just saying that because I'm naked."

"Naked Summer is my favorite, but it's the entire package. I noticed you when I moved back five years ago. You looked different than when we were in high school, but you were still so goddamn pretty… But you were also guarded."

She twisted to face him.

"Then last year at Elle's uncle's birthday, she dragged you onto the dance floor with us. It was the first time since I moved back that you let yourself out. Your smile lit your entire face and you laughed… *Really* laughed." His expression grew thoughtful. "God, I think you stole my heart with that laugh, and then the first time you rolled your eyes at me when I said something too flirty, my heart was completely lost to you."

She took his hand and placed it over her heart. "I promise I'll be kind with your heart and take care of it."

Smiling, he took her hand and placed it on his chest. "I promise I'll be kind to your heart and take care of it."

She didn't need to say it. Her actions told him, that as much as she'd stolen his heart that he'd done the same to hers. Like a drizzle that started before a powerful storm lit the night, this attraction had built quietly. Now it raged between them. Just as she thought she reached the bottom of how she felt about him, she'd find there was still further to go. Even if it took this long to admit it, she knew that the unguarded laugh that stole his heart that night was because of something he'd said. That first crack in her armor was caused by him.

"I know you can't stay the night, but if you could I'd want you to."

"And if I could, I would stay." Raising his hand to her lips she offered a gentle kiss to his palm. "You're getting pruny. Why don't we get out, dry off, and I'll let you hold me for a bit before heading home."

"You'll let me hold you?" That left eyebrow cocked, making her belly flip.

"And walk me home." With a wicked glance over her shoulder, she stepped out of the glass shower.

"As you wish." He shut off the shower.

Dried off, Summer pulled on a fresh Henley courtesy of Todd. He tugged on a T-shirt and sweatpants before pulling back the covers. As she settled into his nook, he told Alexa to set a timer for midnight.

"Just in case we fall asleep," he offered.

"Here I was thinking you thought I turned into a pumpkin at midnight."

"I told you I love pumpkins." He kissed her temple.

She tipped her head up to study his face. The scruff along his strong jawline. The tiny bump in his nose. That sexy left eyebrow with its exclamation mark scar.

Raising her hand, she traced the small scar. "How did you get this?"

He let out a long breath. "My dad and I—" His jaw tightened. "We've always been two very different people. When my mom died the difference between us got bigger. The first Christmas after she passed, he packed up all her decorations. I tried to stop him. We argued and struggled for the box of her things. He let go and the momentum sent me and the box flying. I crashed into the coffee table."

"Oh, baby." She cradled his cheek.

"Dad took me to get stitched up. He just kept saying how sorry he was and that he shouldn't have let go of the box. Only I wasn't angry that he let go of the box. I was angry… still am…that he'd let go of her. He removed every memory of her from the house. Every tradition. Everything that kept her alive for me and Rose was taken away."

Anger and pain radiated within her. Not only had Todd lost his mother, but the parent left behind tried to take away her memory.

"I'm so sorry, baby. You lost both parents." Emotion added a slight wobble to her voice.

"One I lost—" He shrugged. "The other…I'm not sure what happened there. When I left for college, I didn't look back. I tried to come around for Rose, but the strain between us just got more tense over the years. He's made it clear that he doesn't approve of my life choices, so we don't speak or interact."

She sat up, face pinched in outrage. "What life choices?"

"He said he didn't pay for his son to go to college to work in a bar."

"You own the bar! Hell, you own two!" she seethed, holding up two fingers.

He pulled her back against his chest. "I know, sweetheart. His opinion doesn't matter to me anymore."

"I could punch your dad. Although, I won't because I told Liam to never hit, but…" She puffed out an angry breath.

"You really are a mama bear." His lips curled into a small grin.

"Well mama bears take care of their cubs and their…" Her forehead scrunched in consideration of what to call him.

"Papa bear?" he suggested with a smirk.

She swatted his chest. "I'm not calling you papa bear."

"Not yet, sweetheart." He winked.

"Keep dreaming."

"So far my dreams are coming true," he murmured, holding her close.

This is my life. Happiness sighed through Summer with each slice of the knife into the cooled brownies. Her thoughts wandered through the memory of last night with Todd. Him holding her close and losing themselves in conversation until the Alexa alarm went off at midnight. Almost like Cinderella, her night with the handsome prince was over. Only there'd been no lost glass slipper because her prince walked her home. He texted her this morning. Now, she stood in the kitchen prepping one of the few baked goods she'd mastered over the years, boxed brownies.

To say that her culinary skills were limited was a massive understatement. She'd mastered grilled cheese, break-and-bake cookies from the refrigerator section in the grocery, boxed brownies, spaghetti and, according to Liam, the world's best PB&Js. Much of the cooking in the Michaels' household was done by Mom and Dad. Summer's food teetered between undercooked and burnt to a crisp.

"Boxed brownies?" Dad remarked as he walked into the kitchen. "Someone is pulling out the big guns for tonight's dinner."

"Don't be cheeky or I won't leave any for Mom and you to have for dessert tonight," she teased.

"No need since you two will be gone, I plan on your mother being dessert tonight."

Summer blanched. "Seriously, why do you say these things to me?"

"It's just so fun to mess with you." An almost witchy cackle boomed from him.

Dull sadness snaked through her belly, thinking about

how Todd no longer had this. As much as her parents drove her nuts at times, she was so lucky to have Mom and Dad.

Placing a brownie square on a napkin, she handed it to him. "Let me know how they are."

"Wow, you are pulling out the big guns if you're having me taste test." Dad took a bite and nodded. "Nice work," he said through a mouthful.

Summer smiled and placed a few extra brownies on a small plate for her parents. The plate she was taking to Todd's she wrapped in aluminum foil.

"Speaking of nice work, several of the staff at the school were going on and on about the Christmas market."

"Yeah, it turned out really well," she said, opening the cabinet to put the aluminum foil away.

"The new guidance counselor is married to the county supervisor and expressed interest in having you help with some special events related to the county fair this summer. They asked if you had a card or a website."

"Just give them my number." She tried to keep the annoyance out of her voice.

She could feel the chide coming. *You're so talented, but…* Reminiscent of a mosquito, her dad's heretofore unvoiced criticism buzzed around them waiting to suck up her patience. She didn't want to be ungrateful. Both her parents were supportive…*ish*? It just always came to this, to Summer not living up to her potential.

"It would just be easier for your business to have a card, at least. It's more professional. Like a *real* business."

Eyes closed, she counted *1…2…3*. "Dad, it is a real business."

"Then you need to treat it like one. That means business cards. That means a website. Have you spoken to Janet about that class, yet?"

"No, but—"

He puffed out an annoyed breath. "I don't know why you

don't take it seriously. It's like in high school when you didn't apply for college because you said you wanted to do party planning. Then you had nothing but waitressing to fall back on when you came home."

Each word was like a knife slicing into barely scabbed over wounds. How could she be loved so much by someone who always seemed just a little disappointed in her?

Dad blew out a harsh breath. "I just want you to have the best life, just like you want for Liam. I'm really proud of what you've done over the last year with your party planning—"

Event planning. She wanted to scream but bit back the angry protest out of deference to all the ways her dad and mom had been there for her and Liam.

"—and if this is what you want to do with your life, I want you to have the best possible chance for it to be a real career for you."

Swallowing down the many words that whirled within her, she nodded. "I know. I spoke to Janet on Saturday. I'm going to go to the Village Rose tomorrow after my shift to talk to her."

Dad stepped close and placed his hands on Summer's biceps. "I know I push, but I'm a parent. You know that's what we do."

His words still echoed in Summer's heart while she and Liam walked to Todd's. It was a warmer than usual December evening hovering in the low thirties. The crisp air filled her lungs and cleansed the emotions from the talk with Dad. She didn't want to bring that into this happy moment with two of her favorite guys.

Since Liam's bedtime was eight thirty, they were meeting Todd at his house at four thirty. Both the brewery and wine bar were closed on Monday, much like most of the businesses in town, except for Cassie's Café.

"I love the Pepto house," Liam chirped, taking the walkway to Todd's stairs.

"The *what?*" she snorted.

"Pop calls it the Pepto house because it's all pink. I think it's cool, though." Reaching up, he rang the bell.

"Hey!" Todd beamed, opening the door, a tongue-wagging Sheba at his feet.

"Sheba!" Liam exclaimed as he signed.

"Nice job signing her name." Todd gave a thumbs-up and ushered them in.

"I made brownies," she announced, handing him the plate.

A dubious expression covered his face. "You baked?"

Hands on hips, she sassed, "There are a few dishes I've perfected."

"Mom makes the world's best PB&J," Liam offered, looking up from petting Sheba.

"Well, I can't wait to have that PB&J." Flirtation sparked in his expression.

How was he making PB&J sound dirty? Heat flushed her cheeks.

After hanging their coats in the foyer, Todd pulled out two pairs of slippers. A Liam-size black pair with miniature Huskies on them and a red pair with tiny books on them for Summer. The sweetness of this man was almost overwhelming. It wasn't just the thoughtful gesture to keep their feet warm on his hardwood floors, but an offering of that future they spoke of. A future in which there'd be many more dinner nights that started with them slipping off their shoes and pushing into their slippers by his front door.

I am falling so hard. The thought coursed through her as she followed him into the kitchen.

Bowls full of ingredients covered the kitchen island. Three printed sheets of paper lay beside them.

"Liam, ready to learn how to make pizza?" Todd's lips curled as if he was excited by the prospect of teaching her son the fine art of pizza-making.

Liam nodded, pushing up his sweatshirt sleeves.

"Grab the instructions and tell me what our first step is."

Grabbing the first sheet of paper, Liam read aloud. "Wash our hands."

Perched on a stool at the island, Summer sipped pumpkin cider as Todd instructed Liam about how to make pizza. The ingredients were set up assembly line-style, with dedicated stations for dough, sauce, cheese, and the various toppings for the three pizzas they were making: cheese, spicy sausage and honey, and Hawaiian. Each of their favorites. The printed instructions guided Liam through each step.

It was perfect. Not just the preparation of the pizza being made up like an activity allowing Liam to take part in making dinner, but how it was set up in the way that best fit how her little guy did things.

One of the strategies they'd used over the last few years to help Liam thrive was scripts and step-by-step instructions. If he knew what was expected, he could handle it. It made the unknown less scary, quelling the anxiety that sometimes got the better of her son. Happiness swelled in her heart at the effortless interactions between her two favorite guys.

Why did I ever worry about this?

Laughter lit Liam's face as Todd put on an Italian accent, while drizzling sauce on his homemade dough. "You sound terrible!"

"What?" Todd's mouth puckered into a pout. "I sound just like Mario and Luigi."

"It is a pretty terrible accent," she chortled.

"The thanks I get for showing you my'—he slipped into an even more exaggerated Italian accent— "my mama's recipe."

She scooped up flour from the small bowl beside him and flicked it at his nose. "Silly man."

He grinned. "You *love* it."

The butterflies in her belly swooped.

"How come Mom doesn't have to help?" Liam asked, sprinkling cheese onto the sauce-covered dough.

"She made us dessert, so we have to make her dinner." Todd rolled out the dough for the second pizza.

"Oh... It's like how mom does the dishes most nights because Pop or Grandma cook." With a nod, Liam picked up the instruction sheet and read aloud, "Hand to Todd and go to second sheet."

While the pizza baked in the oven, Liam and Summer set the kitchen table and Todd cleaned up the ingredients. Sheba sprawled in her large bed tucked up against the floor-to-ceiling windows that overlooked the back patio. It was so easy how they fell into this little domestic tableau. Like the softest of sweaters, this fit so perfectly.

The herby aroma of pizza filled her nostrils. Todd placed the three perfectly cooked pies on wire racks in the middle of the table. After cutting the three pizzas, he grabbed a metal spatula to serve.

"I'm assuming you want the Hawaiian pizza." Todd grabbed her plate, loading a slice.

"And a slice of your spicy sausage and honey." She winced, realizing she'd just asked for "his spicy sausage" in front of her son.

Wickedness danced in his features. "As you wish, sweetheart." He placed a second slice on her plate.

"Sweetheart?" Liam groaned, but then started laughing immediately. "You're so gushy, now. Like Nat and Noah."

"One day you'll find your sweetheart and then you'll get it." Todd chuckled.

Liam laughingly hooted, "Never!"

"What do you want, buddy?"

"Cheese, please." Liam held up his plate, and Todd scooped up a slice for him.

"Well, I'm having all three kinds." He rubbed his hands together. "As chef, I have to try everything I prepared."

Liam's lips pursed. "Is that a rule?"

"An unwritten rule."

"What does that mean?"

"It means that it's something you know without having to look it up. Like saying hello to someone when you see them or shaking hands when you first meet someone."

Liam nodded. "I was the chef, too. Can I have all three?"

"You got it, buddy."

Summer fixed her gaze on Todd's, trying to communicate her thought. *Did you just get my child to try something besides cheese pizza without asking him to try it?*

The smirk stretched across Todd's face seemed to reply *I sure did, sweetheart.*

Maybe she would have to start calling him papa bear.

Bellies full and pizza almost all gone, they ate the brownies with scoops of vanilla bean ice cream. Todd had put out chocolate sauce, whipped cream, and sprinkles for them to make sundaes.

"A brownie without ice cream is just sad," Todd said, licking his spoon.

"We have homemade ice cream on Christmas Eve," Liam offered, spooning up a bite.

"My Dad's mom made ice cream on Christmas. She'd use the snow saying Christmas snow was the best, so my dad carried on that tradition," she explained.

"It's fun. We have dinner and then go for a walk to look at the lights, while Pop makes the ice cream. Then we watch *Home Alone.*"

Todd leaned back in his chair. "I love that tradition."

Summer tilted her head. "What do you do for Christmas?" It just hit her that she had no idea what he did for the holiday. She knew he ate Thanksgiving dinner at Cassie and Zach's, but after he shared the strained-to-nonexistent relationship with his dad, she wondered how he spent the holiday.

"On Christmas Day, I pick up Grandpa Rice from the

Assisted Living and we go to Cassie and Zach's. Rose and her girlfriend join."

"What about Christmas Eve?" Liam's stare jumped to Todd.

He shrugged. "Sheba and I have dinner here. Then we watch *It's a Wonderful Life* on TV."

This would not do. The idea of Todd spending any holiday alone was unacceptable.

"Sheba and you should have Christmas Eve with us," Liam suggested, taking the words straight from her mouth.

That's my sweet little boy. Admiration and love squeezed her heart.

Todd's mouth opened, but she silenced him. "Please join us."

"Are you sure?" That left eyebrow ticked up.

She reached across the table, threading their fingers. "Very sure."

"So gushy!" Liam grumbled.

CHAPTER NINETEEN

"That is so fetch!" ~Mean Girls

Summer fastened a streamer to the edge of the beam. Silver streamers crisscrossed the wooden beams of the Farmer's Ale. The brewery would open in another hour for a private event. Clusters of regular customers, friends, and family would fill the brewery to celebrate Noah Wilson's thirty-ninth birthday.

"I told you to wait for me before you climbed up there," Todd groused as he walked into the bar area with a box of candles for the centerpieces.

She peered down from the ladder. "Don't go all alpha on me."

Placing the box on a nearby table, he walked to the bottom of the ladder and took hold of it. "It's hardly alpha male to not want my girlfriend to fall and crack her head open."

My girlfriend. Maybe she should climb down because in that moment she thought she might swoon.

It had only been four days since they declared each other "theirs" in his entryway foyer. Since then, the relationship she'd bristled against wrapped itself around her like a luxurious cashmere blanket.

"You shouldn't be climbing ladders in a room by yourself. Where's Nat?" he went on, a perturbed vibe coated his words.

"Nat ran to the bathroom."

"Can you please come down?" he almost beseeched.

"You are adorably overprotective," she teased, starting to climb down.

"Well, papa bears gotta take care of their mama bears."

Laughter rumbled inside her. "I'm *not* calling you that."

His strong hands gripped her waist the moment she reached him. Giggling she let go, her body flying into him. The firmness of his chest pressed tight against her.

He bent close, murmuring, "Oh, you're going to call me it soon, sweetheart."

"Keep dreaming, silly man." She playfully elbowed his stomach.

Spinning her to face him, a roguish smirk kicked across his face. "I'm *your* silly man."

The smile lit up every crevice of her face. "That you are." Encircling his nape, she raised to her tiptoes and captured his bottom lip in a nibbling kiss.

"OMG!" Nat's squeal pierced the room.

Rolling her eyes, Summer twisted her head to face her friend.

"You two are so adorbs!" Giddiness vibrated across Nat's body. "I thought I'd be desensitized to this after last night's support group holiday gathering, but you are too cute."

Henry finally got what he wanted, a man in the group. Todd joined her and Liam for a holiday party at the clinic last night. With the forthcoming holidays, and due to Noah's birthday shenanigans tonight, the group decided to have a potluck since they'd be on hiatus until after the New Year. They set up food and games at the clinic bringing their kids and inviting Nat, Noah, Nat's dad – the other Dr. Owens –

and Nat's mom to thank them for offering their support. LaToya and Felicia's parents, who'd come in for Christmas, Summer's parents, and Pelavi's brother had all joined.

"I should probably go before she starts taking pictures again." Todd tipped his head at Nat.

"Too late!" Nat chirped, holding up her phone and taking a picture.

Eyebrow arched; Summer wagged a finger at Nat. "That's one. I told you last night, you only get two pictures a day."

Her lips puckered in a pout. "But it's a special occasion."

Todd pressed a soft kiss to the center of Summer's brow. "Oh, sweetheart, there's no fighting Nat. You're going to be plastered all over her social media."

That was one thing he was very wrong about. Nat never posted pictures of Summer on social media. Even before telling Nat the full story, she'd asked to be kept off social media posts. Everyone, including her bestie, happily complied. Since leaving Max, she'd mostly avoided being on online social platforms so if a stray picture of her did end up being posted there'd be no ability to tag her. She'd only got on Facebook last year to participate in Autism support groups but used a picture of a sunflower for her profile, kept it private and unsearchable, and went by Summer Joy.

After almost ten years, she hoped Max had stopped looking for her. When she left him, she'd gone to the last place he'd assumed she'd go; home. With the way she bristled at the idea of Perry and the Grand Canyon-sized distance she'd put between her and her parents she'd hoped he'd never suspect it was where she'd went. She'd done all she could to make him think she'd run off to California. He'd never come here looking for her. Even though coming home had lulled her into a sense of safety, she'd always maintained a hypervigilance simmering just below her skin.

"You need to get going or you're going to be late," Nat said, slipping her phone into her back pocket.

Face scrunched, Todd's eyes fixed to the rooster shaped clock over the bar. "Shit. That's right."

"Late for what?" Summer's head tilted to the right.

"Noah and I are meeting with the buyer from Maxwell's in ten minutes."

Meeting? Here? She'd almost forgotten about the negotiations with Maxwell's flagship store in Manhattan carrying a Farmer's Ale sample pack.

"The buyer is here?" she asked, stamping out the catch in her voice.

Logically she knew it wouldn't be Max or his sister Vanesa, Maxwell's head buyer. They'd send a junior associate to work on such a small deal. A small deal for the high-end grocery chain, but a huge deal for Todd and Noah.

"Zoom," Nat blurted, causing Todd to arch an eyebrow at her. "They're meeting on Zoom. The buyer isn't here. Too close to Christmas to travel for an hour long meeting. So, no Maxwell's peeps here," she sputtered as pink crept up her neck.

Summer pushed the ball of dread snaking up her throat back down to her belly. Even if the shadows of her past haunted the corners of the sunshine-filled today of her life, it wasn't here. There'd be no reason for Vanessa or Max to ever come to Perry. If a junior associate buyer came to the village, none of them would know Summer. It had been almost ten years. She looked utterly different.

I'm safe. Liam's safe. She repeated the thought like a desperate mantra.

"You're being weirder than normal?" Todd studied Nat.

Schooling her face into an indignant expression, Nat jammed her hands onto her hips. "I am as weird as I normally am."

"Sure." He smirked, looking back to Summer. His eyebrows knitted together, as if concerned. "You okay, sweetheart?"

"Of course." Summer lifted her lips into a pretend smile.

Like a bloodhound catching a scent, his green eyes bored into her in assessment.

"Just thinking about all the things that I still need to do before I run home to change and pick up Liam for the party." God, she hated lying to him. *I can't take this chance away from him.* She forced her smile to reach her eyes.

"I'll see you tonight." Nodding, he released her and stepped back.

"Wait…" She grabbed his hand and pulled him back to her. "Aren't you forgetting something?"

Leaned in, wickedness filled his features, as he captured her lips in a toe-curling kiss.

"You guys!" Nat's voice hit a glass-shattering pitch.

Lips still locked with Todd: Summer flipped Nat the bird.

"Manners!" Nat *tsked.*

Once Todd left, Nat let out a long breath. "Are you okay?"

"I just forgot about the Maxwell's deal." She opened the box on the table and pulled out several barrel-shaped candle-holders for the tables' centers.

Raking her teeth along her lower lip, Nat stared at Summer.

"What?"

"If you tell them, they'll turn down the deal. Noah and Todd would never—"

"Nat."

"It's not too late. They haven't signed anything yet," she persisted.

"Nat." Summer spoke her friend's name like a warning, causing Nat to flinch.

Of course, Todd and Noah would give up this opportunity. Even without needing to hear her entire story, they'd pull out of the deal. But it wasn't just about her. This deal had the potential to bring so much economic prosperity to the village. They could expand the brewery and hire more staff. It could attract potential visitors to the village to not just check out the brewery but downtown's shops and restaurants. It also offered Todd a chance to showcase his talents on a larger scale. For so many to see how talented he was with his witchy brews. Including his dad.

After what he'd shared Sunday about his father's disappointment in him, she knew this would be more proof to hold up about how wrong Sheriff Jeff Krueger was about his son. Hell, she'd frame the press release when the deal went through, and hand deliver it to the county sheriff's office.

"I'll say this and then I promise I won't bring it up again," Nat said.

Summer shot her a disbelieving look.

"Well, I'll try not to bring it up again." Her face twisted in apologetic realization that she'd likely bring this up again. Nat was nothing but determined and that was something Summer frustratedly adored about her friend. "While you're busy taking care of everyone else, don't forget to take care of yourself. There's a reason they tell us on planes to put our mask on first."

"What does that mean?"

"Sacrificing yourself for everyone else only leaves us without you." Nat stepped close and took Summer's hands. "And I don't want to live in a world without Summer Michaels."

"You're being melodramatic." The chide was soft.

"Maybe"—she shrugged— "but I'm a doctor and I always err on the side of caution. I know it's your past and your story to tell, I just don't want to see it keep its hold on you. The moment Maxwell's was mentioned, you stiffened. Even Todd noticed. You've made such huge strides over the last year pulling away from the pain of your past, I just don't want this to shove you back."

Summer squeezed Nat's hands in reassurance. "It won't.

I'm moving forward. I promise. I even have my first appointment with Dr. Horin scheduled for January fifth."

"Okay." Nat squeezed back. "Wanna schedule a wine and Ben and Jerry's date that night like we did after my first therapy appointment?"

"Yes!" Summer beamed.

Hours later, Taylor Swift's melodic voice greeted Summer as she entered the Farmer's Ale. Beside her, Liam chattered about how he and JJ were shooting free throws during PE that day. After decorating with Nat, she went home to shower and change into the party dress Nat talked her into buying during last week's emergency first date shopping excursion. It was a simple forest-green dress with a sweetheart neckline that hugged her curves in just the right way. Enough to accentuate them without clinging.

"Todd!" Liam shouted, running past her toward the bar.

A big grin broke across Todd's face as he looked up from the open book on the bar, a blue zip-up hoodie molded over his sculpted form. "Hey, buddy."

"I made a free throw today!" Excitement pulsed through him.

"Nice job!"

"And…" Summer prompted her little boy.

"Sweetheart," Todd leaned over the bar and placed a soft peck on her cheek. "You look gorgeous."

"Todd." The impact this man had on her body. Just a chaste peck and heat tiptoed up her spine and invaded her cheeks.

"And I got a hundred on my math test." Liam beamed.

"Someone's earned a treat." Turning, he opened the glass fridge behind him and pulled out a small brown opaque bottle. "I made this special for when you come in here for events with your mom." He placed the bottle on the bar, turning the label toward them.

The Little Man in white block lettering stretched across the orange label. A silhouette of a little boy playing with a dog was just below the writing.

Liam's eyes widened and Summer's heart nearly burst open like a pinata full of all the feels. So many emotions swirled within her. Gratitude. Affection. Admiration. *Love?* It was the only feeling that came with a question mark. An uneasy uncertainty hissed inside her, warning that it was too soon, too much, and too bold. That as much as Todd spoke of a future, telling him that she thought she was falling in love with… correction, may already be in love with him, would send him running.

"What is it?" Liam's question snapped her back to attention.

"It's homemade root beer. I know Mom only lets you have soda on special occasions and since this is a special occasion…" he trailed off, meeting her eyes for approval.

She met his gaze with an agreeable smile.

Liam's little fingers skated across the bottle's label. "It looks like what you buy in the store."

Pride tugged at the corners of Todd's lips. "It's better than what you can get at the store." He slipped a bottle opener out of his pocket and opened it. Grabbing a frosted mug from the little freezer under the bar, he poured the frothy brown liquid into it. "Give it a whirl." He plopped the mug in front of Liam.

Taking a long gulp, his dark brown eyes sparked with joy. "So good!" He let out a tiny belch.

"Manners," she chided halfheartedly.

"How'd you learn to make this?" Liam asked.

"My grandpa. It's his recipe. It was one of the first things he taught me to brew."

"It's so cool that you know how to make soda." Liam's

brow wrinkled. "Is it hard to learn?"

"Nah. It's like science class, it's just doing experiments until you get it right."

"Could I learn?" His eyes darted between her and Todd.

"If Mom's okay with it."

"Mom?" Liam peered up, a plea in his expression.

She ruffled his thick chestnut hair. "Sure, baby."

"Hey, boss man!" Jasper, one of their bartenders, strode in and joined Todd behind the bar.

Summer narrowed her eyes at Jasper's green hoodie. "Nat's going to be mad. Where are the shirts she made?"

For Noah's birthday, Nat had talked the staff and several guests into wearing T-shirts with Noah's face on them. She'd gone a little crafting crazy the last few weeks with her Cricut machine, making T-shirts and even a tablecloth, which sat draped over the buffet table, with Noah's trademark dimpled smile plastered all over it. Thanks to Nat's insistence that she wear one of the dresses they bought on their shopping trip, Summer got a pass on wearing the T-shirt. Although, Liam happily rocked his Noah shirt.

"Don't worry, mama bear." Todd winked, unzipping his sweatshirt and tossing it to the side.

There was a tiny hitch in her breath as she took in the way the black T-shirt hugged his muscular frame as if it was another layer of skin. The white *Say Yes* stretched across his broad chest causing a flutter deep in her core. For a moment, she considered dragging him into his office to peel off that too-tight shirt and lick down his defined stomach…

Simmer down, vagina! Grabbing the mug of root beer, she took a swig to cool down her boiling blood.

"Todd Jebediah Krueger!" Nat bellowed, stomping into the room, face pinched in annoyance.

"Your middle name is Jebediah?" Liam chortled.

"It's a family name." A furrow marred his brow.

"What are you wearing?" She planted herself in front of

the bar and put her hands on her hips. "Et-tu, Jasper?" she shrilled, gesturing at his matching black T-shirt.

"Nice to see you, Nat." He smirked.

"Why are you *not* wearing the Noah shirts?" Her mouth puckered. "Why are you wearing these instead?"

As Taylor Swift's "Love Story" started playing, Todd pulled a bottle from below the bar, placing it in front of Nat. The words *Just Say Yes,* scrawled on the label.

"What?" Her face scrunched. "Say yes to what?"

A charming smile curled his lips, turning the bottle around to reveal a back label reading *Turn around, Nat.*

Eyes rounded into the size of saucers, she nodded. A visible shiver rippled across Nat's body.

Summer pivoted with her friend and her mouth dropped open. Behind them stood Noah, that dimple of his punctuating a big smile. Excitement and hope shimmered in his blue eyes. A fitted black T-shirt—just like Todd and Jasper's—hugged his large frame. Only instead of the word *Yes* it read *I have one question for you.*

Nat just stood there blinking. "What's happening?"

"Let's find out." Summer nudged her toward Noah.

Taking her hand, he knelt to one knee and pulled out a small black ring box. "Nat, I–"

"YES!" she screamed and jumped into the air.

Rising, he caught her in his arms. "I didn't even ask you." He rumbled with laughter between her peppered kisses. "I had a whole speech."

"You had me at the T-shirt." Happy tears streamed down her face.

"She said 'yes', come on out," Todd called, rounding the bar.

The office door halfway down the hallway leading to the back door flung open. Noah and Nat's parents, and Clayton and Elle, ran out cheering.

Tears pricked in Summer's eyes watching her best friend embrace her parents. Joy glistened in all their eyes.

Todd's muscular arms came from behind her, tucking her into his chest. His nose nuzzled into her hair. "Looks like you'll have another wedding to plan."

"And you'll have another one to dance with me at."

He squeezed her middle. "Oh, sweetheart, I never need an excuse to dance with you."

"Ugh!" Liam grumbled. "Everyone's being gushy."

CHAPTER TWENTY

"Can I get you guys anything? Some snacks? A condom? Let me know!" ~Mean Girls

Summer bolted down the stairs at the doorbell's ring. Not solely out of excitement to greet Todd, who'd be joining them for Christmas Eve, but to stop her parents. It would only be a matter of mere moments before they said or did something to mortify her.

Jumping in front of her dad just as he reached the foyer, she positioned herself between him and the front door. "Consider this my Christmas present; please don't say anything embarrassing."

His face twisted with incredulity. "I would never."

Her eyebrows pulled together.

Arms crossed; mom stepped up. "You're being a little dramatic."

"Please." She huffed a heavy breath. "Just don't bring up my aging ovaries or how cute our babies would be."

"I swear, Summer Joy," Dad said, placing his hand on his heart. "I'll restrain myself from discussing your reproductive viability."

Tilting her head around her dad, she shot her mom a harsh look. "Mother?"

"You're no fun," Mom pouted.

"Why are you all standing in front of the door?" Liam appeared in the living room entry way; face wrinkled.

"Todd's here."

"Shouldn't we open the door?"

Summer wagged a finger at them in warning. "Behave." Turning, she opened the door.

A smiling Todd stood, two large bags full of presents dangled from one hand, while a pink leash hooked to Sheba wrapped around his other. "Merry Christmas!" Sheba's tongue was lolling out from her large grin.

"So, you're here for my daughter's hand." Dad's deep voice boomed.

"Dad!" Mortification blazed her cheeks.

"You only said we couldn't talk about your aging reproductive organs," Mom defended with a sassy wink.

"What are reproductive organs?" Liam blinked.

Summer glowered at her mother.

Her mouth slanted into an unapologetic smile. "He's gotta learn some time."

"Let's talk dowry." Dad crossed his arms over his chest.

Todd lifted one of the bags. "How about some freshly brewed beer?"

Dad hooted and raised his arm in the air. "Sold!"

Despite the embarrassing initial five seconds of Todd's arrival for Christmas Eve, her parents cringe-worthy antics subsided. The five of them blended better than she'd imagined. Sitting around the dining room table over Dad's mouth-watering prime rib and Mom's collection of delectable sides, the conversation flowed like a calm river. Sheba sprawled in the corner of the dining room atop a folded flannel blanket Liam brought in from the living room.

"Todd, I thought the beer your granddad used to bring to the holiday faculty party was good, but *this* puts his to shame." Dad saluted with his half-filled mug of beer.

"It's his Christmas ale recipe, but I brew it in a bourbon barrel."

Dad sipped and smacked his lips together. "Is there vanilla and nutmeg in this?"

Summer reached under the table, taking Todd's hand and beaming at him. This was so stark from the last time she'd sat at a table with her parents and a boyfriend. With Max, a harsh edge accompanied the meet the parents dinner. Instead of the stiff spine and curt responses of that day, Dad's posture was relaxed, laughter curved his lips, and he fell in-and-out of easy conversation. Granted, Todd already knew her parents. There'd been countless interactions at parties and BBQs over the last year. Not to mention the random "There's Todd, let's invite him to join us" dinner at restaurants in the village.

Even if that foundation hadn't been there, something about this moment felt inevitable. Like two magnets pulled apart, they'd been drawn to connect to one another, despite her attempts to pull away.

We fit. She leaned back, allowing that knowledge to wash over her like a refreshing rainstorm after a drought. With Max, she'd always been about molding herself to fit his world. With Todd she didn't have to change who she was, nor who he was.

"Todd's going to teach me to make root beer!" Liam announced.

"So you've mentioned," Mom teased, pointing her fork at him, amusement brightening her dark eyes.

"He's really excited," Summer added.

"Me too." Todd grinned, his gaze bounced between her and Liam. "So is Grandpa Rice. I told him when we had lunch today. He wants to be there for the first lesson to make sure I don't mess it up."

She squeezed his knee below the table. "I'm sure you'll be a perfect teacher."

"I don't know. Jeb Rice's teaching shoes are big ones to fill. He's still a legend at the high school. How is your grandpa? I haven't seen him in a while." Dad forked up several glazed carrots.

"He's great. He's the social chair at the Assisted Living. Always planning their parties. That's what he's doing tonight. He hosts a Christmas Eve shindig for the residents who don't have families and staff members who have to work."

"Oh, a party planner like Summer." The laughing lilt of Dad's comment nipped at Summer's nerves.

I'm not a party planner. She swallowed down the growl growing in her throat.

"Not like Summer at all." Todd's strong hand squeezed her knee easing Summer's tightening jaw. "He just puts out a few snack trays and bottles of wine for a night of board games or watching old movies. Summer coordinates huge events. There's a budget, vendors, publicity, logistics, and so much more that she does." Todd threaded their fingers, lifting them to his mouth and pressing an appreciative kiss. "Grandpa Rice has nothing on my girl."

"My girl?" she guffawed.

"You would prefer my woman?" He met her sassy smirk with a roguish smile.

There was no fighting it; that boyish smile and mischief filled gaze left her a puddly mess. Every inch of her became an ooey-gooey glob of affection for this man. *My man.*

"You two," Mom cooed.

Dad cleared his throat. "Agreed that Summer can do more than just party plan—"

Summer held her breath waiting for the *but.*

"—Which is why Sharon and I want her to take some classes at GCC. That reminds me, Summer did you speak to Janet Coates?"

"Yes." Summer pushed the last spoonful of mashed potatoes around her plate. "I spoke to her Tuesday after work."

"Oh honey, that's wonderful" Mom clapped her hands.

"Will you be registering for that class?" Dad leaned forward. "I checked the website and the deadline to register is the third. You can take up to two classes without having to apply to matriculate."

"I–"

"If you're worried about the cost, Mom and I will pay.

"Class?" Liam chirped. "Is Mom going to school?"

"Uh…" Summer's mouth went dry.

There'd been no decision. Her parents asked her to have a conversation with Janet and she'd done that. She still didn't know if she wanted to take the class. A queasiness rolled around her belly each time she thought about it.

"You don't need to pay. Plus—"

"Nonsense." He waved a dismissive hand. "We still have money in the college fund you never used."

"Dad—"

He ignored her protest. "Just register and I'll transfer the money to your account."

"I've got an idea!" Mom jumped in with a loud clap, dragging everyone's attention. "Since it's Christmas, let's save the business chatter for the twenty-sixth. The holidays are for fun, after all."

Summer shot her mom a thankful look.

"How about we clean up—" she nudged her husband "—while Summer and Liam take Todd and Sheba on the walking tour of our favorite decorated houses."

Dad's brow creased. "But you usually go on the walk with them, while I make the ice cream."

Mom trailed her fingers along dad's cheek. "Wouldn't you much rather have me help you *make* dessert?"

"Someone's working on getting on the naughty list." He waggled his eyebrows at his wife. "Summer Joy, you all enjoy your walk and make it long…*very* long."

"Gross," Summer's face twisted into a grimace.

He pointed a finger at her. "You said nothing about your mom's reproductive organs."

Todd snorted.

Fat, fluffy snowflakes waltzed in the cool night air. The world around them almost a replica of a shaken-up snow globe. Colorful string lights enveloped the mixture of Victorian, Dutch Colonial, and Mid-Century box houses making up the neighborhoods they wandered through.

Contentment sighed through her body. By no means was life perfect for Summer. This wasn't a Hallmark movie, its sappy sweetness washing away the struggles of today nor the ones that haunted from yesterday. She'd still have a well-intentioned but intrusive father to contend with. There were still the demons of her past to deal with, both the literal and figurative.

None of that mattered in the radiant glow of this moment. All ills melted away in the gaze of the man beside her and the smiles of the little boy in front of her when he turned to gush about a decorated house.

"I like this." She clutched Todd's gloved hand.

"Me too, sweetheart." Todd's stare flicked between her and Liam, who skipped in front of them with a tail-wagging Sheba in step. "This feels…" A crease formed in the middle of his brow as he seemed to search for what to say.

"Right." She stopped and faced him. "This feels right."

He raised his hand to her cheek, the cool damp fabric swiping across her skin.

The stuttering cadence of her heartbeat roared. "Is it too soon to—"

"So, the rumors are true!" A feminine voice crooned, pulling their attention.

A young woman was jumping out of a gray pickup truck. Coppery-red hair poked out from beneath a black wool page boy hat. Her green eyes—identical to Todd's—fixed on the little foursome of humans and canine.

"When Brenda told me she'd seen my dear brother making out with Summer Michaels behind the brewery after the Christmas Market—"

"Rose... We were hardly making out." Eyes rolling, Todd sighed.

The smirk curving Summer's lips countered his argument. There had been a light make-out session when Todd pressed her up against her car Saturday night.

With a dismissive expression, Rose sauntered toward them. "I told my dear sweet girlfriend that she was mistaken. My doting big brother would *never* start dating someone and not tell me."

"It's not like that, Rose, I've just been busy this week and we haven't had a chance to speak"—he motioned between Rose and Summer— "You know Summer Michaels...my girlfriend."

"Girlfriend?" Her eyebrow ticked up. "Nice work! Glad to see you're no longer pining for the prom queen."

Her use of prom queen caused a bristle to rip down Summer's spine. The phrase had been tossed at Summer so often since she'd returned home that now the word reverberated with derision and judgement.

"Kidding." Rose slapped her brother's bicep and turned to Summer; a warm smile filled her features. "Seriously, though,

I'm really happy you two got together. You make a great couple."

Maybe she'd let the prom queen comment go. The sincerity in Rose's gaze spoke of genuine happiness for her brother. Plus, if being the prom queen meant she had Todd beside her, she'd wear the motherfucking crown with a shit-eating grin on her face.

"Mom." Liam shuffled over, Sheba trotted beside him, and wrapped his arms around her waist.

"Hey, Liam." Rose nodded. "Remember me? I came to talk to your class about stranger danger?"

Releasing his hold around Summer's waist, he turned, straightened his back, and held out his hand. "Hi, Officer Kruger."

"Such a gentlemen," Rose cooed as she shook his hand. "You can teach Todd a thing or two."

A half-scoff, half-snort escaped Todd.

"Are you joining us for dessert?" Rose motioned to the front door of the plain gray house beside the decorated one Liam stopped to look at.

Summer drank in the starkness of the gray house compared to the rest of the neighborhood bedecked in a happy explosion of holiday cheer. The only lights that beamed from the house were several lit table lamps atop the end tables visible from the living room window. No lush pine tree adorned in twinkling lights or tiny electric bulb candles glowed in the windows. A simple wreath with a worn pink ribbon hung on the white front door, the only clue that Christmas touched the house.

Pink? Summer's heart squeezed for just a moment thinking of the blush of pink that washed over Todd's house.

Just as she realized whose house they stood in front of, a tall, broad chested, man with a neat black beard with streaks of gray crisscrossing it opened the front door. Peering at them, shock widened Jeff Krueger's eyes.

Jaw tight, Todd's gaze jumped to his father. For a beat, their eyes held in a silent exchange.

Kicking her boots through the fresh snow piling the sidewalk, Rose cleared her throat. "He'd love it if you'd come in, so would I."

A mournful yet longing expression sat upon Jeff Krueger's face. A soft plea seemed to swim in his eyes that appeared almost evergreen in the porch's dim light. Father and son continued to stare. Their fixed gazes saying everything and nothing at all until Todd cut the visual tether between them, turning back to his sister.

"I'll see you tomorrow at Cassie and Zach's," Todd said with an uncharacteristic hard edge in his voice.

Hurt sliced into Summer's chest. Both for Todd and his father. Taking in Jeff's now downcast gaze and slow nod, Summer saw herself. If anyone understood regret, it was Summer.

"Alright." Rose sighed. "Summer, Liam, will you be there? I'd love to get to know my brother's girlfriend and little boy."

Summer knew that Rose meant to get to know her big brother's girlfriend's little boy, not *his* little boy. That didn't stop the sensation that bloomed inside her at the idea of Liam being Todd's little boy. Of them being a family.

What are you thinking? This was all ridiculous. They'd been dating for eight days, and it was way too soon for delusions of happy endings with marriage and Liam calling him dad to dance in her head. Somehow, his kisses had zapped away any semblance of logic and reason from her. *Relationships go at their own pace,* her very own words taunted her, reminding her that there was a flow for each river. Some fast. Some slow. All flowing. There was definitely a lot of flowing feelings rippling inside her.

Tucking Summer into his side, he pressed a gentle kiss to her temple. "Yeah, Summer and Liam will be joining me at Cassie's."

Every Christmas Day, Cassie and Zach held an all day party at their home. Family and friends wandered in and out of their large farmhouse, snacking on the buffet of food that covered three large tables set up in their kitchen and dining room. The Christmas Day activities at the Michael's house was confined to an extravagant big breakfast followed by a day spent in a vegetative state watching movies and playing games. Todd had invited the entire family to join for the late afternoon. Summer's parents declined, so Dad could take her mom on a movie date in Buffalo.

"Great." Rose beamed. "I'm looking forward to telling Summer all the embarrassing stories from your teens. Like the time you dressed up like Samwise Ganges to attend a midnight showing of *Lord of the Rings: The Two Towers.*"

Both Summer and Liam cackled.

A furrow creased his forehead. "Goodnight, Rose."

Her face twisted into an innocent expression before she strode toward the house. "Goodnight, big bro."

"Sam Ganges?" Liam gaped. "He's the sidekick."

"Yes, but Sam gets the girl at the end." Todd's eyes swept down Summer's form, a roguish grin brightened his face. "The *right* girl."

Smiling, Summer leaned in and presses a gentle kiss to Todd's cheek, causing Liam to roll his eyes with a groaned "So gushy!." As their shared laughter faded, Summer's stare fell back on Todd. Sadness shimmered in his gaze which remained locked on the front door, his father and sister on the other side and he on the outside.

"I always thought Sam Ganges was cute." She bit her lip.

He turned. "*Yeah?*"

"There's something about the good friend character that's *very* sexy." She lifted to her tiptoes, nuzzling her nose against his.

"You two are annoying," Liam mumbled.

Summer's eyes fluttered open. A cozy warmth enveloped her from the sensation of being tucked into Todd's side. Tiny snores filtered through the room from Liam, who lay with his head on her lap, wrapped in a flannel blanket beside her on the couch. Sheba folded herself into a ball, snug behind Liam's knees. The four of them claimed the couch when they'd sat down for tonight's double feature, their annual showing of *Home Alone* followed by *It's a Wonderful Life*, which Todd watched each Christmas Eve. Mom and Dad stretched out in their respective recliners on opposite sides of the living room.

After they'd returned from the walk, Mom announced it was time to each open one gift. When Todd went to grab the presents that he'd brought, she'd *tsked* at him that there was only one appropriate gift to open on Christmas Eve.

"Star Wars!" Liam had hooted at his set of Jedi-inspired pajamas.

Since Summer was a little girl, the only gift they opened on Christmas Eve were PJs. They'd change into them immediately, spending the rest of the night eating Dad's homemade ice cream and watching movies. Embracing the tradition, Todd rocked navy pajama bottoms speckled with orange beer bottles and matching T-shirt that she'd gifted him.

The set mom gave Summer was a little more form-fitting than the previous years. Admiring herself in the mirror before she'd emerged from her room, she knew that there was no bluster in her mom's teasing about making her more grand-babies. Silky pajama bottoms hugged Summer's hips and ass. A matching pink tank with lacy trim and a built-in bra accentuated her breasts but flowed over the swell of her belly in a babydoll fashion. Thank goodness the set included a matching silk robe, which she wrapped tightly to cover herself.

Hours later, they all hovered between sleep and awake in the living room. Mom's head lay at an awkward angle against her headrest, a tiny dribble of drool on the corner of her lips. Summer considered grabbing her phone to take a picture to use the next time Mom said or did something embarrassing, but she was too cozy sandwiched between her two guys to indulge in that idea beyond a mere thought.

Sighing, she tipped her gaze up to Todd, whose expression was pure contentment. "You fell asleep," he whispered.

"You're an excellent pillow." She snuggled in, inhaling his wintry, woodsy scent.

His fingers combed into her loose tendrils. "I'll always be your pillow… Or anything else you need me to be."

A sweet ache, reminiscent of devouring too many tasty things, filled her. Nat would tease her that she was having all the feels, and she was. Like seeds in the wind, each emotion swirled in search of a place to take root deep inside her and bloom. That delicious pang in her heart warned that one of those emotions had already planted itself and sprouted.

Summer broke the stare with Todd, looking to the other side of the room. Dad's dark eyes peered back at her with a knowing grin.

"What time is it?" Mom yawned and stretched in the chair.

Dad lowered the footrest and scooted to the edge of the recliner. "It's after midnight. We need to get this little munchkin to bed, so Santa can come."

"Good call." Summer brushed her hand against Liam's cheeks. "Baby, time to go to bed."

"Come on buddy. I'll tuck you in." Dad said, standing up.

"Todd, will you and Sheba tuck me in?" Liam said sleepily.

"Sure." Todd peered between Summer, her dad, and then Liam. "If that's okay with your grandpa," he added.

Summer looked between her dad, whose mouth was dragged down in a small frown, and Todd.

"Yeah." Dad nodded, a slight bob in his throat. "I need to go put the ice cream maker away anyways." With a shrug, he turned to leave.

"Night, Pop," Liam yawned and stood.

Dad stopped and peered over his shoulder, a small smile curved his lips. "Night, bud," he said and shuffled out of the room.

"Bedtime rules," Summer said, ruffling Liam's already sleep-mussed hair.

"Brush his teeth and then one chapter from the book on the nightstand." Todd flashed her a soft smile.

"Yeah." God, her heart almost exploded with happiness that he knew that. That he'd paid attention enough to know these things.

"Come on, buddy" Todd murmured, placing a hand on Liam's shoulder and guiding him out of the room.

She pressed a hand over her heart. She was done for. Watching the gentleness of this big strong man escorting her little boy upstairs, with Sheba following behind, made her knees wobble. Any moment she'd swoon like a damsel from one of her historical romance novels.

"You're drooling, Summer," Mom snarked, placing a hand on her shoulder.

"I'm not." She wiped at her mouth, just in case. There was no drool. "Do you think dad is upset?" Summer motioned her head toward the empty entry way where her father and then Todd and Liam had just left through.

Frowning, Mom looked between the entrance and Summer. "It's hard for him. He's been the number one guy in your lives for a very long time."

"Me being with Todd won't change anything." Even she knew that was a false promise.

It did and would change everything. It already had.

Tonight was the first time someone else besides she or her parents tucked Liam in. Change was scary. For her parents. For Summer. What may be the scariest thing of all, was how right this felt.

"Most nights we see our daughter and her son on the couch. Tonight, we saw our daughter's family."

Family? She shook her head. "It's too soon for that word."

"Sure." Mom's tone was unconvinced. "Whether it's too soon or not, things are changing and that's tough."

"Isn't that what you want? You all but served me up for the taking." Summer motioned toward the silky jammies gifted by her mom.

"It would help if you loosened this…" Mom fiddled with the robe's tie.

Summer swatted her away. "Stop, woman." She guffawed.

Chuckling, Mom stepped back and offered a wistful smile. "Even if it's something we want, it doesn't make it hurt less… In a good way, though. Every parent wants their child to do these things. Find a partner. Have a family."

"Though I did it in the reverse," Summer said, self-deprecation punctuated her words.

"You've always had your own way of doing things. I know that."

She met her mom's soft gaze. "Does Dad? I know you both encourage me, but he's been—"

Mom let out a hard breath. "He just wants what's best for you. We both do."

What about what I think is best for me? That's the one part of this conversation that never surfaced. Her parents, especially her dad, were so focused on what they felt was best for Summer that they never asked her what she wanted. Had Summer even stopped to ask herself that same question? The last time she'd made a decision solely based on what she wanted had been when she'd left for New York City. *And look what happened there.* Still…

"He's just been pushing so hard and—"

Palm placed on her shoulders; Mom halted her words. "You might have been the cheerleader in high school, but your dad has always been your biggest supporter. It's why he pushes so hard. He knows how special you are. We both do, but I know he can be a little overzealous at times. Please know, he means well."

On the surface she knew Dad only wanted what was best for her. That the little backhanded comments were meant to help. Except all they did was hurt. Each pierced her heart, coursing a poison that dripped along her veins in its knowledge that in her father's eyes she'd been weighed and found wanting.

"He made it through half a paragraph before he conked out." Todd chuckled and strode into the room. "Although, so did Sheba. She is refusing to leave his side. I left them curled up together sharing his pillow."

Mom turned toward Todd. "Looks like Liam got a dog for Christmas after all."

"I guess so." A low chuckle vibrated in Todd's chest. "I can come by first thing in the morning to pick her up."

"In the morning?" Mom clucked. "You're not going anywhere. It's almost midnight and it's snowing. You'll sleep here."

"Uh…" Todd rubbed the back of his neck.

Mom's mouth slanted into a salacious grin. "We're all adults here. Let's not pretend you two haven't…" she motioned between Summer and Todd "Done the deed," she finished.

"Mom!" Summer hissed, cheeks blazing.

"I all but served you up, remember." Mom winked.

CHAPTER TWENTY-ONE

"I know having a boyfriend might seem like the only thing important right now, but you don't have to dumb yourself down in order for a guy to like you." ~Mean Girls

Todd *is sleeping over.* Summer paced the length of her room. After saying goodnight to her parents, she'd slipped into the bathroom to wash her face and brush her teeth. Leaving a spare toothbrush on the counter for Todd, she headed back to her room allowing him to get ready for bed.

Todd in my bed. Not once in her life had a boy slept in her bed in her parents' house. Even that weekend her senior year when her parents went to Thousand Islands and Shane begged to sleep over, she'd declined.

Todd was no boy. A tingle struck up low in her belly at the image of Todd's large form hovered over her. His hand clasped over her mouth, stifling her moans and whimpers for more.

Seriously, vagina, you need to stop!

Hands on her hips, she scanned the room. The plush

cream-colored comforter was pulled tight over the bed and fat pillows covered its top half. A stuffed panda bear, the first gift Liam ever bought her, flopped onto its side on the small, cushy, blue reading chair in the corner. The scent of cinnamon apples danced around the room from a small infuser plugged into the wall outlet.

It was her little corner of the world, and she was doing something she'd never done before, sharing it with someone. Not just someone, but Todd. The truth buzzed within her that he wasn't just a someone but maybe *the* someone.

The creak of the door caused her to turn.

Todd shuffled in with his mouth slanted into a boyish grin. "Hey."

"Hey." Her response breathless. "This is weird." She twirled the sash of her robe around her wrist.

He arched that sexy left eyebrow causing her heart to stutter. "Is it?"

"A bit. It reminds me of the scene in a romance novel when the couple gets stuck at a roadside inn and have to share a bed."

"This is nothing like that trope." With the grace of a tiger, he prowled closer. Something wicked and a little predatory smoldered in his green eyes. "First"— hands on her waist, he pulled her close— "in the books that scene leads to the couple's first time, and we've already had each other."

"Are you saying now that you've had me, you don't want me anymore." The tiniest flicker of insecurity sparked in her. What if she hadn't lived up to his fantasies? What if she was like that sought after Christmas toy, discarded as soon as the last decoration was packed away come early January?

"Sweetheart, that was just a taste." He nipped at the shell of her ear. Gooseflesh sprouted along her arms. "You are a decadent meal that I plan to devour one bite at a time."

"Will you be nibbling on me tonight?" The question dripped with a huskiness foreign to her ears.

"Not when your parents and son's bedrooms are just down the hall." He smirked. "I have no faith in your ability to be quiet when I get my hands on you."

Breath swooshed out of her. The images of his hands and tongue crisscrossing her body heated her blood. A flush crawled up her chest, finding its home in her cheeks.

Clearing her throat, she took charge. "I think it would be *you* that would have trouble controlling yourself."

His left eyebrow quirked.

Stepping back, she untied the sash and opened her robe. The silky fabric fell to the carpet revealing the sexy but sweet pajama set. The pink silk clung as if holding onto her curves for dear life. Reveling in his stare, she slipped her hands into the waistband of her bottoms and pushed them down. Brazenness crackled inside her as she stood clad only in lacy panties and a babydoll top.

He swallowed thickly, his gaze drinking her up like a man dying of thirst. "Someone doesn't play fair."

"Who me?" She batted her lashes, sashaying her hips as she walked to the other side of the bed. Her skin hummed with each step knowing his gaze remained fixed on her.

"You do like wielding your power over me."

Teasing this man ignited a delicious sizzle in her bloodstream. As contented and happy that he made her just with his sweet words and calming presence, the playfulness between them thrummed joy through her. Even before she'd given herself over to this growing feeling—its hold threatening to conquer every inch of her—there'd always been a fizziness in her veins with their banter.

He teased about the power she had over him but he had as much over her.

Pulling back the comforter, she slid in, the cool sheets kissed her bare legs. She patted the empty spot beside her. "Will you be joining me?"

"Two can play this game, sweetheart," he said, voice dripping with sinful intentions. Yanking his shirt off, he tossed it to the ground. The pajama bottoms hung low on his hips. Dark red hair skated down his belly drawing her gaze lower.

Summer tried to swallow, but her mouth grew dry.

"Maybe I will have to have a nibble tonight." A wolfish glint darkened his eyes.

"What are you waiting for?" It came out almost like a squeak.

Turning he locked the door and moved to the bed. With each step her breath grew ragged. Slipping in beside her, he tucked her back until her shoulders were against his chest. His lips whispered kisses down her jawline. The heat of his mouth moved to her neck. Head back against his shoulder, she gave him full access. His hands caressed her breasts, the peaks pebbling from the taunting friction of cool silk against her body.

"Oh," she whimpered with his slow pinch of one taut bud.

"Shh," he murmured. "You have to be quiet, sweetheart, or I'll stop." He rolled both her nipples, igniting her body like kindling.

"Don't..." She bit her lower lip, fighting back the moan wanting to escape.

"Don't what?" He slid the thin straps of her top down, releasing her breasts.

"Please don't stop." A gentle plea strangled her words.

Confusion twisted and turned within her. She shouldn't be doing this. They could get caught. But her entire body melted into his touch. The way he fluctuated between hard pinches, gentle rolls, and soft strokes of her nipples slickened her core with need.

"Todd..." Her teeth sank hard into her bottom lip, pushing back the needy cry.

"You like that, sweetheart?" His right hand snaked down her belly, lifting the hem of her top and skating his fingers along the waistband of her underwear.

"Oh yeah," she purred, rubbing her ass against his growing arousal.

"Summer," he let out a low rumbly growl. "Behave."

"You don't like?" She pressed her backside deeper against his length delighting in the twitching and clenching of his muscles.

"I do, but …" he pushed aside the fabric of her panties and ran his finger along her slick center "…this is about you."

"Ah—" She slapped her hand over her own mouth.

In languid strokes he circled her clit. The tiny nub pulsed with electricity. With each caress she writhed against him. Wildfire erupted within her, its liquid heat coursed along her bloodstream. Her teeth bit into her own hand to stifle her wanton cries. The pleasure coiled tighter and tighter. A pleasurable ache pulsed between her legs wanting only one thing to quell its throb.

"I want you inside me," she whimpered, moving her ass against him. "Please."

"Summer," he groaned. "This is about you."

"Then give me what I want."

"I don't have a condom."

"I have an IUD." She moved his hands to the waistband of her underwear, guiding him to pull them down her hips and legs. "I trust you."

Perhaps it was the haze of lust and want, but she had complete faith in this man. He'd never put her in danger. If there was any risk, he'd pull away.

"Same rules." He kissed below her earlobe. "We have to be quiet."

Shifting, he tugged down his pajama bottoms and boxer briefs, kicking them off the bed. Remaining on her side, she pressed back against his front. His erection poked against her lower back. Moving his fingers down her body, he gripped her leg, lifted, and hooked it over his arm. The head of his cock tapped at her entrance, sending a jolt along her nerve endings.

"Oh," she let out a pleased whine at his inch-by-slow-inch invasion into her.

"Your pussy is like fucking silk," he gritted.

She moved herself against him, urging him deeper. "Aren't you glad you gave in to me?"

A throaty laugh left him. He brushed away loose strands from her forehead and pressed a gentle kiss to her temple. "Only you could make me laugh during sex."

"I never imagined making you laugh during sex," she said breathlessly, rocking against him.

"But you imagined sex with me?" His other hand moved back to her breasts. "Did you lay in this bed at night thinking about me doing this?" Those capable fingers rolled and pinched each nipple, eliciting a strangled groan from her throat.

Her hands flew to her mouth.

"Did you touch yourself in this bed?" The slickness of his tongue dragged down her neck "Did you think about me?"

Words failed her so she only nodded. The decadent assault of the reality of his words and touch collided with the memory of lonely nights bringing herself to climax with just the mere thought of him. The reality and memory blazed inside her.

"Did you touch yourself like this?" He moved his hand from her breasts to the apex of her sex, caressing the pulsating nub.

"Yes." It was muffled beneath her hand, but she didn't trust herself to let go. Even though that was exactly what she was doing with this man. Letting go and falling into his waiting arms.

In a slow dance, their hips moved together. The slide of him in-and-out of her in an almost torturous pace rippled a pleasurable tightening deep in her belly. Her hips quickened searching for release. His fingers moved against her clit in cadence with the increased thrusts into her.

"Todd," she gasped beneath her clasped hands, her head falling back against him. An orgasm shook through her.

Removing her hand, he took her mouth with his. He drank up her muffled moans with a deep kiss. With slow pumps he carried her through her release. The fog of orgasm dissipated.

She broke their kiss. "Your turn." It was a breathless command.

Releasing her leg, he pulled out and flipped her onto her belly. Strong hands wrapped around her middle lifting her hips into the air.

"Same rules," he repeated, driving into her.

Summer buried her face into the pillows, masking her cries.

"Fu—" He stifled a throaty groan.

"Rules, baby." She turned her face, smirking up at him.

A roguish smile curled his lips, and he thrust deeper into her, hitting that spot. She bit back the cry, her nails digging into the sheets, the rising wave of another climax built. With almost relentless pumps, he drove into her. The tension pulsed, begging to come undone.

"Please," she whined, body quaking for release.

He slipped a hand beneath her, finding that needy bundle. "I'll always take care of you."

It was all she needed. "God," she gasped, clenching around him. Like a towel wrung dry, sweet relief dripped through her soaking every tense muscle with release.

With a final pump, he shuddered. Despite the tremble rolling along his limbs, his strong arms gathered her up pulling her into his chest.

Panting, she looked up at him. "Good boy."

A rich laugh left his lips.

After circling back to reality, they cleaned up. The beauty of her room at the end of the hall was it was right across from the bathroom. Her parents had an ensuite bathroom, so there'd be no running into them in the middle of the night and Liam was dead to the world when he slept. Still a joint shower would be out of the question. After Summer rinsed off, she changed the sheets while Todd showered.

Tossing the dirty sheets into the laundry, she tiptoed back upstairs. Mom and Dad's door remained shut, snores drifting from their room. Noticing the crack of light from beneath the bathroom door, indicating that Todd was still inside, she crept to Liam's room to check on him. Liam and Sheba's heads were pressed against each other, sharing his pillow. A hint of a smile on both their sleeping faces.

"She's going to think she can share my pillow now," Todd murmured, coming up behind her, his arms looped around her middle.

"Don't act like she doesn't get everything she wants," she whispered, leaning into him.

"What can I say, I'm a softy for my ladies."

Shaking her head, she closed the door and turned to face him.

"As much as I enjoyed that sexy little number you had on earlier, I really do prefer you in this." He tugged at the hem of the shirt she wore.

After showering, she'd pulled on the white Henley she'd nicked from his place Sunday night and her favorite pair of pink fleece pajama bottoms.

"So, I shouldn't wear that getup for you again?" she said, her voice low and taunting.

He gripped her waist. "Let's not be hasty."

"Let's go to bed." Chuckling, she took his hand leading him to her bedroom.

"Are we going to actually sleep? You have a tendency to pounce on me."

"Shut up." She giggled, pulled him inside and quietly shut the door.

The bed was remade. All signs of what had transpired earlier gone, except for the delicious ache between her legs and goofy grins on their faces. She still couldn't believe she'd done that. That *they'd* done that. She had no regrets. Just shock at her brazen wantonness and frankly a little pride. Piece-by-piece, she'd flaked off all the shouldn't do's, embracing a world of yeses.

"I've never had sex in my parents' house before," she admitted, crawling into bed.

"Really?" He slipped in beside her. "Even with Shane?"

Her face scrunched. "No. I only had sex with him a few times our senior year. Mostly at his house or in his car."

"Shane was your first?" He tucked her into his chest, the scent of her strawberries and cream bodywash clung to him.

"Yeah." She tipped her head up. "Who was yours?"

"Monique Jones. We dated junior year of college."

She blinked. "Junior year of college?"

"As you recall, I was a late bloomer. None of the girls I liked in high school were crushing on the jazz band's trumpet section's first chair."

"First chair? Very sexy." She ran her finger up his torso, enjoying the clench of his muscles.

"One would think." Laughter curled his lips.

"We were all fools." She snuggled into his bare chest. "Did you love Monique?"

"I cared for her, but looking back, I wasn't in love."

"Have you ever been in love?"

"With past girlfriends... No." His hands slipped below her shirt, coasting up and down her spine. "I'd never felt for them the kind of love I'd hoped for."

"What kind of love?"

"The kind where your chest constricts just a little bit each time the person you love walks into a room, whether it's been ten seconds or ten days since the last time you saw them. The kind where you hate fighting with them but can't imagine there could be anyone else you'd rather fight with. The kind where they hold your hand both to walk beside you, but also to drag you forward when you're scared or stubborn. The kind where they see all your ugly pieces."

She caressed his cheek. "And think you're beautiful in spite of them?"

"No." He covered her small hand with his large one. "Loves you because of them. The pretty and ugly pieces make us who we are. Loving someone means loving all of them, even the parts that don't sparkle and shine."

"That's beautiful."

A wistful expression washed over his face. "It's something my mom used to say. She'd say it whenever my dad wasn't showing his best self. When he'd be grouchy after a long workday or do some of the gross things we men wait to let you see until we've fooled you into loving us."

"I have a son and a father. I'm well aware of all the gross things men do." Her mouth tugged up. "Plus, we ladies can be equally gross."

"I'm aware. I have an especially gross little sister. I once caught Rose using tweezers I used for building *Star Wars* models to pop a pimple."

Summer blanched. "I don't know if I should be more horrified by Rose or that the man I just let come inside me built *Star Wars*, plural, models."

"Correction." He cleared his throat. "Not *the* man but *your* man."

"That you are." Running her fingers over his chest, she closed her eyes and listened to the quiet thump of his heartbeat. "I remember your dad always kissed your mom when he'd drop her off or pick her up from cheerleading practice.

He'd even show up at games with flowers for her. My teenaged heart nearly combusted with how adorable it was."

"I used to think they were so in love. God, as a kid I only hoped to be as happy as they were." He let out a hard breath. "But I was wrong. After she died, he just packed memories of her away with all her things. When you love someone, really love someone, you can't do that. Hell, my grandma has been dead ten years and Grandpa Rice has never taken off his wedding ring."

"I'm sorry, baby." She squeezed her arms just a little tighter.

How must it have been for him to go from seeing two people utterly in love to one seeming to forget the other existed. Todd's house erupted in the blush of his love for his mother, while his father's remained plain and gray.

"Do you think that's why you've never been in love?" she asked, peering up at him.

"Are you psychoanalyzing me, Summer Michaels?"

"Just trying to understand why a man with such a big heart, one that pestered me into a relationship—"

"Some men woo, I pester." He purred, making her laugh.

She raised her head capturing his gaze. "Seriously, though. How is someone as wonderful as you single? How are you not married with a gaggle of children? How have you never been in love?"

He brushed his long fingers into her hair. "There's no deep-seated fear or hangup. I'm not the broken male lead of a romance novel who can't love because his heart has been guarded. Yes, my mom died and that broke but didn't destroy my heart. Yes, I was the nerdy teenager who pined for girls who never liked me in return."

"Until now." She grinned.

"Until now." His grin matched hers. "The truth is boring and simple. My heart just hadn't met its match until—"

"Now?" she interrupted, her heart pounding like a fist

knocking on the door asking to come in. Or perhaps, it was asking for her to let it out. To speak the truth wandering inside her, searching for freedom. "I think I'm falling in love with you."

"You think you're falling in love with me?" His response was slow, deliberate, and a little questioning.

What did "I think I'm falling in love with you" mean? The confession felt like a lie coming out of her mouth. Think equaled uncertainty. She knew how she felt.

"No." She shook her head. "I don't think I'm falling in love with you. I am in love with you. I know it's crazy. It's too soon. Maybe I'm dick-matized from your very lovely and capable cock melting my logic with too many orgasms."

"Summer—"

"I'm not done." She sat up, taking in his still open mouth waiting to speak. "Sorry. I'm being rude but I need to get this out."

Nodding, he smirked.

"It's not your dick. It isn't even this last week together. I've been falling in love with you since we danced at Pete's birthday party last year. Every book we discussed. Each time we bantered at the café. All the little moments over the last year and a half. I knew I was falling for you and that's why I pushed you away. You terrified me. You still do because I've never felt this way about anyone. I love you, Todd Krueger." She halted, staring at his unreadable expression.

"Are you done?"

"Yes."

Their gazes tethered for one…two…three beats before his lips ensnared hers. His fingers wove into her hair, pulling her deeper into their kiss. Like a sunflower basking in sunshine, she opened to him allowing the heat of his tongue to meld with hers in a slow embrace.

"I love you, Summer Michaels."

"You do?" A tiny tremble shook her words. "Are you sure? It's not too soon?"

He cupped her face. "Yes, I'm sure... So fucking sure. From the outside looking in this may seem quick, but me and you, we've been in this together long before you kissed me on my couch. Every eye roll, smile, laugh, snarky comment... each moment with you over the last year made me fall just a little bit more in love with you."

He loves me. I love him. This changes everything.

Breath ragged; she blinked. The seedling of fear sprouted in her belly. She'd be a fool to not realize that her entire life as she knew it was about to change.

His fingers brushed her cheeks, the soothing strokes calmed the embers of anxiety that sparked inside her. "This scares the hell out of you, doesn't it?"

"It does." She swallowed hard, moving her stare to her lap.

"What scares you?"

She fiddled with her shirt's hem. "I lost myself in my relationship with Max. After him...after I came home, I was a mess. It's taken me all this time to find myself again, my real self."

"Are you scared you'll lose yourself in us?"

She shook her head. "No, because you'd never let that happen and more importantly, I am stronger than the girl I used to be. I'm not the girl who molded herself to be what others expected just to be *liked*—" Her face twisted into a grimace. "Even though I wasn't really liked. I just did what others expected. I played the mean girl and then the shallow trophy girlfriend. I know that now. It's my past and I don't plan to go back. I'll be working on that and other things when I start therapy."

"I'm in awe of your strength. You're such a fighter. It's just one of the many things I love about you." He caressed her cheek. "If it's not losing yourself in us, then what scares you?"

"When I came home, the way I got myself out of the hot mess that I was, was with routine and my to-do lists. There was comfort in a plan. In knowing what happens next. I never planned on you, and I don't know what happens next."

He threaded their fingers, bringing it to his chest. "I don't know what happens next, but we can find out together."

Worrying her lip, she nodded.

"And if it helps, I can make you a to-do list. Item one, lay down and let me hold you."

"Okay," she murmured, doing just that. "What's item two?"

CHAPTER TWENTY-TWO

"And you can only wear your hair in a ponytail once a week, so I guess you choose today." ~Mean Girls

I t's Christmas morning and Santa left me a very sexy man in my bed. The mix of light and shadow of breaking day caressed the room in a subtle light. Summer lay facing Todd, his arm draped over her middle. The hard angles of his face softened in sleep. An urge pulsed in her to reach out tracing his features to imprint this moment— the first time she'd awakened beside him—to memory.

Had last night happened? Not just the unplanned sex, but the declaration of her feelings. She loved him and—most unbelievable—he loved her in return. True he'd chased her for months, but infatuation wasn't love. Some men loved the chase, not the actual chased. There'd been a pebble of fear that if she'd given herself over to the quiet affection for him that he'd lose interest. That once he had her, he'd find her wanting. That he'd realize she lacked something. Empathy, kindness, warmth, intelligence, success, or a number of other things she'd been assessed as missing over her thirty-seven years.

"Stop staring, creeper," he said, voice hoarse from sleep and eyes still closed.

"I'm not a creeper," she protested, face pinched.

Eyes still closed; he nuzzled into her neck. "You peeped outside my house and now you're staring at me in my sleep. That's textbook creeper behavior. I'm wondering if there's a notebook in your top drawer with Mrs. Summer Krueger scribbled all over it in glitter ink with hearts."

She swatted him. "You wish."

He kissed her neck. "That I do." He moved to her lips.

But she turned her head. "No! I have morning breath."

"So do I. Just makes us a perfect match." Arching that sexy left eyebrow, he cradled her face in his large hands and captured her mouth with his.

Melting into his kiss, she wrapped her arms around his neck. "I guess loving someone's ugly bits means embracing morning breath."

"That it does, sweetheart."

"You really do love me as I am? Scars and all?" She traced circles along his chest. "Like you don't want to change me."

"The only thing I'd want to change about you is getting to go to sleep with you each night and wake up each morning with you." His forehead wrinkled. "What's this about, sweetheart?"

She released a long sigh. "I know this seems like boo-hoo from the former prom queen, but I've never felt like I was sufficient. In high school I was the pretty girl, but also the mean girl, and I played that role so well because I thought it was what was expected of me. I hung out with girls who acted like that when I was in junior high and just stayed in that role. I may have worn the crown, but in everyone else's eyes, I was utterly lacking. I wasn't kind like Elle. I wasn't smart like Carmen. I wasn't talented like you."

He placed his forehead against hers. "But you are all those things."

"Not then." She closed her eyes, unwilling to face his comforting gaze. "Then I left for New York City. It was the same story, but different words. Then I met Max. I thought he was my Prince Charming, sweeping me off my feet. He lavished me with expensive gifts and attention. Then piece-by-piece, he chipped away at me. I twisted myself up to fit his image of me."

He cradled her face. "I would never—"

She silenced him with a kiss. "I know, baby."

Deep in her bones, that truth lived. Not a drop of Max's undesirable characteristic resided within this man. Those green eyes shimmering back at her reflected the truth – she was perfect in his eyes. Just as he was in hers. Every scar and flaw tied up in a splendid package.

"I know I'm just right for you." She threaded their fingers. "A perfect fit."

"Always."

She flicked her eyes to his chest, chewing her lip. "I just wish I was enough for my parents."

"Is this about them pressuring you to take that class?"

She'd told him about both her parents, but especially her dad, pushing her to expand her business and enroll in the class. After speaking with Janet on Tuesday, she'd stopped by his laboratory at the brewery before heading to the school to pick up Liam.

"I know they both mean well and only want what's best for me. With my mom, while sometimes annoying, it's more encouraging, but my dad—" she nibbled on the corner of her mouth. "Like going back to school isn't a bad thing, it's just the sum of many little comments. Since I was a little girl, he'd say these things. If I got a B, it could have been an A. I worry that no matter how many weddings or Christmas Markets I coordinate that I'll be *just* a waitress that plans parties in his eyes." An annoyed huff left her lips. "I feel like such an ungrateful twat saying this. He's done so much for me and

Liam. They both have. I know he loves me, but—" A quake trembled her words.

"First, that's bullshit. You are the best goddamn waitress I've ever had the pleasure of calling me a moron and you know my stance on the party planner comments."

A tiny smile lifted her lips.

"Second, all he's done for you and the love you have for your dad doesn't change that he doesn't accept you as the fucking amazing woman you are."

"I know." She nodded. "I still want to make him happy, though. I love my dad."

"Of course you do." He kissed her forehead. "Is the fear that taking the class or expanding your business won't be enough for your dad stopping you from doing those things? Or is it just not what you want to do? If it's the later, you've got me in your corner. If it's the former"—his long fingers tucked beneath her chin, tipping her gaze up to him— "please don't limit yourself out of fear of other people's expectations."

"But what if taking the class or expanding my business isn't enough? What if—"

"That's his problem, not yours. You are the sun, Summer. So bright and warm. Don't dull yourself because someone else is scared they'll get burned."

"The sun is the center of the universe. You're going to give me a big head."

"Well, you're the center of *my* universe," he murmured, enfolding her into his chest. "Well, you, Liam, and Sheba."

"You're ridiculous."

"You *love* it."

"I do." She kissed the center of his chest. "I love you."

His green eyes snagged her gaze. "And I love you."

"Mom!" Liam's voice called through the closed door.

"Yes, baby?" She twisted her head toward the door.

"Are you decent?"

Joint smiles bloomed across their faces. "Yes," she said as she watched Todd sit up and yank on his T-shirt.

Liam opened the door and shuffled in, balancing two penguin-shaped mugs on a small cookie sheet turned serving tray. Sheba scampered in behind him.

"Merry Christmas!" he chirped, presenting the mugs to them.

"Is this chai?" She smiled, taking one of the cups and handing the other to Todd. The sweet spicy scent of cloves and cardamom danced in her nostrils from the steam rising from the cup.

"Pop helped me make it. He said you two probably needed caffeine."

Conspiratorial glances and quiet snorts passed between her and Todd. Indeed, they'd been up late, but she prayed the comment was spurred only by her parents' wild imaginations and not from actually hearing them.

Please God, I'll never have sex in my parents' house again, if you could do me the solid of them not having heard me and, if they had, erasing their memories.

Todd patted the end of the bed, inviting Liam to sit. "Merry Christmas, buddy."

He climbed onto the end of the bed, sitting crisscross applesauce, and balancing the cookie sheet on his lap. "Merry Christmas, Todd. I'm so excited you and Sheba slept over!" He almost vibrated with excitement. "Are you staying for presents and breakfast? Grandma makes gingerbread French toast."

Summer's gaze met his in a silent exchange.

He nodded. "Yeah. I don't pick up Grandpa Rice until noon, so I can stay."

"Then we're going to Cassie's to meet you?"

He ruffled Liam's hair. "Yep. You'll get to play with Cassie's kids and their dog, Hazel."

"And Sheba?"

As if on cue, Sheba leapt onto the bed, circled twice, and plopped beside Liam.

"Yep, she'll be there. She and Hazel are cousins." Todd grinned, sipping his tea. "I should probably take her out."

"I already did it." A prideful smile curved Liam's mouth. "Pop and I got up an hour ago, but he said I wasn't allowed to wake you before seven."

"Tradition." She sipped her tea. "House rules that you can't wake mom up before seven on Christmas morning." It had been the same rule for her as a little girl and now as the mom in question, she was so grateful for it.

"Pop let me walk Sheba in the backyard, while he watched from the kitchen window. Then we gave her some leftover prime rib." He stroked Sheba's ears.

"Prime rib and sharing the pillow." Todd chuckled. "You're spoiling her, little man. She'll be a real diva when I take her home."

"She's already a diva," Summer teased as the Husky rolled over to present her belly for rubs.

"What's a diva?" Liam's face wrinkled.

"You know how Grandma gets when we go on road trips about the car temperature and insisting only on Tim Hortons coffee?"

Liam nodded.

"I heard that." Mom appeared at the door, phone in one hand, and the other planted on her hip. "Here I was simply coming to get you all to open presents only to find out my only daughter thinks I'm a diva," she said with mock indignation.

"Were you taking a secret video of us?" Summer pointed to the phone, the live video images flashing on the screen.

"Just for prosperity." She tapped on the phone and slid it into her robe pocket. "The four of you were the picture of domesticity."

Summer stood in front of the mirror brushing her hair up into a high ponytail. The happiness of last night and this morning twined around her. Perfect was a word she'd not tossed about throughout much of her life. Not in the truest meaning of it. But at this moment her life felt as close to perfect as she could get. Even with the nipping annoyance with her dad, she'd not trade places with anyone else. Although, she wished her father would embrace who she was.

The sweetness of today almost vaporized the lingering heartache from the incident with her dad. Even the marketing book her dad gifted her for Christmas hadn't marred the perfection of this morning. Her dad's gift and his accompanied comment about discussing the class on the twenty-sixth was washed away as Summer had curled up on the couch with a second cup of tea in hand—cheering Liam and Todd on while they raced remote control cars.

Smiling, she took in her image in the mirror. The happy sensation radiated in her reflection. A large grin adorned her face. There was the hint of a sparkle in her brown eyes. A silver, bear-shaped pendant necklace with tiny emeralds for eyes dangled below her collarbone, exposed in the V-neck red tunic she wore. The argyle fabric clung to her breasts, flattering her figure. Just like the necklace, the sweater had been a gift from Todd. He'd selected the garment with Nat's help, but the necklace and books he'd gotten her was all him.

"You're a mama bear," he'd said, that boyishly charming, yet a little roguish, smile popping. He explained the emerald eyes were selected because they were Liam's birthstone.

Although she couldn't help but notice that they were also the color of his eyes. Somehow the little pendant melded the three of them.

Stop! You're acting like you're getting married. She shook her head, placing the brush down on the dresser.

"That sweater looks nice on you," Mom said, walking into the room.

"Thanks."

"Although, don't you think you should wear that dress you wore for your date? Jeans and a sweater seem a little dressed down and you looked so nice in that outfit."

Summer tightened her smile, reminding herself that her mom was trying to be helpful. "Cassie keeps it casual. She's likely to be rocking leggings, so my jeans are fancy enough."

Mom shrugged. "Alright, but maybe wear your hair down. You always have it up and it's so lovely when you wear it down and do something with it." Mom came up behind her, touching the end of her ponytail.

Summer grabbed her phone from the bedstand. "It's just easier to throw it up."

"I get the allure of easy, but it might be nice to make an effort. Your meeting Todd's family, after all."

"They know me," she sighed frustration simmering. "I don't have to pretend to be someone else for them."

"I'm not telling you to put on a show, but maybe just add a little shine."

Summer massaged between her brows. "Mom, please stop."

"I'm just trying to help."

"What's going on?" Dad asked, appearing at the door.

Mom gestured at Summer. "Just trying to get her to do a little more with her hair. It's the first time she's going to Todd's family as the girlfriend and not just as their friend or employee."

"They already know me." Summer's jaw clenched.

"Doesn't mean you shouldn't make an effort." Dad stepped fully into the room; his tone gruff.

"I—"

He went on, ignoring Summer's attempted protest. "Your mother is just trying to help you. It's just like with your party planning. We bring up a website and you say, 'they know how to get a hold of me'. At some point you have to try. You can't just settle."

Summer blanched.

"Brian, it's Christmas." Mom warned.

He shook his head. "We're always waiting to have the conversation. She'll go to school when she's ready. She'll get a new job when she's ready."

Dad went on as if the "she" he spoke of didn't stand mere steps away. The echoes of the past almost screamed inside her. How many times had she stood in a room where others spoke about her, rather than to her. Erica. Max. Her parents.

Mom placed a hand on Summer's shoulder and squeezed. "He... We just want what's best for you."

"Do you?" she snapped, fire raging in her belly.

Mom's eyes bulged. "Excuse me?"

"Don't speak to your mother like that," Dad hissed, his narrowed gaze locked on Summer.

Take it back, she cautioned herself. She knew they only wanted to help. It was who they were. It came from a good place. At least that's what she'd told herself over and over again. In that moment, the excuse felt akin to using a Band-Aid to coverup a flesh wound.

Dad's forehead creased. "I can't believe you'd say that. We've always been there for you."

"I'm sorry." She looked down, her voice small.

"We've only ever wanted to help you." Disappointment laced dad's words.

She's so ungrateful. She doesn't remember what I do for her. Max's voice hissed in her memory, sending a shiver up her spine. Her parents did so much for her... for Liam and here she was being the selfish, thankless Summer of her past. The one Max's caramel-smooth taunts and harsh slaps reminded her she was.

Summer braced, fighting against the pull of those memories yanking her back to a time when she folded into herself. To a time when she'd molded herself to fit what someone else wanted her to be. A time when no matter how hard she tried, she never made him happy. No matter how much weight she lost, the clothes she wore, and dinners spent with a silent smile on her face, she'd still be treated to Max's cruelty.

"We love you so much, honey, and only want what's best for you," Mom said, dragging Summer's attention back to her parents.

"We may push you, but we know you can be so much *more*," Dad added.

Each word was reminiscent of swift paper cuts, slicing cruelly into her heart. Quick, but exacting and leaving behind a throbbing ache in the stinging truth.

I am utterly lacking in my father's eyes.

That's bullshit! Todd's words boomed inside her, hushing the loud voices.

Meeting her father's gaze, she straightened her spine. "You're right. You do want what's best for me. I know that, but what about what I want?

"What?" Dad tipped his head quizzically.

"It's always about what you think is best. It's not about what I want. Somehow what you feel is best for me is always about ways to make me be who you think I should be. It's all about how to fix the many ways I disappoint you. The ways in which I don't measure up to your expectations."

"We love you, honey…" Remorse filled Mom's dark eyes.

Despite the tremor in her throat, she continued, "I know you do, both of you"— she looked between her parents— "but it doesn't change the fact that I don't think I'll ever be what you think I should be. No matter what I do, you'll always point out how I could have done it differently or better. How I could fit the mold you have for a daughter."

Dad went to speak.

But Summer cut him off, "I know. I know. You just want to help me. I've been telling myself this forever. That it all comes from a good place, but how much help do you think I need?"

"A lot!" Dad snapped, causing Summer to flinch. "The last time we left things up to you, you went to New York City and ended up with Max."

"Wow." It was barely a painful whisper. Summer placed her hand on her heart to still the sharp ache radiating there.

Like a pro/con list Summer's many mistakes lay in front of her. The choice to forgo college to move to New York City. The decision to date Max. The stress of her relationship with Max twisting her up and causing her to vomit almost daily making her birth control pills ineffective. Coming home to work as a waitress, refusing to bend to her parents' will to go to college or find a different job. Each choice stacked up on the con side, tipping the scale over to one conclusion.

"He didn't mean that," Mom said tentatively. "Brian." She shot him a harsh glare.

Dad rubbed at his temples. "Summer, I'm—"

Summer lifted her hand, palm out. "No. He did."

"Mom!" Liam's voice drifted from downstairs. "It's time to go. Are you ready?"

"I'm ready," she shouted, a gentle tremor in her tone.

"Summer, wait." Dad reached for her. "I didn't... I just want what's best for you."

"I understand." She swallowed hard. "I want what's best for me too. I want to be my best self." Tears brimmed in her eyes, but she blinked them away. "But I love and embrace who I am now even if I'm far from where I want to be. I just wish you could do the same rather than only loving who you want me to be."

"Summer, I..." A mix of shock and regret glinted in his dark eyes.

"Mom!" Liam bellowed.

"Coming, baby." Summer turned.

"Summer, wait."

She walked out the door.

CHAPTER TWENTY-THREE

"Finally, girl world was at peace." ~Mean Girls

Summer sat on Cassie's deck with a soft flannel blanket draped over her legs, her palms warmed by the mug filled with peppermint hot chocolate in her hands. In front of her four teams made up of both adults and children readied to square off. Reminiscent of a circus ringmaster Grandpa Rice stood on the sidelines, an old fashioned black top hat adorned with a large red velvet bow rested atop his head.

"You know the rules," he drawled, scanning the clusters of smack-talking adults and giddy children. "You have thirty minutes and can only use the items in this tub to construct your snowmen." He kicked a large red plastic container in front of him.

"Grandpa." Rose wagged her finger.

"Excuse me." A wry grin belted across his face. "Snowpeople."

"We can't say snowmen anymore?" Zach grumbled, a furrow notched in his forehead.

"Snowmen can be boys or girls, because girls can be anything," Liam said, looking between Rose and Todd.

"They sure can be, buddy." Prideful amusement etched Todd's expression as he reached out his hand and fist bumped Liam.

Summer smiled as she watched her guys fist bump. That happiness heightened by the intense pride for her son's unabashed willingness to pipe up that girls could be anything. In that moment she took an extra-long celebratory swig of her hot chocolate, imagining it was a glass of champagne. *I'm killing it at raising a good man.*

"Very true." Grandpa Rice nodded, continuing to go over the rules.

It was the annual Rice Family Christmas Day Snowperson contest. Teams of four, which required at least one child and adult faced off in three categories: best design, most structurally sound, and most Christmasy.

Despite Liam reminding them that Christmasy wasn't an actual word, he and Todd were taunting the other teams that they'd have a clean sweep. Rather it was Todd jeering, while Liam parroted him. Since Rose and her girlfriend competed with Todd each year, Summer chose to reclaim her cheerleader days and root on her guys from the Adirondack chairs surrounding the outdoor fireplace. The blanket across her legs, Zach's homemade cocoa, and the lick of the heat of the flames cocooned her in a cozy respite. Tension still slithered across her muscles from the earlier incident with her parents. Well, mainly her dad. As much as Mom encouraged, dad pushed.

She'd not told Todd the complete story, yet. When they showed up, his Summer spidey-senses flared. Pulling her into a quiet corner of the house he'd murmured, "Are you okay?"

Those three words almost undid her in that moment. She could melt into them and allow all the thoughts, feelings, and tears hidden within her to spill out. Instead, she placed a soft kiss on his cheek asking for just a good day. Taking in the loud hesitation in his eyes she whispered, "My dad." That's all she had to say.

He kissed her temple, nodded, and said, "We'll talk later, but now let me give you a good day."

That's just what he'd done. Afternoon now spilled over to dusk. Sunset's radiant burnt-orange and amethyst consumed the sky. Lights strung in the bare maple trees lit the property. Now she sat, sinking into that good day sensation, listening to Grandpa Rice chastise Zach and Todd for their un-sports-manlike smack talk.

"On my mark!" Grandpa Rice raised an airhorn into the air. "One. Two –"

"May the odds ever be in your favor," Todd said in a faux British accent, bowing to the other three teams.

"Suck it, Krueger!" Zach shouted, playfulness under-scoring his taunt.

"Boys!" Grandpa Rice *tsked*. Smiling, he sounded the airhorn as he shouted "Three!"

With that, adults and children scrambled to the red container grabbing tiny shovels, scarfs, hats, zipper bags full of coal or carrots, and an assortment of random items for their creations. The *woosh* of scampering feet and laughter punctu-ated the scene.

Head shaking and a giant grin covering his wrinkled face, Grandpa Rice shuffled through the scene toward the deck. Despite his ninety-two years, youthfulness radiated from him.

"Mr. Rice, I got you some hot cocoa," Summer said, handing him a polar bear-shaped mug.

"Mr. Rice?" He took the mug, his gaze darted around. "Is the ghost of my father behind me?"

She laughed. "Sorry. Jeb."

It was still weird to call him by his first name. He'd asked her to do this each time he came into the café with Todd. For most of her life, he'd been Mr. Rice, the pun-loving Chemistry teacher. Even if it had been almost two decades since she'd sat in his class, some habits were hard to break.

Like failing my father. The thought stung. Sipping her cocoa, she allowed its creamy sweetness to drown that dull ache. No matter how good of a day it had been, it nipped at her like silent rattlesnakes hidden in tallgrass.

"Now that you're dating my grandson, it's even more important that you call me Jeb or Grandpa." His lips curled into a rakish smile.

"Grandpa?" She almost choked on her hot chocolate.

"Yeah. *Grandpa.*" His expression akin to someone who had fixed the game and already knew the outcome.

Was it too soon to snuggle into the warm blanket sensation of his promise that one day she'd call him "Grandpa"? It wasn't the idea of a replacement grandparent. She'd had lovely grandparents, who'd since passed. Rather it was the deeper meaning of what would bond her to this family.

Todd. A cautious but hopeful feeling coursed through her. Even when she pulled away from Todd, she knew he was the balm for her weary heart. The idea of getting to have him each day was like waking up to find out every day was Christmas. It was far too soon to think this, but she indulged that starry-eyed love drunk girl inside her. The one who would, just as he'd teased her that morning, scribble *Todd Krueger* all over the front of her notebook in glittery ink. Hell, it was scrawled all over her heart.

"Cassie tells me that you're thinking of going back to school?" he said, nestling deeper into the chair beside her.

She worried her lower lip. She'd mentioned to Cassie the possibility of taking a class. Mainly because Janet Coates had come with Elle for lunch at the café on Thursday and chattered on and on about potential future study-buddy dates. Naturally, Cassie teased but was her usual supportive self and offered to alter the schedule to accommodate the demands of the class.

"I'm not sure, yet." Her eyes fixed on Liam and Todd sorting through the spoils from the red tub. All the excuses rasped against her tongue but didn't come out. *I don't have time. I'm a working single mom. I don't want to take time away from Liam.* They stacked up like non-fitting Lego blocks, masking the truth. *What if I fail? Worse, what if I succeed and it's still not enough?*

"I can understand the hesitance to go back to school at your age." He grimaced. "Although, I've got a good fifty-five years on me, so as far as I'm concerned, you're a baby."

A breathy snort huffed out of her.

"I didn't go to college until I was thirty. I was working and had a family, so I didn't finish school and start my teaching career until I was thirty-eight."

"Really?"

He sipped his cocoa. "I was a bit of a hell cat in high school. I even got suspended a few times."

"You?" she gaped.

"I was what Rose would call the OG bad boy of Perry High. Drinking. Fighting. Getting caught in less than polite positions with girls in the bed of my truck." That twinkle in his eyes sparkled just a little brighter.

"What happened?" She twisted her body toward him.

The mild-mannered, slightly dorky chemistry teacher who made an art form out of puns and dad jokes bore no resemblance to the bad boy he'd described.

"After graduation, my dad gave me an ultimatum to go into the Army and get my shit together or…" His lips pursed.

"Or?"

"There wasn't really an 'or what'. Guess it was less ultimatum and more an order." He laughed. "So, I enlisted for four years in the Army. It smoothed some of my rougher edges but didn't make me the man you see in front of you now."

"What did?"

"My Laura." Wistful sadness curved his lips. "When I got out of the Army, I settled in Rochester and worked at the School of the Deaf as a maintenance man." His gaze flicked to Rose, who scooped snow into a bucket. "Excuse me, person."

Summer grinned.

"As you know Laura was deaf. She'd gone there for school and then ended up working there as a secretary. She had the most beautiful eyes, like two giant pools of mossy green ponds. This fiery red hair that seemed to clash with her sweetness. We just smiled at each other for months. Then I left her a note and then she replied. We wrote notes for months. Then, I learned sign language. It took me almost a year to get good enough at signing and get the nerve to ask her out. No girl ever made me as nervous as she did. Three months later, I proposed." A sorry not sorry glint flashed in his eyes "Two months after that we were at the courthouse and Zach's dad was already three months along in her belly."

"You were a *bad boy*." She winked.

He beamed. "I was, but Laura made me want to be a good man. Then, when each of my four children came along, I got a little closer to becoming *that* man. Even if others didn't quite believe it. I still remember the shocked faces of my parents when I told them I was going to go to school to be a teacher. Hell, the school principal at the time was an old classmate. It took them ten years of me teaching until they finally let go of the memory of who I'd been and embrace who I was becoming."

"Becoming?" She blinked.

"I'm still not the man I wanted to be for Laura, but each day I work on it."

"I can understand that." A tiny wobble shook her words.

He reached over and patted her hand. "I know you do. I remember who you were in high school."

She looked away, an embarrassed flush creeping up her neck. Of course he did. There were few in the village who hadn't known who Summer Michaels had been in high school. As a teacher, he'd had front row seats to her Regina George antics.

"We all have rough edges." He squeezed her hand, drawing her focus back to him. "They just wrinkle differently on each of us."

She nodded, allowing his words to wash over her.

"Meanwhile, I'm excited to witness who you are becoming but also plan to enjoy every minute of who you are right now." He lifted his mug to his lips. "I rather like you, just as you are."

"Thanks." She swallowed hard at the insignificance of her response. Emotions twisted in her chest causing both a throbbing ache and an odd sense of completeness. In a single moment she felt embraced by someone who was becoming newly important to her, while one of the most pivotal people in her life didn't accept her.

"He's so good with him." Jeb motioned to Todd, a proud expression lit the older man's face.

Bent in the snow, Todd scooped up fat pieces of charcoal out of a plastic bag. Under Liam's careful direction, he placed each piece along the round belly of their snowperson while Rose and her girlfriend worked on the head of their creation.

"He is." Summer sighed with contentment. "They're good with each other." Laughter bubbled out of her as a snowball hurled toward Todd, only to miss him when Liam tackled him to the ground covering his large body with his little boy one.

"Zachary, no snowballs until after or your team is DQ'd," Jeb warned.

"It was Cassie!" Zach's face contorted into an affronted expression.

"Way to sell me out, hubby." Cassie tossed a snowball at her husband but missed.

While they playfully bickered back and forth, Summer watched Todd and Liam. Amusement filled their features.

"Todd is like his dad." Jeb sighed.

"Excuse me?" She almost choked on her hot chocolate. "Jeff Krueger?"

He chuckled. "I know, but the Jeff who fell in love with my Mandy and gave me those two beautiful grandchildren out there was a different man before she died. If I close my eyes and just listen to Todd and Liam, I can almost go back to a Christmas when Todd was Liam's age and Jeff was his. Before Mandy died, Jeff overflowed with love and playfulness. In losing her, he lost himself."

"And left two children behind to pick up the pieces." She winced at the harshness in her tone.

He placed a gloved hand on her arm. "I like that you're protective of my Todd. He deserves that. Hell, he needs it. He's got such a big heart and needs someone to protect it."

She placed her hand against her chest, remembering how he'd said she had his heart and she'd promised to take care of it. *And I will,* she silently reconfirmed her vow to him.

Jeb let out a hard breath. "You're not wrong, though. For a long time, I was so angry with my son-in-law for shutting himself off. He was there in the sense of making sure Rose and Todd had the things they needed."

Not everything *they needed.*

His nod almost telegraphed that he'd heard her thoughts. "They needed more than things to survive. They needed… need his heart. I don't make excuses for him. Those are choices he'll have to face, but I understand. When I lost my Laura, I thought my heart was gone. For months I was an ornery bastard."

"You?"

A lopsided smile tipped his lips. "I know it sounds far-fetched, but it's true. I hibernated like a grumpy bear until my family coaxed me out of my cave and helped me discover that my heart wasn't gone....it was just broken. They put me back together." He tilted his head to the yard filled with three of his four children, grandchildren and their children. "I understand Jeff better now because he and I both share losing the love of our lives."

"He wasn't the only one who lost someone." Her eyes fixed on Todd, posing with his sister, her girlfriend, and Liam for a picture in front of their now completed snowperson.

"That's true."

"You and Jeff may have lost the love of your lives, but there's a big difference between the two of you. You came out of that cave giving your family you."

"Some bears take longer to come out of their cave." He shot her a thoughtful look.

"But who looks after their cubs while they're in the cave?"

"You're good for my grandson. I'm glad to have you in the family."

Her heart squeezed. Somehow in the last year and a half she'd gone from her world consisting solely of her parents and Liam to all this. To an entire network of friends, who loved and supported her. To a new family that embraced her just as she was. To a man who filled her heart with his love and whose heart she desperately wanted to fill in return.

Jeb stood, raising the airhorn. "Time's up!"

Like a general inspecting his troops, Jeb marched between the waiting teams. A glittery crown sat atop Ryan, Cassie's brother's, snow queen. Thanks to his two girls and Laney, the snowwoman that they dubbed Queen B sparkled with glitter tossed over her plump figure. Link, Zach's older brother, and his family had built a lopsided snowman whose head threatened to fall off any second. In Summer's opinion, Cassie and Zach's Santa Hat wearing snowman squared off against the Krueger's Frosty the Snowman look-a-like to clench the coveted prize, which was only bragging rights.

Jeb cleared his throat. "Team Krueger!"

"Yes!" Todd lifted Liam into the air, who clapped wildly.

"Krueger winning streak stands," Rose taunted and twerked in a version of a touchdown dance. A snowball whizzed across the air and smacked into her chest. Her mouth dropped open and eyes narrowed. "This is war, Cassie."

Cassie scooped up a pile of snow, forming a second snowball. "It's on like Donkey Kong!"

A snowball flew into the air, hitting Cassie's arm. Eyes wide, she turned facing Summer. "You threw a snowball at me? But I'm your boss."

Summer tossed a second snowball at Cassie, who dodged it, but hit Zach in the butt. "You may be the boss at the café, but here you're Team Rice and I'm Team Krueger."

Todd beamed. "With mama bear on our side, we'll have a clean sweep of this year's reindeer games."

"Shut up, Rudolph," Zach snarked, flinging a snowball at Todd and hitting him in the stomach.

"Remember the rules, no hitting the head and no hitting me." Jeb raised his airhorn. "Game on!"

And with that the annual Rice Family Snowball Battle commenced.

After Cassie and Zach's team destroyed them in the snowball battle, they huddled around the outdoor fireplace with cups of mulled wine for the adults and hot chocolate for the kids. Despite the warmth from the flames and alcohol, the damp cold soaked through Summer's jeans making her grateful for the leggings, flannel button up, and extra pair of socks she'd packed for herself. Teeth chattering, Summer ushered Liam into the house to change.

"I'm so glad I remembered to bring a change of clothes," Summer said as she stepped out of Cassie's bathroom.

"Just wait 'til our Fourth of July water balloon battle." Rose chuckled and slipped into the bathroom behind Summer.

"I thought Cassie and Zach always went away for Independence Day." Summer's head tilted to the right.

A wide, almost mischievous, expression covered Rose's face. "Oh, they do. We do it at my dad's sister's house on the lake. You're Team Krueger after all." She winked, shutting the door and leaving a rapidly blinking Summer standing in the hallway.

I'm Team Krueger? She had said that herself in front of some of Todd's most favorite people in the world, half his family, her boss, and her son she'd proclaimed herself Team Krueger. Like a dog pissing on a tree, she'd all but marked her territory. He was hers and she was his.

Her pulse should be racing at that concept. In her mind, she should be uttering a string of excuses for all the reasons this was a bad idea.

Instead, a sense of rightness folded around her like a hug. Reinforcing the knowledge that this was it. The big *it*. The one that Clayton and Elle just committed themselves to. The *it* that Noah just asked Nat to share with him. Her logical side knew this was foolish and rash, but the part of her that still believed in the HEAs of her favorite romance novels pushed her to sink into this.

Shuffling down the hall, she entered the kitchen to find Todd at the kitchen island packing up leftovers. It wasn't anything especially sexy or spectacular, but her stomach swooped, nonetheless.

Coming up behind him, she slipped her hands around his middle and pressed into his back. "Want help?" she murmured.

He leaned against her, his wintry woodsy scent mingled around them. "Nah, just packing up some of grandpa's favorite things."

She squeezed tighter around him. "You're such a good man."

He twisted, pulling her into his chest, and banded his arms around her back. "Not that good. I have half a mind to take you into a spare room and find out if you're commando underneath those leggings."

"Perv." She swatted his bicep.

"Seriously, though. I don't see any panty-lines." His hand brushed the swell of her ass and squeezed.

"Todd!" she squealed with laughter.

"No ass grabbin' in my kitchen," Zach grumbled, striding into the kitchen.

"Jealous that your tush isn't grabbable?" Todd snarked.

"My butt is very grabbable." Zach pouted, hands on hips.

"More like pinchable," Cassie strode into the kitchen and pinched her husband's butt.

"This family," Summer snorted.

"May I remind you that your parents have propositioned me to impregnant you at least half a dozen times since our first date." Todd smirked.

"You'd make cute babies." Cassie clapped her hands, her amber eyes bouncing between them.

Summer tossed a tea towel at her. "Stop!"

"Mom!" Lucas, Cassie's son, barreled into the room with Liam. "Can Liam sleepover tonight? Please?"

Cassie quirked her head to Summer. "Cool with me if Summer is okay with it."

Like adorable puppy dogs both boys looked at her with imploring eyes. "Are you sure it's okay? You've had a house full the entire day and I know tomorrow is your day off."

The café would remain closed tomorrow. Cassie and Zach always gave the day after the holiday off to their staff.

Zach waved dismissively. "What's one more kid for the night. Cassie's brother's girls will be sleeping over too, so

Liam will ensure the boys aren't outnumbered and forced to karaoke Taylor Swift songs all night."

Summer ruffled Liam's floppy hair. "Okay."

He wrapped his arms around his mom's waist, hugging her. "Thanks!"

"I'll head to the house and pack a bag for you." She bent down, kissing the top of his head.

"Come on, Liam, let's go play." Lucas tugged him out of the kitchen.

"His first sleepover," she whispered to herself. Emotion swelled in her chest and rose to her throat, forming a lump.

"He's going to have a great time, mama bear. He's come a long way," Todd said, tucking her back into his embrace.

She nodded, fearing the swirl of emotions inside her would render her voice a mere croak.

Since Liam's diagnosis on the autism spectrum two years ago, she'd done all she could to support him to have a full life. Last year, he'd struggled with social interactions, shutting down. He wanted to belong but at the same time didn't quite fit. In a world run by the non-neurodivergent, of course a child on the spectrum would struggle. Working with the behavior specialist didn't mold Liam into a piece that could be jammed into the world but helped him understand how to cope. She'd surrounded him with people who embraced Liam as he was.

"You're right." She swallowed that lump and pressed harder into Todd's firm chest.

Cassie came up, patting her back. "When you go home to pack that bag for Liam, perhaps pack one for your *own* sleepover."

Fire swept across Summer's cheeks. Not at the blatant sexual undertones of Cassie's suggestion, but because she'd had the same idea. An entire night alone with Todd. No sleeping ears or ticking time to worry about.

"I don't know if she'll need clothes for their sleepover." A salacious grin transformed Zach's face.

"When's the last time I kicked your ass?" Eyes narrowed; Todd almost growled at Zach.

"Easy papa bear." She ran her fingers into his short red strands. "He's not wrong," she whispered in a low purr.

"Papa bear?" An almost feral look glinted in his eyes. His strong hands gripped her waist as he hurled her over his shoulder. "We're leaving."

Taking a deep breath, Summer walked up the front steps of her house. After leaving Cassie and Zach's, Todd drove Grandpa Rice back to the Assisted Living facility, while she headed home. The plan was to quickly pack two bags, one for Liam and one for herself, and leave without running into her dad. She'd thought they'd still be in Rochester at the movies, but both their vehicles were in the driveway. Since it was just after seven, they'd likely still be awake.

I need to move out of my parents' house. Body braced; she opened the door. Even if the argument with her dad didn't linger like a foul stench, coming home to pack a bag to sleep-over at her boyfriend's was mortification enough. It had been almost twenty years since she'd snuck in and out of her parents' house to see a boy, but here she was.

"Summer?" Mom called, her voice soft and a little hesitant, as she walked into the small foyer.

Damn it. She flinched. She'd barely stepped over the threshold. "Yep. Just coming by to pack overnight bags. Liam is sleeping at Cassie and Zach's."

"Is Liam with you?"

Spine straight, she stepped into the living room entryway. Beside her mom on the couch sat Dad. His large form leaned forward, elbows on his knees, and hands scrubbing down his face. He looked up at her, his eyes glossy.

"He's at Cassie's. I just came home to pack—"

"Pack?" Her mom's red-rimmed eyes widened. "You don't need to leave."

"Just for—"

"Fix this," she hissed, her face twisted into a glower and she focused on her husband with a narrowed-eye gaze. "I won't lose my daughter or my grandson. Not again."

Summer blinked. "You're not… You've never lost me."

"But we did," Mom croaked.

Dad met her gaze; weariness deepened the normally happy lines around his mouth. "For three years. No calls. No visits."

It was akin to a knife plunged into her gut. She couldn't argue with that truth. For three years she'd cut them out. At first out of anger about her dad's concerned words about Max. Then out of spite to prove him wrong. To prove that she hadn't made the wrong choice about Max. That spite was strangled away by Max's cruelty, but still shame held her back from reaching out. Shame about what he'd done to her. Shame about not listening to her dad's warning. Shame for closing them out. Almost a decade on the other side of that time and the knowledge that she isn't to blame for what Max did, that shame still hissed inside her.

"I'm sorry," she said, regret quakes her voice.

"No." Dad stood up; his dark eyes glossy. "I'm sorry. I didn't call. I didn't visit. I—"

"Mom did and I ignored her. I—"

He took two steps forward and stopped. "But *I* did nothing—" he slammed his fist into his chest "—I left you with that monster."

Tears brimmed in her eyes. "You didn't know."

"But I did. The moment I met him, I was unsettled. I knew."

"You tried to warn me." She reached out and grabbed his hand. "Max wasn't your fault."

"And he wasn't yours." He squeezed her hand. "I shouldn't have said that. I was angry and...please know that I don't blame you."

"I know." It was barely a whisper.

"But I do blame me. For what I said. For letting my anger get the best of me today and back then. I let my anger stop me from being your dad. If I had done my job as your dad, I would have been able to protect you." A sob almost choked his confession.

"Brian." Mom placed a hand on his shoulder.

He shook his head; a torrent of tears fell down his face. "I failed in my one job as your father.... Keep you safe. That monster almost snuffed out the life in you. When you came back, you weren't the feisty vibrant girl you'd been." He let out a hard breath. "We won't always be around, and I just want to make sure you're safe."

Summer's brow puckered. "Only I can keep myself safe."

Dad stepped back, hurt flashed in his expression.

"I love you, but as you said you're not always going to be around. I got myself away from Max. I've kept Liam safe. Max may have tried to strangle the life out of me, but I'm here. I'm still alive."

"Are you?" Mom sighed. "You may be alive, but you've stopped living. Since you've come home, you've just existed."

"You're an amazing mother, but it wasn't until the last year and a half that you've cobbled out a life outside of being a mom. The event planning, your friends, and now with Todd," Dad said, each word with caution.

The truth of their words settled around her. The effect akin to clearing fog. So much of the last twelve and a half years had been about existing. The first three were focused on survival in her relationship with Max. The last nine and a half about keeping her and Liam safe. In the last year and a half, though, mere existence had slowly become a meal she'd tired of. With cautious steps she'd started to live again.

"I may not have been living, but I am now. Don't you see that?" She motioned between them.

"We do," Mom said, warmth shimmered in her eyes.

"It's why we push. We just want to help you."

"By having me live the life you want for me." She met her dad's stare, a steely resolve in her tone. "And when I don't, pointing out the ways in which I've failed you."

"That's not... I..." He almost winced.

"It is," Mom placed a palm on his shoulder. "There's a fine line between encouragement and intrusiveness and I think we've crossed that."

He shook his head. "Not we; me."

"Dad..." Summer wrang her hands. As much as she knew this conversation needed to happen, regret gnarled inside her at the hurt that filled his normally happy features.

"You're right." Regret pinched his brow. "I've pushed. I've intruded. I've tried to control... You exchanged one controlling man for another one."

"No!" She gripped his hands, forcing his downcast gaze to hers. "You're nothing like that."

"I am so sorry, Summer Joy," he said, his words waterlogged.

"You can be sorry for your actions, but please don't ever give yourself that label." She wrapped her arms around him, pressing her tear streaked cheek against his chest. "I love you, daddy."

Not since she was Liam's age had she called him daddy. But in that moment, it felt right. She may be an adult with her own child, but she knew she'd always be his little girl. They may need to build a path forward on a relationship grounded in mutual respect, but she'd never forget that there'd always be a piece of that little girl that loved her daddy and daddy that loved his little girl.

He kissed the top of her head. "I love you, Summer Joy."

"No hugs without mom," Mom said weepily, folding her arms around them.

For several moments they just stood there. Their joint sniffles and the gentle thump of his heart filled her ears.

"I'll do better," he said, clearing his throat.

"And I'll love you on that journey," she murmured against his chest.

"And I love you."

Summer tipped her head up.

A small smile tugged up at Dad's lips. "You're a good mom. The best. Your ability to speed-read and retain information amazes me. It takes me a month to read the number of books you read in a week. I'm blown away by your memory. You have your checklists, but I know you don't need them. You keep everyone and everything around you humming along."

Summer's brow wrinkled. *What?*

"The support group you put together and all the events you've organized around the village. I don't know how you find the time or energy. You—"

"What are you doing?" Summer raised her hand. An off-kilter sensation took hold of her. The rapid praises giving her whiplash.

Dad's gaze locked with hers. "I'm telling you the things I should have been saying all along. You're right. I pushed you to be more, but didn't tell you all the ways in which you are already everything."

"Dad—"

He shook his head, cutting Summer's protest off. "I told you I want to do better. This is a start."

"Does this mean you're not moving out? Should we get Liam?" Mom asked, stepping back.

Summer turned to face her. "I wasn't packing to move out. Liam is sleeping over at Cassie's and—"

"You're sleeping at Todd's?" Mom cooed.

"Liam's first sleepover?" Dad puffed up, ignoring his wife's salacious expression.

Summer also ignored her mother. "It's huge."

"He's come such a long way."

The brightness of this moment dissolved away the lingering heaviness. They all had. That truth folded itself around Summer like her dad's strong arms.

"It's a big moment for Liam," Mom added, her smile wide. "And for you."

"It is." Summer nibbled on the corner of her mouth. "There are a lot of big moments still to come in our lives and I want you to always be there for them…"

"But it's time for you to move out." Mom's smile dulled just a bit but remained fixed on her face. Not in a sad pretend smile way, but in acknowledgement of the truth between them.

Her parents would always be part of her life. This wasn't like with Max. She wasn't cutting them out, but it was time for her to keep those still cautious steps moving forward toward whatever her living situation would look like. Jeb had talked about her becoming. She didn't know what that looked like, but she knew she wanted her parents with her on the journey to find out.

"I guess today is about a lot of starts," Dad said.

"Good thing we can do it together." She took both her parents' hands.

One conversation didn't fix it, but it was a start.

CHAPTER TWENTY-FOUR

*"I hear Regina George and Aaron Samuels are dating again. The
two were caught canoodling at Chris Isen's Halloween party…
they've been inseparable ever since." ~Mean Girls*

Back *to my good day.* A smile kicked across Summer's face
as she parked her car in front of Todd's house. Like a
puddle after a needed rainstorm, the emotional hangover
from the conversation with her parents dissipated. Pulling
out her phone, she checked the messages that pinged during
the two minute drive from her parents' house. Cassie had
sent a video of Zach singing Taylor Swift's "You Need to
Calm Down" while Liam and Lucas howled with laughter.
Clearly the girls had won.

The second message was her dad, the simple *I love you* text
had warmth surging within her. Over the last hour they'd
started to map out a path forward. It was a map not written in
permanent ink. Boundaries would need to be redrawn as they
navigated their relationship moving forward and what life
looked like after she and Liam moved.

She typed *I love you, too.* The relationship with her father
had found new common ground. Her healing heart was open

to a world of possibility. A world limited only by herself. No longer would her past hold her back from having everything she wanted.

And right now, all she wanted was Todd.

Taking the stairs two at a time, she knocked on his door. Within seconds, the door was flung wide.

"Ready to unwrap your Christmas present?" She batted her eyes.

With a roguish grin, he pulled her into his arms. Their mouths collided in a consuming kiss. His large hands gripped her ass and he hoisted her up. Her legs folded tight around him. Without breaking their kiss, he turned and carried her inside, kicking the door shut.

"Fuck, I missed you." He pressed her against the wall, coasting his mouth down her neck.

"We just—" she gasped at the nip at her earlobe "We just saw each other."

Pressing her tighter against the wall, his erection rubbed her just in that right spot. A tiny whimper escaped with the delicious rasp of the fabric barrier between them.

His fingers traced down her hairline, along her jaw, and to her throat. "I think you missed me, too."

"What makes you think that?" She flashed a coy smile.

Spreading open her unbuttoned coat, his hands ran down to the taut nipples peeking through the thin flannel shirt. "Just a guess," he drawled, pinching one hard peak.

With a breathy moan, she moved her hips against his hardness. "Fine. I missed you a little bit."

"Just a little bit?" He moved himself against her. A liquid sensation tingled at her core.

"Todd…" She moved against him, the needed friction not enough.

"You did miss me." His tongue rasped on her skin as he licked down her neck.

"Put me down," she commanded.

He gently lowered her, his sexy left eyebrow arched as if in confusion. God, how could an eyebrow turn her blood into molten lava?

Placing her hands on his chest, she pushed him into the foyer's opposite wall. Summer slipped her coat off, tossing it onto the coatrack in the corner. "Let me show you how much I missed you," she purred and kicked off her shoes.

With a sultry expression, she unbuttoned her flannel. Reaching the last button, she pushed it off her shoulders and let the soft fabric flutter to the ground.

Todd's eyes blazed.

Biting her lower lip, she glided her hands over her aching breasts which overflowed the white pushup bra's cups, then lowered to the waistband of her leggings. Eyes locked with his, she shimmied the buttery leggings downward. Stepping out of them, she dropped them atop her shirt and slipped her socks off.

His gaze raked across her body. "You were wearing *that* under your clothes all day?" he almost groaned with pain.

"*This*?" She rolled her nipples through the bra's almost transparent fabric. "It's just a simple bra and panties set," she cooed, turning her backside to him knowing that the satin booty shorts barely covered her.

"If I had known you were wearing that all day..." He reached for her.

But she pushed him back and wagged her finger. "No. No. This is about me showing you how much I missed you."

"By torturing me in your sinful angel costume?"

She placed a hand on his heart. "By thanking you for giving me a good day."

His expression sobered. "Sweetheart, you never have to thank me for that. I love you."

She cupped his face. "I know, but I want to." She pressed her lips against his. "You're always taking care of me. Let me take care of you, baby." She lowered to her knees in front of him. Gripping his sweatpants' waistband, she tugged them down. "Why, Mr. Krueger. You aren't wearing underwear?" she teased as his cock sprung out.

"They'd only get in the way for what I have planned for you."

"What's that?" She looked up through her lashes.

"To make you come in every room of this house."

Summer's core clenched. "That sounds like a lovely way to spend an evening." Licking her lips, she ran her hands up his muscular legs. "But first, I have plans for you." Taking him in hand, she pumped his shaft twice.

"Summer," he groaned, leaning his head against the wall.

Brushing her lips to the tip in a chaste kiss, she grinned when his cock jerked. Wrapping her mouth around his thick length, she moved in a slow rhythm. Swallowing beads of salty sweet pre-cum, she moaned with pleasure.

"Fuck," he groaned, his hand fisting her hair.

Gripping the base, she pumped. Inch by inch her mouth took more of him, lathering his thickness in playful tongues strokes between hardening sucks. The gentle tugs of her hair combined with his moans slickened the space between her legs. Relaxing her throat, she took him deeper. Muffled moans escaped her.

"Goddamn, sweetheart," he growled, thrusting his hips. "You like when I fuck your pretty mouth, don't you?"

She answered with a harder suck, taking even more of him.

"You're so fucking beautiful with your lips wrapped around my cock."

His filthy praise coiled need tighter within her. A tipsy sensation flooded her senses with each thrust of his hip. She may be on her knees, but he was the one losing control. That knowledge not just made her drunk with power, but burn with want.

"We need to stop or—"

With a hummed, "Mmhmmm," she took him deeper.

His tip hit the back of her throat. Fingers woven in her hair; he moved his hips faster. She knew he was getting close and that knowledge thrummed within her. With each "Fuck, Summer," and "That's it, sweetheart," he came more undone.

"No." He yanked himself out of her mouth.

"But—" Her words cut off by him pulling her up.

"I have plans for you, remember." He lifted her into his arms.

Her legs wrapped around him and her back hit the wall's cool surface.

He pushed aside her panties, sliding his finger along her center. "Look at you… Your pussy is weeping for me."

"I want you," she whined, need spun tight within her.

"You've got me." With one quick thrust he pushed into her.

The sudden fullness made her cry out his name. He moved in a slow tortuous pace. Nails dug into his shoulders, she clung to him. Their hips meeting in a languid dance. The pleasurable tension wound tight. Each pump tipped her closer, but not quite close enough.

"Please…" she whimpered.

His fingers slid between them; one rough pad stroked her clit. "I know what you need."

"You always do." Like the turning of a crank, her body inched closer and closer until… "Todd!"

Drawing out her climax, he slammed into her until… "Summer!" he shouted, spilling into her.

Breathless, she lay her head on his shoulder. Aftershocks rolled through both their bodies. The whispered "Oh, sweetheart" and gentle strokes of her hair wrapped her up in the sensation of being precious. Being cared for. Being loved.

She lifted her head to capture his gaze. "You have me. All of me."

"And you me." He pressed a gentle kiss on her cheek.

Todd was a man of his word. Summer's back molded to the cool tile; the fifth orgasm of the night rioted through her. The shower's hot kiss seared against her scorched skin. Her fingers threaded into his wet hair while he lapped her up.

They'd not hit every room of the house but had gotten close. On all fours in front of the Christmas tree in the living room, he'd made her see stars with his relentless thrusts into her. She'd rode him hard on the dining room chair, while he feasted on her breasts. The force of his fucking her up against the bookshelf in his office resulted in books tumbling to the floor.

He looked at her, face glistening both from the water and her arousal. "I love when you come over for playdates."

Laughing through her panting breaths, she swatted him. "You may like it, but my vagina may not survive."

He pressed a simple kiss to her core and rose. "I'll nurse it back to health."

"I bet you will." She wrapped her arms around his neck, rising to nuzzle her nose against his.

"Let me start now." He reached for a washcloth and the bodywash.

The aroma of mint mixed in the tendrils of steam dancing around them. Squirting a dollop into his palm, he gestured for Summer to turn. Tucked into his chest, his hands swept along the front of her body, lathering the bodywash and swiping it clean with the wet washcloth. Eyes closed; she melted into his tender touch.

"You're a cinnamon roll with some seriously sexy alpha tendencies," she said, her head lolled against his shoulder.

"I like to think I give more golden retriever vibes."

"You do like to hump my leg," she snarked.

He stepped back. "Just this." He slapped her ass, making her giggle.

"There's been no ass play."

"Not yet," he teased pressing her back into his chest and running the washcloth down her stomach.

"I have to save something for your birthday," she said saucily.

He chuckled. "What's this from?" His hands brushed along the thin scar across her abdomen.

"Liam." She moved her hand to guide his over the puckered skin. "He came early and there were some complications, so they did a C-section."

"Complications?"

"He was in distress, and they needed to get him out. He spent the first few days in the NICU. He was so little."

He palmed her abdomen. The warmth of his hand was protective as if he wanted to keep her and Liam safe from the first few terrifying days of their lives as mother and son.

She placed her hand atop his. "He's okay and so am I. In the end, it was all worth it, because I have my beautiful boy."

"Do you want more children?"

This question had been rattling around in Summer. Over the years of isolating her heart it had been an exercise in the theoretical. But now, with Todd's strong hands lovingly gliding across her skin and the gentle thump of his heart pressed against her back, theory melded with the actual.

"I do," she admitted.

His lips pressed against the back of her head. "Me too."

She turned facing him. "With me?" A wave of insecurity accompanied the question.

All the warning bells inside her blared. *This was too soon.* He'd run for the hills. Who wouldn't when a girlfriend of barely a week proclaimed she wanted babies with them? Still, there'd been a flutter of something in her chest with each joking comment from her mother—though those weren't that unserious—or Cassie about the possibility of future children. A little girl with her thick chestnut waves and his emerald eyes, or a little boy with her chocolatey eyes and his roguish grin.

"Yes." His lips ticked up.

She placed her hand on her belly, soothing the Herculean swoop. "I'm thirty-seven, which is ancient in baby-making years. What if I can't have another baby?"

"Then we have Liam." He moved his hand to her back and caressed along her spine. "Which is more than enough."

"But he's not—" she stopped herself.

He took her hand, placing it on his heart. "But he is. He may not be mine by blood, but he's mine in here. I love Liam and I love you. When I close my eyes and daydream about my future, I picture the three of us. Making dinner together. Teaching Liam all the brewing recipes I've learned over the years and having you try them. Curling up on the couch and holding you while you read a book and Liam plays with Sheba. Being a family."

Leaning into his firm chest, she closed her eyes, getting lost in his daydream. Such a sweet picture he painted. The image, something she'd never dared dream for herself, was so clear that she could almost reach out and touch it.

"One day," she murmured, melting into the crisscross of his fingers along her back.

As much as her body sighed with hope at the idea of that future, her logic knew it was too soon. Deep in her bones, she knew Todd was the piece she'd been waiting for. The demons of her past couldn't be allowed to delude her into questioning how much he loved her and the truth in his desires for their future. It was easy to lose oneself in a fantasy of a future when swept away in the love drunkenness of the early days of a relationship. Time would sober the early days to reality. She only hoped in the afterglow, his eyes still glinted with the promise of a future.

"One day." He kissed her forehead.

They slipped into a companionable silence, swaying beneath the spray of hot water, lost in the promise of one day.

"What's this from?" He traced the small scar below her right shoulder blade.

She exhaled a sharp breath at the feel of his finger pads over the raised skin. "Max."

"How?"

"He got angry one night and slammed me into the mirror. The shards cut into me. I had to have stitches."

"Did it happen just that once?" Concern and anger darkened his eyes.

"No." The single word confession was strangled in emotion.

His hand stilled. "You said—"

"I lied." Tipping her head to him, she met his gaze. "I wasn't ready to talk about it. To have you see me like that."

His brow knitted. "Like what?"

"Broken."

"I don't." Sincerity penetrated his gaze and bore into her.

"I know. At least…now I know."

"Do you think you're broken?" He combed his hands through her wet strands.

Her eyes fluttered to the ground; the water swirled down the drain. In the twisting and turning water she could almost see the swirl of feelings that once tangled inside her. The belief that Max hadn't broken her but had chosen her because she was already broken. Like a wolf sensing a wounded animal, he'd sniffed out the flaws that made her ripe for the picking. That somehow it was all her fault and she'd have always been destined for *a* Max, whether that one or another.

That's bullshit. She met his gaze. "I was never broken. He tried, but he failed. I may have been wounded for a bit, but I am healing."

"You are so strong," he murmured, caressing her cheek.

"I know. I'm a mama bear." A small smile formed.

"That you are. I wish I had been there to protect you... I know you didn't need me nor anyone else to protect you because you protected yourself and your son by getting out. All things that make me fucking love you more." He turned off the shower and stepped out. "Let me take you to bed. I just want to hold you all night.

She nodded, stepping out of the shower and holding out her hand to him. "What happens in the morning when you have to let go?"

He took her hand. "I'm never letting go."

And he didn't. Cocooned in his arms and the assurance of how much she loved this man she had the most peaceful sleep of her life. After waking and gifting her a sixth and seventh orgasm, he lived up to his cinnamon roll hero status and cooked her breakfast. Perched on the barstool at the kitchen island, the sweet aroma of freshly baked muffins collided with the savory scent of the ham and cheese omelet he prepared.

"I'm going to have to take back all the snarky comments I've made to Elle and Nat about the obscene amount of sex they have." She sipped her tea.

"Pretty sure Prince Charming and Mr. Elle have stored up lots of retorts to toss at me." He flipped the omelet onto a plate and placed it in front of her.

"You call Clayton Mr. Elle?"

"That man is whipped." He placed a muffin on her plate.

She arched an accusing eyebrow.

A sardonic grin popped. "We're all whipped. You ladies are a trio of goddesses who have made us all adoring acolytes."

"Trio? Don't forget Carmen. Mathew may be the most

devout of you all." She forked up a bite. "So good," she moaned.

He grabbed a fork and speared a bite.

"I'm adding official chef to your acolyte duties." She broke off a piece of the cranberry orange muffin. "How'd you learn to cook?"

"My dad."

"Really?" Her mouth hung open, the piece of muffin suspended on the fork in front of her.

He shrugged. "When my mom got sick, he took on the things she used to do. Cooking. Laundry. Dishes. I wanted to help, so he taught me. It was nice. We'd look up recipes to try. We even learned to bake. When she felt up to it, Mom would sit in the kitchen instructing us or just watching. Dad used to speak in a horrendous French accent when we cooked." A hint of a smile played in his expression.

Summer nodded, thinking of Jeb talking about the Jeff Krueger before Mandy died. The playful father who adored his wife and made his children laugh. Was Todd's anger not just about the supposed forgetting of his mother by his father, but rather his father forgetting himself? Todd hadn't just lost his sweet mother, but the goofy and attentive father.

"That was a long time ago," he said, sadness shimmered in his eyes.

Her heart ached to smooth away the remorse. To hold him close; the past's painful pull drowned by their love. Even good memories could leave a heart battered and bruised when tied up with regret and loss.

"Be right back." She leapt up and pressed a peck to his cheek.

Running out of the kitchen, she bounded upstairs and found her overnight bag. The desired item in hand, she ran back to him and presented a small book-shaped item wrapped in shiny green paper with a gold bow.

"What's this?" His head tilted. "We already did gifts."

"Yes." She returned to her perch on a stool. "But I had something else for you. It's a little cheesy, so I didn't want to give it to you in front of my parents. Open it." She gestured to the package.

With an uncertain grin on his mouth, he untied the bow and tore at the paper.

"I made it with Nat. It may be a little silly," she offered, tugging a loose tendril from her messy bun.

"All The Things?" he read aloud, his fingers traced the words etched on the small book's leather cover.

"It's a coupon book. On our first date you said you wanted to do all the things with me." Their gazes locked. "Each coupon is for a different thing to do together."

Flipping the pages, his lips ticked up into a wide grin. "There are a lot of things in here."

"That's because there are a lot of things I want to experience with you."

He flipped to the back of the book. "What are these blank pages for?"

"They're for all the things I haven't yet thought of that I want to do with you."

Rounding the counter, he lifted her off the stool and pulled her into his arms. "I love it, and I love you."

"And I love you." She snuggled into his firm chest, listening to the sweet cadence of his happy heart.

"And I'm calling in one of my coupons." He ripped a coupon from the book. "Wanna go on an adventure?"

CHAPTER TWENTY-FIVE

"Hey buddy, you're not pretending anymore. You're plastic. Cold, shiny, hard plastic." ~ Mean Girls

An adventure he'd indeed taken her on. Taking his hand in his kitchen on Monday morning, she'd said "Yes," and the happy whirlwind of the week unfolded in front of her.

After picking up Liam at Cassie and Zach's, they bundled up and zigzagged through Todd's uncle's twelve acres of gentle hills, thicket of woods and quiet clearings, on his snowmobile. Liam sandwiched between she and Todd, Summer squealed while the snow's icy spray kissed her reddened cheeks. Later, Summer stood, phone in hand, taking a video while Liam drove the snowmobile in a slow, not-quite straight path in the open field. Behind Liam, Todd's large protective hands curled around her son's waist.

"I'm doing it!" he'd cheered.

After, they purchased all the fixings for a hearty Italian smorgasbord and headed back to her parents' house. Now, her mom played videographer as Todd taught Summer and Liam to make his Grandma Rice's lasagna with spicy Italian sausage, and pumpkin spice tiramisu. The fivesome sat around the table devouring the meal, while Sheba slept beneath.

Tuesday, they added his laboratory at the brewery as places he'd made her come so hard that she saw stars. In stolen moments between the ending of her shift at the café and opening of the brewery for the day, he'd bent her over his desk fucking her so hard she broke a nail digging into the desk's smooth surface and his thrusts knocked his laptop to the ground.

The next day, he and Liam bent their heads over an iPad at the café to research the best laptop for him to purchase. Noah smirked as he sneaked extra fries onto Liam's plate despite Summer's protest that he'd had enough.

The three nestled in the café during the last hour of Summer's shift for a guys' lunch before Nat arrived. Then, they'd head to Rochester for a *Star Wars* inspired pop-up experience complete with Jedi training and a Millennium Falcon replica.

"How'd you and mom break your laptop?" Liam asked between bites of grilled cheese.

Eyes wide, Todd's mouth went slack.

"Todd's *very* enthusiastic when *working* with your mom," Noah drawled.

Summer glared at Noah with pursed lips.

No more brewery sex! Despite Todd's hand clamped over her mouth in the heat of the moment, it was clear they'd been caught.

"At least Todd didn't need to go to the chiropractor after *working* too hard." She flashed him a saccharin expression.

Noah gaped. "She *told* you that?"

"They tell each other everything, Prince Charming." Todd dipped a fry into the ketchup.

"Which means she'll tell Nat all *your* secrets."

Realization creased his forehead. "Uh… Sweetheart—"

"Sisters before misters," she interrupted, walking away with a sly smile.

With most of her tables mid-meal, Summer covered the front counter so Cassie could make a few calls to suppliers. A to-go order sat ready beside the register.

Waiting, she pulled out her phone and flipped to the saved page for the GCC class. The deadline for registration was coming up. She'd waffled back and forth about taking the marketing class since Christmas. All the 'what ifs' churned in her stomach at the prospect of going back to school.

"Pick up order." A gruff voice pulled her attention.

"Of course." Glancing up, she met a stone-faced Jeff Krueger.

Shit! Why hadn't she looked at the name on the order ticket?

Her eyes bounced between Sheriff Krueger and Todd, whose focus remained on Liam. A small thankful breath escaped that he'd not seemed to have noticed his father.

"I have your order here." She touched the bag, but her gaze stayed fixed on Todd.

It's not like father and son never ran into each other. Perry was a small town, after all, but she desperately wanted to avoid the anguish that had marred Todd's features both Christmas Eve and day.

Jeff's stare followed hers. With a thick swallow, his gaze remained transfixed on Todd.

A bright smile lit Todd's face as Liam howled with laughter. For a moment, Summer wondered if a flicker of the past played in Jeff's vision. Of a time that a grin anchored his face while his own son laughed? Did that memory ache or comfort?

"You two are together?" Jeff's fingers went to the collar of his sheriff's uniform and grasped something, a flash of silver glittered in the mid-afternoon sunshine that filled the café.

"Yes," she murmured, her eyes fixed on his fingers.

"That's your boy?" He tipped his head to Liam, whose wild arm gestures elicited a chuckle from Todd and Noah.

"Yes."

"He looks happy."

"My son? He is."

"No… My son." A gentle tremor shook his voice.

She stared at Todd. "He is."

"Good." He faced her with regret gleaming in his green eyes. "How much do I owe you?"

"Fifteen ninety-three," Summer said, the circular shape that dangled beneath his shirt's brown fabric snatched her stare.

Jeff pulled out twenty-five dollars and handed it to Summer. "Keep the change."

"That's too—"

He waved her off and took the to-go bag. "It's likely not enough. Thank you for giving him what I failed to." He turned and headed to the door, leaving her stunned and confused.

Her eyes flicked back to Todd, whose gaze snapped toward his father. For a moment father and son stared at each other.

She could read the emotions telegraphed in their different, but mirrored expressions. Regret. Sadness. Anger. Hurt.

With a long sigh, Jeff shook his head and walked out.

Todd swallowed hard and then refocused his attention on Liam.

What did I give him?

Without thinking she turned to Laney, who came out of the kitchen with a tray of drinks. "Watch the front. I'll be right back."

Rounding the counter, she flew out into the cold. Jeff was halfway down the street, headed toward his police cruiser.

"Jeff, wait!" she called, running and almost falling on a slick patch of ice.

Face pinched; he spun to face her.

"What did I give him?" she said, a little breathless.

A heavy breath rolled along his brawny frame.

Like his son, Jeff was broad shouldered, tall, and muscular. While Todd hadn't grown into his large structure until late in his teens, stories from her mom about the handsome former high school basketball player confirmed Jeff had always been big. But somehow in front of her, his hand pressed against the cruiser's window, the to-go bag clutched in the other, he seemed small. Like a lost, sad little boy.

"What did I give him?" she repeated, stepping closer.

"A family," he said gruffly.

"You could still give him that." Her words were reminiscent of tentative first steps across a rickety bridge that could collapse at any moment.

"It's too late." He opened the door.

"Is it?" She reached for him, halting his movements. "The necklace you wear says otherwise."

His hand went to the chain visible in the open collar of his shirt. "What do you know about that?"

"It's Mandy's ring, isn't it? The pink sapphire wedding ring."

She hadn't actually seen the pale pink, emerald-cut gemstone, but she knew what it was. She'd seen it on Mandy's hand many times. And the way his fingers curled around it almost as if gripping a loved one's hand confirmed her suspicion. He hadn't packed Mandy away, not fully. He'd kept her close.

His hand dipped beneath his collar, revealing the chain. Mandy's ring sat aside a simple larger silver band, one that would be worn by a man with thick fingers like those that held tight to the necklace.

"I keep them close." Pain twinged his words.

"You should tell him."

"What would that do?"

"It would show him that you didn't forget her. That he'd not been alone…" She twisted her head toward the café and then back to him.

"But he was alone. So was Rose. The three of us lived in a house together, utterly alone. I did that." He looked up to the gray sky.

Placing a hand on his forearm, she pulled his attention back to her. "Why did you pack up Mandy's things but wear her ring?"

It made no sense how someone so deeply in love with his wife could pack up every tangible memory into boxes to be donated or stored in the attic. Then turn around and hold the symbols of their promised forever close to his heart every day.

"In big and little ways, I watched my children's hearts break daily when they saw a picture, or one of Mandy's knick-knacks. I thought packing up her things would help them move on. I thought if I was the only one haunted by her memory, that they'd be unencumbered to live. Unlike me, whose spent the last twenty-three years as the living dead. Just a heartless husk of a man."

"You're not heartless." A steady certainty underscored her words. "I know heartless men. They don't carry keepsakes of the people they love around their neck. They don't have regrets."

He nodded. "I have a lifetime of regrets."

"It's not too late."

Shaking his head, he opened his mouth. A protest played on his lips.

She cut it off. "Don't add one more regret. Like you said, you have enough."

"How can I expect him to forgive me? He's so angry and I don't blame him."

"Sometimes hurt masks itself as anger."

His mouth dragged down.

"Your son has the biggest heart of any man I know. When he loves, it's forever and he still loves you."

Todd had never said the words to her. Not directly. But the expression that swam in his gaze each time she'd seen him come face-to-face with his dad spoke of love. She knew his anger covered up all his hurt. It was clear for anyone to read if they spoke the language of Todd's eyes, and she was fluent.

"Talk to him."

"What if he doesn't want to talk to me?"

"Then keep trying. You're the parent. Be the father you want to be… The man I've heard about in stories. The man that I still see in you, behind all the grief and regret." Her brown eyes squared off with his wavering gaze.

Perhaps she was being too rough. A bit of the no-nonsense mean girl still seemed to live inside her. That girl only came out when fighting for the people she loved. He'd never asked her to intervene on his behalf. Part of her worried that she'd crossed an invisible barrier, but the rest of her stood resolute in the knowledge that sometimes when you love someone you cross lines to protect them. She was a mama bear, after all.

"Thank you for loving my son." He placed a palm on her shoulder and squeezed.

"You never have to thank me for that. His love is gift enough," she said.

"I can see that."

Turning, Summer came face-to-face with Todd, her jacket in his hands and a confused expression on his face. She could slink back and apologize for overstepping, but the days of apologies for things she didn't regret were over. If he was angry with her, she'd face it because she knew they'd talk about it. There'd be no cruel words or firm hands from him. That assurance was solidified by the fact that he knew exactly why she left the café but still came after her with her coat to keep her warm, to care for her.

"I understand if you're angry with me." She stepped to him.

He placed the jacket around her shoulders. "I'm not. I'm just confused about what you're doing."

She looked between Jeff, who still stood by his police cruiser, and Todd. "To tell you the truth, so am I. My mama bear tendencies may have gotten the better of me."

"She's a good one." Jeff cleared his throat.

Todd nodded. "I know."

"I'm happy for you."

Todd's expression remained blank.

"You've grown up to be a fine man."

"No thanks to you," he sniped, as he guided Summer down the sidewalk.

Halting her steps, she grabbed his forearm. "Todd!"

"I deserve that." Resignation dripped from Jeff's tone. "You deserved better. I want to do better by you and your sister. To be the man I promised your mother I'd be. The man I failed to be for her and for you two."

"Don't you fucking use her to get what you want. You threw her away, just like you did the rest of our family," he snarled.

"Show him!" she ordered, spinning to face Jeff. "Show him!"

Todd's brow furrowed. "Show me what?"

A gentle tremor rolled across Jeff's lip as he unclasped the chain around his neck and held it out.

Eyes wide, Todd took slow steps toward his father. His gaze locked on the rings nestled in his father's palm. "Mom's ring?"

"*Our* rings. I've worn them since she passed. I promised to love her until my dying day, and I have never stopped." Jeff's confession rattled with pain.

"You packed her up."

"For you and your sister. I thought I was protecting you. That I was helping you… And I was wrong. So goddamn wrong." Jeff hung his head. "You lost your mother and then I took myself away from you."

"Why?" Todd croaked.

"Because every time I looked at you kids, I saw her. Instead of falling to my knees with gratitude that I had you two, a daily reminder that for too brief a time I had Mandy, I pushed you away thinking it was best for you…but in truth I thought my heart was broken."

Todd's stare jerked to his father. "Thought?"

Tears brimmed in Jeff's eyes. "It was never broken because Rose and you are my heart. Despite everything, both of you have grown up to be amazing. Rose and I still see each other but I've only been able to watch you from afar. Getting your Masters. Opening your business. Starting your family." He gestured to Summer.

"You said you didn't pay for your son to go to college to become a bartender," Todd hissed.

"I was an ass for saying that. I spoke out of anger. More at myself than at you. I'm sorry."

Todd's face remained stoic.

"I don't expect your forgiveness, but that doesn't mean I won't try to earn it." He opened Todd's clenched fist and placed the necklace in it. "I want you to have this."

"Why?"

"Because I took so much of her from you, it's time I give something back."

Todd's lip trembled.

"How are you going to do that?" Todd looked between his closed palm and father.

"I don't know," he murmured. "As you know, I'm not good at feelings, but I'll figure it out. Maybe I can come by your brewery or wine bar. We don't have to talk if you don't want to, but I could just sit at the bar, drink one of your famous beers, and do something I should have done a long time ago."

"What's that?"

"Be there." Determination glinted in his eyes.

Todd blew out a long breath, the silver chain dangled from his tight fist. "Take this back."

"No. It—"

"It's yours. I'm not ready to have it... Not yet." He gnawed on his lower lip. "Maybe someday."

Taking the necklace, Jeff nodded. "Someday."

"You know the brewery and wine bar hours?"

A tiny hopeful smile curved Jeff's mouth. "Yes."

"Alright." Todd turned, took Summer's hand, and headed toward the café.

They walked in silence for a beat until the guilt boiled over inside her. The sorry, not sorry stance that squared her shoulders dissolved.

"I am so sorry." Her voice cracked, tears spilling over.

Eyebrow quirked; he stopped. "Are you?"

"I'm sorry I overstepped." The apology came out like that of a child getting caught with a cookie.

"Oh, sweetheart." He pressed his smirk to her temple. "We'll talk later, but for now just give me a good day."

"Always." She dashed away her tears. "If I promise we can do butt stuff later, will that get me out of the scolding I have coming?"

Laughter barked out of him. "God, I love you."

CHAPTER TWENTY-SIX

"If only you knew how mean she really is..." ~Mean Girls

Butt stuff was not necessary. "After all, what will we do for my birthday?" he'd teased her while they'd taken Sheba for a long walk after tucking Liam in for the night. She'd kept her promise. It had been a good day. The tension from earlier dissolved away with every squeeze of his hand, press of his lips, and wrap of his arm.

Twenty-four hours later, none of the guilt remained. Glass of wine in hand, while she sat in the nail salon, the pedicurist's nimble hands gliding down her long legs, contentment drifted through her. They'd talked about it. He'd listened. She'd listened. Not once did he use her actions to paint her as undeserving or use it as an excuse to.... She shook that thought off.

Because he's not Max. He's Todd... And I deserve him.

She'd waded into the relaxed state of her present. A good man. Good friends. Good family. A relaxation only rivaled by the orgasm Todd brought her to this afternoon. Amongst the stacks of classics in the dimly-lit basement of the village library, his hand covered her mouth as the other one played her like a violin. Returning library books had never been so sweet.

"Someone is positively glowing." Jerome waggled his dark eyebrows at Summer.

"Is that a post-orgasm glow?" Elle grinned.

Summer sipped her wine.

They all squealed.

"Get it, bestie!" Hooting, Nat raised her pint of cider.

Carmen studied Summer. "I think it's more than the sexy-time glow."

"It is." Summer's lips tipped up into a broad smile. "We're in love."

The days of hiding from the people she cared about were over. Like flakey layers of a croissant, she was shedding the pieces of herself that held her back. For the first time in her life, Summer was unapologetically Summer. *I'm free.*

"Love!" Carmen clasped her hands to her heart.

Nat beamed.

"Summer and Todd sitting in the tree, f-u-c-k-i-n-g," Jerome and Elle sang, their teenaged-like giggles causing the nail technician to snort along with everyone else.

Mortification should blaze through her, but the happiness that dripped along her veins wouldn't allow her to feel anything but incandescent bliss.

That joy radiated in her through the next day's shift at Cassie's Café and lit her smile while she sat huddled at a corner table in the not-yet-open brewery with Nat going down a Pinterest rabbit hole.

"What theme do you want? Modern chic? Country sweet? Fairytale?" Summer flipped through images of decorated altars on her iPad.

"Can Taylor Swift be a wedding theme?" Nat tapped her glittery pink fingers against the table.

"Taylor Swift?" Face scrunched, Summer leaned back and crossed her arms.

"I know. When I mentioned it to my mother she said and I quote "This is not a sixteen-year-old's birthday, Natalie. This is your wedding." I guess we'll just have our first dance be to a T-Swift song and call it a day." Her entire body deflated.

A Taylor Swift-themed wedding seemed ridiculous, but so did an outdoor pondside wedding in early December. Still, she'd found a way to make Clayton and Elle's vision a reality.

Biting her lower lip, her mental gears started to turn rapidly. "Noah and you have been in each other's life during all your individual and collective eras. We can use the color schemes and vibes from her albums for each wedding event. Then we can use love songs from each of her albums for the table's décor."

"Yes!" Nat bounced in her chair.

"Clearly the head table will be 'Today Was A Fairytale' and you should walk down the aisle to that song. Even the bridesmaids' dresses can be inspired by the different eras." Summer jotted ideas in her notebook.

The ideas flowed out of her. She'd need to finesse the concept, but she could do this. She could take the vibrant colors of Nat's ideas and use them to paint a picture perfect day for her and Noah.

"I see the Summer Michaels' brain at work."

"I should have a firm proposal for Noah and you by next Friday."

"Do you think Noah will go for a Swiftie wedding?" Nat's forehead crinkled.

"I think Noah would walk down the aisle wearing only a whip cream bikini if it would make you happy," she deadpanned.

Nat's lips formed an *O*.

"You're thinking about Reddi-whipping Noah, aren't you?"

Deep pink crept up Nat's neck.

Summer snapped her fingers. "Tell your vagina to focus. We have a wedding to plan."

"Fine." Nat picked up her to-go latte. "I can't believe I say I want to have a T-Swift wedding and you A; don't laugh me out of the room, and B; actually come up with a way to do it. Goddessdamn, you're good at this."

"Thanks." Summer closed her notebook. "I am good at this, and I really enjoy it, so last night I registered for that class at GCC. I'm going to start slowly but I want to make this a thriving business. Something I can do full-time."

"Summer!" Nat squealed, hurling the full force of her pixie-sized body at her and almost toppling them to the ground.

"Easy, She-Hulk." She laughed, pushing Nat off her.

"Sorry." Nat winced. "So, what made you change your mind?"

Her lips pursed. "I don't want to be scared anymore. I was scared what it would mean if I failed and a little bit about what it meant if I succeeded."

Nat's head tilted to the right.

"I've spent the last nine and a half years hiding from my past, who I used to be, and Max. Part of me feared that if I made this into a real business with a website and all that that he'd find me, but that's silly. It's been almost ten years. While I did a good job redirecting him to look for me in California, I'd be a fool to not think he wasn't smart enough or had enough money to pay for someone to find me here. There's no reason for me to hide anymore, because he's not looking for me. I'm not letting the fear of Max control me any longer."

Nat placed her hand atop Summer's. "Plus, you have an entire army of people that would stand between him and you and Liam. Don't let Noah's cuteness fool you, he was a Marine and knows a hundred and fifty ways to kill a man. Some including spoons."

"Spoons?"

Nat shrugged. "Maybe we should use Taylor's Fearless album as the theme for the head table."

"Why?"

"Because the wedding party will be full of the bravest people I know."

Each member of the wedding party, who'd all been asked within minutes of Noah and Nat's engagement, shimmered with a fearless spirit. Elle had overcome the trauma of her past to find an everlasting love with Clayton. Jerome loved with no boundaries. Carmen overcame the obstacles of backward thinking board members to shepherd the village into the modern era.

"It's only because our bride and groom are two of the most fearless people I know. Especially the bride." Summer linked their hands. Since Nat Owens waltzed into her life seven months ago, she'd fallen in insta-love with the spunky and vibrant young doctor. Like the rest of their ragtag bridal party, she'd faced her monsters to reclaim her heart.

"I love you, bestie," Nat cooed.

"I love you." Summer leaned in, tucking Nat into her side. "Enough sap. Let's finish this up. Amy will drop Liam off in twenty-minutes from his playdate with JJ, then I have a hot Friday night of playing Uno in my future."

"That's right, the parental units are away for the weekend leaving you two home alone. Does that mean someone is sleeping over?"

"*Maybe.*"

It did indeed. Todd would be over after the brewery and wine bar closed. Thankfully, both closed at ten, so he'd be over after Liam went to bed. The guys would have a later night tomorrow. Both bars would be open until one a.m. for New Year's Eve, so Summer planned to take full advantage of playing house with Todd tonight.

Though it didn't feel like playing house. Something felt so right about him coming home to her. About them checking in on Liam, fast asleep in bed, sharing his pillow with Sheba. About tugging on one of his Henleys and snuggling up together in bed.

"OMG! Are you daydreaming about your sleepover?" Nat poked Summer's side.

"Shut up!" Summer blushed.

"You know if you two move in together, every night would be a sleepover." Eyes narrowed; she wagged a finger. "Don't give me that face, Summer Michaels."

"What face?"

"That *it's too soon* face," she mocked Summer's voice. "You, yourself, said relationships move at their own pace. Look at Noah and me. Look at Clayton and Elle. They moved in after a month of dating."

"Technically I think it was after five days."

Both laughed about the impatient Clayton asking Elle to move into his farmhouse within five days of their initial reunion. It was a wonder he'd waited as long as he had to propose. But there was a big difference between Elle and Nat's romances and Summer's.

"I hear you, but neither of you had a nine-year-old to think of. I know Liam and Todd adore each other. I couldn't ask for a better…" she stopped herself, not allowing the word to pass her lips. "It would be a big change for all of us. As you are well aware of, after the epic 'put the toilet seat down' argument Noah and you got in last month."

"It takes two seconds to put it down!" Nat tossed her hands in the air.

Smiling, Summer continued, "Cohabitation is a big adjustment for a couple. Then you add a kid. I'm not saying I'm opposed to it someday, but I need to be practical."

"I get it." Nat's momentary frown ticked up into a cheeky grin. "Well, at least it means you get to keep having sneaking around sexy times. Oh, I remember the days of sneaking a quick sex sesh in Noah's office."

"You still do that. Todd and I heard you two last week."

"We may need to start a calendar to coordinate our brewery sexy times so there's no overlap."

Summer covered her face. "If the health department only knew the things the owners were doing when this place is closed."

Nat winked. "Who says it only happens when they're closed."

"Gross."

"Those who get caught making out in public library stacks shouldn't judge."

"I need to stop sharing all my secrets." Summer picked up her pen. "You do make a strange point about the sneaking around for time together. While I realize Christmas Eve, we"—she made a sexual gesture with her pen and hand— "but I'd not like to make that a habit in my parent's house, so I've decided to find an apartment for Liam and me. Todd aside, it might be good for us to stand on our own two feet. My parents and I discussed it on Christmas and while they don't want us to go, they hesitantly agreed."

"I assume we're stressing *hesitantly*?"

"They're supportive but will miss the little life we built. Though, we're not losing it, just reshaping it a little. I still want them to be a big part of our lives. I'd wait until the summer to pull the trigger to give me time to socialize the idea with Liam and to make the adjustment when he's not in school."

"First, I want to say I am a hundred percent supportive of you moving out."

"But?"

"But... if you're going to move out and have Liam and you go through that adjustment period, wouldn't it make sense to do it once instead of twice?"

"Nat." Her mouth formed a straight line.

"Since you have your crabby face on, I'll relent." Nat

picked up the iPad. "Let's scout some bridal shops where we can go dress shopping next weekend. I have six months to plan this shindig."

Noah's low baritone and the click of heels drifted down the hallway. "Todd will be here soon, and we can show you our brewing setup. We do plan to expand in the spring." Noah entered the bar area and grinned. "Hey, ladies. Sorry to interrupt. I was just giving an unexpected tour to—"

The roar in Summer's brain drowned out Noah's words. No introduction was needed. Beside him stood Vanessa Maxwell, her red lips drawn in a half smile.

"—Vanessa, this is my lovely fiancée, Dr. Nat Owens, and the amazing event coordinator I told you about, Summer Michaels." He motioned between them.

Nat's wide eyes snapped to Summer, whose gaze was locked on Vanessa. Her whiskey-colored eyes, identical to her brother's, assessed Summer. In their linked stares so much was said and left unsaid.

Why was she here? Would she tell Max? Did Max know she was here? Wait, was Max here? *Liam!* Amy would drop him off soon. What if Vanessa saw him? Everyone talked about how her son looked just like her with his chestnut hair and brown eyes. But she knew that his eye color was more a shade of whiskey and less chocolate than hers. She knew the tiny dimple on his right cheek matched the one on Max's.

Rising, she scooped up her things and stuffed them into her canvas bag. "I'm sorry, I have to run."

Forehead puckered, Noah asked, "Summer, are you okay?"

"Yeah." She flung her bag over her shoulder. "Just...uh...I have something I forgot."

Vanessa looked to her watch. "Sorry to push, but could you take me on the tour of your brewing facilities. This is meant to be just a quick trip. Plus, I don't want to keep Ms.

Michaels." She tipped her head between Summer and Nat. "Nice meeting you both."

It was an unexpected kindness from Vanessa, who never liked Summer. Something unreadable flashed in Vanessa's features.

"Nice meeting you, too." Not taking the time to study that look, Summer nodded and strode toward the back hallway.

Get to your car. Call Amy and get her to meet somewhere else. The plan formed quickly with each slap of her sneakered feet against the hardwood leading to the back door. Opening the door, brisk air and a hard chest slammed into her.

"Easy." A deep voice dripped in smooth caramel cautioned.

Thick fingers curled around her arms, steadying her. The scent of patchouli invaded her senses.

"Why if it isn't *my* warm Summer day."

Forcing her gaze up, she met a pair of whiskey eyes. "Max."

CHAPTER TWENTY-SEVEN

"You dirty little liar!" ~Mean Girls

No! No! No! Panic's gnarled fingers gripped Summer's throat cutting off needed air. Chest heaving, she tried to blink away the image in front of her.

It didn't work. He was there.

Max's chiseled features were drawn into a serpentine grin. An expensive looking black trench coat and suit accentuated his lean muscular form. Gray whispered at the edges of his neat dark hair. He looked like a prince, but she knew a monster hid beneath that handsome mask.

"It's good to see you," he drawled, his hand coming up to her cheek. "You look good. Only you could put on weight and make it look appetizing."

"Don't touch me." She slapped his hand away, pulling out of the fog that had temporarily paralyzed her.

With a smirk, he pushed his hands into his pockets. "Just trying to be friendly."

For a time that smile, full of innocent charm, blinded her to the beast behind the Prince Charming façade. A time when she'd debased herself just for an approving 'She's a good girl that likes to please me, isn't she?' from him. Only, unlike the praises Todd murmured in the heat of passion, Max's were tied to breaking and controlling her, not worshiping and loving.

"I've missed you, Summer." His face sobered. "There hasn't been a day since you left that I haven't thought of you."

"I doubt that."

"She forgets to never doubt me." With a gentle movement, he reached for a tendril of hair that had escaped from her ponytail.

She flinched.

Disappointment tugged his lips down. "I still love you, Summer. I never stopped."

"You never loved me."

"But I did," he insisted, the low timbre of his voice like a knife point against her skin. "And you loved me."

"I loathe you," she hissed.

"Now she's being rude." Shaking his head, he *tsked*.

"*She's*"—she enunciated the word through gritted teeth—"not playing your games any longer. Get the fuck out of my way."

With an almost boyish twinkle in his whiskey eyes, he stepped to the side and motioned for her to pass. "Such a filthy mouth."

She walked past him.

"Although, I always liked the things your filthy mouth could do."

Head high, she kept walking. She wouldn't look back. Nor would she drop her gaze. Any trace of vulnerability and he'd pounce. *Just get in my car and call Amy. Get Liam and…* She wasn't sure what to do after that. If he'd found her here, then he'd find her at her parents' house.

"Aren't you going to ask how I found you?" he called.

Summer yanked out her keys. "It doesn't matter."

"All this time I thought you were in California. So did our family's PI. You can imagine my shock to see a contract on Vanessa's desk for a brewery in your hometown. All these years and all it took was a quick Google search. And there you were."

Her steps slowed.

"After thousands of dollars and almost ten years, I find you from a small local newspaper. As you can imagine, I'll need to fire that PI. But there you were in a black and white photo at the grand opening for this place, tucked in the corner completely unaware of the camera. Like an innocent doe, there was my warm Summer day."

She clenched her fists, the teeth of the keys bit into her palm. The endearment once so sweet, now soured in her ears. The words rolled off his tongue like honey after each insult, slap, slam into the wall, or gripped fingers around her throat. As if the idea of her being his warm Summer day absolved him.

"I'm finding this village not at all the way you described it. It's actually quite charming."

Her heart outran her ceasing steps.

"There are these beautiful summer cottages going up on the lake. A perfect escape."

She spun. "What do you want from me?

Stalking closer, that dimple on his right cheek popped. "To take you to dinner."

"No." She whirled to walk away.

"Perhaps, I'll stop by the café you work at in the morning and try again. Maybe you'll change your mind."

"I will never change my mind. You don't love me. You never did."

"But—"

"Men who love someone don't do the things you did. They don't make their loved ones do the things you made me do." Fury built in her belly and spewed out in acidic venom in her words. "Your ego is just bruised that I left. You're like a child who lost their favorite toy. Well, I'm not your plaything anymore. You don't get to dress me up, tell me what to say or do and then punish me when I don't meet your fucked-up expectations."

He stepped close, the heat of his breath a clammy caress against her skin. "I don't think you remember who you are talking to," he snarled.

"Oh, I remember. You just don't realize that I'm not the same girl that use to cower at your threats. Now step back."

He stepped back. "I do like this fiery side you now have."

"Hey, sweetheart." Todd rounded the corner, a bouquet of pink roses in his hand.

"Todd." Her heart stuttered. Relief and fear fought within her. She wanted to sink into his arms but also shield him from this. From coming face-to-face with her monster.

"I was hoping I'd catch you before you finished up with Nat." He reached her, pressing a kiss to her cheek. "This is for you to celebrate registering for your class."

Last night, hands clasped as they walked Sheba, she'd told him her decision. Afterward, she sat alone in her room, the glow of the laptop screen's piercing the darkness, and registered for the class. Clicking *submit*, she'd shot off a text knowing he'd still be awake. Seconds later his *I'm so proud of you, sweetheart*, filled her cell phone screen.

"Class? Are you going to school, Summer?" A dismissive laugh punctuated Max's question.

Todd's brow wrinkled. "Sorry, I don't believe we've met. I'm Todd Kruger, Summer's boyfriend." He turned to Max reaching out his hand, the other banding around her lower back.

"Todd Krueger? One of the brewery owners." Amusement lifted Max's lips, his gaze flicked to Summer. "I see you haven't changed. Always going for the biggest fish in whatever waters you find yourself swimming in."

"Excuse me?" Todd started toward him, but Summer grabbed his hand, halting his steps. "What's that supposed to mean?"

He raised his hands. "Easy, Lancelot. Just a joke between old friends."

"We're not friends," Summer snapped, tightening her hold around Todd's hand.

"Who are you?" Todd glowered.

"Max," she croaked, meeting Todd's eyes.

"George Maxwell, Junior, actually." Max picked at nonexistent fuzz on his coat. "Max is what my friends call me, but since our relationship will be purely professional you can call me, Mr. Maxwell."

"Max?" Hurt shook his voice.

"I'm sorry." She clamped her eyes shut, and guilt clogged her throat.

Why hadn't she told him? At the time it made so much sense. Keep it from him to ensure he, Noah, and the village had this opportunity. In the glare of daylight, the decision she'd made in that bathroom with Nat almost three weeks ago seemed like one of the worst choices she'd made.

"She didn't tell you?" A taunting guffaw rolled out of Max. "She hasn't changed one bit. Still can't be trusted."

Lip quivering, she nodded. He was right about her.

Todd squeezed her hand and let go, turning to Max. "Don't speak to her like that."

"Or what?" Max mocked. "Did Summer get herself a brute?"

"She already had one of those."

Max's glare turned stoney. "You don't know anything."

"I know what she told me."

"I think we've established that *she's* a liar."

Teeth gritted; Todd advanced. "I warned you." His large hands tightened into fists.

"Mom! Todd!" Liam's happy shout halted Todd's movements.

"Mom?" Max's face contorted with shock.

No! No! Summer's pulse matched the cadence of a charging cheetah.

"Hey, buddy," Todd said, his tone not matching the stern glaze in his eyes fixed on Max. His arms wrapped around Liam, who hugged him.

"Hey, baby. You have fun?" Summer came to Todd's side, positioning Liam between them.

"Yep!" he chirped.

"Hey, Summer! Hey, Todd!" Amy waved, rounding the corner. "Just wanted to make sure he got to you. I've gotta run. JJ has a dental appointment, but are we still on for Sunday?"

"Yep." Summer forced cheerfulness into her voice.

Amy walked away.

Silence twined around them. The only words spoken were in each of their stares. Max's assessed. Summer's pleaded. Todd's targeted like a wolf ready to strike a threat.

"Hi. I'm Liam." He reached out his hand to Max.

"Max." Swallowing hard, he took his hand. "How old are you?"

Todd's palm rested on Liam's shoulder.

"He's nine," she breathed.

All her lies had been dragged into the light. She met Max's stoney gaze. The silent plea brimmed in her eyes. Was he enough of a monster to say it out loud? *Is he the monster, or am I? I'm the one who lied.* There'd been justification for each. One to guard. One to protect. One to give. At that moment, none of them cleansed her of her sins.

"Todd, there you are." Noah stepped out of the back door, Nat and Vanessa following behind. "I gave Vanessa the tour without you, but I'm glad she gets to meet you."

"Yes, it's rather impressive and..." She halted, her gaze

jumped between her brother, Summer, Todd, and Liam. Her eyes widened and fixed on the little boy. "Max." The gasp-like quality of his name telegraphed her immediate understanding.

"I'm sorry, Vanessa. but the deal's off," Todd announced, his stare still lingered on Max.

She nodded.

Confusion marred Noah's cheerful expression. Nat took his hand, meeting his eyes.

"Max, we should go," Vanessa said, coming beside her brother. Something akin to remorse flashed across her face.

"You'll be hearing from my lawyer, Summer." He stormed away.

CHAPTER TWENTY-EIGHT

L*awyer?* Summer's breath stammered. In one assessing look of his whiskey-colored eyes, Max knew Liam was his.

He's not Max's, he's mine. She swallowed the bile crawling up her throat. His blood may mingle with hers in Liam's veins, but her little boy was a hundred percent hers. Not an ounce of what made Max – outside of his DNA – roamed in Liam's tender heart. *That won't stop him from claiming my son.* Her fingers curled tight around Liam's shoulders connecting with large masculine protective hands already there like a sentry guarding a precious gift.

"Who were those people?" Forehead creased, Liam peered between her and Todd.

"Um..." she started but stopped.

What to say? *It's your father and aunt?* She'd never lied to him exactly. Although, she knew that a twist on the truth was nothing but a lie. In nine years, he'd only asked about his father once. Three years ago, he'd asked, "Why don't I have a dad?" She merely explained that some people have just a mom, or two moms, or two dads, or one dad, or no parents at all. It was the truth… but it had also been a lie. His little face lit with understanding as he'd said, "I have a mom, a pop, and a grandma." Then he'd asked if he could have a dog.

"They were people that wanted to help with the brewery," Todd offered.

Todd's unreadable gaze held hers. So much swirled in them making it hard to place where his thoughts were.

Hell, she didn't know what she thought. Anger. Fear. Regret. Guilt. Protectiveness. They knotted in a tangle inside her.

Noah cleared his throat. "Todd, can we talk?"

"Later. I should take these two home. I'm sure Nat can explain things. I'd imagine she knows everything." Todd's almost accusing gaze shot between Summer and Nat, who stood wringing her hands.

Noah turned to his fiancée, who nodded.

"Let's go." Todd guided them toward his SUV.

Wordlessly, she walked beside them. After Liam climbed into the backseat, Todd shut the door and faced Summer.

"I know you're angry," she whispered.

"I don't know what I am right now."

"That's fair." She fought the tremor in her voice. "If you want to take Liam, I'll drive my own car and meet you at the house."

"No."

She almost winced at the fierceness in his response.

He closed his eyes, let out a loud breath, and then opened his eyes. "I *need* you two close."

"Okay."

Wrapping his hands around her shoulders, he tucked her

into his chest. "I know we need to talk, but first I need to make sure you two are safe. Second, I need you to know even if I'm hurt or angry with you that I still love you. That hasn't changed."

"I love you so much," she barely croaked out her response.

"Let's get some of your things. You two are coming home with me. We can talk later, but let's focus on giving our boy a good night." He glided his fingers across her cheeks, the rough pads soothed the riot of fears inside her.

And they did just that. Nothing of the fear about Max crept into their time together. After she packed two bags to stay the entire weekend at Todd's, they headed back to his place. Liam vibrated with excitement about sleeping at Todd's.

After sharing a plate of fish frys, from Daryl's, a Western New York staple, Liam made root beer floats. He beamed as he poured the first batch of root beer he'd brewed over the two scoops of vanilla ice cream in each glass. Sheba curled on his lap, while they sat around the coffee table battling one another for Uno supremacy.

A war raged within Summer. Some muscles relaxed into the bliss of the three of them together. The effortless way they sank into Todd's space. Although, later that night as the four of them snuggled on his couch with a movie, it didn't feel like just his place. But she couldn't completely unknot the tension gnarled inside her. They still needed to talk. Max was still there. The threat of an attorney, and what that meant, loomed. Not to mention the need to tell Liam who his father was and what may or may not happen. Would Max want visits, partial custody, or – she gulped at that thought – *full custody*?

True, he'd not been part of Liam's life, but that was because of her actions. She'd hidden the pregnancy. She'd never given him a chance. But could she? There was always a possibility that his cruelty was only for her and wouldn't extend to Liam, but her precious boy's safety wasn't worth the risk. She could tell people what he'd done to her, but would anyone believe her? Max was rich, powerful, and respected. His family was well-known and beloved.

"We should get him to bed," Todd murmured, tipping his head toward Liam.

Just like Christmas Eve, his head lay on Summer's lap. A crocheted blanket draped over him, and Sheba was tucked behind his knees.

"Come on, buddy," Todd murmured, gently nudging Liam awake. "Let's go to bed."

"Can Sheba sleep with me?" Liam asked sleepily.

"Of course." With his large palm on Liam's shoulder, he guided the little boy toward the stairs, a tail-wagging Sheba in pursuit.

"Will mom and you read to me?" He rolled off the couch.

Todd looked between Summer and Liam, affection filling his features. "Of course."

Taking a moment, Summer folded the blanket and placed it on the couch. A few quiet tears escaped, but she dashed them away before heading to the guest room, where Todd tucked Liam in. Flipped on to his side, Liam nestled beneath the heavy comforter on the queen-size bed. Todd sat on the bed's edge, a copy of *Charlie and the Chocolate Factory* in his hand. Summer sat on the other side, listening to the melody of Todd reading aloud and Liam's quiet breaths as he slipped closer to sleep.

"Goodnight, buddy," Todd said softly, shutting the book.

Summer rose and kissed Liam's forehead. "Goodnight, baby. I love you."

"I love you too, mom." Liam yawned. "I love you, Todd."

"I love you too, buddy." The affection in Todd's gaze outshined the lamp's glow.

Her heart almost combusted. Even the fear about Max couldn't dull this moment for her between her son and the man she loved.

"Mom and I will be just down the hall if you need us, but Sheba will be here to keep you company." Todd clicked off the lamp and tipped his head toward Sheba who curled up beside Liam and dropped her head on his pillow.

Taking her hand, Todd stood beside her for a moment watching Liam sleep. A silent conversation passed between them. Liam may be tucked in safe for tonight, but a monster still lay outside. Slipping out of the room, they left the door ajar in case he needed them.

Per Noah, who'd called this evening to check on them after Nat filled him in, Max and Vanessa were still in the village and wouldn't head back to New York City until tomorrow evening. During Todd's brief chat with Noah, Summer texted Nat who assured her that Noah understood the decision to cancel the deal, but wished Summer had said something sooner. Summer had to applaud her friend for not saying, "I told you so," during their short text exchange. In the rearview mirror of today, Summer lamented her decision. She'd thought it was best. She'd thought they'd be safe, but...

He's still here. Spine stiffened, she stood beside the Christmas tree near the front window, her stare locked on the world outside. In the shadows lurked the one man with the power to rip her entire world a part.

"How are you?" Todd came up from behind her, looping his arms around her middle.

"Regretful. Remorseful. Angry with myself." She swallowed back the tears. She'd kept them at bay most of the night with only a few daring ones escaping, but the rest pricked for release. Turning, she faced him. "I'm so sorry. I should have told you. I should have done a lot of things."

"Sweetheart—"

"Don't be understanding," she cut him off. "I don't

deserve it… I don't deserve you. I did this. I cost you the deal." Her gaze dropped.

Framing her face, he guided her to look at him. "You cost me nothing. You saved Noah and I from being tied to a man like that."

"But the deal meant something to the village. For your business. For you."

"Is that why you said nothing?" His brows lifted. "For me?"

"It's such a big opportunity." She pulled away from him. "If you weren't with me, none of this would have happened. You'd never have known. You'd never have lost this chance. I've done nothing but fuck up your life."

"You are my life!" He snapped but then quieted.

Your life? Eyes wide, her pulse ticked up. Both with the fear that Liam would hear them arguing and at his confession.

When no noise or movement manifested, he continued in a quieter voice, "My family is my life. You and Liam are *my* family. I know you're going to say it's too soon, but we promised each other we'd make our own rules. I love you and I adore that little boy. My first thought every morning and last thought every night is about you two. I could have a million Maxwell's lined up to sell my beer, but none of that would matter if I didn't have you and Liam." He closed the space between them, cradling her face between his large hands. "So, please hear me…you have ruined nothing. You're not just my family…you're my home and there's no living without you."

Unbridled tears coursed down her cheeks, coating his fingers in salty wetness. Somehow, he'd squeezed even more love out of her. Unable to speak, she captured his lips.

"What am I going to do about Max? What if he takes Liam from me?" Her voice shook.

"Nobody is taking our boy from us."

"Max never loses."

"But he has lost before. You beat him. You got out," Todd insisted.

"For him to come back like my own personal Michael Myers." She stepped away from him, tossed her hands into the air, and paced the length of the room, hoping the movement would settle her frayed nerves. "He's too powerful. Too rich. I'm just a waitress. A single mom. A—"

"Marry me."

It wasn't a question. It was an almost desperate command. One she was unsure she'd heard correctly.

She blinked. "What?"

"Together we can fight him."

"Todd…"

Taking her hands, his beseeching gaze met hers. "You're not *just* anything. You're the woman I love. You're the mama bear of all mama bears."

Despite the ache in her heart, a watery laugh slipped out.

"They're not going to take Liam away from a loving and stable family. Max may have his millions and high-priced lawyer, but he cannot offer Liam what we can… A real home."

She swallowed thickly. "I don't want you to marry me because of Max."

"I'm not."

"But you are." She gestured at him.

"I was always going to marry you. Max is just pushing up the timeline. You deserve a more romantic proposal than this, but I promise you I'll make up for that with the rest of our lives, together."

"Todd."

"I won't push if a life with me isn't something you want, but if all that is holding you back is the belief that I'm doing this because of Max, then toss that idea out with the rulebook, sweetheart." An earnest plea swam in his green eyes.

"I want a life with you. For tonight to be our every night, minus the horrible baby daddy drama."

A silent laugh pulled at the corners of his mouth. "Is that a yes?"

"It's a let me think about it. Is that okay?"

He pressed his forehead to hers. "It's more than okay."

"Will you take me to bed and hold me?"

Without a word, he scooped her into his arms. Snugged close against his chest, he carried her to his room. Scratch that, *their* possible future room if she said yes.

Todd's muscular arm draped over her waist, both protective and a little possessive. The idea of being possessed by anyone had curdled in her stomach until him. Belonging to Todd wasn't about ownership. In his embrace, she was supported not bound. She was loved and it freed her.

Creeping out of the bed, she grabbed her cell phone from the nightstand and tiptoed downstairs. The furnace's gentle hum filled the living room. In the glow from the still lit Christmas tree, she dialed a number she'd blocked from her mind, but not her phone. It was just after midnight, but she knew he'd be awake.

"Hello."

"Max," she said, her spine straight.

"I wondered if it was you when that 585 area code flashed on my phone," he said, his tone dismissive.

Of course, he'd not know her phone number. When she left, Summer left her phone. She got a new number and a new phone in order to assure he'd not be able to track her.

"So, what does the mother of my child want at this hour of night?" Max's caramel-dipped voice taunted.

"I'm sorry I never told you about him," she said, trying to hide the placating tone.

"I don't think you're sorry at all."

"You're right, I'm not. You never wanted children. You made that perfectly clear."

"That was then, this is now. Age brings perspective… It's time to think about my legacy." The clank of ice against a glass accompanied his words.

She could picture the amber liquid. So much of this man's habits remained cataloged in her memory. The nightly glass of scotch before bed. The gold Princeton class ring tapping against the table's surface in consideration of a decision. His serpentine smiles after a cruel jab. The cooed "Why does she make me do this?" with each slap.

"What do you want? Do you want custody because I will fight you," she hissed.

"And you'll lose."

"I'll tell people what you did."

"Nobody will believe you," he scoffed.

"They will."

"They won't." Assured venom filled his voice. "Especially after they learn who you really are. How do you think Liam would feel to learn what a whore his mother was, probably still is. What would that bartender of yours think? Would he still want someone so damaged?"

"What are you talking about?"

"I told you I missed you. Thankfully I had those videos we made to keep me company."

"You're a bastard!" she snarled.

"You're the expert on bastards since you made *my* son one," he quipped.

"Fuck you. He's not *your* anything. He's *my* son."

"You're right," he said, his tone almost bored. "Vanessa did counsel restraint. She reminded me that my lifestyle isn't conducive to fatherhood."

A furrow puckered her forehead. *Vanessa advocated for him to back off?*

"If you recall, I can be very generous. I'll forgo the attorney. You can keep him on one condition."

Closing her eyes, she straightened her spine. "What condition?"

"Give up the bartender."

"What?" she croaked.

"I don't like to share what's mine," he seethed. "Plus, if you're going to mother my child I want no distractions. I'll even send child support and pay for Liam's education. I'd expect my son to go to an Ivy and I'd imagine you couldn't afford that on a waitress's tips."

"Would you be part of his life?"

"Not as long as you're a good girl. Adhere to my condition and you can keep the boy and I'll even pay for it." He clucked his tongue. "I leave for the airport at three tomorrow. Stop by my Airbnb at noon with your decision."

CHAPTER TWENTY-NINE

"I'm sorry that people are jealous of me… but I can't help it that I'm popular." ~Mean Girls

A chill crawled down Summer's spine, but not from the icy breath of the last day of the year. Snow crunched beneath her boots as she moved closer to the old primary school that had been refurbished as Airbnb apartments. With each step closer to the red brick building, anxiety crisscrossed within her.

"This is for Liam," she whispered.

This morning watching Liam, his face bright, flipping pancakes with Todd, she knew exactly what she needed to do. Her priority had always been, and would, remain her son.

Reaching the building's side entrance, she pulled out her phone and texted Max.

Summer: I'm outside.
The Asshole: I'm in 103, come in.
Summer: No, you can come outside.

Holding her breath, her eyes locked on the phone screen. In no scenario would she willingly go inside his Airbnb.

The Asshole: Fine.

Minutes later, face drawn with annoyance, Max emerged. "This is a little dramatic, even for you, Summer," he grumbled, rubbing his hands together.

"I don't trust you." She narrowed her eyes.

"Now, now... Should thieves talk about trust?" The tut was playful but underscored with venom.

"I'm not a thief!"

He placed his hand on his heart. "But you are. You stole my heart, and then my son."

She rolled her eyes. "You don't have a heart, and you don't care about Liam. You, yourself, said fatherhood didn't fit with your lifestyle."

"True." He crossed his arms over his broad chest. "But I'll make it work if you don't agree to my demands. Perhaps, boarding school."

"You're an asshole."

He stepped closer, crowding her. "She should mind her manners. I'm being kind to her with my offer."

Stepping back, she let out a hard breath. "You're right, I should remember who I'm talking to."

"Good girl." A sardonic grin slithered across his face.

"I want to make sure I have this correct... please explain your terms again."

"Give up the bartender and I'll let you keep the boy. I'll even give you three grand in child support a month and pay for Liam's college."

"And you don't want to see Liam? Be part of his life?"

He made a dismissive gesture. "No. As long as you remain single, I'll keep my distance."

"What about the videos you have of me? The ones you

threatened to show people." She swallowed thickly, not wanting to say it aloud. The memories of the things he'd made her do were still too hard to talk about.

He quirked an eyebrow. "Those are my insurance policy that you'll remain obedient."

"How do I know you won't use them against me, even if I do what you ask?"

"You've gotten shrewder." He tapped one long finger against his chin. "Perhaps, we could negotiate then."

"What do you want?"

Stalking close, he brushed a wayward tendril of hair behind her ear. "Come inside with me."

Acidic bile snaked up her throat. "Are you saying if I have sex with you, then you won't use the videos?"

The smooth pads of his fingers coasted to her lips. "You know you'd enjoy it."

She flinched.

"Call your bartender. Tell him it's over. Then come inside and keep me company until I leave for the airport. After we're done, I'll let you delete the videos yourself and I'll write you a check. For child support, not the sex. Although, if you're an extra good girl I may tip you." He stepped back, pushing his hands into his pockets.

This is for Liam. She reminded herself, pulling out her phone and dialing Todd.

"Put him on speaker."

She complied.

"Sweetheart." Todd's voice filled the space between her and Max.

"Todd." Her stare met Max's.

"Yes?"

"I love you, baby. I'll be home soon."

Angry clouds darkened Max's eyes.

"I love you too, sweetheart."

Ending the call, she slipped the phone into her pocket. "I don't accept your terms."

Max blustered. "Some mother you are, choosing a man over her son."

"I'm doing this for my son. Teaching him to not back down to bullies. To fight not just for the people he loves, but for himself. You can post those videos. You can hire all the overpriced attorneys in the world. But you will not beat me. You will not own me, not ever again." She pivoted.

"I'm not done with you," he snarled, fisting her hair, and yanking her back against him. "She needs to remember who's in charge." His hand came up to her neck, his fingers curled tight.

"Let go," she choked out, slamming her boot hard onto the top of his sneakered foot.

"Bitch!" He tossed her to the ground.

"Summer!" Todd shouted, racing around the building with Noah beside him.

Eyes wide, Max's head jerked toward the two men charging toward him.

"I got him. You get her," Noah hollered. Reaching Max, he barreled into him, knocking him over. "Stay down, asshole!" He held a squirming Max on the ground.

"I got you, sweetheart." Todd scooped her into his arms. "Are you okay?"

She nodded. "I am. I swear."

"Get off me!" Max seethed.

"Not up to you… Summer?" Noah drawled as if he was asking if she wanted another cup of tea.

"Let him up. He's not stupid enough to try anything with you two here."

"You're the boss," he said, standing up.

"You're going to jail, pretty boy," Max grumbled, rising up and wiping at his clothes.

Noah's head tilted, his lips ticked up into a sarcastic grin. "You only wish you were as pretty as me."

"Was this a game, Summer?" Max glowered.

"No, it was a set up."

After hanging up with Max, she'd woke Todd and told him everything. He'd said they'd fight Max together and she knew her plan was the only way to win. Not for a single moment did she consider Max's condition. That single condition would easily become more and more demands until he'd stripped away every bit of her. She knew this because that's what he'd tried to do before. Liam deserved, no… needed, his full mother, not a stripped down version.

"So, your boyfriend and his friend came in like knights. This changes nothing. All it shows is that two men attacked me after we canceled their deal. At least that's what I'll tell the police." He pulled out his phone.

"You'll tell the police nothing," Vanessa ordered, emerging from behind the SUV parked in front of the entrance.

"Vanessa?" His forehead pinched with confusion.

"Did you get it?" Summer gestured at Vanessa.

"Sure did." She held up a cell phone. "You?"

Summer pulled out a second mobile. "Yep. Between your video and my audio, I think we have more than enough evidence."

Jaw slack, Max's gaze bounced between his sister and Summer. "Vanessa, what have you done?"

"What I should have done a long time ago." Eyes narrowed; she stepped close to her brother.

The worry that shimmered in Vanessa's expression after she'd walked into the brewery had nipped at Summer. How remorse rather than shock filled her gaze at seeing Liam. She'd cautioned her brother to show restraint. It all spoke of someone that could be a potential ally, not foe. It was a chance, but Summer would risk it to protect her son.

Early this morning, she called Vanessa and the entire truth

came out. The Maxwell family's PI had found Summer eight years ago. Only Vanessa paid him to continue the California myth. When Summer asked why, she simply said, "I know who my brother is."

Now, Vanessa stared down her brother. "You will leave Summer and Liam alone. Never contact them. Additionally, you will step down from the family business."

"Or what, you'll play the video and audio for our parents? The board? Make it public? This is blackmail!" he spat.

She wagged her finger. "Silly big brother. I'm going to do all those things. There's no extortion, unlike what you tried to do to Summer. I'm just telling you what you're going to do, but I'm certain the legal ramifications of your actions will help ensure that."

"You wouldn't."

"But I would… And here comes my ace in the hole now."

Everyone turned. A white police cruiser parked, and a stoic faced Jeff Krueger jumped out of the car.

"Dad… What are you doing here?" Todd asked.

"I called him. We've interacted at several fundraisers for the police union and cervical cancer organizations. He's how I heard about your brewery. He went on and on about his son's famous brews," Vanessa explained.

"You did?" Todd faced his dad.

An almost bashful smile curved Jeff's mouth.

Todd opened and closed his mouth.

Jeff cleared his throat. "What seems to be the problem?" His gaze moved to Max, dirty wet splotches dotting his now rumpled clothes, and then landed on the red hand marks around Summer's neck. "Summer? Are you okay?" His gruff tone was warm and concerned.

"I am, but I'd like to file a complaint." She squared her shoulders.

Hands in restraints, Max sat in the back of the police cruiser while Jeff called the village police to take their statements. As county sheriff and the father of one of the witnesses, he thought it was best to hand it off to the local authorities. While the police took Noah and Todd's statements, Summer leaned against the building with Vanessa.

"You said you knew who your brother is, what does that mean?" Summer asked, her stare fixed on the police cruiser.

"He's always been controlling and quick to anger. There were a few things that caused me to pause with his past girlfriends. Never anything I witnessed, but… I just knew." She fiddled with her jacket's sleeve. "I wasn't nice to you when you came into the picture, hoping that it would scare you off. It worked with other girlfriends, but…"

Summer sighed. "I stuck around."

"Max is charming. He has a way of making you feel like you're the most important person in the world, while simultaneously tearing you down. He's like the Picasso of head fuckery." Her face fell. "I saw what happened the night before you left. I saw him slam you into the wall and slap you. I had come back to his apartment after leaving because I'd forgotten my cell phone. I saw what he did, and I did nothing. I should have intervened. It ate away at me, so the next day I came back to check on you and offer help, but you were gone. The doorman mentioned you gave him the key and asked if I was there to pick it up for my brother. I knew you'd left, so I vowed to do whatever I could to help you stay gone."

"Did you know about Liam?"

"Yes." Her eyes casted down. "I had the PI keep tabs on you for me."

"If you vowed to keep us safe, why did you offer a deal to Todd and Noah?"

She closed her eyes. "I knew about your event coordination work. Max showed zero interest in the buying side of things. I thought it was a way to funnel more money into the village and ultimately help you financially. It was risky and stupid. I never thought he'd notice and find out. I'd managed to keep everything about you and Liam from him. I'm so sorry, Summer."

She faced her. "I'm not." And she wasn't. Max's arrival was the sledgehammer breaking down the wall that had held her captive. She'd faced her jailer and was now free.

Sighing, Vanessa pushed off the wall. "I should probably pack up and head out. I need to call my parents and tell them everything. Then head to the airport."

"Stay." She reached for Vanessa's arm. "Come meet your nephew. Plus, there's a New Year's Eve bash at the brewery. We can both celebrate our liberation."

They'd both been bound by Max. Each hiding from him in different ways. Today marked the start of a new life for both women. A future unshackled from the secrets that they'd been forced to keep.

"Are you sure?" Vanessa shuffled foot-to-foot.

"Yes."

"Okay." She pushed her dark hair behind her ears.

"Come by Todd's house at six. You can have dinner with us, then I'll show you the Perry nightlife." She grinned.

After a stiff, but still warm hug, Vanessa headed inside. Summer remained pressed against the brick wall as Todd and his father talked. A small smile bloomed on Todd's face while his father spoke. She placed her hand on her heart, warmth surged and dripped along her veins.

Patting Todd's shoulder, Jeff mumbled something and then strode to his car.

Todd turned, their gazed tethered from across the small courtyard. With each step he took closer, her heart soared. Lifted by that feeling, she bolted and jumped into his arms.

"Oof," he huffed as he caught her.

"Am I too heavy?"

"Nope. Just need a good grip." He squeezed her ass.

"Oh, shut up." She swatted his chest.

"Make me." He smirked.

"Gladly."

Her mouth slanted over his. Banding his arms around the small of her back, he pressed her tight into his embrace.

"Take me home to our boy," she demanded, breaking their kiss.

CHAPTER THIRTY

"Ma'am, do you have this in the next size up?" ~*Mean Girls*

Fingers threaded with Todd's, Summer strolled into the brewery. Until nine p.m., the bar hosted a family-friendly New Year's Eve Party. Partnering with Cassie's Café and the bakery, patrons were treated to an array of tidbits and desserts. The Little Man, the official kid-friendly drink, made its debut alongside hot cocoa and juice for the kiddos. After nine, all the little ones would be shuttled home and the adults would get to play.

The brewery overflowed with laughing patrons. Their friends and Summer's support group members claimed a cluster of tables near the buffet. That group now included Amy, her husband Joseph, and JJ. His little face lit when Liam entered the room.

"Aunt Vanessa, come meet my friend!" Liam tugged Vanessa along, his small hand folded in hers. He'd taken to the idea of having an aunt.

Liam had many questions, which required many, many more future conversations. Summer knew this. She didn't have all the answers but started by introducing him to his aunt. They'd start there and she'd figure it out, but not alone. Not anymore. She had her parents, whom she'd called to give them the CliffsNotes version of today's events. They'd drive back in the morning, knowing she and Liam were safe. She had Nat, Todd, and above all, she had herself. With her support people in place, she knew she and Liam could navigate this and anything else that came their way.

"Let's get a drink." Todd pressed a kiss to her cheek, guiding them to the bar.

"Oh, are you going to buy me a drink?" she cooed, batting her eyes.

"No, you're going to buy me a drink."

She nuzzled into him. "Good thing I'm sleeping with the owner."

Later, she leaned against the bar and sipped her glass of rosé chatting with Nat, while their guys helped the staff. Friends funneled in-and-out. Her vision snagged on a tall, broad-chested figure entering the bar. A pair of slightly weathered green eyes darted around the room.

"Is that…?" Nat pointed.

"Yup." Summer grinned, waving at Jeff Krueger.

"I can't believe that he was the one shipping the brewery for Maxwell's''. He's never stepped inside either bar."

"People aren't always what we think they are." She knew that better than anyone. She'd never been whom people thought she was or whom she'd thought she was.

Todd moved toward his father. The two men met halfway between the bar and the entrance. The space between them seemed not as vast anymore, though, it still required steps to close it. Raking his fingers into his coppery locks, unsure hope danced in Todd's eyes as he looked between his father and Summer.

"I'll be back," she said, placing her drink on the bar and sauntering over to Todd.

"Summer." Jeff's normally stoic face softened. "How are you doing?"

"I'm okay." She leaned into Todd, who tucked her in close.

"Good. I just wanted to come by to let you know that Max was bailed out, but I personally made sure he was escorted to the airport and the judge issued a temporary stay-away order. The DA will reach out on Tuesday. I spoke to Chief Martinez from the village police. His officers have Max's description and will drive by your place and the café a few times a day just in case. I also plan to have my lunch there the next few weeks, but I doubt we'll see him back."

"Dad put the fear of god in him," Todd offered, a thankful expression on his face.

"Nobody messes with my family. Ah..." Jeff cleared his throat. "I mean, my son's family."

Todd placed a hand on his dad's shoulder. "Do you want to meet Liam?"

And just like that she fell just a little bit more in love with Todd. His ability to forgive and move forward. His kind heart. His strength. He was everything she'd always wanted and never thought she'd deserved. But she did deserve it. At least, she was starting to believe it. Just another thing to work on in her journey toward becoming.

"Liam!" Todd called, motioning for him.

"Coming!" Liam signed something to JJ and then ran over. "Yup."

"Liam, I want to introduce you to my dad. Sheriff Jeff Krueger."

With a broad smile, Liam outstretched his hand. "Hi. I'm Liam. Nice to meet you."

"Nice to meet you." His large hand eclipsed Liam's. "Call me Jeff."

"Hey, baby, wanna have Jeff try some of your root beer?" Summer placed her hand on his shoulder, the little boy bookended by her and Todd. *Just as it should be.* The thought sparked joy across every nerve ending.

Liam's laughter danced around the table as Jeff told funny stories about Todd as a little boy. His green eyes sparkled as he looked between his son and Liam. Summer leaned her head against Todd's shoulder, melting into the relaxed muscles of his body. The tension that once spooled his body tight at the mere mention of his dad dissolved. Just like with her and Liam, there'd need to be many, *many* more conversations between father and son, but the expression on both men's faces telegraphed their willingness to have those. They'd start here.

"Have you met my aunt?" Liam gestured to Vanessa, who approached the table with Noah in tow.

"Yes." Like a hero from one of Summer's historical romance novels, Jeff stood up. "Ms. Maxwell."

A soft pink caressed her cheek. "Please, call me Vanessa."

"Vanessa." His smile popped brighter. "If you call me Jeff."

Nudging Todd, Summer whispered. "Do you think they're into each other?"

Todd's nose wrinkled. "He's so much older."

"You read romance. Total age gap. He's fifty-four. She's thirty-six. Plus, he's a total DILF."

"DILF?" He grimaced. "I'm not letting you near my dad."

"Don't worry, papa bear, you're the only person ILF." She placed a chaste peck on his cheek.

Vanessa schooled her expression from a little girl with a crush to serious business lady and addressed Noah and Todd. "I need to talk to you about business stuff."

"I'll take Li—"

"I got him, Summer," Jeff interrupted. "Liam, why don't we take some of your root beer to Grandpa Rice and Rose. I don't think they've tried it yet."

"Okay," Liam jumped up.

"Thanks, Dad." Todd smiled.

"Of course, son." A hint of a tremor wobbled his words.

Summer took Todd's hand, squeezing it tight. Today had been a big day for them both.

"I've spoken to my parents. Even if Max refuses to resign, there's a morality clause in our employment contracts as executives. Something my parents and the board take very seriously. Dad called an emergency board meeting for Monday to remove Max. He doesn't represent the Maxwell's business or our family. If you're open, I'd like to move forward with our deal. So would my parents," Vanessa said.

"Are you serious?" Todd looked to Noah, who made a *yeah I know* expression.

"Yes. Your beer is amazing. I have a feeling that other stores will be sniffing around you two soon enough and I'd like to be the first." A determined smile anchored her face.

"You should do it." Summer met his questioning eyes.

"Are you sure?"

"Yeah. The world deserves to try your witchy brews."

Max may be a monster, but his parents weren't. They'd always been kind to her. Now, understanding that the prickly interactions with Vanessa were an attempt to protect her from Max, Summer knew Vanessa was just as kind. With Max no longer associated with Maxwell's, there'd be no reason to not proceed.

"Before you answer, one more thing." Vanessa smoothed down her sleek black hair. "My parents would like to meet their grandson. If you're okay with that, Summer. The deal and my parents' request are not contingent on each other. Take one. Take none. Take both...please. They're all on the table. No strings attached. I wanted you to know their ask before you agree to anything. No more secrets."

"Agreed. No more secrets. Let's set up a call with your parents, you, Todd, and me to discuss them meeting Liam. When I left, I was so focused on protecting him from Max that

I didn't think about what I'd be taking away from him. His aunt. His other grandparents. I'd like to give that back to him, but I also know we need to figure out what that looks like."

"Of course." Vanessa nodded, then addressed Noah and Todd again. "Think about the deal and give me a call next week."

Soon after, Summer and Todd collected Liam to head home.

Since it was a special occasion, Liam's eight-thirty bedtime had been extended. He'd begged to stay up for the ball drop, so they'd curled up on the couch together. As Summer shuffled back in the living room from using the bathroom, a silent laugh curled her lips at the sight of her guys fast asleep on the other end of the couch. Sheba sprawled beneath the Christmas tree, snoring. It had been a valiant attempt. They'd made it until eleven-thirty.

Scooping up the now-empty bowl of popcorn from the coffee table, she padded into the kitchen. She'd load the dishwasher, killing a little bit of time before the ball dropped. Then she'd rouse both her guys, so that Liam could celebrate with the noise makers he'd been chattering on about all day. Not to mention, she could get a midnight kiss and maybe ring in the New Year properly once she and Todd tucked Liam in for the night.

"Caffeine," she muttered through a yawn. Tea was needed to keep her awake for what she had planned to do with Todd.

"Tea, at this hour?"

"Eek!" she squeaked, spinning to find Todd standing in the kitchen. "You scared me."

"Sorry, sweetheart." He crossed the checkered floor and twined his arms around her.

"What are you doing here?"

His face scrunched. "Last time I checked, I lived here."

"Smartass." She poked his arm. "You were fast asleep."

"I set an alarm on my phone to ensure I woke up in time."

She raised her brow. "For the ball drop?"

"To claim this before midnight." He lifted up a white slip of paper.

"Is that a coupon for a New Year's Eve quickie?" she teased, taking the slip of paper from him.

"Nope."

"Todd," she gasped, reading the words *This Coupon is Good for One Lifetime Together.*

"Summer Joy Michaels." He slipped a ring out of his pocket and bent to one knee in front of her.

"Your mom's ring." The words rasped out.

"I told my dad to give it back to me when I was ready. I'm so ready." He took her hand. "Tonight, he asked me what I wanted for the coming year, and this is it. I want to come home every night to you wearing my clothes." He tugged on the hem of the Henley she wore. "I want to be your husband. I want to be Liam's father. I want to make a home with you. I love you. Please marry me?"

"Yes!" Happy tears rolled down her cheeks.

No more excuses. She knew—she'd always known—he was the missing piece. The fear. Her past. None of it held her back anymore. Those things were still there, but she took back her power from them.

"Yes?" The brightness in his eyes lit the room.

"Yes, you fool. Now kiss me!"

"As you wish." He chuckled, pushing the ring on her finger. The pink sapphire gleamed in the light from the pendant fixture. Jumping up, he lifted her and spun her around the kitchen and kissed her thoroughly.

That delicious, almost-too-full feeling pulsed in her chest. Each time she thought she'd hit the limit on her love for him, he coaxed more out of her.

"What's happening?" Face wrinkled, Liam appeared at the door, Sheba beside him.

"Todd asked me to marry him." Summer looked between her son and Todd.

"Does that mean we're moving in?"

"How do you feel about that, buddy?" Todd tipped his head toward Liam.

"Can Sheba sleep in my room?" He scratched Sheba's ears.

Todd chuckled. "Of course."

"Okay." With a pleased smile, he shrugged and headed out of the room with Sheba.

"I think he approves."

"He sure does." She grinned. "I think he and I are both getting our happy ending thanks to you." She caressed his smiling face.

"Oh sweetheart, this isn't our ending, it's our HEA, so it's just the beginning."

EPILOGUE
SIX MONTHS LATER

"Regina seems…sweet." ~Mean Girls

"French Fries and Wedge Salad is here." Cassie waltzed into the kitchen.

"Oh?" Summer said, not looking up from her cell phone. She'd refreshed GCC's student page three times, willing it to flash the final grade from her class. The semester wrapped up last week and grades were supposed to be posted today. No matter her grade, she'd already registered for two more classes over the summer term.

"He's got an entourage with him. I sat them in your section *Mrs.* Wedge Salad and French Fries." The waggle in Cassie's eyebrows was audible.

Yep. Mrs. Wedge Salad and French Fries. It was still a little dizzying to wrap her head around. Their courtship, as her dad teased, had been a whirlwind, yet a long time coming. After the proposal, they didn't wait long to start their HEA. By the end of January, she and Liam moved in. On Valentine's Day they had a simple ceremony at a historic courthouse in Canandaigua followed by an intimate reception with their favorite people at a lakeside inn. Her parents. Their friends.

The entire Rice Clan. His dad and sister. Support group, which Todd attended, along with Amy's husband, Joseph, each week fueling Henry's elation to no longer be the only man in group.

"Your parents and Liam are also with them." Cassie sauntered up beside her. "So is *Big Daddy Krueger*," she purred with a salacious punctuation.

"Gross," Zach groaned from the stove. "It creeps me out that you think my uncle is hot."

"He's a DILF!" Summer and Cassie cackled in unison.

Neither Todd nor his cousin appreciated the women in the village swooning over the handsome Jeff Krueger, which made Cassie and Summer do it just a little more. Over the months, father and son built a stronger relationship with weekly lunch dates. Jeff even came by the brewery for Liam's brewing lessons.

Finally! They'd posted the grades. Smiling she slipped her phone into her back pocket. "I should get out there."

"Yeah, don't keep *Big Daddy Krueger* waiting. Wouldn't want you to get spanked. Although…" Cassie wiggled her hips.

"Seriously, woman!" Zach bellowed.

Laughing, Summer pushed into the dining room. Instead of the front booth that Todd claimed most days when he and Noah came in for lunch, her people sat at three tables pressed together. Grandpa Rice. Nat and Noah, fresh from their honeymoon. Rose. Her parents. Jeff. In the middle sat her guys, smiles stretched across their faces.

"Sweetheart." Todd rose and greeted her with a tender kiss.

"Did you get your grade? Is that why you wanted us all to come?" Dad asked. There was a moderate amount of fathering he'd do from time-to-time. No journey was without its bumps, but the path forward with she and her dad had smoothed over the months.

"I got an A!" she announced.

The table erupted in cheers, claps, and whistles.

"That's my smartass." Pride curled Todd's lips.

"Let's celebrate. Tater tots for the table!" her dad boomed, waving to Laney who replied with a thumbs up signal and disappeared into the kitchen.

"Actually, I have gifts to thank you for all your support." Summer smiled.

Laney and Cassie reemerged from the kitchen with several gift bags. Her bench was deep, but these were her core people. Her family.

Each of her people's names were scrawled in glitter on the front of a rainbow bag. Cassie and Laney distributed them.

Summer gave one to Todd, their gazes tied. "Thank you for loving me just as I am and supporting me on my becoming."

Dad lifted his coffee cup. "To our Summer Joy."

They all raised their drinks and that full feeling in her chest swelled just a little more. Wiping escaped tears, she smiled. "Open your bags."

"Oh my god!" Mom squealed, holding up the T-shirt with *Grandma* written on it. "Are you..."

The table filled up with *Grandpa, Aunty, Uncle, Great-Grandpa,* and *Big Brother* T-shirts. Nat held a onesie with *Future Bestie* on it over her still small belly.

"We're having a baby,' Summer cried.

Todd pressed a protective hand to her abdomen. Her guys already knew. She and Todd pulled the goalie in March. By April she was pregnant. Today marked the end of her first trimester, so they felt it was safe to tell people. Last night, they'd told Liam, who vibrated with excitement and insisted it meant they needed to get a second dog, so the baby had their own.

Happy tears and hugs surrounded them. Everyone

quickly donned on their shirts and Summer nudged Todd to open his.

"I love you, mama bear." He beamed, holding the shirt featuring a family of four bears beneath the words *Papa Bear*.

"I love you, papa bear." She pressed her smile against his.

The End.

Keep turning the page for a sneak peek of Melissa's upcoming release, **Book Boyfriends.**

SNEAK PEEK: BOOK BOYFRIENDS
CHAPTER ONE

Not A Book Boyfriend

I wish I were on a date with Captain Wentworth. Davis Mackenzie is *no* Captain Wentworth. In fairness, none of my dates ever hold a candle to my dream book boyfriend. They don't have to be top-tier Austen male romantic leads, but at least in the ballpark of the book boyfriends that cause my pulse to race. In the pages of my favorite romances are the perfect men. Men who do battle, traverse distant lands, and say all the pretty words while still ensuring their lady is well-sexed.

In real life, I'm sitting across from Davis. He's thirty-six, single, and breathing. Just my type. At least, that's what my younger brother Jackson must think.

"It's fascinating, Georgia. It all happened on Bainbridge Island," Davis says, his focus fixed on his phone.

"The island off Seattle? What happened there?" I cock an eyebrow, which he'll not notice since his vision appears permanently fused to his phone.

We're twenty minutes into this meet/cute orchestrated by my younger brother, and the only connection here is between him and his phone. Even my breasts, served up on a platter thanks to this gravity-defying pushup bra, aren't dragging his attention.

"Joel Pichard and Bill Bell founded pickleball in 1965 on Bainbridge Island," Davis goes on about the one topic that's dominated this blind date: pickleball.

I'm not anti-pickleball, even if I am not a sporty girl. It would just be nice to talk about anything else or for him to ask about me. Right now, it would be nice if he'd look at me.

Note to self: never again accept a date with someone Jackson has raved is 'just my type'. I bite the inside of my cheek, attempting to force my face into a serene expression.

My younger brother means well. Everyone means well. Our soon-to-be-a-dad, older brother, Rem. My best friend, Hope. Colleagues from work. They all want me to have a relationship that lasts beyond the first date.

This isn't the best first date but it isn't the worst. It's not like the guy who robbed me after I went to the bathroom or the one who asked for the server's number in front of me.

At least Davis is attractive. If you're into neat, dark stubble brushed across a strong jawline, thick raven hair, and ashen eyes rimmed in gold which peek out from behind trendy black-framed glasses. With his height, which I clocked at just over six foot, and the lean physique visible beneath a blue short-sleeved button-up, he has the "hot nerd" look that sends a tingle to my lady bits. It's almost enough to wash away the simmering annoyance at the tick of checking his phone every three minutes. *Almost.*

"You've never played pickleball?" Right eyebrow arched, he looks up.

Well, that got his attention. Grinning, I lean against the chair's cushioned back. "Nope."

"How is that possible?"

"I'm more of an indoor kind of girl." I sip my pineapple cider. Its crispness explodes on my tastebuds. At least, for this blasé date, I'm at Fisher's Landing, my favorite—and the only —local gluten-free brewery with their unrestricted menu of tidbits and ciders for my consumption.

"There are indoor courts," he says, his stare—again— drags back to his phone.

Seriously, dude? "Do they now?" My tone skews flippant.

I could be flirty and bat my lashes. The only promise I made to Jackson was to go on this date, and here I am. I don't have to feign flirtation for someone whose focus is elsewhere. I may be single, but I'm not desperate. It's far better to be lonely than unhappy. It took a devastating heartbreak and the last five years to drill that lesson into my head.

He leans against the chair's high back. "Maybe on date two, I can introduce you to the sport. On an indoor court, of course."

Second date? I almost choke on my drink. Beyond our shared basket of steak fries, there's no commitment. Drinks are all I promised my brother. This happy hour meeting is for Jackson's sake, not mine. An evening in with a good book and takeout is far superior to the squeeze of these Spanks, and this black mini-dress Hope talked me into.

But I promised… At least, I get french fries. Bad dates— really anything—are always better with french fries. I rarely get a chance to indulge in the salty treat while I'm out, due to my celiac disease. Most places lack a dedicated fryer or kitchen to ensure gluten-free options. That oversight often results in stomach cramps, migraines, and too much bonding time with the toilet for me.

"Have you been here before?" I pluck a fry from the basket.

"Nope." His long fingers tap against his phone screen.

"It's a favorite spot for my best friend, Hope, and me."

He simply nods.

"Do you have a best friend?"

"Yep." His focus remains tethered to his phone.

With a tap of my kitten heel against the chair's leg, I force my mouth into an almost painful smile. "Besides pickleball, what kinds of things do you enjoy doing?"

A vee forms front and center on his brow. "Hike."

"Guess you're an *outdoorsy* guy."

"Sure." With a shrug, his attention moves back to his phone.

I bite back an annoyed breath. "My older brother, Rem, is a big hiker. He loves Chino Hills. Which trails do you like?"

"Lots of them."

Seriously! The fries here are good but not worth this. Blind dates aren't my thing either, but at least I'm present. Davis appears more décor than an engaged partner. Granted, what hiking trails do you like isn't going to whip me into a verbal frenzy, but I'm at least trying.

I brush my long brown hair behind my ears. "If you need to be doing something else, it's okay. If you need to leave—"

"What?" Confusion twists his features when he looks up.

I wave between us. "You've been looking at your phone a lot."

"I... I didn't realize... Sorry." He places the phone on the table.

"If you need to go, it's okay."

He rubs the back of his neck. "No. I'm here, Georgia."

My nose crinkles. "Are you sure? Because we can call this if you want..."

"Yes—" His face scrunches "—I mean, no. I don't.... We don't need to call it. Let's do this. I promised your brother, and I hate breaking my promises."

Promised my brother? Great! Did Jackson call in a favor for this blind date? My dating history is less than stellar, but I had no idea it was *younger brother calls in a favor* bad. When Jackson told me there was a guy he wanted me to meet, I assumed it was because he thought we'd get on. However, Davis's engagement screams uninterested.

Is this how my younger brother sees me? Desperate? Shifting in my seat, mortification blazes my cheeks.

For several beats, we stare at each other. The clank of dishes, chatter from other patrons, and muffled music from the bar's speakers spin around us. It's the trademark awkward first date pause, where neither of the participants knows what to say. In a book, my *actual* love interest would rescue me from this awkwardness. My real-life book boyfriend isn't in sight. No dashing duke, cinnamon roll baker, or devoted werewolf alpha is coming to my rescue.

"You're not athletic like your brothers."

My spine stiffens at the *statement of fact* aspect of his question. True, I'm not cut out of marble like the pickleball champion of Southern California across from me. With my round hips, thicker thighs, and squishy belly, I'm built for comfort. I detest running, love pastry, and adore my soft curves. Still, I bristle at the undertone of his accusation about my lack of athletic prowess.

"Why do you say that?"

"You're an indoor girl, remember?" He smirks.

"I can think of some *very* athletic indoor activities." I skate my fingertip around the glass's rim.

Interest sparks in his eyes.

"Yoga," I say with a *dream on, buddy* lilt.

Davis may have this whole hot nerd aesthetic thing going on, but I don't plan to engage in *indoorsy* activities with him. I've been fooled by a handsome face before. Though fooled seems a poor choice of words for what Will did and its impact on my heart. *But we're not going to think about that.*

"Yoga?" Davis huffs a breathy chuckle. "Can't imagine someone from Jackson's gene pool not being into competitive sports. They call him Beast at the pickleball courts."

"It's a deep genetic pool... Lots of options." My gaze flicks around the crowded bar.

This isn't the first time someone's noted the difference

between me and my siblings. Rem and Jackson are your poster children for Type A personalities. Sports. Grades. Careers. It's all a competition for them.

Then there's me, Georgia Lane. Sometimes, it's as if the only thing we have in common, besides a shared last name, is each being named after one of Dad's favorite artists.

"Jackson says you write." He dips a fry into the ketchup.

"He did?" Queasiness swirls in my stomach at the idea that Jackson is telling people about my writing.

"He says it's a hobby of yours."

And there it is, the reason for that churn in my belly. Hobby may be the kindest term my brothers used to describe my writing.

I clear my throat. "It's not exactly a hobby. I've published three novels."

"Really?" His head tilts. "Impressive. Jackson didn't mention that. Who's your publisher?"

"I am."

After years of scribbled story ideas and starts/stops with manuscripts, I completed my first novel four years ago. Instead of the traditional path of querying agents even to have a chance at a publisher, I took a different route. Not waiting, I got a freelance editor and cover artist and did all the things to independently publish. And honestly, that's a big deal, all businessy and stuff.

"Did you self-publish because you couldn't get an agent?"

"No." I narrow my gaze. "I prefer to have control over my career."

He nods. "And you make a living at it?"

"Not yet."

It's *the* dream, though. Even if my bank account sometimes reflects my older brother's concern that this is just an expensive hobby, just like Jackson's many intramural teams. Somehow, our younger brother's pickleball, flag football, and basketball leagues don't seem to drum up the same level of disapproval.

Still, I do okay enough… Enough to keep me going. To reach for the dream of days spent crafting my stories and seeing my book on the shelves of all bookstores instead of just a few indie ones in Southern California.

"In the meantime, I'm a hospice social worker. Not sure I'd want to give that up. It's a tough job, but I love it."

His smile dips. "All that death must be hard."

"It's not a giggle-fest, but it fills me up. The end is just the beginning for so many, and I get to help those left behind find their way." I slosh out a breath at Davis, whose gaze is fixed to his phone. "What do you do again?"

"I work with your brother at No Boundaries, remember?"

That's right, Mr. Glued To His Phone works at the new startup where Jackson is deputy chief financial officer. My love for my younger brother is unquestioned, but he's a finance bro.

Forbes and spreadsheets are my brother's porn. No doubt Davis shares that same predilection. I've interacted enough with Jackson's finance bros to know the type. In every romance novel, Davis is the man the main character drops for the grumpy mechanic with a heart of gold.

"You must enjoy writing if you're paying to do it." He takes a long drag from his habanero strawberry cider.

"I do," I say, determination tightens my expression. "Everyone needs a heart to live. Writing is mine."

It's something my dad says. Nolan Lane isn't the sitcom dad with pretty speeches and sage advice outside the belief that a life without passion is not worth living. This truth is rooted so deep inside me that it's almost the steady beat pulsing me toward my passion. No matter how many times the voices, both inside and outside, try to steer me away, I always come back to writing.

"I get it," he murmurs.

"You do?" I say softly, my gaze linking with his.

Something akin to understanding glints in his dark pupils. So few people in my life seem to get this, let alone understand my passion for writing.

Davis blinks out of our tethered gazes. "Surprised you'd keep doing it, even though you don't make a living at it." He dips a fry he's already bitten into the ketchup.

Eww… Double-dipper. My stomach twists at both his action and question. "Most authors don't make enough to support themselves. A lot of us keep our day jobs to supplement."

"You're not George R. R. Martin or J.R.R. Tolkien level yet."

Not a single woman or marginalized author. Perhaps shared french fries were too hopeful for this date. Rem lectures that my standards are too high, which is why I'm single, but there is a bare minimum. A man who doesn't double-dip into the joint condiment before we've even had our first kiss and whose writer references aren't only white, heterosexual, cis, non-disabled men isn't too much to ask.

He juts his chin at me. "What do you write?"

"Romance."

"Really?" He snorts.

Brows knitted, my smile flattens. "What's wrong with romance?"

"It's all hitched breath and happy endings."

"It's about people. What drives us—"

"Into bed," he guffaws with a dismissive wave of his french fry.

"If you're doing it right." I lift a brow.

"There's more to life than sex."

"Said no man ever," I retort with a huffed laugh.

Challenge flashes in his eyes, and his mouth flexes into a teasing grin. "Someone's judgmental."

"Says the man that judges an entire genre of novels that he's *never* read."

His forehead creases. "What makes you think I've never read a romance novel?"

"Have you?"

He leans back. "Well…"

"Just as I thought." I pick up my drink.

He grabs another fry from the basket. "Romance has just never appealed to me. I prefer to read things with more substance."

A scowl forms on my face. "But you've never read a romance."

"I know what I like. I don't need to try something to confirm that." He dips his fry and then bites it in half.

"But we're not talking about you liking it, we're talking about you *not* liking it… About you denigrating an entire genre, one that makes billions annually, without having read a single romance novel. You don't need to try peanut butter to confirm you like Nutella, but you do need to try it to confirm you don't like it." I motion wildly between us.

The corners of his mouth quirk. "Your brother says you're choosy."

"Excuse me?" Face scrunched, I tilt my head.

"Do you go on a date with every man who shows interest?" He dips his half-eaten fry back into the ketchup.

"Of course not. What does that have to do with anything?"

"If we follow your logic, how do you know you wouldn't like to date them if you don't go on a date with them?" He gestures with his fry before tossing it into his mouth.

My jaw slackens. *Is he serious?* These are two different things. Not to mention, staring longingly at his phone for most of this date and only asking me questions about myself to dismiss or insult me doesn't scream *I'm interested*.

"You may be missing out on someone who gives you hitched breath and the happy ending you crave."

"Who says I crave those things?" I purse my lips. "What has my brother been telling you?"

"A few things... Also, you write romance, and I'm sure you have an entire bookshelf filled with swoony page-turners."

My mouth opens and then closes. He's not wrong. But he doesn't get to paint me as the lonely spinster—the patriarchy's word, not mine—who writes happy endings and dreams of the day she gets hers. Even if he's sort of right. *Emphasis on sort of.*

"There's nothing wrong with wanting a happy ending."

"Our happiness shouldn't be contingent on another person, especially when most people fail you or won't always be there." He leans back and his lopsided smile flattens into a firm line. A wisp of sadness shades his expression.

I bite back the urge to say, "Who hurt you?" The wounded male main character whose heart just needs a plucky love interest to heal him may cause a flutter in my belly in a book, but in real life, it's a red flag. We'll add this to the many reasons there will be no second date with Davis. Skeptical men with emotional baggage are for my books, not my heart. It's already been tattered by one commitment-phobic man. It doesn't need another.

"It's unrealistic to wrap one's happiness up in a single person. Romance just feeds us the delusion that it is." Forehead pinched, he waves another half-eaten fry between us.

"The happy ending in a romance isn't just about the couple. Yes, that's part of it. We root for them, but it's about their individual journeys. It's also about their relationships with others, not just each other or themselves. The best romances show that."

"Again, that's not real life. Most people are on their own."

"It's some people's lives."

"Not everyone is lucky enough to live in a fairy tale, Georgia," he says, his voice a little gruff.

Indignation simmers in my bloodstream. What Davis knows about me wouldn't fill a page's footnote. My life is hardly a fairy tale. If it were, I'd be here with someone else—the someone else who, despite my hope and heartbreak, is now someone else's Prince Charming. Instead, I'm here with Davis.

"I'm well aware." I meet his stare.

"Are you?"

"Very much so," I hiss through a tight smile.

So predictable. It's as if it's in one of my books. He's the jaded finance bro, and I'm the hurt but still hopeful romance author. The girl who believes so much in happy endings that she spends hours crafting them. Happy endings may be my business, but none of my characters get them without getting a little scrappy.

Scrappiness isn't something I'm known for, at least with my friends and family. But Davis is neither. *He's* just a bad date, and I'm done with bad dates.

My mouth curves into a sardonic grin. "You're right, though. Life isn't a romance novel. In one of my books, a handsome stranger who turns out to be *my* love interest would have rescued me already from this *terrible* date. From a date with a man who spent the first twenty minutes checking his phone and the next twenty insulting me." I drain my drink and slam the glass onto the table with a *thwack*.

"I didn't insult you—"

"Nothing makes me swoon like someone referring to what I write as *lacking substance*." Expression tight, I scoot from my chair and grab my purse from where it's hooked on the back. "But since this isn't one of my books and it's real life, I'll rescue me."

"Wait, Georgia... Are you leaving?"

"Yes. Whatever favor you did for my brother, please consider it paid." I pull out fifteen dollars from my wallet and toss it onto the table. "For my drink. You can pay for the fries since your double-dipping ensured I wasn't touching them. Manners dictate that you forgo double-dipping of a shared condiment until after the first kiss. Everyone knows that."

"Wait? Kiss?" Befuddlement laces his words.

"*Never* happening." I sling my purse over my shoulder. "Though, maybe you're right about that too… I've never kissed you, but I can say for certain I would not enjoy it… I like a man with more substance."

And with that, I turn and march out.

ACKNOWLEDGMENTS

Just as Summer had an entire team of people surrounding her on her journey of becoming, so do I with each book. Making Home wouldn't happen without the love and support of so many people. Let me gush about them!

None of this would be possible without my real life book boyfriend; my husband Liam. Thank you for being the inspiration for all the green flag men in my books, and showing me that good men do exist.

A huge thank you to Meghan Fisher. You are the wind beneath these author's wings. Thank you for your support and alpha reading skills.

This book would NOT be without my literary mama bear and editor Gemma Brocato. I am so grateful you took a chance on me and continue to work with me to tell my stories.

This beautiful cover to curtesy of Su from Earthly Charms and @croquith (on Instagram).

Thank you to Autumn Blevins for the amazing job with copy edits and proofing.

A huge thank you to the village of Perry, N.Y. Like Summer who frequents the library to foster she and her son's love of reading, I discovered my love of books in the stacks of the Perry Public Library, and inspiration for storytelling in the picturesque place I grew up in.

ALSO BY MELISSA WHITNEY

Available wherever you get e-book, paperback, and audiobooks

All books are available in e-book, paperback, and audio. You can get books at Amazon.com: Melissa Whitney: books, biography, latest update or by requesting at your local library or indie bookstore. Signed copies can be purchased through Heartbound Book Shop: Where Every Page is a Love Story.

The Home Series

Finding Home - Book One

Coming Home - Book Two

Making Home - Book Three

The At First Series

At First Smile

Stand Alone Titles

In the Hello and in the Goodbye

Happy Ever Afterlife

Book Boyfriends

Recovery Run (Coming Soon)

ABOUT THE AUTHOR

Melissa Whitney, who hails from Western New York, is a contemporary romance author. As a legally blind woman much of Melissa's work focuses on the exploration of disability, mental health, and trauma through a heartfelt, sexy, and comedic lens.

Melissa's debut novel *In the Hello and in the Goodbye* released in April 2024, with a warm reception from readers for its thoughtful autism and mental health portrayal. Since then, she's released *Finding Home*, a Jane Austen inspired small town romance, *At First Smile*, an own voice hockey romance with blindness rep, and *Coming Home*, a *Little Women* inspired small town romance. Her work has been featured in several publications and on podcasts for its thoughtful, sensitive, and accurate representation of disability and mental health.

Ms. Whitney lives in Southern California with her husband and their rescue pug Milo. When not crafting her swoony stories, she's on the hunt for a pastry, brewing a cup of tea, and diving into her latest swoony romance.

To learn more about Melissa Whitney, you can visit www.melissawhitneywrites.com. Sign up for her newsletter to stay in the know with all things Melissa Whitney. Connect with her on social media (IG: @melissa_whitneyatuhor, Threads @melissa_whitneyauthor or Facebook: Melissa Whitney Author).

www.ingramcontent.com/pod-product-compliance
Lightning Source LLC
Chambersburg PA
CBHW060821120726
47909CB00006B/2018